First

First

Kim Pritekel

P.D. Publishing, Inc.
Clayton, North Carolina

ISBN-13: 978-1-933720-00-5
ISBN-10: 1-933720-00-X

First Printing 2002 (ISBN: 0-9718150-7-0)

9 8 7 6 5 4 3 2

Cover art and design by Stephanie Solomon-Lopez
Edited by Day Petersen/Betty Anderson Harmon

Published by:

P.D. Publishing, Inc.
P.O. Box 70
Clayton, NC 27528

http://www.pdpublishing.com

For my big sister, Tiff. Thank you for being my biggest fan.

Chapter One

The line hung silent on my end.

"Emmy? Are you there?" my big brother asked, worry marking his deep voice.

"Yeah, Billy, I'm here. Are you sure? Dead?" I couldn't bring myself to believe Beth could possibly be gone at only thirty-four. Breast cancer? That couldn't be. She's far too young for that. Isn't she? "I have to go, Billy. Someone is calling on the other line," I lied.

"Okay, Emmy. I'm sorry I had to call you at work. Are you sure you're okay? I mean, I know you two were such good friends when you were kids and all."

Friends. If only they had known the truth about Beth and me. Wiping those thoughts and memories from my mind, I said, "That's okay. I'm glad you told me. Thanks, Billy."

"Yeah. Hey, come home every once in a while. I know they give you parole now and then in the Big Apple."

I grinned into the phone. "Yeah. Now and then. Bye, Billy."

I gently set the receiver into its cradle, sat back in my chair, and looked around my cramped office. I was an up-and-coming lawyer at the firm of James/Parks/Stone, where I had worked my butt off to curry favor with the sexist partners. Not an easy task, but one I performed with gusto.

Perhaps I would take some personal time and go to the funeral. I was due for a vacation anyway. I could catch a flight to Denver, Colorado, and head south to Pueblo, the town where I grew up and had not been for years. I could still picture the neat rows of modest-sized homes, all painted similar colors, gray barbecue smoke wafting up over the six-foot wood privacy fences. The perfect Norman Rockwell neighborhood. The town held nothing for me anymore. Not that it ever really had. Still, it had been a while since I'd seen my parents and Billy. His kids were growing up so fast, and I'd never even met them.

I stood and walked to the window that looked out over the park next to the building, and I watched as a man was yanked by his overly enthusiastic Great Dane. The last time I had seen Beth had been in that park. I rested my forehead against the cool glass. She had come up to New York to see me, and the short visit had been uncomfortable and strained at best. I remember how tired she had looked. Thin, too, which made her tall frame seem lanky and gaunt. I realized that day would be one of those that can haunt a person for the rest of his or her life. *What if?* I sighed. I didn't believe in wasting time on "what ifs". It helped nothing to worry and think of all the things that were over and done and couldn't be changed. But still...

With a sigh, I turned back to the stack of files and papers on my desk. I really should clean it up. I smiled to myself. Never could keep my mind on one thing. Suddenly, with the force of a blow to the stomach, a malformed sob ripped from my throat and I plopped down into my chair, gripping the arms of it with a fierceness that surprised me. I closed my eyes, squeezing them tight as I fought the emotion that was trying to make its way to the surface. Finally, I could breathe again. After a couple of deep breaths, I had myself under control, but I decided maybe it was best to start that personal time today.

I sent a quick e-mail to one of the senior partners to explain my sudden departure, gathered my belongings, and headed toward the door.

"Ms. Thomas?" Lois asked as I closed and locked my office door, suit jacket and briefcase in hand.

"I'm leaving for the day, Lois. If anyone calls, please transfer them to my voice mail. If any of the partners wish to speak with me, transfer them to my home phone. It's in the Rolodex."

"Why certainly, Ms. Thomas. Is everything all right? You look a bit out of sorts today. Are you feeling okay? Shall I call Ms. Kelly?" Lois Wutherman, my trusted secretary of two years, was a kind, older woman who had been born and raised in London, where she lived until she immigrated to the U.S. with her husband after World War II or what she called "the big one". She looked at me with large brown eyes hidden behind enormous bifocals, her silver hair piled on top of her head. I often wondered just how long her hair actually was; she never wore it down. She probably thought that would be bad form for a lady. I smiled to myself.

"No, that's not necessary. I'm fine. I've got some personal business to take care of," I said, although for just a moment I fought the urge to perch at the corner of her desk and spill my guts to this woman who had mothered me through disappointments at work, fights with my lover, and a car accident two years ago. For some reason, this was something I could not share with her.

"Well," she said, taking one of my hands in both of hers and patting it in her usual motherly way, "whatever it is, t'will all be fine."

She smiled, although I knew she could read the strain in my eyes and see that annoying wrinkle that appears between them, revealing my level of stress. "Thank you, Lois. I'm sure it will." With a deep breath, I walked past her desk and left the firm.

The early afternoon air of downtown Manhattan hit my face with an intense force, the cool autumn air sharp and biting. I found my car in the covered parking garage next to our building and pressed the button on my keychain to deactivate the alarm and release the door locks. I climbed behind the wheel, tossed my briefcase and jacket onto the seat beside me, and stared out at the busy street, my hands placed on the wheel, my mind in another place, another time. *Beth.* I could still see the expectant look in those blue eyes as she stood beside the park bench and stared at me.

"Don't I even rate a hug?"

I shook my head to clear it and turned the key in the ignition.

I shared a modest townhouse in one of the outlying boroughs of the city with my lover, Rebecca. It was spacious, with big windows that allowed in the sunlight of the day. The brick-faced front opened to a small yard, the autumn yellow grass lining the driveway on either side. Come spring, flowers would pop up in the planters Rebecca had scattered around the yard.

My black Persian, Simon, met me at the door, his thick tail waving in confusion at my being home so early.

"Hi, baby," I crooned as I picked up his considerable bulk and rubbed my cheek against the soft fur of his neck. After a few moments of greeting, Simon let me know he'd had enough and fought my tight embrace. Letting him down to return to one of his numerous daily naps, I headed for the kitchen. I could not get Beth out of my head. *Why hadn't she told me she was sick when she had the chance?* I could feel my shock begin to succumb to anger. I walked over to the sink and leaned on its sturdy surface, my head hanging. I could feel the tears welling up in my throat, wanting to spill forth and overtake me completely. The myriad of emotions was overwhelming. I fought the urge to cry, but suddenly my cheeks were wet with the onslaught of tears that ran down my face and landed in the stainless steel double sink. Plop. Plop. My pain and self-pity were interrupted by the shrill ring of the phone, which lay on the counter next to the Mr. Coffee. I decided to let the machine pick up.

"Hello. You have reached Emily and Rebecca. We cannot come to the phone right now, so leave a message at the beep and we will get back to you as soon as possible." Beep.

"Yes, this message is for Emily. Hi, this is William Parks, and your secretary told me—"

I pushed away from the sink and wiped at my eyes as I walked toward the cordless. Snatching up the receiver, I said, "Hi, Bill. ... Yes, I did. We've had a death in the family, and I had some personal time coming—"

"Of course, of course. By all means take care of you. The criminals of New York will wait and be happy for your return, I'm sure," Parks said with one of his famous fake laughs. He lowered his voice for dramatic effect. "You take all the time you need. These things can be so difficult."

I fought the urge to tell him to stick his pity up his ass. Bill Parks cared about nobody and nothing except Bill Parks. However, he was one of my bosses, so I thanked him for his kind words and assured him that John Dithers would cover the Holstead case in my absence. I was grateful to hang up and end my conversation with the pretentious, pompous man. He was my least favorite of the three senior partners, the kind of lawyer about which jokes are made.

I tuned off the ringer and walked to the fridge. The remainder of our leftover linguini stared me in the face, as did the two-day-old pizza, still in its blue-and-white Domino's box. Disgusted by the thought of food, I entered the living room and lowered myself onto the couch, my hands lying limply next to me. I stared out the French doors into the small backyard. I felt so empty, as if everything inside had been removed and I was left with nothing. I sighed deeply, then an idea occurred to me. I walked to the hall closet and on tiptoe reached for and grabbed the three white photo albums that had been the source of much comfort, as well as painful memories, in my life. I felt a need to delve into the past, a past when Beth Sayers was still alive, a time when she was my neighbor, my best friend, my lover, my confidante. I felt a need to rediscover this woman who had stolen my heart and had never really given it back.

With sweating palms, I carefully flipped open the cover, almost as if I were entering a sacred realm. The first half of my photo album was filled with baby pictures of Billy and then of me. There's a picture of me at age three heading to my first day of ballet lessons — which, I am told, I hated — but my mother thought I looked so darned cute in my white tights and pink tutu. There's a picture of Billy and me in Halloween costumes. The caption indicated he was nine and I was five. I don't remember ever wanting to dress as a princess, but I guess at one time I must have felt the urge. Billy was dressed as a sheriff and holding my hand, and we both had impatient smiles plastered on our cherubic faces. Ah! Now that one was more like me. I was sitting in the middle of a large sandbox with some little redheaded girl who I don't remember at all, a large green bucket of sand forever poised over that mane of red hair. I had to smile despite the fact that my heavy heart was beating limply in my chest.

Skipping a few years worth of photos, I finally came across the pictures taken after Beth became part of my life. It didn't seem like there was ever a time when she hadn't been. Now, I would never hear her wild laugh again, never see those twinkling blue eyes looking into mine with so much love.

I closed my eyes and took a deep breath before opening them again to stare down at us. In the beginning, it had been I who pursued her for a friendship. During the summer of my tenth year, many of the families in our neighborhood had decided to leave the area, taking most of my friends with them. The Sayers family moved into the house next door with their soon-to-be ten-year-old daughter, Elizabeth, who refused to answer to anything other than Beth. She was a shy girl and later told me I had intimidated her, though I never understood why. Finally, as the summer slowly crawled by with nothing to do and nobody to do it with, she agreed to cross over that sacred boundary between their small, green postage stamp lawn and our small, green postage stamp lawn, and we played four square. From that day, the two of us were attached at the hip.

I turned the page to reveal a photograph of us standing in front of my childhood home, the garage door open to show the old Dodge my father refused to give up and still has, except it isn't gold anymore: it's now an interesting shade of avocado green. My father never did have any color sense. In the picture, I was wearing an old football jersey Billy had outgrown and handed down to his tomboy sister. My dark blonde hair was haphazardly pulled back into a ponytail. My knees had two painful-looking scrapes that were just beginning to scab over. I was linked arm in arm with Beth, who was wearing that Mickey Mouse shirt I swear she would have worn day in and day out if her mother would've let her. We had great big goofy smiles on our darkly tanned faces. So young. So carefree. I read the caption my mother had written neatly below the Polaroid, "Emmy and Beth, 4th of July, 1977." That was our second summer together. That was also the year we kissed for the first time.

I looked up from the photo album, suddenly aware that I was hungry. Putting the album aside, I went to the kitchen and made a PBJ — peanut butter and jelly, the food of choice. I hadn't had one since college. Looking at the old pictures was bringing out my younger self. I smiled and shook my head.

With sandwich and can of Dr Pepper in hand, I grabbed the photo albums and sank down to the floor. I got to my knees and unzipped my gray, pinstriped skirt, pushing it down over my hips, then sat to remove it and toss it aside, followed by my nylons. As I sat in my camisole and underwear, I looked at some of the other pictures on that page: Emmy and Beth at the zoo; Emmy and Beth in the pool; Emmy, Beth, and Billy playing basketball. Then I saw it. The night of the school play and Beth's first starring role. It was a silly little play entitled "Who Calls the Wild Wylde?" It was about a family named Wylde who lived in the backwoods town of Looneyville. Beth played the son, Joseph Wylde. That year she discovered her love of acting. In one scene her character had to give Miss Thelma Rooster a peck on the cheek, and she decided she wanted to practice. On me.

~ ~ ~ ~ ~

The weekend before the play, Beth was spending the night at my house. We were up in my bedroom running my extensive collection of Matchbox cars over the many roads and highways, stopping at the good places to eat and visiting all our numerous friends along the way. Suddenly she stopped, tiny white VW Bug in hand.

"Let's practice!" she said, her eyes wide with this new idea.

"Practice what?" I asked as I rammed my truck into the post of my bed, causing a great avalanche of rock and other such debris to fall from that massive mountain that was in the middle of our town.

"Practice my scene with me and Thelma Rooster."

I could feel my stomach tighten with a strange sort of excitement. I looked at her as if to ask, "Are you serious?" although I knew she was, and I prayed deep down she wouldn't change her mind. So I said, "Which one?"

"You know, the one where I have to..." she looked back over her shoulder to make sure Billy or my parents weren't listening through my closed door, "...where I have to kiss her."

"Why? You know how to kiss. You do have a father, after all."

"Yeah, but that's different. He's a boy; this is a girl."

"But you're playing a boy, so it's the same thing."

"No it's not! And I don't kiss my father like he's my girl-friend," she said matter-of-factly.

"I hope not!" I giggled, liking this game of playing hard to get.

"Come on, Em!" She eyed me with those intense blue eyes that even at the tender age of eleven threw my senses out of whack and made me agree to anything.

"Okay. But first wait." I threw my forgotten car on the floor and ran to the door. I opened it ever so slightly and looked at as much of the hallway as I could, then shut the door and leaned my huge, trusty brown teddy, Ruffles, against it to guard us. Next, I went over to my window and shut my blue pastel curtains, and then walked to my original spot and sat cross-legged in front of Beth.

"Gee. You'd think we were hiding in Fort Knox," she said.

"What's that?"

"Never mind. Okay. You have the first line." She looked at me expectantly.

"I don't know what the line is."

"Oh yeah. Okay, you look away from me and try to be all ladylike and flustered because you're in my presence." I stifled another giggle. "Then you say, 'Well, good morning, Joseph Wylde. How are you on this bright and sunny day?'"

"Well, good morning, Joseph Wylde. How are you on this bright and sunny day?" I asked, batting my eyelashes at her. Real serious-like, Beth grabbed my hand and brought it to her full lips, just barely brushing my knuckles. A bolt of excitement raced up and down my spine. I didn't remember Joseph doing that to Thelma in rehearsal, but I didn't say anything. I would let Beth do whatever she wanted. After all, she was the acting expert, not me.

"Thelma Rooster, you are looking lovely as always. Why are you out here all alone?"

"Oohh! I remember this line!" I exclaimed. "Mother's gone inside the store, Joseph."

Beth smiled at me and nodded. "Good. Then you say, 'But you can walk me home, if you like. I'm sure she'd be understanding of my taking my leave with such a kind gentleman like yourself.'"

I began to repeat the line when she stopped me and pulled me to my feet. "Let's really act it out." She grabbed my hand, put it through her bent arm and held it with her other hand. "Your bedroom door will be the door to your house, okay?" I nodded, then proceeded to say my line quite nicely, I thought. We walked along our path until finally she stopped short of the door to my "house".

"It has been an honor to walk with you, Thelma. ... That is, may I call you Thelma?"

I didn't know the next line, and Beth seemed to be a bit too much in character to remember to tell me, so I just nodded. She smiled at me and released my hand from her arm. Her breath came in shallow puffs of air as her body moved closer to me. I was nervous, scared, and excited all at the same time. She rested her hands on my shoulders and brought her head up next to mine. I was surprised when our lips met. I had been expecting her to kiss me on the cheek. My blood began to pound through my veins with enough electricity to short out all my thoughts. I had once seen a movie in which a woman closed her eyes when a man kissed her. Thinking that must be the correct procedure, I closed mine and sighed.

When the kiss ended, Beth pulled away and looked me in the eye. A look of wonderment filled her face. I was almost breathless and certainly speechless. I had never kissed anyone before except my parents and my Aunt Kitty, who insisted on giving me a big wet one every time I saw her, which was often. I had never liked any of those kisses. This was different, and I think we both knew it. Beth rolled a tendril of my summer-lightened hair around one of her fingers and smiled. "Can we rehearse again?" she said quietly.

I could only nod. She took one of her hands and brushed some hair from my forehead and brought her face to mine again. This time I wrapped my thin arms around her neck and leaned in to her.

~ ~ ~ ~ ~

My rock. Beth would always be the strong one.

The play met with critical acclaim among the fifth grade class and their families. Mrs. Arbuckle thought Beth's performance was "much too dramatic for such a cheerful story." What did she know? Beth was not cast again until middle school.

Chapter Two

It was getting late, but I wasn't ready to give up on my stroll down memory lane. I shifted my position on the floor and turned the page of the photo album. I saw more school pictures of Beth and me and snapshots taken at home. Did my mother have nothing better to do than run after us with a camera? As a kid, it never occurred to me that she took a ton of pictures. Now it took an act of God to get me in front of that lens.

As the years went by, Beth became more and more detached from our peers, especially the girls. The only time she'd have anything to do with them was if they would challenge or make fun of either of us or if some other girl became their target. Beth was a champion of anyone who became the "underdog". If an injustice was done, she wouldn't hesitate to fight anybody, and she did so often. Beth could mostly be found with the boys. She was incredible when it came to running, basketball, or any game involving physical activity. I smiled as I remembered Beth's slam-dunks.

~ ~ ~ ~ ~

"Come on, Em. Don't be such a wimp. Take the ball, run up the court, and jump. Slam it in there."

I stared at Beth like she had just landed from another planet. "Beth, have you forgotten that you're the one who is a hundred feet tall? I'm short, remember?"

"So," she said as she ran by me, whacking the ball out of my hand and dribbling it down the cement, until she pushed up on her left leg and slammed the ball into the hoop with a satisfying whoosh. "It's not about height, Em. It's about ability." She landed with a smug smile on her face, her eyes daring me. I raised my brows. She knew I could never refuse a dare.

"Fine. I'll show you height, *and* I'll show you ability." I grabbed the ball that continued to bounce down the court and ran.

"I'm so sorry, Em. I really thought you could do it," my best friend said as she sat next to me on the front porch, my mother holding the towel to my nose. I glared at her with my black eye.

~ ~ ~ ~ ~

Beth had a difficult home life. Her parents married when her mother became pregnant at the age of sixteen. Her father, Jim, made no secret of his doubts that Beth was even his, but I believe he loved her. He raised her as his, and Beth loved him dearly. Her parents remained married until she turned thirteen, then, no longer able to tolerate his wife's tirades and drinking, her father left the family to return to his home state of Tennessee. Beth did not see him for years at a time.

To stay away from her house and the steadily increasing abuse by her mother, Beth came over to my house, and I think in her mind she saw my mother and father as her own. I know Billy loved her. In his eyes, it was almost like having the younger brother he'd always wanted. Beth and I would lie on my back lawn and stare into the night sky, trying to count all the stars we could see. She would often cry silently, the tears flowing down her cheeks, rolling over the sides of her face to collect in her ears. She would shiver and blame it on the cool night air.

I have to give my mother credit. She tried to be everything that Nora Sayers wasn't. She coddled Beth, taught her things, showed her that she counted and was loved. By all of us. Beth clung to that sense of security, wrapping it around herself like a blanket.

I came across a picture of Beth, Billy, and me on a fishing trip *before* the Sayers separated. Billy had just turned seventeen, and my parents decided to give him a chance to prove he was responsible by taking his thirteen-year-old sister and her twelve-year-old friend fishing.

~ ~ ~ ~ ~

"I am not going to bait anything for you two, so you better get over that squeamish girl stuff and learn to do it yourself," he scolded as we backed out of the driveway. I turned to Beth, who sat with me in the back seat of our huge Suburban, with a look of fear-spawned doubt on my face. She smiled at me. I felt my fears melt away.

"I don't need no one tying on my worms, if that's what you mean. Heck no. I bet I could do it better than you anyway!" she said proudly.

"Girls," Billy mumbled to himself, although in the rear-view mirror I could see the small smile play across his maturing face.

After a long three-hour drive, we finally reached Carter

Lake and found a good place to set up for the night. The campsite was surrounded by huge, beautiful trees. Beth and I got out of the car and made a slow circle of the area. The day was warm, but the presence of so many trees made it absolutely incredible with endless shade. The maze of trees and vegetation went on and on, and any number of adventures could be played out.

"You thinking what I'm thinking?" Beth asked mischievously.

I gave her a smile and said, "See you later, Billy!" I grabbed her hand and we ran toward the thicket of dense fantasy.

"Hey! You guys gotta help me!" my brother yelled.

"We're just girls! We can't do it anyway!" Beth yelled as we disappeared into the forest, our giggles the only clue we were there.

After a bit, we slowed, for fear of running headlong into a tree trunk. We walked hand in hand, looking at the incredible beauty of God's planet. The hillside was sloped slightly, the ground soft from recent rains. We stepped over fallen trees and ducked under low branches. I looked up in wonder at the huge trees, so stoic in their existence. Chipmunks called warnings to each other; mosquitoes and butterflies fluttered about our heads.

"I think we should live here forever. Never go back to school; never get jobs when we get older. Just stay here and live off the land like Tarzan," I said wistfully.

"Me Tarzan, you Jane," Beth said, pounding her developing breasts with her fist.

I giggled. "No way. Me Tarzan, and *you* Jane."

"Unh uh. I want to wear the loin cloth." We walked on in silence. "No, I think we should be more like Huck Finn and Tom Sawyer," she said after a few moments.

"I want to be Huck Finn!" I exclaimed, thinking of the possibilities.

"No way! You're too brainy to be Huck. You would make a much better Tom Sawyer."

She let go of my hand and began to dance in a clearing we had come upon. The late afternoon sun hid half the small valley in shadow; the large hill covered with wild grass on the opposite side rose like a golden giant behind the trees, a small stream dissecting the wild grass and flowers. She lifted her arms to the sky and tilted her head back.

"I want to be free!" she yelled to the silence of the mountains, her loud cry echoing in the expanse. Only a far-off bird answered.

I stood back and watched her as she danced and jumped around. Beth would soon turn thirteen in October, but I could already tell she would be a great beauty some day. She had hair that was dark, almost black, reaching to just below her shoulders, and it shone so brightly in the sunlight. She had amazing blue eyes and beautiful skin. I was already getting pimples, but she had none. She was tall for her age, and I guessed she would one day be much taller than my mother was, with long legs and an athletic build. Her incredibly active life kept her young body hard. She was beautiful.

Suddenly, Beth stopped yelling and dancing and turned her back to me, her hands in the pockets of her shorts. Her shoulders slumped in defeat.

"Beth?" I asked, my brows drawn in confusion. "Why'd you stop?" She said nothing, but I could feel an immense sadness radiate off her in waves. "Beth?" I asked quietly again as I walked to her. "What is it?" I put my hand on her shoulder. She would not look at me. "Tell me."

Without a word, she turned to me and grabbed me in a hug of desperation. Her hands linked behind my back, her head bent down to lay on my shoulder, and she sobbed. Alarmed, but knowing she would tell me when she was ready, I wrapped her body in my hopefully comforting embrace and stroked her hair as I whispered encouraging words into her ear just as my mother always did when I was upset.

We stood like that for maybe two or three minutes when, with a final sob, she said, "My father is leaving my mother."

"Oh, Beth," I said stroking her back. "I'm so sorry. How do you know?"

She tightened her embrace a little and said, "I heard them fighting the other night, so I got up and walked to their door. It was closed, but I could hear them yelling and my mom crying. She was telling him not to, but my dad said he had to. He couldn't do it anymore."

"Do what?"

"I don't know. I guess put up with her. She's been coming home real late again. Usually drunk. In some ways, I don't blame him. I don't know." She sniffled and was quiet. We stood there holding each other, each with her own thoughts and fears running through her head.

"Are you going to go with him?" I asked, almost not able to breathe as I waited for the answer.

"No. He won't let me."

I slowly released the pent-up breath of relief, then felt guilty. Beth had always been much closer to her father than to her mother.

   With a sigh, Beth pulled away from me, her hands resting on my hips. I wiped the tears off her cheeks with my thumb. She stared down at me, her eyes red and her face swollen with the upset. As I looked on, a single tear slid lazily down her cheek.
   "Don't cry," I whispered. I leaned forward and reached up to kiss her forehead. She looked so miserable. Then I kissed her lips softly, just the barest touch of mine. I pulled back and looked at her, trying to gauge her expression. Her eyes were dark, burning into mine. She moved in for another kiss, but I backed away.
   "Billy will be looking for us," I said, and dropped my hands from her body. Beth and I had only kissed the one time the previous year when we rehearsed her play. She had looked at me this way several times since then. Before, I never really understood what that look meant, but now she used it again. It was a look of wanting, like when you saw the greatest bike in a store window and wanted it so badly it hurt. Had she wanted to kiss me at another time? Was that what her look of wanting was for?
   We began to walk back through the trees as these thoughts whirled around my immature mind. Had I ever wanted to kiss her before? Yes. There had been a couple times, but I felt too funny about it, so I never brought it up. Now, looking back, I know Beth would have gone along with it, and perhaps would have even started a situation or two on her own. She found her security and stability in me. But we were girls, I reasoned. We should be kissing boys or at least talking about it. All my other friends did. Weren't boys the ones who were supposed to get my heart racing like this? Make me feel dizzy and dumb and yet alive, all at the same time? My hormones probably just hadn't kicked in yet. This made me too nervous for it to be right.
   We emerged from the trees into the clearing where Billy had started setting up camp for us. His big blue tent was already up; our much smaller red one was in process. Hearing us approach, he looked over his shoulder.
   "There you two nuts are. Don't ever do that again, Emmy, or I'll nail you to a tree, right before mom nails me to the one next to it!"
   "Sorry, Billy," I said quietly. Both Beth and I were in much more somber moods now than when we had run off. Hearing the difference in my voice, he looked at us again. His face held an expression of concern and curiosity, but he asked nothing. Billy never did.
   "Well, since you two think you're such land rovers, go and

get some sticks to start a fire for marshmallows tonight. But you two get your butts back here in fifteen minutes!" he yelled to our retreating forms as we headed back into the trees.

That night, Beth and I lay in our tent in our separate sleeping bags. I lay on my back staring up at the red canvas that was our protection from the rain outside. The heavy drops pelted down on our tent like the rain was knocking on the door, begging to be let in. I could hear the portable radio Billy was listening to in his tent; it sounded like Led Zeppelin, but I had never liked my brother's music.

"Em?"

"Yeah?" I turned my head to look at Beth. She was curled up on her side facing me. In the darkness, I could just barely make out her form and could not see her face or the expression in her eyes.

"Do you think you'll ever get married?"

"Married?"

"Yeah. You know, with a husband and kids."

"I don't know. I've thought about it, but I'd rather go to college. I've decided what I want to be."

"What?" she asked with interest.

"A lawyer." I turned on my side so I could talk to her easier. "I saw this really neat story on TV last week where this woman became a lawyer, and she won this case where this little boy was kidnapped by his father."

"Why would his father kidnap him?"

"I don't know. Anyway, the woman, I think her name was Terry, she helped the police get the boy back for the mother, then she tried the case in court and won. She got to go on Donahue."

"That is really neat. I want to do movies. I don't ever want to get married. Do you think we'll be friends when we're old?"

"Of course we will!" I exclaimed, almost offended by the question. "We'll be friends forever."

~ ~ ~ ~ ~

I loosened the plastic covering over the pictures and removed that one to study it. We had met an older couple at the lake who volunteered to take our picture so all three of us could be in it. We stood by the lake, Billy in the fishing vest our father had given him for his birthday, with the fish he had just caught proudly held high by the line. Beth and I were standing next to him, our arms around each other, smiles pasted on our faces. Now, as I looked into Beth's eyes, I could see how unhappy she was. I wonder why I didn't see then how much her parent's splitting up had affected her. Perhaps the innocence of youth does not allow you to see these things. Beth should never have seen so many of the things she was handed as a kid.

The caption on the bottom of the picture read, "Billy, Emmy, and Beth catch dinner, Spring 1979." Below that I had written in my childish scrawl, "Emmy and Beth, Friends For Life."

I looked up from my past to see Simon staring at me. He had been asleep next to me and I hadn't even noticed. I picked him up, a rag doll in my hands, and held him close to me, his eyes closed, purring in contentment. I looked out the windows of the French doors that led to the backyard. Night was approaching swiftly, the sun taking one last curtain call before the entrance of the moon.

"How's my boy?" I asked into his thick fur. "What do you think, Simon? Should I let her go? Huh?" I stroked his ears as I got lost in thought once more.

~ ~ ~ ~ ~

When we returned home from the lake, my mother rushed out of the house to meet the car.

"Wow. Your mom must have really missed you guys." Beth laughed.

I did not share her amusement. I could see it on my mother's face; something was wrong.

Billy saw it, too. "I wonder what's up," he said as he put the Suburban in park and cut the engine.

My mother ran to the back window where Beth and I sat. "Beth, honey, you need to get home just as soon as possible. Your mom called me this afternoon and told me your parents have something very important to talk to you about."

"They're getting a divorce, aren't they?" Beth asked quietly, looking at her hands as they played with the hem of her T-shirt.

My mother looked at me, her pretty face lined with worry. She looked back to Beth and put her hand on Beth's shoulder. "Why don't you go on home, hon. If you can come back for dinner later, you know you're more than welcome. I know Emmy won't mind." She smiled in an attempt to lighten the mood. Beth smiled politely, then slowly got out of the car.

"Want some help with your gear, Beth?" Billy asked.

"No thanks, Billy. I've got it. Em, will you walk me home?"

I looked to my mother to see what I should do. She nodded. "You can walk her to the door, then you need to come back here and take in your camping things. Okay?"

"Okay." I climbed out of the car after Beth and helped her lift her big duffel bag out of the back. With a thud, the heavy bag hit the driveway, where she left it to drag on the ground by the long strap.

"Thank you for everything," she said over her shoulder to my mother and Billy, who watched from the car.

We walked side by side, our steps perfectly matched. I looked over at her profile. She walked with her head up, her eyes straightforward. I wished I could have known what was going through her mind at that moment. We both knew the inevitable end to that journey, yet neither wished to acknowledge it. I turned my gaze forward again, and we reached her front porch.

She dropped the bag and faced me. "Wish me luck," she said with a quick hug, then headed into the house.

I stood there for a moment thinking about what this could mean. I stared at the front of the small house, the light blue paint peeling. Chips of paint were mixed in with the dark green of the bushes that lined the front wall. I'd never before noticed how badly it needed painting. Two or three coats, maybe? Maybe that's what the Sayers needed — another coat. I turned when I heard footsteps coming toward me. It was Billy.

"Come on, kiddo. Help me lug in all those fish you caught." He mussed my hair and gave me a light punch on the shoulder. Slowly, I turned from Beth's door and headed home. Billy put his arm around my shoulders as we walked.

"Will they have to leave, Billy?" I asked, looking up into the face of what would be a very handsome man someday, his eyes dark like our father's, his hair the same light color as our mother and me.

"I don't know, Emmy. I just don't know. What is it that Aunt Kitty always says? 'Keep hope alive and doubt at bay.' You never know. Maybe everything will be fine. Grown-ups can do some pretty stupid things sometimes."

We reached the house in silence. Billy grabbed his camping gear and disappeared into the confines of his room. I watched as he closed his door and read the signs displayed there. One read, "*Teenager Intelligence! They say the A-bomb was dangerous*," and the other,"*Beware, boy bites.*"

With a sigh, I went to the kitchen where my mother was beginning to make dinner. I sank heavily into one of the kitchen chairs and watched her work.

"Want to help?" she asked, turning to me, the dishtowel over her shoulder.

"No. I'm never getting married, so why should I learn to cook?"

"You're not, huh?"

"Nope. I've decided," I said with finality.

She smiled. "You do have to eat still."

"I'll eat out."

"Well then, I hope you're rich. So, why aren't you ever getting married?"

I shrugged. "I don't know."

I looked at the pile of dinnerware waiting to be placed on the table. A stack of yellow linen napkins were folded neatly, topped by five wooden napkin rings that were in the shapes of elongated cats, each one carved to touch the tip of its nose to the tip of its tail. I picked one up and swung it around my finger. "Why five?" I asked, showing my mother the napkin ring.

"Your Aunt Kitty is coming over for dinner."

I nodded acknowledgment. "Why did you marry Dad?"

"Because I loved him," my mother said as she turned back to the stove to stir the mashed potatoes.

"Can I do that?" I asked, eyeing the pan.

"Sure you can. But you may not want to ruin your non-domestic reputation." My mother gave me a sly smile over her shoulder.

"Can you keep a secret?" I giggled.

"You got it, kiddo."

I leapt from my chair and took the big wooden spoon from her hand. "But why did you get *married*?"

"Well, when a man loves a woman—"

"Oh, Mom, I know all that stuff. But why get married? Can't people just live together or live close by each other? Aunt Kitty isn't married to Ron."

"You could, I suppose, like Kitty, but that is just what we do. I hope she will marry Ron someday. Lord knows he's proposed enough times. Being married is the better way to go, for many reasons. When you meet that certain someone, you'll understand. You'll want to be close to him all the time, and you'll want to do things with him and go places with him."

My mom put a pan of rolls in the oven.

"Can I marry Beth?" I asked, turning to look at her. She nearly dropped the plate she held as she studied me. I knew it was a ridiculous question, but wanted to see what her response would be.

"Why would you want to do that?" she asked slowly.

"Well, we do things together, and I want her around. Isn't that what you said?"

"Yes, but honey, girls don't marry girls. You'll find a nice young man."

I turned back to the stove and watched with interest as the lump of mashed potatoes slid off the spoon and fell back into the pan with a plop.

"You know, maybe you and Beth should make some other friends besides just you two. You would have a lot more fun with a whole group of girls, don't you think?"

I rested the spoon handle on the side of the pan and mumbled something about having to put away my camping gear as I walked out of the kitchen and out the front door.

Beth never came back over that night. I was disappointed; I wanted to know what was happening, but my mother told me Beth would tell me when she wanted to. Later that night, as I sat on the front step, Mr. Sayers packed up his car and, with a small wave to me, drove away, his taillights in the darkness the last thing I saw.

~ ~ ~ ~ ~

I hadn't seen him since.

Chapter Three

I put the photo album aside and stood, stretching my screaming back. I looked around the living room. The thick rugs covering the hardwood floors were a light gray, the furniture, soft black leather with red accent pillows. The walls were lined with framed black-and-whites of the places Rebecca and I had been together, or separately, and the places we wanted to visit together someday. Despite the sharp colors, the room was soft and warm. The mantle on the fireplace in the corner held a beautiful piece, sculpted for us as a housewarming gift by a young artist we knew. Made of black onyx, it was the figure of a woman reaching to the sky, perhaps reaching for her salvation.

My life was so different now than I had once imagined. For one, Beth was not at my side as she had always professed she would be. I sat on the couch. The thought occurred to me that although she had not been in my life for over a decade, I still relied on her strength from a distance; the memory of her sustained me. Now the connection was gone forever. I rubbed my burning eyes.

I looked down to see Simon leaning against my leg, his tail entwined between my calves. "You hungry, little man?" Simon answered with a loud meow. "Okay, okay. I need to make something for your other mom, too, or she will not be happy with me."

I walked through the dining room and looked at the table that would seat twelve when fully extended. Rebecca and I had recently bought it, and its rich cherry wood finish shone from the last bit of light coming in through the two double windows that lined the wall just above the matching cherry wood buffet table. I ran my fingers lightly over the silk flower arrangement at its center.

Entering the kitchen, I heard the garage door open. I began to take vegetables out of the refrigerator to start preparing the salad. The inner door opened, Rebecca walked in, and I looked at her for a moment. Her long red hair was taken down to lie around her shoulders after a long day of teaching high school science, and her dark blue-green eyes looked alive and radiant. A feeling of urgency suddenly filled me. I walked over to her and held her to me, almost knocking her off balance.

"Hi, babe! I'm glad to see you, too, but you already swept me off my feet long ago you know," she said with a surprised laugh, her arms holding me tightly.

I laid my head on her shoulder and wept silently. The sight of this woman with whom I shared my life now and forever brought me to my knees. Her loving smile was just the permission I needed to really let it all out so I could finally begin to let go.

"Hey, hey," she said, gently starting to pull away.

"No. Can I just cry for a minute?" I asked, my hold on her like a vise.

"Of course you can, Emily. Of course." She pulled me back into her arms and was silent.

~ ~ ~ ~ ~

"Don't cry, Beth. Come on. You have to be strong."

"I hate them," Beth said with a final sob, her voice bitter.

"No, you don't. They're your parents; you're not allowed to hate them." I ran my fingers through her hair. We were in my bedroom and I was lying on the bed with Beth next to me, her head on my stomach, her favorite position. We were quiet for a long time. I glanced down to see if she had fallen asleep. She was awake, her gaze far from my house.

"What are you thinking about?" I asked as I braided a couple strands of her dark hair together. She didn't answer for a minute.

"Do you think I'm weird, Em?" she asked, her focus remaining on the wall, almost as if she was afraid of my answer.

I laughed. "Of course I do. That's why you're my best friend!"

"Gee, thanks." She grabbed the hem of my blue- and purple-striped T-shirt and wiped the drying tears from her eyes.

"Thanks, Beth. Wasn't one of my favorites anyway."

"Be grateful. At least I didn't blow my nose."

I grinned at her and swept her hair behind her ears. She pushed the thin material away from my stomach and examined the white skin beneath. I could feel her warm breath as she traced small circles above my belly button with her fingertips.

"Find anything interesting?" I asked, curiosity keeping me in check.

She smiled, patting the skin of my stomach. "Just like a baby's butt." She lifted her head and stared down at her hand as she flattened the palm against one side of my rib cage. "Isn't it incredible how there are so many strange little curves and bumps on a woman's body?" She traced the center line of my stomach up to where the fabric of my shirt began, just below my burgeoning breasts.

"I guess I've never given it much thought," I said, feeling unsure about Beth's explorations and feeling naked in my uncertainty.

"Hmm," she said absently, then sat up and pulled my shirt back into place. "Let's go down to the Soda Jerk and get some ice cream."

I stared at her as she jumped off the bed and began to pull her hair back into a ponytail, the black hair band clamped between her teeth, her weight shifting from one foot to the other. My eyes narrowed as I watched her. This was her habit when she was nervous. I slowly stood, my legs shaking.

"Sounds good," I said, silently releasing the breath I had been holding.

~ ~ ~ ~ ~

The late September chill of New York was chased away by the fire Rebecca had built to accompany our after-dinner coffee. This had become a tradition we hadn't realized we'd started until one night a couple years ago when we didn't do it, and we both realized how much we missed it. I lay on the couch with my legs resting on Rebecca's lap and stared at the strange shadow that danced on the walls from the trance-like light reflecting from the fireplace.

"So, Beth's parents split when she was thirteen?" she asked, her hands caressing my calves and ankles.

"Yup. Thirteen. Actually, that was when they divorced. They separated the year before." I let out a sigh, took a sip of my mocha fudge coffee, and looked at the ceiling. "We were on summer break, soon to be going into seventh or eighth grade. I don't remember which one now. I think eighth."

"How old were you?"

"I was just a couple months shy of turning fourteen."

Rebecca sipped her coffee, then asked, "Why didn't you tell me any of this before, Emily?"

I looked at her for a moment as I thought of an answer. Why hadn't I? "I told you she was in that play we saw. I pointed her out to you."

"You did, but only in passing. You never really told me anything about her, just that she was someone you used to know. I remember exactly what you said, in fact. We were sitting there in the dark theater, and when she came on stage you said, 'You see that girl playing Pippa? I used to know her.'"

I smiled. "Well, yeah, but—"

Rebecca patted my leg to shut me up. "Yeah, but nothing. I'm not mad at you, sweetie; I just want to know, that's all. I want to know about someone who meant this much to you. I want you to share this with me."

"Okay." I sat up, kissed her lightly on the lips and caressed the side of her face with my fingertips, and then lay back down. "To be honest, I don't know why I didn't tell you. I guess because it was so long ago, and it really doesn't matter anymore."

"Emily, if it didn't matter, then Beth's passing would not be affecting you as much as it is." She looked at me in the way she always did when she knew I was full of it. I smiled to myself. It reminded me of how my mother used to look at me.

"We used to do everything together," I said quietly. I looked at Rebecca and smiled, then found myself looking past her, through her, to all the adventures Beth and I shared together.

~ ~ ~ ~ ~

After Beth's parents divorced, she and I became even closer than we had been, if that was possible. Any other friends either of us had at school became secondary, some disappearing altogether from the world we created for the two of us. Every weekend, she spent the night at my house, or on the rare occasion when her mother would allow it, we stayed at her house. By that time, Beth was heavily into the theater and acting. She would come up with short one-act plays or scenarios for us to act out.

In the beginning she had to use some pretty heavy powers of persuasion to get me to participate, but then I got into them as much as she did. I remember one of them where she was a shy James Dean-type character and I was a beautiful girl he had seen on the street and just had to have. Halfway through, I stopped her, her bold written script in my hand.

"Beth, why do you always have to play a guy?" I dropped down on my bed, untying the scarf from around my neck, a "prop" that I had stolen from my mother's closet. Beth grabbed the end of it and tried to pull it out of my hands.

"No!" I slapped her hand. "Mine."

"Why? Do you want to be the guy?" she said with one of her crooked smiles.

"No!" I exclaimed. "But why do you have to be?"

"Well, someone has to be. You see, Em, to be a good actor you have to be able to embody other types that just aren't like you in life." She ran her hands down either side of her head to re-slick her water-slicked hair.

I chuckled. "What textbook did you read that in? So, why don't you ever play a girl, then?"

She looked at me through her long bangs. "Very funny. I already play one of those in life; I don't want to typecast myself already. The acting world does that enough." She threw herself down on the bed and stretched out beside me on her stomach. Resting her chin on her hands, she stared at my headboard. I lay back and gazed at the ceiling. I noticed the small spot in the corner where the roof had leaked three years ago. We both were quiet, the only sound coming from the tick of my alarm clock on the tall dresser across from the bed. I began to imagine that the ticking of the clock matched my heartbeat. My heart jumped as the bed squeaked when Beth changed positions to get closer to me. I looked over at her to find her lying on her side, her head resting on her hand, looking down at me. She didn't say anything, just looked. I began to feel like a lab rat. A strange heat was making its way from my feet to my head. I found it hard to breathe, my midsection tingling.

"What?" I asked, slight irritation marking my voice for being made to feel uncomfortable. Or was it vulnerable?

"Nothing. I'm just looking at you. Am I not allowed to look at you?" Beth sounded hurt.

"Yeah, but why would you want to? I look the same today as I did yesterday and the day before that." I sat up and stood from the bed. "You are so weird sometimes. Jeez." Beth followed my movements, surprise filling her eyes. I walked over to my dresser and began to rearrange my small collection of unicorns. Why was I getting so upset?

Looking at my reflection in the dresser mirror, I saw that my shoulders were tight, almost like I was ready to pounce. Surprised, I relaxed them, felt the tension flowing out. On my face, my mouth was shut tight, brows drawn in stubborn anger. I looked at Beth's reflection in the mirror. She still lay on the bed, having rolled back onto her stomach. She was facing the opposite direction, her legs bent at the knee, crossed at the ankles, and slowly swinging up and down in a hypnotic rhythm. I could get lost in that rhythm. She was resting on her elbows and looking at something in her hands. Through the thin material of her shirt, I could see the sharp edges of her shoulder blades. It reminded me of the sleek back of a tiger as it sneaked up on its prey.

"What are you playing with?" I asked, my voice quiet from guilt. Beth cleared her throat, but did not look at me.

"Later in the script, I'm supposed to give this to you." She half turned and showed me what she held. It was a small gold plastic band. "Remember, I propose?"

"Yeah," I said quietly as I sat next to her. I took the ring and looked at it, turning it over in my hand. I smiled at her. "It's so sudden, Beth. I thought we'd at least live together first." She laughed. I slid the band onto the ring finger of my left hand. It was a bit loose, but it would work.

"Well, honey, if I ain't even allowed ta look at ya, how do you ever 'spect us ta git married?" she said in one of her Southern hillbilly accents.

"Beth, I'm sorry! I don't know why I got so mad." Beth had moved onto her side, and I snuggled up next to her, tucking my head against her neck. She wrapped her arms around me and held me. I could hear her heartbeat racing in her chest, her breathing getting faster. Off in the distance, I thought I heard the doorbell.

"I wonder who that is. Probably Aunt Kitty. She's supposed to come over today."

"Your mom and her are pretty close, aren't they?" Beth ran her hand down my back, rubbing out any remaining tension, turning me to jelly. I could only nod. Her hand slid to the hem of my shirt and then slipped underneath. The warmth of her skin felt so good, I didn't stop her. I didn't want her to stop. She ran her hand up my spine, then back to my waist, then a bit further over to my side, then around my ribs.

Even after her hand had passed over an area, I could still feel its heat. A burning sensation started in my lower stomach and spread. I could feel my chest tighten. I wasn't sure what Beth was doing, but surely it couldn't be anything other than a massage to comfort me, could it?

I closed my eyes when her hand reached the underwire of the bra that covered the mounds of my newly formed breasts. Her fingers stilled, hand stopped in its tracks, almost as if she wasn't sure what she was doing and was surprised to find it there.

With my head tucked down, I couldn't see her face. I wished I could see her eyes to be able to read them. Beth was like an open book to me. My skin felt cold when she removed her hand from under my shirt. I didn't say anything; I stayed how I was. We lay there for a moment, until there was a knock at my bedroom door. We both froze.

"Emmy? Are you two in there, honey?" my mom said from the other side.

"Yeah," I said, still in Beth's arms.

The doorknob rattled. "Open the door, honey." I rolled away from Beth and stood, my legs unsteady as I walked over and unlocked and opened my door just wide enough to look at her.

"Why did you lock your door?" I just stared at her expectantly. "You girls were so quiet I didn't even know if you were still here or not." She smiled. I just looked at her, impatient yet grateful for the interruption. "That Newman girl came by. She wanted to know if you want to go out and do something. I didn't know if you were here or not, so I told her you girls would go get her when you got back."

"Mom! We don't want to play with Darla Newman!" I exclaimed. We didn't want to play with anyone.

"Now, Emily, I know you two have an incredibly busy schedule, but Darla Newman is new here, and she has no friends. There is no reason why you and Beth can't go out and play for a while."

"Mom!"

"It's not for the rest of your life, Emily. Just a couple hours."

I looked back at Beth who sat Indian style on the bed, looking at me and shaking her head. I turned back to my mother.

"We don't want to. Let her go find somebody else."

My mother sighed and shrugged. "Okay," she said and walked back down the hall. I closed the door and leaned against it, my arms crossed over my chest.

"Jeez. I am almost fifteen, nearly an adult, and she still treats me like I'm a kid! I don't even like Darla Newman!"

"Come on, Em, Darla's not that bad." Beth stretched out her long legs and stood from the bed. "Besides, you didn't have a problem with her the other day."

"Yeah, but I had to go with her; you weren't home."

Beth quirked an eyebrow and studied me. "What is wrong with you lately, Em? You are so short-tempered. Everything and everyone is making you mad."

"I don't know!" I yelled. I walked over to the bed and plopped myself down face first. "I hate my mother," I whined into the wrinkled bedspread.

"No, you don't either. What did you tell me? They are your parents; you're not allowed to hate them," Beth said from somewhere near me "Come on. Let's go down to the creek."

There was a small creek about half a mile from our houses. It ran along a distant bike trail and emptied into a large pond that was walled in by a ring of huge rocks. This pond, dubbed the Toilet Bowl by the kids who lived in the area, was the neighborhood swimming hole. The "Bowl" was surrounded by trees and dense wild foliage that provided shade and much privacy for the older kids who would go skinny-dipping.

Beth and I sat on the lip of a large rock ledge that sidled up to the water, our feet in the pond's coolness. We sat side by side, me looking into the murky depths, Beth looking at me.

"What's going on with you, Em? You are acting really strange." She chuckled to herself. "I thought I was supposed to be the one with an attitude. You're the good kid, remember? At least, that's what my mom always says."

"Why?" I asked, not looking at my friend, my eyes riveted on the water as the sun beat down on it, making it glow.

"I don't know." Beth shrugged. "That's just what she says."

"Well, that's stupid. You don't have an attitude. You're perfect." I could feel my friend's eyes boring into me. I felt a wave of heat rush over me for the hundredth time that day, and I began to feel uncomfortable. "Let's swim." I jumped up and tugged my shirt over my head and unbuttoned my white cut-offs. In my underwear and bra, I dove into the shallow depths of the pond.

"Emily!" I heard Beth call out as my head broke through the surface. I rubbed the water out of my eyes and turned to look at her as she stood on the rock ledge, my shorts in her hand.

"What?"

"Look. You're...you're bleeding!" she exclaimed, showing me the red stain in the crotch of the denim.

"What?" I swam over to her and looked at the material with disbelieving eyes. Sure enough, there was a spot of blood the size of a silver dollar. I pulled myself out of the water and looked down at my underwear, where I found a similar stain made pink by the water.

"Oh my God!" I swallowed as I felt hot tears sting behind my eyelids. I felt emotions flowing through me at an alarming rate and I had no idea why. I wanted to cry, laugh, and yell all at the same time. Beth put her arm around my shoulders.

"Are you okay, Em? Do you need to sit down? Your mom said that it can make you feel weak or even cramp up. Are you okay?"

"I'm fine!" I raged, suddenly feeling more than a little embarrassed. I pushed her away from me and tugged my shirt back on. I took the shorts from her hand and began to rinse them in the water of the pond, praying to God I could get most of the stain out so I could walk home. The red stayed where it was. "My mom's gonna kill me," I sobbed as I rubbed with my fingertips.

"No, she's not. She'll understand, Em." I stood on shaky legs and struggled to pull the wet denim over my legs and butt. "Well this explains a lot." Beth smiled one of her crooked grins, her blue eyes twinkling.

"What is that supposed to mean?" I fired back. How dare Beth make jokes during a crisis like this?

"Your mom said that a woman will experience mood swings, and girl, you have definitely had them."

"I have not! I have been perfectly fine. Besides, what does my mother know, anyway?" I began to walk away from her, my wet feet making my sneakers soggy, every step producing a squishing sound. That made Beth laugh even harder, which only added to my misery. Although I was being childish and terribly difficult, deep down I was so thankful Beth was at my side at what I knew, even at the downside of fourteen, was a pivotal moment in my life as a woman.

~ ~ ~ ~ ~

Rebecca grinned. "SO, did your mom get mad?"

"No, of course not. In fact, to add to my humiliation, she grabbed me in the front yard, with neighbors all around us in their yards, and hugged me and made a huge fuss about her baby becoming a woman. I was mortified!" Rebecca threw her head back and laughed, her hand rubbing up and down my calf. "But then what self-serving teen wouldn't be?"

"So Beth hadn't started yet, obviously," she observed, still chuckling.

"No. That came a few months later. She was lucky; she started in the middle of the night, though it was my mother who helped her through it."

"Why?"

"Oh, Beth's mom was just too far into herself. She couldn't find the time, I imagine. Between the drinking and the men," I said dryly, remembering how often Beth's mom would leave her daughter to sort out her own problems. We were silent for a moment, each lost in our separate thoughts. "Oh," I said, grabbing the hand that rested on my knee, our fingers intertwining. "How did the doctor go today?"

Rebecca leaned her head back against the couch, her tired eyes looking at me. "He said that if it doesn't take this time, we'll try once more. If that doesn't take, then he suggested you and I start thinking of another plan of action. Maybe we should think about stopping—"

"No." I shook my head sternly. "We'll try again." One of us had to stay strong.

"Oh, baby, what if this doesn't work?" she whispered, that little line appearing between her eyes as it always did when she was worried or upset. I reached out my hand and rubbed it away with my thumb.

"It will work, sweetie. It has to." We stared into each other's eyes for a moment, neither wanting to break the connection. I needed to feel her tonight, to know that she was really here and everything would be okay.

With a sigh, Rebecca smiled. "Well, babe," she said finally, giving my thigh a squeeze, "we should get to bed. It's getting late." She leaned over and kissed me softly, but I grabbed on to her and deepened the kiss, holding her to me with both hands framing her face, leaving us both breathless.

"Wow," she breathed. "It is definitely time for bed."

Chapter Four

I lay in the dark, wrapped in Rebecca's arms and listening to the sound of her steady breathing. I could not get Beth off my mind. There was still more — more I needed to remember; more I needed to figure out before I could finally let her memory rest. There was so much left unfinished between us, so much left unsaid.

I could picture her face: her bright eyes shining, her hair loosely held in a ponytail or braid, most of it usually spilling from its bonds. She was smiling at me, that special little crooked smile that she saved for only me. Her eyes were so full of life and her adventurous spirit.

I gently disentangled myself from Rebecca and slipped out of bed. With a sleepy murmur of protest, Rebecca released her hold and turned onto her other side. On quiet feet, I headed into our bathroom, shutting the door with a soft click before turning on the light. I studied my reflection. My hair, which Rebecca calls golden, reaches to just below my shoulders. This is the shortest I've had my hair for a few years. I ran my fingers through the strands and tucked it behind my ears. My green eyes looked dully back at me. I saw no life in them right then. The skin under them was slightly puffy from the crying I had done earlier. Something told me I was not done crying, either. I felt so emotional, like I had a carbonated bottle of tears inside that someone had shaken to the point where the cork was going to shoot off into space leaving the contents to overflow.

"Babe, you okay?" Rebecca called sleepily from our bedroom.

"I'm fine. Go back to sleep." She mumbled something I couldn't understand, then all was quiet again. I splashed some cold water on my face, then tiptoed out of the bedroom.

Simon met me at the top of the stairs, his long, black tail swishing curiously in the air, his large gold eyes looking at me questioningly as he escorted me down. I trailed my fingers along the wall as I descended, my eyes focusing on the images in the pictures that lined the staircase.

The moonlight that filtered through the large downstairs windows allowed me to see Rebecca and me smiling with our arms around each other standing in front of the beautiful castle of Sleeping Beauty in Disneyland. Our friend Camille had taken the picture while her partner, Dana, had stood off to the side with a wide grin across her tanned face. I smiled to myself. That had been such a wonderful trip, our first together. We had been living with each other for less than a year.

I proceeded, looking down to make sure Simon hadn't planted himself between my feet, making us both fly down the remaining stairs. Unlike him, I knew I would not land on my feet. My heart beamed as I saw the picture of my lover and me on our dream vacation to Ireland, the land of her late mother's birth. We planned to go back in a couple years.

A bit further down was my college graduation picture. My mother had taken the shot, and my father and brother were-on either side of me, all three of us smiling broadly. I was the only one in my family to get a degree, Billy opting to join the service instead. I looked into the tired eyes of my father. He looked older than his years, and I worried about him. I knew his health was not great, and my mother just didn't want to worry us. My father was a kind man and had been a good father to grow up with, albeit a stern figure.

~ ~ ~ ~ ~

"So, what's this I hear — you and Beth wouldn't play with that Newman girl?" my father asked, a forkful of mashed potatoes halfway to his mouth. I could only stare at my father, for I had no answer. Instead, I decided to be angry with my mother. I looked at her, silently calling her a traitor. She didn't take the bait.

"Darla's mother said that she was awfully upset, Emmy."

"Well, we don't like her, Mom," I stammered in lieu of an explanation.

"You don't like her," my father said dryly. "Why? 'Cause she's not Beth?"

My father's comment took me by surprise. I looked across the table at my brother, who seemed to find his meat loaf very interesting. I knew I would get no help from him, mainly because I knew deep down Beth and I were wrong, but I wouldn't allow those words to pass through my lips. I looked back at my mother, who met my gaze with her own dark eyes burning into mine.

"I want to see you playing with kids other than Beth. Do I make myself clear, Emily Jane?"

"But—"

"Don't argue with your mother! That girl has got way too many problems. She's a bad influence on you. I won't have my daughter hanging out with that girl. Her parents aren't married anymore, and her mother whores around."

"But, Dad, that isn't Beth's fault!" I exclaimed, my face red with anger.

"Don't you talk to me that way, young lady! You are fourteen years old, still a child. I don't give a damn if you've started your monthly or not." I turned even redder at this announcement to the family. I could not even look Billy in the face, terrified of what I'd see there.

"Henry," my mother said quietly to my father, placing her hand on top of his. My father glanced up at me with apologetic eyes for a moment before they became serious again.

"Girls your age should have lots of friends. Right, honey?" He turned to look at my mother. "Didn't you have lots of girlfriends at Emmy's age?"

My mother didn't answer, but turned to me instead. She placed her soft, warm hand over mine.

"Sweetie, we're not saying that you can never see or play with Beth again, only that maybe you should give some other girls a chance. Okay? There have been a few new families that have moved into the neighborhood, and I've seen some girls and boys your age with them."

"Frances, don't act as if this isn't serious!" my father said to my mother.

"Honey, I will handle this." My mother gave him the "look". He shut his mouth and took a drink of his milk, his eyes focusing elsewhere.

"Okay?" my mother asked me again.

I glanced down at my half-eaten dinner and pushed my fork into the mountain of mashed potatoes. Feeling a lump in my throat too thick to speak over, I simply nodded.

"Good." My mother patted my hand before releasing it.

"So, Billy, how did try outs go? Did you make the team?" my father asked with barely controlled excitement edging his voice. I didn't bother to listen to my brother's answer. Why should I care if he made the stupid baseball team? I picked up my fork again and pushed my food around until it was a big pile of meat loaf, mashed potato, and green bean mush.

I leaned against the counter as I watched the sink fill steadily with billowy suds. My head jerked to the right when I heard a crash. Billy ran into the handle of the oven as he tried to catch the dishtowel he was tossing into the air. He drew his brows together and groaned, holding his stomach. I smiled to myself. Served him right, the big dope. He wouldn't even stand up for Beth.

"Is that water done yet?" He walked over to stand beside me.

"Almost," I said absently, watching the hot water stream

from the faucet.

"Good. I don't wanna be here all night with you."

"Thanks." I slugged him in the gut. He doubled over and glared at me. "This is just not fair, Billy."

He grinned. "Why? We always have to do dishes. It's like a national pastime."

"Not the dishes, you dope, this whole stupid thing with Beth. It sucks! Dad is being so unfair." I looked over my shoulder to the doorway of the kitchen to make sure neither of my parents was within listening distance. I could hear Captain Kirk giving orders to Spock in the next room. I turned back to my brother. "Why is he doing this, Billy?"

He shrugged his broad shoulders. "I don't know, Emmy. You know Dad. He usually has a reason for what he does, even if he's the only one who knows what it is." He smiled and slugged me lightly on the arm. "He loves us and is always trying to do what's best. I think he just worries because Beth has so many problems with her family, and that whole thing with her mom having that fling with the president of that bank she works at."

My head snapped around to stare at him. "How do you know about that?"

Billy shrugged indifferently, grabbing the handful of knives I had just washed and put into the sink to rinse. "Everyone knows about that, Emmy. It's no big secret."

"But, they never throw a fit because you and John spend so much time together. And his dad's a drunk, too! And he beats his wife! So what's the big deal about Beth and me? God, this is so stupid!" I could feel my anger building. It was not fair that my parents were trying to dictate who I spent time with. My blood began to boil. How dare they try to come between Beth and me!

"Come on, Emmy. You know you guys can still play, or whatever it is you do."

"Don't pacifize me, Billy!"

My brother grinned. "That's patronize, you dip. And I'm not." I slammed the freshly washed glass into the hot water so hard that a stream of it fountained into the air and splashed me in the face. My brother fell against the counter laughing, his hand holding his stomach. "Dang, girl, calm down." I just glared at him and wiped my face.

~ ~ ~ ~ ~

Having reached the foot of the stairs, I made my way into the kitchen and brewed a pot of Ginger Peach tea. Sitting with my steaming mug at the table, I opened the photo album once again. The year

1981 came in with a bang. My father had just been promoted to sales manager at the car dealership in December, and my brother would be joining the military after his high school graduation in June. Beth and I would be going into high school in the fall. Ronald Reagan would be elected president and shot before the year was out, and MTV, the greatest of all Eighties TV phenomena, would begin. During that twelve-month period, two hundred and ninety-six people would die from a disease given the short-lived title of "the gay cancer".

I flipped to a picture that immediately brought a smile to my lips. The Polaroid showed Beth and me in the living room of my parent's house, our arms around each other's shoulders, glasses of red Kool-Aid raised high for the camera. Our young faces had huge smiles plastered on them. In the background my parents could be seen in each other's arms, caught forever in a New Year's kiss. Billy had snapped the picture right at midnight. The caption read, "Mom, Dad, Emmy, and Beth celebrate the New Year: 1981."

~ ~ ~ ~ ~

"That looks like such a rad movie!" Beth exclaimed, staring at the commercial for the incredible adventures of a new hero, Indiana Jones. Steven Spielburg's "Raiders of the Lost Ark" was due out in theaters soon.

"I can't wait!" Billy agreed from the couch behind us as we sat on the floor. He dumped a handful of popcorn into his waiting mouth.

Beth looked over her shoulder at him, a lopsided grin on her face. "I bet Harrison Ford kicks as much ass as he did as Han," she said, referring to her hero playing Han Solo in "Star Wars" and "The Empire Strikes Back".

"Beth," I said in surprise, "my parents might hear you. Watch your mouth." She stuck her tongue out at me and turned back to Billy.

"Not to mention Karen Allen." He smirked and Beth smiled back at him and nodded before she turned to me.

"Who's Karen Allen?" I asked, looking from one to the other.

"A really cute chick," Billy informed me.

"Hey, ready for bed?" Beth grinned as she wiggled an eyebrow, letting me know she had something planned.

"Hey, don't leave me down here alone, guys," Billy complained. "It's bad enough I had to stay home tonight."

"You had a chance to go with Sarah and her family, Billy," I chastised without the slightest bit of sympathy.

"Yeah, but her dad hates me. No way am I gonna spend a couple days with that old geezer watching us every minute.

Talk about a shitty New Year's."

"Guess he just doesn't want a bunch of pups left after you leave," Beth said with a wicked smile. "Sorry, Billy boy, gotta go."

I shrugged at his incredulous look and stood to lead the way toward the stairs. My bedroom hadn't changed much over the years. I still had pastel blue curtains hanging over the large window, but had talked my mom into letting me paint the room. Now instead of the curtain-matching blue, my walls were white. Not a big victory, but life is made of small victories. Posters of Harrison Ford, the musical group Toto were plastered on my walls. Olivia Newton-John was on one closet door, with Bonnie Tyler on the other. Clark Gable and Vivian Leigh graced the wall on one side of my dresser mirror, while Judy Garland and Tom Drake graced the other in a still from "Meet Me in St. Louis", forever frozen in the classic Hollywood pre-kiss pose. On the wall opposite the dresser was a poster with Bogie and Ingrid Bergman from "Casablanca". Beth had gotten me into the great classics.

"Oh, man. What a long night." Beth plopped down on my bed and grabbed her overnight bag from the floor. She unzipped the largest pocket and dug around for a few minutes, then with a smile, she withdrew a small bottle nearly filled with clear liquid. She gave me a grin full of mischief.

"What's that?" I asked, walking to the bed to sit next to her.

"Rum."

"Rum?" I repeated, my curiosity piqued. "Where did you get it?" I took the bottle from her and read the label. "Ron Rico Silver Label. Puerto Rican Rum."

She took the bottle back and unscrewed the cap. "It's my mom's."

"Uh, won't she miss it?" I asked, still eyeing the little glass bottle warily.

"Nah. Are you kidding? She's got enough to last her ten New Year's. She won't even know it's gone." Beth put the opening to her lips and, with a deep breath, took a drink. I had to grab the rum from her as she began to cough and sputter, almost dropping it to the carpet.

"You okay?" I asked as I thumped her back in concern.

"Ugh! Yeah, I'm fine. Try some." Her voice was low and rough from the coughing fit and the burning liquid. I gave her one last glance to make sure she wasn't going to keel over and took a swig. The sweet fire filled my mouth, and I clenched my eyes tightly shut so I wouldn't spit it all over my bed. I managed to swallow, feeling the rum sear my insides as it finally landed in my stomach with a whoosh.

"Good God!" I cried after my own coughing fit. I handed the bottle back to Beth. "That stuff is awful! Your mom actually drinks that stuff on purpose?"

Beth laughed at me. "I know. It's better when you have it in something like a daiquiri."

"How would you know?"

"I've had them before. They're really good."

I eyed her with a raised brow and then shrugged. "So, what do you think of that new kid. What's his name? Scott something?" I asked, looking at her profile as she took another drink. She closed her eyes as she swallowed, not looking at me as she handed over the rum. She swallowed a couple of times, but did not cough or show any other sign of discomfort. Finally, she took in a mouthful of air as though to cool her tingling mouth. Something told me this was not her first experience with straight rum.

"Scott Mathews?" she supplied. I nodded as I took a drink. "I think he's a dork. Why?"

"Darla likes him. He's all I heard about last week. Scott this, Scott that. Isn't Scott cute; he's got a cute butt."

Darla Newman had become one of my close friends, completely against Beth's will, but it pleased my parents. Beth and Darla didn't get along that great, but Beth tolerated her for my sake. Darla thought Beth was weird because she didn't like makeup, nor did she do anything with her hair. Many of the girls our age wore their hair at shoulder length or shorter, but Beth, as usual, went against the crowd. She wore her hair long and straight, though usually pulled back in a ponytail or smashed down by some hat. Her long bangs were always being pushed out of the way by her hand or mine. She did not constantly talk about boys, and she had no interest in clothes. She just didn't fit in, and she relished her differences. She said they made her unique. I thought it just made for hard times with people snickering behind her back and making jokes about her. Beth didn't mind the names they called her, some of which I really didn't understand. One frequent name directed at her from the boys was dike. I mean, what does a water embankment have to do with her? Once, I told Billy how silly and strange it was for Beth to be called that. He turned bright red and walked away mumbling about homework. All the same, I thought it was interesting that the reasons people didn't like Beth were exactly the reasons that I did.

"I think he's a dork, too. I mean, he's not even cute." I looked over at Beth and waited as she took a drink.

"Ahh!" she exclaimed, smacking her lips together with a smile.

"You've got to be joking. That stuff is awful." I took the bottle from her outstretched hand and looked at it again, making an impromptu decision that I did not like rum. "What is this stuff supposed to do to you, anyway?" No sooner had the words left my mouth than I felt a surge of energy run through my body, making it tingle from the soles of my bare feet to the end of my ponytail. My eyes opened wide as I tried to stifle a giggle that sprouted straight from my gut.

Beth laughed. "You were saying?"

"Whoa." I turned to her. "I feel reeeally strange." I smiled. It felt as though my head was as light as a feather, strange thoughts floating around like billowy clouds in a clear, blue sky.

"Really?" Beth said, trying to hold back her own giggle. "You don't look strange."

"No?" Beth shook her head, her bangs falling into her eyes. I reached out to try and move them, but my eyes weren't working as well as they usually did, and my perception was off. I snickered as I poked her in the eye. "Sorry, Bethy, honey."

"Quite all right." She giggled, rubbing her red right eye.

I couldn't keep my head still so it began to bob on my neck like it was hooked to a spring, which made us laugh even more. I would always be a lightweight when it came to alcohol.

~ ~ ~ ~ ~

I smiled as I ran my finger over the glossy faces in the photograph. We were so young. Then my smile became bittersweet. The year I turned fifteen would also be the year our friendship would take a severe turn for the worse. But I didn't want to think about that. My thoughts turned back to the first night Beth got me drunk.

~ ~ ~ ~ ~

After many silly attempts at playing cards, acting out scenes from our favorite movies, and singing, Beth and I decided to go to bed, the alcohol draining the energy out of us both. Beth switched off the light and stumbled her way back to bed, hissing a curse as her foot smacked into something. I lay on my back staring at the ceiling, my mind caught between a state of total exhaustion and one of utter clarity. It was a strange feeling. I felt the mattress shift as Beth lay beside me on her back, her eyes on my profile. She was quiet, but I could hear her breath come in quick bursts. She turned on her side facing me.

"Em?" she asked, trying to whisper, but not quite managing it.

"Yes, Beth?"

"You're a fun drunk." She giggled.

"I am not a drunk. You're the drunk. You drank a way lot more than I did, you fish."

She giggled again. "Na ah. You did."

"No, you did." I rolled over to face her and stuck my finger in her side. She cried out and shifted away from me.

"Shh." I laughed as I began to attack again. "You'll wake my parents." I reached out with both hands, groping for her most ticklish parts.

"You better quit," she said through clenched teeth, grabbing my hands to still them and give her aching sides a reprieve. "I'm warning you, Em. You'll be sorry."

I giggled as I looked into her eyes, which held an evil gleam in the near darkness of my bedroom. I stuck my tongue out at her. She raised her eyebrows and leaned up on her elbow, looking down at me. A burst of heat roared through my body, landing squarely between my legs. I swallowed.

"Are you gonna stop?" she asked quietly.

"No," I croaked. Why did I say that? I could end this all right now and get her to stop looking at me that way if only I'd agree to behave. Then we could go to sleep.

"No?"

Say yes! Say yes! "Do you think I'd actually listen to you, Miss Smarty Pants?" I could hear a groan inside my head. I shoved it away and glared playfully back at her. I reached an experimental hand toward her stomach again, only for it to be taken in hers. She pushed me onto my back and rolled on top of me, holding both my hands securely over my head. My head was in a daze from the alcohol that ran though my system, and from the heat and weight of Beth's body stretched out on mine. Wherever our skin touched, mine flamed. I felt like I had a full-body fever. Our legs were bare, leaving our underwear and T-shirts as the only barriers between our blazing bodies.

"Are you still going to fight me?" she breathed, her lips just inches from mine. I could only shake my head. She smiled vaguely. I'm not sure who finally bridged the gap between our mouths, but the next thing I knew, her lips were pressed to mine.

She let go of my hands and ran her own down to my shoulders. My hands automatically reached across the expanse of her back, her voracious body heat nearly burning me through the thin material of her T-shirt. Our bodies shifted slightly, and I nearly cried out as I felt her leg go between mine, her thigh pressed to the throbbing between my legs. I had no idea what was happening, but I was enjoying it thoroughly. I felt wet, as if I had peed my pants. I could feel Beth's own strange wetness against my thigh. I began to pull away from her, but she grabbed me tighter. Then I felt the wetness of her tongue against my swollen lips. I had heard about this from Billy. French kissing. Curious, I eagerly opened my lips to her.

Beth's tongue was soft, and I could faintly taste rum mingled with Crest toothpaste. She ran her tongue over mine and seemed to search for something just out of reach in my mouth. I heard her whimper as she pressed her lower body into mine. I gasped as her thigh rubbed against me, and then she started a slow, rocking motion with her body. She pulled her mouth from mine and buried her face against my neck. I closed my eyes, reaching my hands down to press her into me, to intensify the contact. She grabbed my thigh that wasn't between her legs and raised it so it rested near her hip. I sucked in my breath at the heightened sensation. I couldn't help the moan that escaped my throat. This seemed to affect Beth; her rhythm quickened.

I felt hot breath on the side of my neck followed by her lips. I arched in response and noticed additional sensations coming from my breasts where they rubbed against hers. There was a tight tingling feeling, almost painful, throbbing from my nipples, which were hard like when I got out of the shower. I reached my hands up and put my fingers between our bodies and onto Beth's nipples. They were just as hard as mine felt. She groaned into the tender skin of my throat.

"Oh, Em."

A pressure was building in the pit of my stomach, and it was working its way down with every thrust of Beth's thigh against me. It moved quickly to spread out like a blanket of warmth onto my butt and the tops of my thighs and sailed like a comet through the sky to between my legs. My breathing quickened as the wave of heat began to turn into a pulse like a heartbeat. As if they had developed a mind of their own, my hips arched to meet Beth's rhythm. I dug my fingers into the hem of her shirt as I felt that pulsing pressure explode from my body with a blast of light behind my eyes. My mouth opened as my eyes closed; my breathing and heart stopped. I could feel Beth tense against me, her breaths coming in gasps against my neck, her hands curling into the sheet on either side of my head, until her hips stopped altogether.

Slowly, slowly, my sense of the world returned, and I could breathe again. Beth pushed up so she was above me with her weight on her arms. We stared into each other's eyes, not sure what else to do. She opened her mouth as if she were going to say something, when we both started at the knock on my bedroom door.

"Emmy? Beth? Are you two okay?" my mother's voice said quietly from the other side. I swallowed hard, but managed to bring my voice to its normal level.

"Fine, Mom."

"I heard a noise."

I looked up at Beth who shrugged; her eyes looked as mortified as I felt. "Uh, Beth fell out of bed. She had a bad dream." I closed my eyes at how lame I knew the lie sounded, but my mother seemed to buy it.

"Okay, sweetie. See you in the morning."

"'Night." I heard her soft, slippered steps fade and disappear altogether.

To my doleful relief, Beth moved off me and rolled onto her back on her side of the bed, careful not to touch me in any way. With the loss of her body heat, my body felt chilled in the cold January night air. I stayed where I was, but looked over at Beth, noticing that her breathing still had not completely returned to normal. She put her forearm over her eyes.

"I am so drunk," she whispered.

"Yeah." I groaned dramatically. "Me, too." I actually had never felt more sober in all my fourteen and a half years. I could still feel a faint pulsing between my legs. *What had we just done? Was that normal between friends? Between girls?* Darla Newman and some of her friends had told me stories about how they would lie down with a pillow or a teddy bear and rubbed against it.

I turned to look at Beth expecting to meet eyes made dark by the night, but she had her back to me. Her breathing was fairly normal now, and I couldn't tell if she was asleep or not.

"Beth?" I whispered in a voice that was barely audible to my own ears. Her only reply was a slight moan as she resettled her shoulder against the mattress.

The light of the morning came quickly, its brightness stirring me out of a restless sleep. I glanced at the alarm clock that sat on the dresser across from the bed. It was only 8:15. I laid my head back down on the pillow with a sigh. My head hurt, and I didn't feel like I had fully returned to the land of the living yet. I looked over at Beth. She lay on her stomach, facing me, arms crossed underneath the pillow. She was still very much asleep, her breathing slow and deep. As last night came back to me, I studied her face. Her mouth was relaxed and there was a slight smile on her full lips. Maybe she was reliving the experience in her dreams. I closed my eyes as a now familiar heat blossomed between my legs. *No, no. Never again. We can never do that again.*

~ ~ ~ ~ ~

Chapter Five

I stood at the counter with my hand on top of the coffeemaker as it perked to life, my mind a million miles away. I saw Beth and me that morning as we dressed for breakfast. We joked around as usual, both complaining about our common headache, and shared a giggle or two about getting away with becoming drunk. To the untrained eye, it would have seemed as though nothing was wrong or different. But I knew, and I could not meet Beth's eyes. I thought if I looked into those ocean-blue depths, I would see something that would scare me, and I wouldn't be able to turn away from it. Our usual, easy connection was gone, and I missed it.

I jumped slightly when arms encircled my waist and warmth pressed along my back, but then relaxed into the familiar body.

"What time did you come back to bed?" Rebecca whispered into the side of my neck.

"Late. Too late." I closed my eyes when I felt a hand snake its way up to cup my breast through the cotton of my T-shirt. My body responded immediately, already electrified from the memory of my first time with Beth.

"Mmm. If only I didn't have to go to school today," she whispered.

"Oh, the things I could do to you."

Rebecca chuckled into my ear. "You are cruel, Emily."

"You have no idea." I turned in the circle of her arms and looked deep into my lover's eyes. I saw so much love and compassion there. How had I gotten so lucky?

"When are we going to fly to Colorado?" she asked, gently kissing my swollen, red eyes one at a time.

"We?" I said breathlessly, my hands slowly caressing her back and rear.

"Mmm hmm. I'm going with you to the funeral." Rebecca's lips traveled to my ear, taking the lobe between her teeth.

I closed my eyes. "Uh, what...what about school?" My hand reached around the front of her robe and slowly pulled the belt loose, letting the material slide through my fingers.

"I'll take a few days personal leave. It's not a problem."

"Oh, Becky, honey. I don't want you to get in trouble. It's not that important." I swept the ends of the terry cloth aside and stared hungrily at her naked breasts just before my hands engulfed their softness. Rebecca groaned and her lips found mine.

"It's important to you, baby." Rebecca gently pushed me back toward the countertop and motioned that I should hop onto it. I did as instructed.

"I can go alone....Oooh." Her hand slid between my thighs, her fingers finding my already-soaked underwear. She gently slipped a finger around the edge and slid into me. I threw my head back, my bottom lip caught between my teeth. Rebecca ran her tongue along my exposed throat.

"You'll never have to go alone, Emily," she whispered as she added a second finger and slowly began to pump in and out of me. Her lips found mine again. "You want me to go, don't you?"

"Oh, yes...yes, I want...want you to go." I closed my eyes tightly. She increased her rhythm as her tongue found my rock hard nipple through my shirt. I groaned, opening my legs wider for her. Rebecca moved the silky material of my underwear aside a bit more and reached in with her thumb to rub me with slow, measured movements.

"Oh, God," I moaned.

I began to rock my hips when I felt myself getting close. Rebecca increased her thrusts as my moans came faster and closer together. I grabbed the handles on the cabinet doors behind me and clenched my eyes shut, my mouth open as I felt myself slip over the edge. Rebecca quickened her movements, her fingers coaxing the orgasm out of me, one stroke at a time. I cried out her name and my body collapsed against the cabinets, my breathing heavy. Rebecca removed her hand and leaned into me, kissing me softly. I held her for a moment until everything slowed to normal speed. Finally, I pulled back. With a wicked gleam in her Irish eyes, she placed her index finger covered with my wetness to her lips and sucked gently. I stared, transfixed. After a moment, she pulled the finger free.

"Now I can taste you all day."

A short time later, Rebecca hustled out the door with a quick peck on my lips, our countertop interlude making her run slightly late for work. I closed the door behind her and leaned against it, thinking about all I had to do today to prepare for our trip.

~ ~ ~ ~ ~

I laid out my big beach towel with a faded Popeye winking at me on the front lawn and carefully arranged myself on it, one leg bent up, the other straight out in front of me. I leaned back on my elbows, my face raised toward the rays of the uncharacteristically hot early May sun. I pushed my sunglasses up slightly, leaving a smear of Coppertone across the lens. "Damn." I closed my eyes and waited for the sun to do its job.

"You know that's really bad for you," I heard a voice say, a slight dry tone to it. I opened my eyes and squinted against the silhouette of Beth standing over me. I didn't need to see her face to imagine the lopsided grin that was surely there.

"So? Darla said that all the girls are doing this."

"What do you care what the other girls are doing?" Beth dropped down to the grass next to me, her long, shorts-clad legs bent at the knees, her hands dangling over the tops. She adjusted her Denver Broncos cap, lifting the bill slightly so I could see her face to the bottom of her eyes, the rest cloaked by shadows.

"I don't know why on earth you bother wearing that cap. The Broncos suck."

"You just wait, Em. One of these days, we are going to get the greatest quarterback ever to play the game, and then you'll laugh. Craig Morten is okay for now, but you just wait. You mark my words. Can you say Super Bowl Champions?" She adjusted the cap again.

"Whatever. So why are you so late? I thought you were coming over earlier this morning." I grabbed a small brown bottle of suntan oil and squirted some into the palm of my hand. "Want some?" I extended the bottle to Beth.

"No. I don't intend to sit out here and bake, thank you."

"Hey, just 'cause some of us aren't naturally tan like some people I know." I glared up at her. "Besides, a tan looks really good," I argued as I began to spread a second layer of the coconut-smelling oil over my very white legs.

"Yeah, in June or July. Em, this is the first hot day we've had this year."

I chose to ignore that obvious fact and returned to my first question. "So where were you?"

"I was talking to my dad," she said, trying to hide the grin that slowly spread across her face.

"He called? Oh, Beth, that's great! I know he hasn't called since Christmas." I smiled, truly happy for Beth. Her typical nonchalance was a complete act. She was always beyond thrilled when Jim called or wrote. "What did he have to say? How's his new wife? What's her name?"

"Lynn." I nodded and began to spread the sticky oil on my other leg before starting on my arms. "They're fine. Happy.

Guess what, Em?" The level of excitement in her voice qua-drupled in those last three words. I looked at her, sensing she would need my full attention for what she had to say. "I'm going away for the summer!"

She had my attention, all right. "What!"

"Yeah. My dad is going to send me to a camp for talented kids. I'm going to do theater! Isn't it radical!" Beth glowed.

I felt my heart sink. What would I do for an entire summer without my Beth? My heartbreak immediately turned into anger. "What, so your dad has nothing to do with you for like almost two years, and now you're going to drop everything and run at his beck and call?"

Beth's face fell. She looked at me for almost a full minute before she spoke, her voice very low. "I am not running at his beck and call. I love my father and would do anything to see him and be with him, even for just a little while. And besides, this isn't about him. This is an amazing opportunity for me to do different kinds of theater, gain some experience. Some of the best instructors in the country are going to be there." She stood and wiped her hands over the seat of her shorts to knock off any loose grass. "Besides, someone like you wouldn't understand. You're too busy trying to look like Darla Newman." Beth stepped over my beach towel and walked across our yard to her own before disappearing through the torn screen door.

"You'll miss my birthday and the Fourth," I said to myself, feeling beyond miserable. My stomach felt strange; my chest felt...empty.

~ ~ ~ ~ ~

I slowly lowered the lid of the suitcase, the solid click of the snaps bringing me back to the present. I wiped a finger under my eye and collected the wetness with the tip. I had hurt Beth so badly that day in late spring. I should have been thrilled for her. It was the chance of a lifetime. She knew it, and I refused to care.

~ ~ ~ ~ ~

I opened the screen door, careful not to let it slam behind me and chance being skinned alive by my mother. Hopping off the step of the porch, trying to gather my courage, I had moved a few feet toward the Sayers' yard when I stopped dead in my tracks.

"You're worthless! You'd rather run to that bastard who left you! You got that, Beth? He abandoned you, sayin' you ain't even his kid anyway!" Mrs. Sayers was screaming, her shrill, drunken voice carrying on the late evening breeze.

"That's not true!" Beth screamed back, her voice just this side of tears.

"No? Ask 'im! Ask that rotten son of a bitch if you don't believe me. Him and that slut wife of his."

"You're just jealous because you can't find anyone who'll put up with you, because you're a drunk!"

Slap!

I jumped as I heard the sharp sound of skin hitting skin.

"What you sayin' to me, you little bitch! Huh? Talkin' to your mother that way? Huh?"

Slap!

"Get off me, woman!"

I dared to take a couple steps forward, my eyes welling with unshed tears. I had to be careful that Beth not see me cry; she would be mortified if she knew I had heard everything and felt any pity for her.

"You're worthless, Elizabeth! You got that? Rotten and worthless!"

"Fuck you, Mother!"

I jumped again as Beth's front door was shoved open so hard that one of the hinges protested just before it snapped from the wood. Beth flew out at a quick walk, about to break into an all-out run, when her head snapped in my direction. I could see the wet trails that led from both pain-filled eyes as well as a bloody trickle that began at the corner of her mouth. The moonlight caught in her eyes for just a moment as our gazes locked, then she turned away from me and began walking at a brisk pace down the street.

I wasn't sure what to do, but then I reasoned that she didn't start to run because deep down she wanted me to follow. She needed me to be there for her right now, as I had refused to be earlier that afternoon.

My heart was pounding dangerously fast as I jogged down the driveway past my dad's old Dodge. I could see Beth up ahead, her dark figure illuminated every few yards by the street lamps that lined the way. I could barely hear her sobs above my own thundering heartbeat. Beth turned down the narrow path that would lead toward the Toilet Bowl, completely shrouded in darkness now. We had traveled this path so many times, we could have done it with our eyes closed. I followed, increasing my speed so I could catch up to her in case she decided to duck into the trees.

"Beth?" I called out when I was only ten feet behind her. She didn't answer, just kept walking, her hand snapping a small branch from a tree, which she began to strip of its new leaves as she walked. "Beth? Please stop. Please."

I closed the distance between us and grabbed her by the shoulder. She turned cold eyes on me, her tears still silently falling down her cheeks. She said nothing.

"I'm so sorry. I heard all those terrible things she said to you." I couldn't control my own voice and began to choke on my words, the pain and guilt from earlier mixing with the pain I felt looking at her face now. "It's not true, Beth. It's not." Tears began to tumble from my eyes as quickly as my words fell from my mouth. "What she said to you. You're so beautiful, so talented, and you're loved, Beth. You're wanted. You must know that. She doesn't know what she's saying."

A guttural sob ripped from Beth's throat, and she fell into my arms. I held her to me, absorbing the shocks of her quaking body. I felt her knees give, and she began to sink to the ground. I stayed with her, never losing contact as we slowly hit the dirt path. Her tears came in earnest now, our sobs breaking the silence of the hot, late spring night. I held her to me as if letting her go meant letting go of a part of myself. I cried for her and for me, realizing I had thrown her father in her face earlier, just as her mother had done a few minutes before.

"I'm sorry, Beth. I didn't mean it. I'm sorry. I was being selfish."

Beth took a deep breath and tried to get herself under control. She took in several more breaths, never leaving my embrace. "It's okay, Em," she finally said, her voice thick with emotion still needing to be shed. "It's not your fault."

"Yes, it is. I should have been there for you today. You were so excited. I'm sorry."

In response, she tightened her hold on my arms, which encircled her side.

We sat on the path for what must have been close to an hour, both of us lost in our separate memories of what had just happened. I felt numb, impotent to do anything.

"Let's go sit by the Bowl," Beth said, her voice startling the stillness of the night.

As one, we stood. I gave her a last tight squeeze before I let her go. I looked at her face and gently ran my thumb over the blood that had seeped from the corner of her mouth. In silence, we walked toward the small pond.

It wasn't lost on me that this was the first physical contact between us since New Year's. I wondered if she was thinking about that, too. Probably not. Beth had too much else on her mind to worry about something that had happened five months before. We never discussed the significance of that night, if there was any, both claiming to have been too drunk to remember much. But I remembered, no matter how much I tried to forget.

We sat at the pond's edge side by side, our hands in our laps as if in fear they might wander over to the other's body.

"When do you leave?" I asked, my voice hushed as though the very night was listening.

"Mid-June." She turned to look at me. "I'm going to miss your birthday, Em. I'm sorry. I'll leave about two weeks before."

I sighed deeply, then smiled. "I know. That's one of the reasons I was upset when you told me." I looked into the water, black as tar without the sun's rays to make it glow. "Pretty bad, huh?"

"No. I nearly said no because of that."

My head shot up. "What? Beth, no. You need to do this. You're so good at acting, and this is only going to make you better!"

"But I'm always there for your birthday. I know how much it means to you...to me." Her pained eyes pleaded with me.

"I'll survive." I nudged her shoulder with mine. "Besides, we always have yours in October."

She smiled at me. "Will you write me?"

"Of course I will. You don't need to ask that, Beth."

~ ~ ~ ~ ~

I walked to my home office and sat heavily in the comfortable, high-backed chair behind the antique desk Rebecca had given me last Christmas. I leaned my head back and to the side so I could look out the window to my right. Our neighbor, Alison Briggs, was raking the leaves between our two townhouses. She and her husband Howard had lived in the house next door for seven years, ever since he had retired from the Air Force. They were just a few years older than my parents and were very nice to Rebecca and me, but I always felt they were not completely comfortable with our relationship, especially Howard. Rebecca thought I was being too sensitive.

I turned my attention back to my office. This room had been one of the reasons why I'd wanted this place. My home office was bigger than my office at work. The top half of the walls were painted white, the bottom half were rich cherry wood paneling that matched the woodwork around the door, windows, and ceiling. Bookshelves were built into the walls behind my desk and across from it. I had filled the shelves with every type of book from V.C. Andrews to Stephen King, from Nicole Conn to Homer. Behind me was my prized set of leather-bound law books, given to me my first year of college.

I looked at the computer in front of me, its dark screen mirroring my image in its glossy finish, the vibrant, random lines dancing in geometric patterns. With a sigh I moved the mouse slightly; the screen came to life. I logged on to the Internet, found the phone directory, and clicked onto an airlines page. I was about to click on United when the cordless phone rang.

"Hello?" I said into the handset, which I balanced on my shoulder as I continued to gauge prices.

"Emmy, honey?"

"Hi, Mom. What's up?" My mother sighed on the other end of the line. I closed my eyes as I steadied myself for what I knew would follow.

"You heard about Beth, honey?"

"Yes. Billy called me at work yesterday and told me."

"He shouldn't have done that! Call you at work to tell you such terrible news. What was he thinking?"

I was surprised at how emotional my mother sounded. I decided to go easy on her. "It's okay, Mom. I was glad he told me as soon as he did." I left United and clicked on American.

"So you're coming home?" she asked, her voice quiet yet filled with hope.

"Yes. Rebecca and I are coming." I took out a legal pad and a pen and began to jot down the prices of tickets to Denver International Airport.

"Oh, I'm so glad, honey. I wasn't sure whether or not Rebecca would be able to get the time off. That is so wonderful of her to do that, don't you think? She's such a nice girl."

I could hear the smile in my mom's voice. She and Rebecca got along just like old friends, much to my initial relief. "Well, Mom, what did you expect? She *is* my partner. It would be no different than if Dad were to take some time off."

"The difference, honey, is that your father wouldn't have bothered."

We both chuckled at the truth in that statement. "Okay, Mom. So get to the point. What's up?" I asked, beginning to get impatient. My mother was not one to call just to chat. She usually had a purpose.

"Well, honey. I...I just wanted to say that I am so sorry. I know how much Beth meant to you...at one time. I think maybe your father and I overreacted a bit when you two were girls. Maybe we weren't being fair. You know, last year she came back here, and she actually had lunch with me one day. I made her peanut butter and jelly with the thin-sliced bread—"

"Cut in half diagonally?" I asked, not able to keep the grin off my face.

"Of course! Just what kind of hostess do you think I am, anyway?"

I grinned. "Why on earth did you make her PBJ?"

"That's what she asked for."

I dropped my pen, rested my elbow on the arm of my chair, and covered my eyes with my fingers, sighing heavily.

"Are you okay, Emmy?" my mother asked, her voice just above a whisper.

"Yeah...yes. I'm okay. You know she came up here right after she left there. She never mentioned she'd seen you."

"She probably didn't want to upset you, sweetie."

"I had no idea, Mom. None. I had no idea she was sick. Did she tell you she was?"

"Yes."

"What!" I sat up in my chair, my hand flying from my eyes. "Why didn't you tell me?"

"Would it have mattered, Emily?"

I sighed again as I looked out the window. Alison had moved to her small front yard, her thin jacket blowing away from her body in the increasing gusts of wind as she bent to pull some stray weeds.

"No. And to be even more honest, I'll never forgive myself. I wasted my last chance, Mom. Once again, I wasted my chance. She needed me, and I couldn't be there. I slunk away from her. Again." My voice began to quiver as the emotions sailed to the surface.

"What do you mean, Emmy? Again?" My mother's voice betrayed her confusion.

"Nothing. Look, I'd better go. I was just about to order our plane tickets off the Net when you called."

"You know, that must be so handy — having a second phone line for the Internet. I keep trying to get your father to get a second line here."

"What, so your solitaire game won't be interrupted?" I laughed.

"Hey, don't knock it, kiddo. I am the neighborhood champion, you know."

I chuckled before turning serious again. "So what time? When?"

"What? The funeral? Uh, hang on. I have it right here." I could hear the shuffling of newspaper in the background. "Okay, here we go. It's Monday afternoon. Uh, it starts at 3:00."

"Where?" I held my breath.

"Pioneer Cemetery."

I closed my eyes again. "Okay. Talk to you later, Mom." I clicked the off button and set the phone on the desk harder than intended.

~ ~ ~ ~ ~

"I didn't really know my great-grandmother; I thought her funeral went really good, though. So where do you think you want to be buried?" I asked Beth as I climbed to the top of the monkey bars.

She dug the toes of her tennis shoes into the gravel at her feet and twisted the swing first to her left, then to her right, the heavy chain coiling like a rope in front of her nose. "Pioneer. It's the oldest cemetery in Pueblo."

"Really?"

"Yup. But I am no way gonna be buried here. No way!" She let go of the chain, her swing sharply twisting to the left, then smoothly to the right, before stilling in the middle again. She grinned. "Have you ever been there?"

"Nope." I hooked the back of my knees onto a bar and let myself fall through the opening. My hair fanned out under me, my arms stretching for the ground that was just out of reach.

"We should go there," Beth said, her voice wistful.

"Why? Ugh!" I pulled myself back up with my stomach muscles.

"Because. It's peaceful. It's beautiful and full of history."

"Hmm." I shrugged. "Okay. We'll go there someday."

~ ~ ~ ~ ~

The midday Friday traffic was grating on my nerves. With an exasperated groan, I swung my Taurus off the main road and decided to take the back route. This city amazed me. No matter what time of day or night, the streets were so overloaded with traffic that road rage never surprised me, and in fact, I could relate.

Every Friday at this hour, Rebecca had a chemistry class, and they would usually be doing a lab. Rebecca should be able to talk for a couple minutes if I stopped by on my way to the store.

The conversation with my mother was playing through my mind, tying my nerves into knots again. I couldn't believe Beth had told my mother about her sickness but not me. There was a time when I would've been the first person she turned to. The first to know, the first to comfort. Sadly, I was forced to realize that time had come and gone many years ago. Then my thoughts returned to that day in the park. Did she call me there to tell me? Had my apathy toward her made her hold her tongue? These were questions for which I would never know the answers.

With a sigh, I grabbed a CD from the portable carrier and slipped it into the car's player. Immediately, my nerves settled as the soothing tones of Sarah Brightman coaxed me into a more relaxed mood. I began to sing along with her angelic voice to "All I Ask," a duet with Cliff Richards. The tune from "Phantom of the Opera" filled the confines of the car as I cranked the volume, losing myself in the music and trying to forget about Beth for the first time in two days.

~ ~ ~ ~ ~

"How in the hell can you listen to that opera crap?" I asked, my hands on my hips as I watched Beth, her eyes closed, brows rising and falling with each resonating chord of "La Traviata".

She let out a long, slow breath as the aria came to an end and hit stop on her cassette player. "Have you ever listened to it?"

"No."

"Come here." She pushed play and quickly grabbed my hand to stop me from running out of her room. The man's tenor filled the small, dark room and my ears.

"This sucks."

"No, Em. Don't you hear it?"

"Yeah and it sucks!" I tried to pull away, but she kept me in an iron grip.

"No, don't just hear it, Em, really feel it. Let it enter you and fill you up inside." She turned to face me. "Close your eyes." I just stared at her like she was crazy, my arms crossed over my chest. "Please? For me? Do this, and if you don't like it, you never have to hear it again. Okay?"

"Fine." I closed my eyes with a heavy sigh.

"Now, listen to what he's saying," Beth said close to my ear, her voice soft and wistful.

"I don't know what he's saying. He's singing in Italian."

"You don't have to understand the words, Em. Just understand the music and the emotion behind it."

Still determined to believe Beth had lost her mind, I listened anyway, and, suddenly, I knew what she was talking about. I felt a chill run down my spine, and my chest literally expanded with emotion, as if I had just taken a deep breath even though I couldn't breathe at all. As the singer's voice rose in his anguish, so did my eyebrows and my heart rate. I felt his sorrow, his loss. Before I could do anything to stop it, I felt twin tears slip from my eyes, lazily sliding down my cheeks to be followed by two others. I couldn't stop. The music rose to a hypnotic pitch, his voice leading the way up the hill, only to fall down the other side, slowly fading until all I heard was the ringing in my own ears. My eyes slowly opened to see Beth staring at me intently, waiting for my response. I could not speak as I felt my nose wrinkle and my eyes squeeze shut, more tears coming in a sob.

Beth smiled in understanding and gathered me into her arms. "It's okay, Em. Pretty powerful stuff, huh?" I nodded and continued to hiccup against her chest. "It got me the first time, too. Still does, sometimes."

"It's amazing. Better than therapy," I finally managed. I could feel her chuckle vibrate against the side of my head.

~ ~ ~ ~ ~

Chapter Six

I pulled into the visitor's parking lot at Rebecca's school and glanced up at the large red brick building that was Bovine High. I made my way toward the front doors, my hands buried deep in the pockets of my coat, my head bent against the brisk wind.

"How you doing, Frank?" I asked the security guard who held his post at the double front doors.

"How goes it, Emily? Cold one today, eh?"

"You know it." I smiled at the older man and entered the building. Since class was in session, the halls were mostly deserted. I could hear the click clack of someone's high heels in an unseen hallway to my left. I removed my bulky London Fog coat, carrying it in my arms as I headed toward my lover's classroom on the third floor.

"Ms. Kelly? I need your help over here. This isn't turning out right," I heard a student say as I walked through the open doorway of Rebecca's room.

"Okay, Brian. Hang on a minute."

I spotted Rebecca, her dark red hair shining under the fluorescent lighting. I loved to run my hands through its thick, silky strands. She looked stunning in the green mid-calf skirt that hugged her hips just so and her creamy silk blouse; she had removed the matching green jacket at some point during the day. She was bent over, looking into a microscope. Her very shapely legs ran smoothly from underneath the fabric of the skirt and slid easily into cream-colored heels, the strong calf muscles defined and delicious.

I leaned against the doorframe with my arms crossed over my chest and stared in appreciation. I was so proud of Rebecca. When we met nearly six years earlier, she was a teller at a bank during the day, and taking classes at night to earn her teaching degree. I had fallen in love, not only with the woman but also with her drive and her dedication to anything she did. She was breathtaking in every way.

Rebecca's mother, Shannon, had emigrated from Ireland to the United States as a young woman, meeting Rebecca's father shortly after and becoming pregnant by him. He soon abandoned her, leaving Shannon to give birth to and eventually raise her daughter alone. Shannon never married, choosing to devote all her time and energy to her only child. Rebecca and her mother had been very close, and she had been devastated when her mother had died three years earlier.

"Ms. Kelly, someone is here."

I straightened when I heard my presence being announced by a nasal-sounding girl.

Rebecca looked over her shoulder and smiled. "I'll be right back, Carrie," she said with a light pat on the arm of the student she was helping. She walked over to me. Her sensual eyes — which were either blue or green or sometimes both, depending on what she was wearing — were a deep emerald green to match her suit. She wore no makeup, relying instead on the peaches and cream complexion of a true redhead. "Hey, you," she said, her voice low and sultry for my ears only, bringing back memories from that morning. "This is a surprise."

I grinned sheepishly, feeling conspicuous with thirty-five pairs of eyes staring at us. "I got our tickets today. American, just under nine hundred round-trip."

"Not too bad. La Guardia?"

I nodded. "My mother called today, too. The funeral is Monday at 3:00."

"When is our flight?" She unconsciously tucked a restless wisp of my hair behind my ear.

"Tomorrow morning at 6:15. I figure we'll get there early enough that I can do any visiting and get it out of the way." Rebecca looked at me strangely. "What?"

"Honey, you haven't been back to Colorado in years, and yet you feel it's a burden to see them?"

I stared at her, completely oblivious as to why she might be surprised. She could see my confusion and led me a little further into the hall.

"Emily, do you know what I would give if I could just hop on a plane and go see my mother?" I sighed and glanced down at my fidgeting hands for a moment before I felt my chin being nudged up. I met her gaze. "You take your family for granted. And your friends." Her features softened and she briefly took my hand, squeezing my fingers. "So, how are you?"

"I'm okay," I said quietly, her words bouncing around in my mind. "I'll get through this. It's just kind of a shock, you know?"

"Ms. Kelly, is this stuff supposed to smoke?" one of the students asked as he stared down at a Bunsen burner.

"Oh, boy," she said with a look of apology in her eyes. "I'd better get back in there. Where are you off to now?"

"Lexy's. I need to pick up some of those little travel doodads. Do you need anything?"

Rebecca shook her head and moved in close to me to whisper in my ear, "Just you." She gave me a kiss on the neck. "I'll be a little late. Dr. Landis wants me to stop by his office before I leave today."

"Why? Is everything okay?"

"Fine. I'm not real sure what he wants. I'll tell you all about it tonight." With a soft smile to ease my worry, she walked back into her class.

I watched her for a moment, not able to take my eyes off the way her butt moved under the skirt, the sway of her hips.

"Who was that woman?" I heard that same nasal-voiced girl ask as I headed back down the hall.

As usual, I had to park clear out in the Antarctic in the Lexy's Grab & Go parking lot. The bitter cold tried to sneak in around my coat, biting at the exposed skin of my neck and creeping up my sleeves to my arms. By the time I reached the double doors of the store, I was shivering. I nodded to the old man who stood just inside greeting customers, and headed toward Health and Beauty Aids to get what we needed.

~ ~ ~ ~ ~

"No! Beth, I— oomph." I sucked in my breath as the giant teddy bear flew into my stomach. "You're going to pay for that!" I picked up a previously thrown Nerf football and pulled my arm back to launch it when the ball was taken out of my hand from behind. I turned to see a man standing over me, his brows drawn and an extremely unhappy look on his face.

"You two need to leave," he hissed.

I looked back at Beth, who was trying to control her hysterical laughter, then I glanced at the aisle, which was filled with stuffed animals, balls, and a rubber pool toy that littered the floor around our feet so thickly the white tile could barely be seen. I turned back to the disgruntled employee and gave him my best, most innocent smile, only to have him lift his arm and point in the direction of the front door. Beth and I ran out of the store, trailed by our giggles.

~ ~ ~ ~ ~

I chuckled as I loaded my cart with mini bottles of shampoo and travel cases for soap and toothbrushes. Beth and I could turn almost any location into a playground. Unfortunately, where two was always company, three or more were nearly always an unwanted crowd.

~ ~ ~ ~ ~

Darla invited me over for a movie night while her parents were out, but I refused to go unless Beth could, too. Finally, Darla agreed.

"No. Don't make me, Em. Please?" Beth was lying on my bed on her stomach, my teddy bear in her arms. She watched me as I sat on the floor in front of my full-length mirror, brushing my hair.

"Beth, you leave in what, like five days? I want to spend as much time with you as I can." I stuck a barrette in my mouth and pulled one side of my hair back with my hands.

"But does that have to mean at Darla's house?" She groaned as she buried her face in Ruffles' thick, brown fur. "That chick is strange, and she does not like me." She rolled over onto her back, pulling the bear with her, and stared at the ceiling, connecting the little dots of insulation thingamajigs with her finger.

I glanced at her in the mirror. "Come on, Beth. She's not *that* bad. It'll be fun."

"Yeah, so was Auschwitz," she mumbled.

I ignored her comment and tucked my pink polo shirt into my shorts, lifting the collar so it framed my neck and the very bottom of my chin. Beth looked at me through narrowed eyes and turned back to her stomach. "You've never worn your shirt like that before. In fact, I don't think I've ever even seen you in a shirt like that before." She sat up.

"It's Darla's. Do you like it?" I asked, standing and turning around to face her, my arms out to the sides, palms up in expectation.

"Can do without the pink."

"I knew you'd say that." I turned back to the mirror, putting the last couple of touches to my feathered bangs and adding a final squirt of Aqua Net.

"Then why did you ask?" Beth grabbed Ruffles and hugged him again, looking at my reflection critically.

"I don't know. Maybe I thought for once I'd get a straight answer out of you or something." I added some light pink, bubble gum lip gloss and smacked my lips together.

"You smell like a gumball machine." She wrinkled her nose. "Em, you look so much better when you go just as yourself, without all that crap."

I turned to look at her, my hands on my hips. The attitude that I wore like a cloak when around Darla slid into place. "Well, I really don't care what you think, Beth. I happen to like *all that crap*. Is that okay with you?"

She looked at me for a moment, surprise washing briefly

over her face before she became expressionless again. "Since when?" She tossed Ruffles aside and stood from the bed. "Fine. So, are you done? If I have to do this, I want to get it over with as soon as possible."

I watched in stunned silence as she walked out of the bedroom.

"Emily! Hi!" Darla exclaimed when she opened the front door to her house. She looked as though she wasn't expecting company and was beyond thrilled at the surprise. I was slightly annoyed at how fake she could be sometimes. I looked at Beth in time to see her roll her eyes. "I see you brought your little friend." She turned to Beth, a smile plastered on her face. "Beth, isn't it?"

"Yup. Since the day I was born."

I glared at Beth. Darla looked down to take in Beth's faded blue jeans that were getting thin in the knees and her scuffed cowboy boots that were planted wide, as if she were waiting for a fight. Dark eyes traveled back up to see the tight, black tank Beth wore, her tanned, muscled arms crossed over her chest. She briefly took in the worn Broncos cap and finally stopped at annoyed, vibrant blue eyes that met her gaze with a raised brow in a silent challenge.

Darla's focus immediately turned back to me. "Come on in. Hurry, before we let any flying or crawly things in." She turned away from us and disappeared into the dark house.

"Does that include the resident?" Beth muttered as she followed. I stifled a grin. The Newman house was one of the biggest in the neighborhood and looked out of place next to all the smaller, two- and three-bedroom homes that surrounded it. Darla had told me happily one day that her house contained "approximately six and one-half bedrooms and three bathrooms. Oh, four if you count the little half-bath Daddy put in last year."

The Newmans were a pretentious family who had lots of money and even more arrogance. I frequently wondered why I hung out with Darla at all. Beth asked me that question often. My parents seemed to approve, and I knew that, through Darla, I would get to know the right people once we hit high school. The right people would be helpful in getting into important clubs that colleges liked to see. I had already decided the next four years would be dedicated to getting the best grades and the best scholarships I could. Being a lawyer was an obsession.

"Em, who gives a damn what your folks think of Darla? She is a little rich bitch," Beth had said one night, her vibrant eyes ablaze. "You have got to learn that what other people think is not *that* important. What do they know, anyway? Sometimes I don't think I'm heading where you're heading." That had hurt me to hear, mostly because I knew Beth spoke the truth.

"So, do you guys want anything to drink? Eat? Candy? Ice cream? Chocolate?" We followed the sound of Darla's voice and ended up in the kitchen, where the only source of light was that coming from the open fridge.

"I'll take a cola," I said brightly, finding one of the bar-stools and hopping onto it. Beth looked at me as if she wasn't quite sure what to do. I indicated that she should sit on the stool next to mine.

"I don't want—"

"So, Emily! Guess what!" Darla ran right over Beth, not even checking her rearview mirror to see if she was still alive.

I looked at Beth with surprise clearly evident in my eyes. She was staring at the floor, a hand on her hip as she chuck-led lightly to herself. I didn't know what, if anything, I should do. "Uh, what?" I stammered. My blood began to burn as I felt an automatic need to protect Beth from Darla's harsh judg-ments, but I lacked the courage to do anything.

Darla walked over to the breakfast bar in front of us and leaned her elbows against the countertop. "Remember that guy, Scott Mathews?" I nodded as I popped the top of the Coke. "You know, the guy with the really cute butt?" Again I nodded. "Well, the other day, me and Laura and Sandra and Mary were at the mall, and oh my God! There he was! He looked so cute in his shorts and shirt. Oh, I could have just died!"

I could hear Beth groan next to me, just barely audible. I tapped her leg under the bar with the toe of my Ked.

"Well, he walks over to us, and he has Spencer Milton and Brett Kylor with him. So it was like, oh my God! The three most popular, rich guys in our school, right?" Nod. "Okay, so they walk up to us, and Scott says hello to me!" Darla screamed and clapped her hands. "Isn't that great?"

I smiled, trying to show my support. "That is so cool, Darla." I ignored Beth, even though I felt her eyes on me.

"Don't you think that he is just like sooo cute?" she exclaimed, eyeing me expectantly, her dark blonde brows raised to her hairline in anticipation.

"Um, oh yeah. Scott Mathews is so totally cute, Darla. You are so lucky."

"Em, you said you thought—" Beth began to say.

I quickly turned to her and cut her off. "Beth, do you want a sip of my Coke?"

She looked at me strangely. "No."

I gave her a look that told her to shut her mouth. She shook her head slightly, her eyes taking on a dull sheen, but she said no more about it. Darla walked back to the fridge and began to pull out different kinds of meats and cheeses, throwing them on the counter behind her. Then she headed for a cabinet above the microwave, tossing boxes filled with different types of crackers next to the meats and cheeses, rambling the entire time about school, boys, hair, makeup, and clothes.

Beth tossed her cap onto the bar in front of us and ran her hands through her hair. I could tell she was being pushed far beyond her limits, and the only reason she hadn't throttled Darla was because of me. Finally, with a sigh, she put her cap back on and rested against her forearms on the bar, staring down at her fingers.

"Oh my God! You have got to see this!" Darla turned back to us, nearly scaring the bejesus out of me. Her brown eyes were wide with excitement, and she hurried out of the room, half-made snacks forgotten on the counter. We followed her toward the spacious family room. I had been in Darla's house before, but I watched Beth as she looked around, her mouth slightly open and her eyes wide. I could tell she was trying to hide her reaction to all the beautiful things the Newman's had, but she wasn't doing a very good job of it.

The white carpet was thick, like walking on a cloud. The large screen TV was in an oak cabinet against the far wall. On either side were shelves lined with hundreds of different figurines and strange knickknacks. Darla looked over her shoulder at Beth, who had a strange expression on her face as she gazed at the figures. "Daddy is sent to other countries for his job, and so he always buys some stupid little statue for my mom. She collects them or something. So, I wouldn't become too attached to them if I were you." She looked at me and winked, then she broke out into a wide grin. "I'm just kidding. Sit." She pointed toward the comfortable-looking couch that was covered in a pastel green pattern with bits of blue and gray mixed in. I did as I was told. Beth walked over to the Elizabethan wingback that was upholstered in gray with the same colors of green and blue to match the couch. I looked at her with a question in my eyes. Why wouldn't she sit with me? Beth wouldn't even look at me. I could tell she was angry at having been dragged here and was just biding her time before she could escape. Beth knew Darla's comment about the figurines was meant as a deliberate insult. Didn't she understand that Darla was shallow and simple? That she had to belittle others to feel better herself? Why couldn't Beth just fit in like everybody else? I wanted all my friends to get along.

"This is my father's newest toy. It's called a VCR. I don't know what that stands for, though." She grinned sheepishly.

"Videocassette recorder," Beth said dully as she looked at the international figurines again, her chin resting in her hand.

"Yeah! That's right. I'll have to remember that. Anyway, we got *Ordinary People* with that really, really cute guy, Timothy Hutton. And my mom made me get that boring movie, *Kramer vs. Kramer*, but it has Dustin Hoffman in it, and he's kinda cute."

"That's a great movie!" Beth exclaimed, sitting up a little more in her chair. "That has Meryl Streep in it. She is one of the greatest actresses to ever grace the screen."

"Whatever," Darla said dryly. She took one of the videos out of its box and slid it into the large, silver machine. The TV clicked on with a static-filled whoosh, and the movie began. Beth was transfixed by the images she saw on the screen, which was bigger than any television her mom or my parents had ever owned.

Darla sat on the couch next to me and talked incessantly about boys and hair and clothes and makeup and jewelry and Scott Mathews. She droned on and on and I occasionally nodded my head and said "Uh huh." Then she said something that caught my attention cold. "So, why do you hang out with her, Emily? She is a freak." My head snapped around from watching Dustin Hoffman fighting with his little boy over eating ice cream instead of dinner. "What?"

"You heard me. Beth is a total freak and will bring you down. You must know that." I quickly turned to look at Beth to see if she had heard any of this. "Don't worry about her. She's so wrapped up in that stupid movie that I doubt a tornado could bother her."

"Please don't talk about Beth that way, Darla. She is my best friend," I said weakly. I didn't know what to do. Beth was indeed my best friend, and I didn't want her to get hurt, but Darla was the only other friend I had around the neighborhood, and with Beth gone for the rest of the summer, I didn't want to be left alone.

"Emily, that is the problem! People talk about her at school all the time. And," she leaned in, almost conspiratorially, "they're starting to talk about you, too."

"Darla ..." I stopped as I turned toward Beth, who had stood from her chair. She looked at us, her face expressionless, but her eyes burning.

"Been a hoot. I better get going. Later." She walked toward the front door, fists clenching and unclenching at her sides.

"Beth!" I called as I raced after her. I could feel my heart sink.

"Emily!" Darla called after me.

I ignored her. Beth was just about to descend the steps of the porch when I caught her. "Wait, Beth, please don't go."

She turned on me, and she was furious. She took a step forward until her face was mere inches from mine. "I am not going to stay here, Em. That little rich bitch may have you wrapped around her little finger, but I know her game. I've known conniving little debutantes all my life, and why you'd put yourself in the path of one on purpose is beyond me." She turned and began to walk again, her foot on the first step.

"I'm sorry, Beth." I threw my arms into the air, at a loss about what to do. Beth kept going. She hit the second step, her boot about to touch the path that would lead to the sidewalk and her salvation. I watched her, feeling my anger build. "God, I feel like I am always saying that to you, saying that I'm sorry!"

She stopped and looked up at me, her face resigned, her eyes sad. "Maybe that's because you keep screwing up." I stared, dumbstruck. "Em, I am used to people looking down on me, laughing at me. I have a mother who is a drunk and couldn't keep her husband. I *am* different. I'm not like all the other girls. And all that is fine. I don't care about them. But you, Em, you're my best friend. Aren't you supposed to stand up for me like I stand up for you?" She turned from me again, only to turn back. "And one more thing, Em. I got news for you, no matter how much you try to be like the Darla Newman's of the world, you're different, too. Someday you just might realize that."

I watched, paralyzed, as Beth walked to the end of the path and onto the sidewalk toward her home. I looked back at Darla's house, staring up at its massive structure, so torn. My eyes were drawn to the silhouette at the door.

"Why did she leave?"

I stared at my "friend", something telling me she had been standing there the entire time and knew exactly what was going on. "Look, Darla, I'm not feeling too good. I'm gonna go home."

She didn't say anything for a moment and then shrugged her shoulders. "Okay. See you later." I heard the heavy front door slam shut as I headed for the path.

As I walked home, I thought of what had just happened.

When had Beth and I grown so far apart? When we had first become friends, we'd been so much alike my parents used to tease us and say they could take home Beth and no one would ever know it wasn't me. Then one day I woke up, and we were two completely different people with two completely different goals in life. It wasn't fair.

I picked a ripe apple off the Nivens' tree as I passed, and took a large bite of the sweet fruit. With a quick glance at my house across the street, I decided to keep walking, not ready to go home. I knew on a gut level that once we started high school, Beth and I would be no more. She would go her way, and I would go mine. All the same, Beth Sayers was a part of me, a part of my heart and soul, and I hoped she always would be.

I thought about the future. What would it bring? Would I end up as a big lawyer in some big city as I hoped? Where would Beth be? I dropped to the curb in front of the McKinzey house and ate my apple as I reminisced about a time when Beth and I had been about eleven or twelve. We promised with a pinky swear that we would buy houses on the same block, maybe even next door, and always go over to each other's place to have lunch and watch movies together. I smiled ruefully as I chewed. That sure had gone out the window. Even at just a few weeks shy of fifteen, I knew that was no longer to be.

Did I have to choose between Beth and my new life, my new friends? I know Beth had been hurt both by Darla's words and by my inaction. She had every right to be, but did she have a right to place me in a situation where I had to choose? I didn't know. I stood from the curb, threw the apple core into the McKinzey trash barrel, and walked on.

~ ~ ~ ~ ~

Lexy's was busy as usual. I pushed my buggy strategically around slow and inconsiderate shoppers who felt the need to park their carts in the middle of the aisle and talk. I barely managed to miss being hit by an old woman who was staring down the aisles she passed instead of watching where she was going.

Finally reaching the health care products, I ducked down an aisle containing mouthwash and toothpaste. So many brands to choose from. I smiled as I continued to think about Beth. She had the straightest, whitest teeth I'd ever seen. She'd been one of those lucky people who never had to see the inside of an orthodontist's lair. I located a travel-size bottle of Scope and tossed it into my buggy.

As I found the rest of our travel toiletries, I wondered if maybe I was giving my past too much thought. I remember my father once saying that people should let the past lie with the dead. Perhaps he was right.

Two little girls, who looked to be around eight or nine, walked by me arm in arm. One had bright red hair and sparkling green eyes. Her friend's black hair was woven into tight braids with brightly colored barrettes. Her chocolate complexion was bright with youth, and her dark eyes laughed as they giggled together. I stood for a moment and watched them. They were the perfect combination: one dark and one light, a balance to each other. Beth and I had been like that once.

~ ~ ~ ~ ~

I wandered around my house restlessly for four days after Beth left Darla's so abruptly, not sure what to do. I sensed somehow that Beth would not want to see me, and I wasn't going to force yet another apology on her if she didn't want it. My mother kept glancing at me with an odd expression on her face, like she wanted to ask what was going on, but something held her back. She gratefully accepted my extra help, but finally, the day before Beth was to leave for camp, she placed her hand over mine, stopping me in the middle of folding a pair of socks. I looked into her concerned eyes.

"Honey, Beth is going to be leaving tomorrow, right?" I nodded. "Why don't you just go and talk to her?"

I shrugged, once again amazed at how perceptive my mother could be. "I can't," I said simply.

She shook her head sadly and continued to fold laundry. I knew deep down I was wrong this time, but I lacked the courage to face Beth. The plain and simple truth of it was that I didn't know what to say.

It was turning out to be a record-breaking summer with temperatures in the upper nineties to the low hundreds every day. My parents had bought Billy and me a huge trampoline a couple summers before, and I laid on it, feeling the weight of the hot June night as I stared at the stars. I was miserable. My parents were asleep. Billy was gone and I missed him terribly. At the beginning of the month, he had left for the Army, sent somewhere in the South for boot camp. I sighed heavily as I thought of the start of high school in the fall. The idea scared me as well as excited me. I wanted to make getting good grades my focus. I didn't care about anything else, as long as I could get a good scholarship and go on to law school. Everything else was just fluff.

My thoughts turned to Beth again. What would she do once she hit high school? She hated school. I figured she would probably pursue theater. I smiled to myself as I thought back to the production of Andrew Lloyd Webber's "Joseph and the Amazing Technicolor Dreamcoat" that was staged as the summer musical our final year of middle school. She had played Mrs. Potiphar. It wasn't a big part, but she had been wonderful. I honestly thought theater was the only thing that kept Beth here. She had nothing else, no other connections.

"What are you thinking about out here all by yourself?"

I looked up to see Beth staring down at me. She wore cut-off jean shorts with a tank top, her hands buried in her hip pockets. "School," I said quietly.

She nodded and climbed onto the trampoline with me. "Yeah. I've been thinking a lot about that, too." She sighed as she flopped down on her back, the entire tarp bouncing us both slightly at the quick movement. It always reminded me of water, of what it must be like to sleep on a ship.

"I was also thinking about that musical you did last summer." I could almost hear the smile spread across Beth's face.

"Oh, yeah. 'Potiphar had very few cares, he was one of Egypt's millionaires,'" she began to sing. I joined her, "'Having made a fortune buying shares in Pyramids.'"

We broke into a healthy stream of laughter. It felt so good to laugh with her again. We didn't laugh as much as we used to.

"That was probably the best time of my life so far," she said wistfully. I turned to look at her profile. She still wore the smile, her eyes lost in memories.

"This summer theater camp is going to be really good for you, isn't it?" I asked.

She looked at me and nodded. "Yeah, I think so. I can't wait. I only feel complete when I'm on that stage, doing a play."

"Has your mother calmed down any?"

Beth turned to look at the stars again. "She'll get over it. She always does." She placed her hands on her stomach and began to beat out a simple rhythm that kept time with the tune in her head, probably something from "Joseph".

"Do you remember that song 'Close Every Door' from the musical last year?" she asked, eyes glued to the stars.

"Yes. It's a beautiful song."

"You think? I always thought it was so sad." She began to sing the song about being isolated from love and from all those who would support you and I closed my eyes as I listened to Beth's smooth voice. After a few lines, she tapered off and started to hum the song softly, her thoughts a million miles away. Suddenly, she stopped. "I always felt like that song was about me, you know? I could relate."

She was quiet for a moment then looked over at me with a grin. "Have you ever noticed that the tarp on a tramp smells like the seats on the school bus?" She turned to me when I didn't answer and found me staring at her like she was crazy. "You've never noticed that?" I shook my head. "Yeah, well, you smart, uncreative types..." She sat up and looked down at me. "I'm sorry about that whole thing at Darla's, Em. I know you're just kind of stuck in the middle."

"It's okay, Beth. You don't have to apologize. It's not your fault; it's mine. Darla isn't a real friend. I realize that."

"So why are you friends with her?"

"Someone to hang around with. I don't know."

"With friends like that." Beth smiled and I smiled back. "I better go. I'm leaving in the morning and didn't want to leave mad or with you mad at me. This has been a tough few days." She scooted to the side and lowered herself to the ground.

I stared at her back in awe. How can she be so forgiving? Beth had the biggest heart of anyone. What would I do without her? She turned to look at me.

"What?" I asked, confused at her expectant expression.

"Don't I rate a hug?"

I grinned and jumped down from the tramp and into her arms. We stood in each other's embrace for nearly five minutes, neither wanting to be anywhere else in the whole world.

"I'm going to miss you," she whispered in my ear.

A shiver ran down the length of my body. "I'll miss you, too."

"You'll write, right?" Beth asked when we finally parted.

I nodded and swallowed against my rising emotion. "Sure. But you have to write back, Beth Sayers!" I admonished.

She grinned shyly. "I will. I promise. Maybe I can call you on your birthday."

"You better," I said, using every ounce of self-control not to cry.

Beth smiled as if she could see my inner turmoil. She ran a quick hand through my hair and turned away. "See ya."

I watched her walk to the wooden fence that separated our two yards. She climbed onto the trash can there and, with a mighty heave, pulled herself up to balance for a moment on top of the wood. She looked at me over her shoulder again and smiled, then jumped down to the other side.

~ ~ ~ ~ ~

Chapter Seven

I took the mail from the box and put the envelopes between my teeth, fumbling with one hand to get the right key into the lock, my other hand and arm burdened with blue plastic shopping bags. After my third attempt, the door opened and I hurried inside to drop my load before my arm came off. I dumped everything on the kitchen table and returned to the car for the rest.

With a sigh, I deposited my keys on the table amidst the mass of bags and hung my purse on the doorknob of the pantry.

"Hey, lover boy," I crooned when I felt Simon's tail weaving its way between my calves, leaving a black trail of fur on my jeans. "Well, looks like we're going to have to make Mommy brush you tonight, huh, little man?" I rubbed the top of his head and down between his eyes, which were tightly shut; his loud purring filled the quiet kitchen.

I turned back to the table and began to sift through the mail. "Bill, bill, junk mail, bill, hmm." I tossed all but one envelope back down, the handwritten name and address catching my eye. I flipped the letter to see if there was a return address on the back flap. *Monica Nivens, Pueblo, Colorado.* I drew my eyebrows together, then a small grin spread across my lips. I slid my finger under the flap and tore open the paper. A single sheet slipped out with a short, neatly hand-written note.

Dear Emily,

I want to tell you how sorry I am about Beth. She was an incredible woman and was a very good friend to have. I am looking forward to seeing you if you come back home for the funeral. Please come, Emily. It has been far too long since you've been home.

Your mother tells me you are happily involved with a teacher named Rebecca. Why didn't you tell me! If you come down, and I hope you do, I am looking forward to meeting this special woman who was finally able to keep a hold of Emily Thomas. Lord knows the rest of us couldn't!

Take care, Emily, and know that my thoughts and prayers are with you right now.

Love Always,
Monica

P.S. If you'd like, Connie and I would love for the two of you to stay with us. Which brings me to...

P.S.S. I can't wait for you to meet Connie. I wish you could have come to our commitment ceremony, but I do understand the life of a lawyer. Boy, do I! Connie and I constantly fight about it!

I laid the letter on the table and smiled. *Monica.* She was right; it had been far too long. I chuckled as I began to take my purchases from the bags and arrange them for packing or putting away. I could easily recall my mother's voice when she first mentioned Monica to me.

~ ~ ~ ~ ~

"Did you hear that Claudia Nivens' girl is going to law school?" My ears perked up immediately. *A real life law student? And so close!*

"She don't look smart enough to be no lawyer," my father said, sitting in his recliner with his feet up and the newspaper in his hands.

My mother looked over at him, laying her *Redbook* on her lap. "Henry. That's not nice."

"Well, it's true." My father looked at her from around his paper. "She looks like a damn idiot with those glasses of hers always just halfway on her nose. Who in hell wears glasses half on and half off?"

"I thought glasses were supposed to make you look smarter?" I said from my place on the floor in front of the TV, where I was watching my favorite character, Jo, on *The Facts of Life.*

"Not her."

Claudia Nivens' husband had died in the early Seventies from a terrible accident at the CF&I steel mill, and she and their only daughter, Monica, lived off his meager life insurance dividends and the salary Claudia earned as a nurse at St. Mary Corwin Hospital. Monica was much older than I was, so she had little to do with us kids. She started law school when I was only twelve. On more than one occasion, I sat on the banana seat of my bike and watched from our driveway across the street as Monica would hurry out her front door with a full backpack slung over one shoulder, usually more books in her arms, racing toward her beat-up light blue Volkswagen Bug. She'd often look over at me, her black hair pinned up on the sides, the dark length blowing around her pretty face, and give me the slightest smile, before disappearing into her car and driving off.

~ ~ ~ ~ ~

I returned to the kitchen after running some packages upstairs and I once again eyed the letter on the table. I thought back to the summer Beth had spent at camp. She had been gone for two months, but it had seemed like two years. Our main communication was through letters and that just wasn't the same as having her there with me. I sighed as I thought of those days.

~ ~ ~ ~ ~

June 23, 1981
Dear Emily,

Hey, Em. Um, I'm not real good at writing letters, so you're going to get what you get, okay? Anyway, I made it all the way here to Tennessee all on my own. Man, was that scary! I never flew before. It's really kind of cool in a way. When you take off down the runway, the plane starts to go really, really fast, and you feel almost like you're stuck to your seat. Then when that huge, metal bird lifts off, your stomach goes, too. Kind of like being on a roller coaster, but not as bad.

My dad was so happy to see me; I really thought he was going to cry! I have never seen him so emotional before, yikes! His wife Lynn is really nice, too. She's pregnant, so in a few months I'll have a little brother or sister! Isn't that great? I never thought I'd be an older sister, though lord knows I'm surprised I haven't been five times over by my mother.

Well, I got to camp three days ago. It is really nice here. The camp is huge! There are kids here from all over the U.S. I met a girl from Alaska the other day! Isn't that wild? I'm in a cabin with seven other girls, not counting our counselor. They are all pretty nice for the most part. Only three of us are here to do theater. The others I'm not real sure about. It is really hot and humid here. Ugh. I guess it's like that here in the South. They have the coolest accents here. You know how I pick them up, so I'm sure it won't take long and I'll be say-ing things like y'all and fixin' to and usedtacould. It's so funny. Like it's all one word! Love it.

I guess this will have to do for now. I miss you a lot!!!!! I'll write again soon. Oh, and I'm sending you a birthday card, too. Hopefully you'll get it on time!

Love,
Beth

A birthday wish for a special friend on her special day
Happy Birthday from that
special place in my heart.
June 24, 1981

Hey, Em. I know this card is kind of dorky, but it was all I could find. Happy Birthday! I miss you!!!!

Beth.

P.S. The food here is awful! One girl said that this stuff tastes like prison food. I wonder how she knows that.

6/27/81

Dear Beth,

Hello. I was so excited to get your letter! I got your card today, too. Thank you. I can't believe I am going to be 15 tomorrow, can you? Sometimes, I think we are getting so old. Mom says that Dad is going to start teaching me how to drive, and he's going to stop at the driver's license place and get me a driving book to study! Isn't that exciting? I can't wait.

Everything here is pretty much the same. It has been sooo hot here, too. But as you know, it's dry heat. What's humidity like? I hate it. I've heard that humidity can cause all kinds of pimples. Is that true? I sure hope not! If I plan to live in New York or Los Angeles someday, I'll get the hugest zit on my face as I'm trying some huge case in court! Wouldn't that be awful? The judge would probably laugh his butt off.

Darla and I went swimming yesterday. It was fun, but we ran into Scott Mathews there. I am so sick of hearing about him and having to see him. I mean, Jeez, I don't care about him or any of his stupid friends! They tried to invite us over to Scott's house for some stupid pool party. Darla was thrilled. I didn't want to go, so I didn't. Besides, I think my parents would have flipped! My mom says we are way too young to date, and she thinks that Darla's parents are just asking for trouble by encouraging her to. I don't know if I agree with them, but all the same, I'm not interested. I have too much else to worry about other than some boy.

I better go for now. It is so late and I am so tired. I think my mom has a big day planned tomorrow. She won't tell me. I miss you, too. Please come back soon!

Love,

Emily Jane Thomas

July 3, 1981

Dear Em,

I am so happy! We had to write a short one-act play to act out with ourselves and two or three other people, and then we performed them for our teacher. He's this strange guy named Buck. That's what he wants us to call him. Wild, huh? Anyway, so we perform them, and he'd pick the one he liked the best, and then the winner would do their play for the entire camp. I won! Isn't that great? See, Em, I told you those scenes that you and me acted out would be useful.

I met the coolest counselor today. Her name is Casey something. I don't know her last name. She is so much fun. She isn't in our cabin, but the one next to it. I think she is good friends with our counselor, Kim. She is from Montana, but lived most of her early life in England and has this wicked British accent. She is really big into the theater. She is seventeen. Em, you should see her. She has long blonde hair with these big expressive brown eyes. Eyes kind of like a puppy dog. She has the most beautiful smile. I think you'd like her. She's so nice.

I've heard that about humidity, too, but I don't know if that's true or not. I've actually noticed that my skin is healthier here. Don't know. Either way, Em, no judge in his right mind is about to kick you out of a courtroom! If he does, tell me, and I'll kick his ass for you.

Better go. Happy 4th of July! I miss you so much! I hope these next two months fly by.

Love,
Beth

7/8/81
Greetings!

Hi, Beth! I was so happy when you called me. When I didn't hear from you on my birthday I was so sad. But then you called the next day, and it was all okay again. Just the sound of your voice made me happy and not miss you quite as much. At least for a while, anyway.

Mom and I went to the store today. We both ran out of eye makeup. That stuff is so expensive, you know? Jeez. Those cosmetic companies must think we are all rich. Good thing my parents give me a generous allowance.

I am so proud of you, Beth. I knew you would do well there. I saw your mom today. She asked if I had heard from you. Why haven't you written her? She got a job finally. I think she said she's at the grocery store. I hope she'll like it there. I know it's been hard for you guys since she got fired from the bank after that whole deal.

I didn't know you guys were allowed to be friends with the counselors. Better go. Darla is taking me to the movies tonight. I have to start getting ready.

When are you coming home?
Love,
Emily Jane Thomas
P.S. Do you think I should use my full name once we get

to high school?

7/14/81
Dear Beth,
Beth, why haven't you written? Are you okay? Please write soon. I miss you! I miss your letters, too.
Emily
P.S. My dad took me driving today. It was so scary! We went driving around the cemetery so I could see what it's like with a curvy road. Plus my dad said that if I killed us we'd be in the right place. He's such a goof!

July 21, 1981
Dear Em,
Hey, Em. Sorry I haven't written in a while. I've been really busy. Buck has us working our butts off. Me and this guy Chris had to write a 2-act play together. It is really good. That took a lot of time, though. We couldn't decide on a script forever, but then he finally decided to agree with me. Of course, I had to persuade him just a little. I'm glad he came to his senses. I hate the sight of blood.
Oh! I have got to tell you about this. Last night me and Casey, remember the counselor I told you about?, snuck out and went swimming. It was so fun! It was so bad. We are not allowed to be out of our cabins past ten, but we waited until about one in the morning and met out behind our cabins. She really surprised me, though. She took off her clothes! She wanted me to "skinny dip" with her, but I was like, no way! But there we were at the lake, and she is completely nude. She is beautiful. I really admire her a lot. If I could only have half the body at seventeen that she has!
So my mother got a job? Good for her.
Better go. Miss you.
Love,
Beth
P.S. Why did you have to buy eye makeup? You don't wear eye makeup. Do you? Oh, and the humidity is beginning to get sticky hot. We're in the middle of a major heat wave right now. Ugh!!
P.S.S. To answer your question about your name. Why would you go by your full name just because it's high school? You said you always hated your full name.

7/25/81
Dear Beth,
I was glad to hear from you. I was getting worried. This

Casey sounds kind of like trouble. She can get you both in so much hot water if she's not careful. She is the counselor! Be careful, Beth. Why on earth would she take her clothes off in front of you?

Scott Mathews finally asked Darla out. She was so excited. She set me up with one of his friends, Seth Lewis. I think it's kind of ironic that his name and yours rhyme. Anyway, I am so glad that you'll be back in a month. How is the acting going? I miss you.

Love,

Emily Thomas

P.S. Yeah, I do hate my full name, but it sounds a lot more grown up than Emmy. Don't you think?

August 1, 1981

Dear Em, Hey. Wow. Casey went on a trip with some of the other counselors to a town called Cropville (no kidding!), which is only about ten miles away from camp. She bought me this really beautiful bracelet. I'm laying here on my bunk right now looking at it. It's silver (I told her how much I like silver) and it has a bunch of charms on it. Like this one is a heart, this one is a happy face, and this one is a sad face. She was tying to get as close to the comedy/tragedy masks of drama as she could. Isn't that sweet? We've snuck out every night for the last two weeks. It's been amazing. We almost got caught last night. It was pretty close.

Better go. Miss you.

Don't grow up too fast, Em.

Beth

8/5/81

Dear Beth,

What are you doing, Beth? Are you crazy? You are going to get into so much trouble! What is it with this girl? What are you doing that is "so amazing"? What, does she let you lay on top of her, too? Do you two kiss and do other stuff, too?

Emily

8/7/81

Dear Beth,

Hi. I'm sorry. I had no right to say that, Beth. Please forgive me? How is camp going? Have you written anything else lately? I miss you a lot.

Love, (if you can)

Emily Thomas

8/12/81
Dear Beth,
Are you ever going to write back to me? Where are you?
What is going on? Do you still see Casey? Talk to me, Beth.
Please?
I broke up with Seth. He wanted to kiss me. I thought he
was just way too much of a dork. It's been really hot. Billy is
going to be able to come home for Christmas. We just found
out. Have you written your mother yet?
I miss you, Beth.
Love,
Emily Jane Thomas

8/15/81
Dear Beth,
????????????????????????????????
Emily Jane Thomas

August 20, 1981
Dear Emily,
Hello. Camp is good. They made Casey leave. She left yes-
terday. Bastards. I should be coming home in about a week.
Probably around the time you get this. I hope you're doing
good. See you soon.
Beth

I stared at the short letter in my hand. I wasn't sure what
to think. Was she mad at me for letting my mouth get away
from me yet again? Why did her friend have to leave camp? I
had so many questions running through my brain, it made
my head hurt.
I sat on my bed and stared out the window. I re-read the
letter again before I tossed it on the comforter beside me. I
grabbed Ruffles and held him to me, lying back against the
pillows. My teddy always comforted me. All of Beth's letters
from over the summer were stacked on my dresser. It had
been so exciting to come home from wherever I'd been that
day and see the newly arrived letter waiting for me to tear it
open. Beth's large, sloppy writing called to me. I smiled as I
realized her scrawl was as carefree as she was. The smile just
as quickly disappeared when that new girl, Casey, entered my
thoughts. Was she Beth's new best friend? It sounded that
way to me. I sighed as I finally admitted to myself that I was
jealous of this counselor. Why did Beth like her so much?
Was it because she was older? Was she prettier than me? I
rolled my eyes at this last thought. Who cared what she

looked like? Blonde with big, brown eyes. Sounded ugly to me.

I rolled onto my side, taking Ruffles with me, and sighed as I stared at my closet door with the poster of Olivia Newton-John. Olivia had blonde hair, but she had beautiful hazel eyes, not dorky brown like Casey. Her glossy lips smiled at me, her over-sized shirt left her bronzed shoulder exposed, and her short hair was swept back from her face with a head-band. I smiled back at her. I wished that someday I would be beautiful like that. Suddenly, I needed to hear the soft voice of the goddess and I rolled off the bed, went to my stereo, and put on the soundtrack record to "Grease". I closed my eyes and smiled as the pianist began to pound out the bluesy beat to "You're the One That I Want".

"'I got chills, they're multiplyin','" I sang as I danced around my small room with Ruffles in my arms. The sound of my bedroom door slamming open startled me, but then my Aunt Kitty leaned into the doorway, closed her eyes, and sang along with me.

"'You better shape up, 'cause I need a man. ...'" I giggled as Kitty entered the room, grabbed my hands and swung me around. We launched into the chorus, our voices blending as we sang at the top of our lungs.

When the song came to an end, we both collapsed on my bed out of breath. We turned to look at each other, finally exploding in a fit of giggles.

"You're so silly, Aunt Kitty."

"Yup. I am." She sat up, grabbing my hand as she stood. "I have been sent to get you for dinner." She pulled me off the bed and out the door.

"Wait! Aunt Kitty!" I cried as I tried to keep up with her quick pace. We began to race down the stairs.

"Come on" was all she would say.

We walked through the family room; that is, she walked, and I was dragged. My parents were sitting on the couch watching *Family Feud*.

"Mom?" I asked as we passed. She smiled up at me and waved. I finally relented and kept pace with my crazy aunt. We left the house, settled into her car, and drove toward town.

"What's going on, Aunt Kitty? I thought we were going to eat dinner?"

"We are. Just you and me."

I smiled and my aunt returned the look. She was the type of woman who made every person she came in contact with feel special. She had an easygoing personality and was loads of fun. She was only about ten years older than I was, what my mom called a "late-in-life baby" for my grandparents. She had long, light brown hair, just a shade lighter than my mom's and mine. Her dark gray eyes were kind and usually smiling.

"So, where are we going?" I asked, my arm resting along the open window, the breeze flowing through the car blowing hair in both our faces.

She smiled at me again. "Somewhere."

"Gee, thanks."

"Anytime, kiddo."

We had driven toward town and then right past it. My aunt turned onto a dirt road that led to what looked like nowhere. I glanced over at her only to meet with a warm smile.

"Almost there."

We approached a small lake surrounded by trees and wild grass. A tiny dock bobbed offshore. It was beautiful. The late afternoon sun shone overhead, giving the water a glowing life all its own. Aunt Kitty parked the car under the shade of a massive tree and got out. I followed suit. She pulled a large picnic basket from the trunk.

"Come on," she said, heading to an almost nonexistent path that led through the dense foliage.

"How do you know about this place, Aunt Kitty?" I asked, happily following.

"Your grandfather used to bring us here when your mom and I were younger. I was pretty little, but I never forgot it." She smiled over her shoulder at me. Finally, we emerged from the mini-forest and ended up right on the bank of the small lake. "I think this is a man-made lake that some crazy old man had put on his property in the Twenties." Aunt Kitty opened the basket and brought out a large red- and white-checkered tablecloth, which she spread on the wild grass. I reached toward the basket only to have my hand slapped. I looked at her with surprised eyes. "No. You sit and relax. I do the work."

I sat cross-legged and watched my aunt as she brought out a container of Kentucky Fried Chicken mashed potatoes and another of gravy. She opened the box of chicken and waited expectantly for my approval. I giggled and nodded. She nodded in response, then took out four biscuits and several little pats of butter.

"And to wash it all down, our house wine." She produced two bottles of Dr Pepper, handing one to me, which I immediately opened to take a long drink. As we ate, we talked about the upcoming school year, which would begin in just under two weeks.

"So, are you nervous?" she asked around a mouthful of biscuit.

"No," I said, a little too quickly. She glared at me, just the hint of a smile at the corner of her lips. "Yes." I grinned. "But I'm looking forward to it. I've always wanted to go to high school. I remember when Billy started, I was so jealous."

"Yeah, I know what you mean. When your mom started I was only...Jeez...how old was I?" She stared off into the past. "Five, six? But I remember it clear as day."

I chewed a mouthful of chicken, then regarded her seriously. Well, at least as serious as I could ever get around Aunt Kitty. "So, why are we here?"

"Why to eat, of course."

"No, no. I mean why just you and me?"

Aunt Kitty put her hand on her chest and looked stunned. "I am wounded, child. Can I not enjoy a day with my favorite niece?"

"I'm your only niece." I giggled.

"Yeah, so, all the more reason for me to spend time with you, yes?"

"Yes. But this isn't usual, Aunt Kitty. You always just come over to our place."

My aunt's face turned serious, which worried me. "Okay, kiddo. Yes, there is a reason we're here." She stopped as a coughing fit wracked her small frame for a few moments. I watched, a shard of concern filling me. Aunt Kitty had gotten sick the year before with a severe case of pneumonia and had never been able to completely shake the cough. She took a deep breath and started to speak again. "Your mom is worried about you."

"What! Why?" I could feel myself beginning to get angry.

"Now, now. Calm down. Don't have a brain explosion. Emily, your folks love you very much, and they just want you to be happy. Which, I got to tell ya is a pretty stupid thing for a parent to want. I mean, a teenager happy? Yeah. And they think I'm crazy? Puhleeze!" I smiled, feeling myself start to calm. She grinned at me and reached out to gently brush some hair out of my eyes. "They want what's best for you. But, see, I am not here to tell you to do anything special with yourself. No, no. That's what your mom would want me to do. Unh uh. That's not what you need. What you need is for someone to listen. Someone who can be objective. So spit it out." Aunt Kitty leaned back on her elbows, her legs stretched out in front of her crossed at the ankles, her eyes boring into my very soul.

"Spit what out? What do you want me to tell you?" I asked as I lazily made patterns on the tablecloth with my fingertips, not wanting to look at my aunt. I was afraid everything I was feeling would just tumble out of my mouth. My aunt always had that effect on me.

"Tell me what's going through that noggin of yours. Even I've noticed that, for about the past six months or so, you have been acting a little on the strange side. Your mom seems to think your friend Beth has something to do with it." My head shot up at the mention of Beth. This caught Aunt Kitty's attention, and she raised a brow. "Ah, Houston we have contact. Okay. So we talk about Beth."

My mind raced as I thought about how much I should tell her. She studied my face, her eyes filled with infinite patience. I knew I'd always been able to tell Aunt Kitty anything in the past, my secrets safe with her. But this...this was something different. I wanted to tell her all about Beth and me on New Year's and all the fights we'd been having since then. About how jealous I felt now.

"Come on, Emmy. Talk to me."

I looked at my aunt again. I could feel my throat constrict with restrained emotion that threatened to spill out and embarrass me, so I decided to talk before my tears could beat me to it. "See, Beth and I, we have a very special friendship. Oh, Aunt Kitty." I cried. I ground my fists into my eyes like a five-year-old child, angry at the tears that leaked out.

Aunt Kitty smiled and gently rubbed my leg. "I thought so," she said, almost too quiet for me to hear. "Tell me about it."

An hour later, I felt drained. Everything I told Aunt Kitty hung in the air between us as if it had a palpable existence of its own. Aunt Kitty, who was now lying on her back, looked up at the gathering clouds. It appeared as though it might rain. She sighed. I stared at her from my own position, also on my back. I was terrified to hear what she would say. Through my entire tale, she remained completely silent, her full attention on every word I spoke.

"Oh, Emmy." Her voice was full of sadness. "I had a friend like Beth once, too."

My eyes opened wide in surprise. "Really?"

She nodded. "Yup. We met when we were in about the seventh grade. We were friends until we were, oh, I'd say eighteen, nineteen, maybe."

"What happened?" I asked, breathless.

Aunt Kitty smiled, but there was no humor in that smile.

"I met Ron," she said simply. I didn't understand. She saw my confusion and smiled as she continued. "See, Karen...that was her name, Karen; she and I moved out of our parents' houses when we were seniors in high school."

"Why?" I was intrigued by this idea and surprised I had never heard about it.

"Because we were young and stupid, that's why. We thought we were old enough to handle the world and anything it had to throw at us. Boy, were we wrong." She grinned at me. "Anyway, we found this run-down, cheap apartment and moved in together. We were roommates. Karen wanted to be 'special' roommates, like when we were younger. I went along with it for a little while, but then I met Ron."

"Um, by 'special', do you mean like Beth and me at New Year's?" I asked, my voice timid.

She nodded. "Yes. I loved Karen very much, but I didn't want to live the rest of my life with her, like that. She did."

"Why? Why didn't you want to spend the rest of your life with Karen, as her roommate?" I was somewhat confused. "If you loved her?"

"Because. Don't get me wrong. I enjoyed my time with her." Aunt Kitty was quiet for a moment, a smile spread across her lips. She blinked and continued. "But I felt more comfortable with Ron. I felt like my life belonged with him, not with her. Karen was a very strong person. Those kind of people, with strength like that, fill the emptiness in their own lives. It's a special breed, Emmy. It sounds like your friend Beth has that same inner strength."

"Like Karen."

"Like Karen," Aunt Kitty agreed with a smile. "You should be glad that you've had this special bond with her. I will warn you, Emily, you two will eventually go your separate ways. Maybe not today or two years from now, but Beth will go out to find her own life and her own fulfillment. Don't try to stop her, and most importantly, Emmy, don't try to change her. Okay?"

"Okay, Aunt Kitty. I promise."

"Beth is who she is, just as you are who you are."

I helped Aunt Kitty clean up our mess and load the basket back into her trunk. I slammed the heavy door and turned to Aunt Kitty. She looked at me with raised eyebrows, waiting for my question.

"Have you seen Karen since you moved out, Aunt Kitty?"

"The last time I saw her was a few years ago. I ran into her at the mall. She smiled and waved, and that was the end of it."

"Oh." I walked around the car to the passenger door, my mind spinning. I couldn't stand the thought of Beth and me just waving at each other from a distance. That could never happen to us.

As we headed home, it began to rain. We laughed wildly as we ran from Aunt Kitty's car, trying to avoid the downpour. We were drenched when we stumbled through the front door, our clothing stuck like paint to our bodies. My mother took one look at us and burst out laughing.

I was annoyed by her laughter until I realized how red and swollen her eyes were. "Mom? Are you okay? Why have you been crying?" I walked over to her, my shoes squishing with every step.

"It's nothing, sweetie. I'm just a little worried right now." She gathered my wet body into a tight embrace. Out of the corner of my eye, I saw Aunt Kitty nod at her, my mother nodding in return as if they had a secret conversation over my shoulder. Slightly irritated at that, I pulled away from my mother.

She held me in place with her hands on my shoulders and smiled at me. She gently brushed away some strands of hair that were plastered to my forehead. "I love you so much, Emmy," she said, her voice full of pride.

"I love you, too," I said slowly, not sure where this was heading.

She gave me a quick hug before pushing me in the direction of the stairs. "Go change your clothes before you catch your death." She smacked me lightly on the rear end. Aunt Kitty followed me up the stairs and headed toward the bathroom.

"Why was she crying, Aunt Kitty?"

My aunt shook her head sadly. "When the steel mill went under last spring, it hit this town hard. Your dad is having a difficult time at the dealership. No one is interested in buying a new car right now when they can barely afford to keep their houses. Your mom just gets real worried sometimes."

I looked at her, my face etched with worry. "Are we going to be okay?"

Aunt Kitty smiled at me and ran a hand down my back. "Fine. Your parents are fighters."

As the summer marched on with its sizzling heat, I began to notice more and more *For Sale* signs dotting the front lawns of houses throughout our neighborhood. It was scary to watch the families I had grown up with disappear almost overnight. The CF&I steel mill had provided employment for thousands of men and women in town, and now those people were having to find work somewhere else. Many moved to the bigger cities of Colorado Springs or Denver; others left the state altogether. Despite Aunt Kitty's assurances, I couldn't help but wonder if we would be okay.

~ ~ ~ ~ ~

Chapter Eight

I sat up in bed, my back resting on the pillows propped against the headboard. I sighed as I looked through the depositions for the Holstead case. John Dithers was to pick up the file in the morning. With another sigh, I removed my reading glasses and rubbed my eyes, placing the manila folder on the small table beside the bed. What a time for this to happen. We were so close to a favorable settlement in this case.

"What do you think?" Rebecca said, a smile in her voice.

I looked up and a pang of pain slithered through my heart. Rebecca stood at the foot of the bed in her oversized T-shirt. She had stuffed a pillow up its long length, making a bulge at her middle. She posed for me, showing off her profile. I climbed out of the big bed and walked over to her, hugging her from behind. I placed my hands over hers where they rested on the pillow. "Soon, baby," I whispered in her ear. "Soon."

"Oh, I know, babe. I am just so impatient." She groaned. "I am almost thirty-five. That clock is echoing in my head everyday. Gets old after a while."

"Good things come to those who wait." I kissed her neck, inhaling the sweet scent of her skin after her shower. I could still smell the Irish Spring. "After all, you got me, right?"

She smiled. "Oh, yes. That took all the patience in the world. I didn't think I had it in me. Did you ever teach me a thing or two about myself!"

I grinned. "See? This should be a walk in the park then. This at least shouldn't take three years."

Rebecca brought one of my hands to her lips and held the palm against her cheek for a moment. With a shaky voice, she said, "Go take your shower."

I turned her around, removed the pillow from beneath her shirt and held her to me. "It just takes time, baby. It'll happen. I promise you. And when it does, you are going to look so beautiful pregnant."

She sniffled once and then seemed to get her emotions under control. "I don't know what gets into me. God, I am so damn emotional lately!" She pulled away from me gently.

"Tell me about it." I grinned and she returned the look, smacking me playfully on the arm. "At least you have an excuse with all those hormones they have you on." I kissed her quickly on the lips then walked toward the bathroom.

"Emily?"

"Yeah, babe?"

"I love you."

"I love you more."

I stepped out of my sweatpants and T-shirt quickly. The chill of the cold night whispered against my skin, making goose bumps erupt all over the cool surface. I clamped my teeth together as I played with the knobs of the shower trying to get the water to the right temperature. With a sigh, I stepped under the hot spray, closing my eyes and letting the soothing water wash over me, loosening my tense muscles. I ran my hands through my hair to smooth it back, rivulets of water streaming down the sides of my face and dripping off my nose and chin. Beth appeared in my mind's eye again and I let the memories come, my mind wandering back to that late summer afternoon.

~ ~ ~ ~ ~

I paced the floor of my room. Somehow, I knew Beth would be coming home today, and soon. What would I say to her? I had no idea. Even after the talk with my aunt, I still felt that nauseating monster, Jealousy, happily munching away at my brain. I stopped pacing and looked into the full-length mirror anchored to the back of my bedroom door. I smiled at my reflection, practicing what would be the best smile to give Beth when she came over. If she came over. *Would she?* I began to pace again before stopping to look at myself once more.

"Hi, Beth." I grinned. *No. You look like an idiot.* I wiped the grin from my lips and tried to look serious. *No.* What about pouty? Maybe she'll want to know what's wrong. I grinned again. "Hi, Beth. How was camp? How did your acting go? How is that little tramp, Casey?" *Ugh!* I buried my face in my hands, peeking at myself through my fingers. Then I froze and swallowed hard when I heard a car outside.

Hurrying around my bed, I glanced out the window and saw Mrs. Sayers' white Chevy slowly make the turn into their driveway. Gripped by uncertainty, I took a deep breath. *Should I wait for her to come over? That could take a while.* I sighed and looked at my reflection once again. I pulled my hair from its perpetual ponytail and brushed the long blonde strands until they shone. I adjusted my denim overall shorts and headed out to bravely face what I was sure would be the storm of Beth's wrath.

As I walked across our lawn, I watched Beth's mother help her daughter heave her heavy bags out of the trunk of the car. Neither spoke a word, the operation silent and efficient. Mrs. Sayers did a double take when she spied me, perhaps not expecting me to appear so soon after Beth's return. I felt funny, like I was a stalker or something. "Hi there, Emily," she said, then headed toward the front door.

Beth looked at me, her large duffel bag slung over one shoulder and a smaller canvas bag gripped in her hands. I noticed a bracelet dangling from her left wrist — silver, with lots of little charms hanging from it. A bitter chill ran down my spine.

"Hey," she said with a wide smile. She almost seemed hesitant. Almost.

"Hey."

"I was hoping you'd be home. I wasn't sure if you'd be off somewhere with Darla or something." She readjusted the bag on her shoulder.

"Nope. Not today." I smiled. My hands began to fidget with my watch, twisting it back and forth around my wrist.

"Cool. I have so much to tell you." She looked over her shoulder at her house and, with a sigh, turned back to me. "I think I should spend some time with her, though. She'll be ticked if I don't. Want to meet at the Bowl later?" Her voice was hopeful.

"Yeah, okay." I was disappointed. I didn't want to have to wait until later. "After dinner?" I heard myself say, grimacing inwardly. That would mean even longer!

"Yeah. Sounds good." She dropped the canvas bag and walked over to me, gathering me into her one free arm and holding me to her for just a brief moment before releasing me. She turned away and grabbed the bag again before heading toward the front door that her mother had left open for her.

My parents and I sat around the dinner table. I stared at the empty chair across from me, still missing my brother very much. I unenthusiastically returned my attention to my plate of spaghetti. I twirled my fork in the long noodles trying to see how big I could get the ball of pasta before it all fell off my fork.

"Emmy," my mother said quietly. "Don't play with your food."

"Sorry." I stuck the whole thing in my mouth so I could chew and not have to worry about thinking or talking while I concentrated on trying not to choke on the massive bite.

"Good God, Frances, didn't you teach our children any

manners?" my father said.

"Emily?" The slightest hint of a smile twitched at my mother's lips. I looked at her with wide eyes and shrugged my shoulders. I glanced at the wall clock to see that it was nearly 7:00. Beth and I had a mutual agreement that after dinner generally meant 8:00. By the time I finished the dishes, it would be time to head to the Bowl.

I stood at the kitchen sink with a dishrag in my right hand and a sauce-covered pan in my left. I scrubbed absently as I stared out the window into the backyard. I didn't really see the big cottonwood tree, the small shed tucked into the back left corner of the yard, or the big trampoline whose black tarp dully reflected the light of the full moon. I was thinking about how I was going to react to Beth tonight. The dishes were all washed except for the pan I was slowly working on. After that, I only had to wipe the dinner table and take out the garbage. I had to meet Beth in fifteen minutes, but I knew I would have no trouble getting there on time.

I thought again about Beth's new friend. I chastised myself, realizing I had absolutely no right to be jealous of this mystery girl. Beth was allowed to have other friends; after all, I had my own friends. But I relied on Beth so much and, at the same time, I had a sinking suspicion that Beth and Casey had been more than just friends over the summer. Had Beth done the same things with her that she had with me? Wasn't that just something for Beth and me alone? Other girls didn't do that, did they? But, then I thought about what Aunt Kitty had told me about Karen. Did all girls do that at one time or other? Either way, I hoped Beth and I would work things out.

With a swish of the dishtowel into the double sink, I left the kitchen and headed toward the living room where my parents were reading the newspaper and watching the evening news.

"Did you read this article, Fran?" my father asked, his voice distracted as he continued to read. I could see a picture of what appeared to be a parade of some kind on the paper in his hand. Men and women were walking down a street with signs in their hands, and their mouths were open as if they were talking or yelling.

"Which one?" my mother answered just as distracted as she focused on her own section of the *Star Journal*.

My father began to read aloud, "Nearly four hundred marchers participated in Friday afternoon's rally in front of City Hall in Denver, demanding equal rights for gays and lesbians. The rally started off peacefully with mild chants and rainbow-colored banners; however, things took a turn for the worse when anti-gay protesters began to throw rocks and glass bottles at the marchers. Several marchers were rushed to a nearby hospital with head wounds and severe cuts. After twenty minutes, Denver police were able to bring things back under control, and the rally was disbanded. No arrests were made." My mother looked up as my father put the paper down. "Those damn carpet munchers and fudge packers," he muttered. "Why can't they just keep it to themselves? No one cares about that...lifestyle. Why can't they just be normal?"

"Henry!" my mother looked at me to see if I had heard the degrading remarks. "Be fair. They didn't deserve that. Someone could have really gotten hurt. They weren't harming anyone. You just read that it was a peaceful march."

"What are carpet munchers and fudge packers?" I asked as I stopped at the front door. Both my parents turned to me, looking as if I had just asked if I could shoot them in the head.

"They're a bunch of sickos is what they are."

"Henry." My mother was silent for a moment as she thought of how best to answer my question. "Well, honey, they are homosexuals. You know, someone who, ah, well, who loves the same sex."

I absorbed this information for a moment before I realized that I had heard both derogatory terms used before at school. I had never known exactly what they meant and had never bothered to find out, because Beth got called things like that all the time, and I just assumed the other kids were being cruel, as usual.

I swallowed uneasily. "Oh. I knew that." I didn't want my parents to think I was a complete idiot. "Well I'm going."

"Don't be out too late, Emmy," my mother said, turning her attention back to her newspaper. As I stepped through the front door, I heard my mother say, "You'd think she'd know what those words mean at her age, wouldn't you, Henry?"

"Well, I'm glad she doesn't. That's nothing she ever needs to—" My father's words were cut off when I pulled the door closed behind me.

I walked somberly down the street, replaying my mother's definition again and again in my mind. Were we? *No. No way.* I did not love Beth in that way. Was Beth? *No.* I smiled to myself. She wasn't one of "those" people. Not a carpet muncher. I shivered. What a horrible name! So vulgar. Beth just always felt more comfortable physically around girls, that's all.

I wound up on the dirt path to the Toilet Bowl. Up ahead I

could barely make out the white of a T-shirt. The moon was hidden behind some rolling clouds, its suffocated light unable to break through the dense branches of trees that surrounded the pond. As I neared, I could see Beth sitting with her knees against her chest, her arms wrapped around her shins. Her eyes stared into the water, but did not really focus on anything. I could tell she was deep in thought as she drew her bottom lip into her mouth to lightly chew on it before releasing it once again.

"Hey," I said quietly, not wanting to disturb the hush of the late August night.

She looked over her shoulder and smiled. "Hi."

I dropped down next to her and sat cross-legged, my arms resting on the sides of my thighs. "You beat me here this time."

"Yeah, I know. I had to get out of there. I've been here for about an hour, I think."

"Oh. I would have been here a little sooner, but with Billy gone, I'm the only dishwasher." I looked off into the trees for a moment before turning back to her. "So, tell me about it. How was camp?"

She smiled. "It was great. I won a ton of awards and trophies. You should see my dresser top. It's loaded with them." Her eyes sparkled, filled with so much pride.

"Oh, Beth." I was truly happy for her. "I knew you would do really well there. You are so talented. If I only had this much of your talent." I held up my hand, placing my index finger about half an inch from my thumb.

"Hey, don't be too hard on yourself, Em. You've got some serious stuff upstairs. I wish I was smart like you. And beautiful." Her smile was disarming.

I grinned shyly. "Yeah, right. All that won't get me a standing ovation or awards and trophies like you get."

"Maybe not, but it sure will get you far in life. You will get far, Em. I know it." Her bright blue eyes bored into mine. They were filled with a mixture of seriousness and sadness. She continued with a grin. "Just remember me when you're a big successful lawyer in some great city."

"Always." I smiled. "As long as you remember me when you give your speech after you win your first Oscar."

Beth grinned, lost in the thought. We locked eyes for a moment as we connected. I had never been linked to another human being like I was to Beth. We were able to say so much with our eyes that our mouths would never say. Right now, I was seeing something flash through hers that told me she was in a great struggle over something. She looked so lost that I felt the need to touch her, to comfort her. I reached out and placed my hand on her right knee, which was still being held securely to her body. I knew she wanted to talk but was unsure if I wanted to hear about it, so I took the plunge to get her started.

"Why did she have to leave camp?" My words came out slowly and quietly. I could see the storm building in the expanse of ocean that was her eyes.

She tore them from mine and looked down at her crossed ankles, silent for a moment. "Someone saw us," she said so quietly I had to strain to hear.

"Saw you? Swimming?" I asked, confused.

"No." She smiled at the memory. "No, they saw us on the shore. We were...we were kissing." She glanced at me quickly to see my reaction. With careful control, I managed to keep my face expressionless. Now that I had gotten her talking, I wasn't going to let my petty jealousies get in the way. When she saw it was okay, she continued. "Casey was naked. I only had my shirt off." Suddenly she buried her face in her hands and groaned. "Oh, Em," her voice was muffled, "it was so embarrassing." She looked at me again.

"So, you and Casey were doing what we...well, you would kiss and stuff?"

A slow blush traveled up her neck and stained her cheeks crimson. "At first." She gave me a lopsided grin and raised a brow.

"At first?" I squeaked. I cleared my throat and remained silent while I waited for her to continue. It became painfully obvious that she wanted me to drag it out of her. Did I really want to hear this? Curiosity got the best of me. "So, um, what else did you do?"

"God, what didn't we do?" It was my turn to blush. I swallowed reflexively and stared into the water for a moment before I could face her. When she had my full attention again, Beth continued her story. "Casey would use her tongue, and she would start sucking, then with her fingers—"

"Fingers?" I interrupted. "Why would she use her fingers to kiss your mouth?"

Beth smirked. "Who said anything about my mouth?"

I sucked in my breath as realization dawned on me. With an audible gulp, I shivered. Beth grinned wildly at my reaction. As my mind began to form a mental picture, I was startled to feel a wave of heat crash against my lower stomach like a tidal wave onto the shore. The wave spread south as Beth continued.

"She would rub my breasts with her fingers and the

palms of her hands. I had no idea they were so sensitive! And then when she'd use her mouth—"

I shut out Beth's rambling as my mind reeled. My mother's voice echoed through my head.

"... at first she started using just one finger, but then ..."

I heard the schoolboys' voices ring in my ears, "Hey! It's Beth the lesbian! Hey, my dog's in heat, ya interested?"

"... Oh, Em. It felt so good. I couldn't walk for a ..."

"They're a bunch of sickos is what they are. ..."

"... is coming here next week."

"What?" I asked, my head snapping to look at Beth. My reverie was shattered in a million pieces. "What did you say?"

"Jeez, girl, where did you go?" Beth grinned at me. "I said Casey is coming here next week before we start school."

"Oh." I felt my stomach drop to my knees.

"I can't wait. Everything happened so fast, we didn't even get to say goodbye. I really want you to meet Casey. She's great. Can you do something with us? Maybe we could all catch a movie or something." Beth looked at me, her eyes hopeful and alive.

"I don't know. Darla and I have plans next week." I regretted the lie as soon as it flew from my mouth, and I cringed when I saw the hurt spread across Beth's face.

"Oh. Em, it's only one day, an afternoon. A couple of hours."

"What, a couple hours is all you want me around for?" I pouted. I knew I was being childish, but could not help myself. Whoever said jealousy kills the soul was a very wise person indeed.

"Of course not!" Beth was getting mad now. "But I figured with your busy schedule and all, a couple of hours was all you'd be able to spare!"

"Well, maybe it is! Let me check my calendar!" I jumped to my feet.

Beth opened her mouth then clamped it shut again. She closed her eyes and took a deep breath before standing and looking me in the eye. "Em, this is stupid. Why are we fighting?" I didn't have an answer for her, so she continued. "I just want you to meet her. You are my best friend, and Casey is really important to me. I just want you to like her."

"What does it matter if I like her or not? She's your friend."

"It just does, Em." She searched my eyes, desperate for a safe place to hold on to. "Okay?"

With a tired sigh, I relented. I could see the fork in our road just up ahead, and it scared me. Which way would we both go? It hardly seemed likely that we'd choose the same path.

Chapter Nine

~ ~ ~ ~ ~

In the days preceding Casey's arrival, all I heard about were the hikes she and Beth had taken, the day Casey had shown Beth how to sail, and the countless other things they had done together. Beth told me Casey was heading back to England after the summer to live with her grandmother and go to school at Oxford. Casey this, Casey that, on and on until I wanted to scream at the top of my lungs! The thing I think I hated most was that Casey actually sounded interesting to me. I just didn't want to admit it to myself, and I certainly couldn't admit it to Beth. I was in my bedroom putting away laundry when I heard a car on the street outside, followed by Beth squealing in delight.

"Oh, goodie," I mumbled to myself as I walked to my window so I could sneak a glimpse of Casey without the pressure of Beth's gaze on me. A large orange and white Ford pickup pulled to the curb and squeaked to a halt. The driver fussed with something on the bench seat for a moment as Beth raced up to the truck door. Even from my window, I could see Beth was almost vibrating with excitement. Finally, the driver's door opened and out stepped Casey. She was tall, nearly as tall as Beth, with long, golden blonde hair. Her back was to me so I couldn't see her face, but her body looked lithe and tan in cut-off jean shorts and a baby-doll tank top. Beth flew into her arms, and they hugged tightly for a long minute. I couldn't tear my eyes away as I watched the two embrace. When Casey finally pulled away, Beth smiled at her.

"Did you find it okay?" I heard her ask.

"Yes, luv. You gave me terrific directions." I was surprised to hear an accent even though Beth had told me about it. "This is a lovely neighborhood. Is your mum home?" Casey said as they walked arm in arm around the front of the truck. When they reached the sidewalk, I was able to see her face. Her hair was pulled back with barrettes on either side of her head, and she had finely sculpted features, with delicately arched brows and large brown eyes that looked kind. Her smile was a brilliant white against her summer-bronzed skin. Beth was right; she was beautiful.

"No. She's at work, I think. She's going out tonight, so we

have the place to ourselves." Beth grinned at her guest. Casey said something too low for me to hear, but whatever it was, it made Beth blush and smile wider. I gritted my teeth and fought the pang of jealousy. Casey turned and looked at my house; I quickly ducked out of view of the window.

"Is that Emily's home?" she asked. I raised a brow in surprise.

"Yup."

"How beautiful 'tis. I can't wait to meet her!"

Was this a joke? She *wanted* to meet me? I snorted at the prospect. Yeah, right. Probably just wanted to rub it in my face that she had basically taken my place in Beth's life. I walked back to my bed and finished folding my laundry. They could wait. I certainly was in absolutely no hurry to meet Casey whatever-her-name-was.

~ ~ ~ ~ ~

I stepped out of the shower and went to the sink, wiping the towel across the smooth surface of the mirror to remove the steam. I picked up my brush and ran it through the long, water-darkened strands of my hair to comb out the tangles. I stared at my reflection, amazed at how much my physical appearance had changed over time. Looking at the pictures of myself when I was younger was quite humbling. I still looked young for my age; so many thought I was in my early twenties. But all the same, I could see the signs of aging, especially in my eyes. Growing up, and in my college days, people used to tell me my eyes held a constant question and reflected a wonder for life, as if I was always seeing things for the first time. Now, looking into my eyes as an adult, I could see how hardened they'd become. The wonder and curiosity had been replaced by suspicion and indifference, brought on by exposure to the complexities of human nature courtesy of my chosen career. I had seen the best of man, but also the worst.

I opened the bathroom door and was surprised to find Rebecca already asleep. She was lying on her side with her back toward me. Her hair spilled over onto my pillow and I smiled as I imagined the clean smell and silky feel of it. Sitting on the edge of the bed, I paused and watched the slight movements of her body as she breathed. I thought back to when we met.

I had been out of law school for two years and was working for a small-time lawyer in Queens while trying to secure a position with James/Parks/Stone. Back then, the fact that I'd reached my goal of becoming a lawyer meant only that I would have a future filled with money, success, and fame. The thought of settling down and being domestic was alien; a past filled with betrayal and bad decisions poisoned any thoughts in that area. But when I ran into Rebecca, literally, at a laundromat three miles from my tiny one-bedroom apartment, my ideas on the subject, and my life, began to change.

I reached out my hand and placed it on her hip as I scooted under the blanket behind her, pressing my body to hers. She moaned softly, covering my hand as it slid to her stomach and entwining our fingers. "You okay, baby?" she asked groggily. I raised my head and placed my chin on her shoulder. She squeezed my hand, letting me know she was awake to talk if I needed to.

"I'm nervous about going back."

"Why?"

I sighed, staring out the dark window across from the bed. *What a good question.* "Well, I guess because I haven't been back for so long, and I still have so much to sort out. I can't get Beth out of my head. She haunts me."

Rebecca rolled onto her back and stared at me as I rested my elbow against the bed, my head in my hand. "Why, Emily? You really loved her, didn't you?"

"Does that bother you?" I asked, laying my other hand on her side.

"Maybe a little. I don't know. I guess it's just because I don't really understand what happened with you two."

I chuckled ruefully. "In truth, neither do I."

She covered my hand with hers, tracing the veins with her fingertips. "Tell me more about Casey. It seems she had a lot to do with things."

I nodded slowly. "She did."

~ ~ ~ ~ ~

The late August heat was taking its toll on the city, and people tried to spend less and less time outside. The previous day's newspaper had mentioned a rise in deaths among the elderly, many of whom were succumbing to heat stroke, and the weatherman reported there was no relief in sight.

I sat on our front porch, the sun-heated cement burning through the material of my shorts and searing my butt. I squirmed but did not move. I was nervous and knew if I stood, I would only start to pace, and that was not how I wanted my first meeting with Casey to go. So I endured the hot seat and stared out to the street. A group of boys were riding their Huffy dirt bikes, playing cards attached to the wheel spokes to create the sound of a motorcycle.

Monica Nivens steered noisily into the driveway across

the street. It sounded like her Bug was about to die. My
mother told me Monica had only to pass the bar before she'd
be a full-fledged lawyer. She pulled a green duffel out of her
back seat and then looked over at me. I smiled and waved,
then began to fidget as she walked across the street, careful
to stay out of the way of the boy's riding, and stopped at the
edge of our lawn.

"Hi," she said with a smile.

I could only smile back. I had been watching this woman
in awe for the past three years. She was my real-life hero and
here she was talking to me. Then I noticed she had cut her
hair. Short. "You cut your hair," I blurted, then wanted to
slap myself or find a deep hole. I must have sounded so stupid.

She chuckled. "Yup. Sure did." She ran a hand through
the short, black strands. "A lot cooler, I can tell you that. My
mom says you want to be a lawyer."

"Yes. More than anything." I felt pride puff out my chest.

She smiled and nodded again. "Good. Good luck to you."

"Thanks. You, too." She smiled one last time before turning to head back across the street. I watched as she walked
up her drive and disappeared into the house. *Wow.* I felt ten
feet tall. Someone had noticed and acknowledged my dream. I
was so excited I barely noticed when Beth walked across the
lawn.

"You look happy." She followed my gaze across the street
to the Nivens' house and looked back at me with questioning
eyes.

"Monica finished law school and is studying for the bar
exam," I explained, but Beth only shrugged. "So, where's
Casey?" I asked, keeping my voice as even as I could.

"She's coming. I wanted a few minutes of you to myself."
Beth smiled that lopsided grin she reserved for me. "I really
missed you this summer, Em."

My heart soared. "I missed you, too, Beth."

"Look, I really want to thank you for doing this for me
today. Your opinion means so much to me, Em, and I just
want you to meet Casey and tell me what you think, okay?"

Beth's eyes pleaded with me to understand. I smiled and
took her hand. "Okay." She squeezed my fingers in response.
"You know, I saw you two through my window, and she is
beautiful, Beth."

Her face lit up, and she nodded. "Yeah, she is, isn't she?"
As if on cue, out of the corner of my eye, I saw Casey walking
toward us across Beth's lawn, a wide, genuine smile on her
face. Beth saw me looking and dropped my hand, turning to

watch the blonde walk up to my front porch.

"Hello," Casey said, her voice light and very feminine. Beth colored slightly as Casey smiled at her. I swallowed the bitterness in my throat. I promised Beth I'd be nice and do my best. I could completely understand why she was so taken with this girl. Casey turned to me and extended a long, petite hand. I glanced down at it then took it. "Emily, it is so lovely to meet you. I have heard so very much about you this summer."

"Likewise," I said through my plastered smile. Her handshake was firm, but not painful; her confidence obvious in her every move. I was amazed at how someone could be so self-assured in beauty and grace, yet not for an instant come off as arrogant or boastful as Darla often was. This appeared to be true security in one's self. I had to admit, I was impressed. Wish I could be like that.

"So!" Casey clapped her hands together and looked from one of us to the other. "What's on the agenda for today? I can't wait to see your city and learn more about you, Emily. My grandmum's name is Emily, you know? It's an old family name."

Beth lead us toward the orange and white truck as Casey fell in step with me, commenting on my house, our flowers, and even the weather. At the curb, Beth opened the passenger side door for me. I glanced at her questioningly. She raised her brows and nodded toward the cab. Okay, so I was to be stuck between the two lovebirds. That should prove interesting. I climbed into the high truck and belted myself in. Casey smiled at me and did the same, slamming the driver's side door and turning the ignition. I glanced over to see Beth sitting happily by the door, her arm hanging out the open window. "I thought maybe we could hit the State Fair," she said, looking down at me. "Don't you think, Em?"

"Uh, yeah. It's the last weekend and all."

"Sounds like gobs of fun!" Casey chipped in.

Beth told Casey which direction to go, and the blonde skillfully steered the large truck onto the street. Beth was good at keeping the conversation on safe subjects like school and Colorado, and we both asked Casey questions about England. It didn't take long to reach the fairgrounds. Beth directed Casey to park in the church parking lot across the street, and we walked to the main gate. The three of us stood in line, and I glanced around to see if I recognized anyone. Part of me hoped I wouldn't, because I didn't want to explain who Casey was. People talked enough about Beth already.

"So, Emily." Casey was smiling down at me. I hated being

short sometimes. I never felt intimidated by Beth's height, but this girl intimidated the hell out of me! "Beth tells me you want to be a lawyer." I glared at Beth for just a second before turning my attention back to Casey. I smiled and nodded. "Oh, was Beth not to tell me that?" she asked, a worried look crossing her features as she once again looked from me to Beth. Beth shrugged and narrowed her eyes at me.

"No. Not at all. That's fine," I said finally. Things had started to get uncomfortable for me, but the blonde had done nothing wrong. "Yes, I do. More than anything." Casey turned back to me with a lovely smile. *Lovely? I never use that word! Ugh.*

"That is so wonderful, luv. I am going to be attending Oxford Medical, but for a long time I was torn between the two: Oxford Medical or Oxford Law. Medical won out, though, I'm afraid."

We moved forward in line, and Beth insisted on paying for all three tickets, much to my disdain.

Casey looked around the grounds. "This is all so charming," she gushed. "How wonderful to have this in your hometown every year."

Without discussion, Beth and I automatically headed for the concourse to get our ride armbands. Casey followed our lead and let the man snap a neon pink band around her wrist.

"What shall we ride first, girls?" she asked, staring at the attractions surrounding us.

"I wanna do the Zipper!" Beth exclaimed.

I glanced at the ride, the small covered cars that held people flopping every which way, and shook my head. "Unh uh. No way. You know I won't go upside down, Beth."

She grinned at me. "Still a chicken, Em?"

"Absolutely."

Casey chuckled. "I'm afraid I'm with Emily on this one, luv," she said, placing her hand on Beth's shoulder.

Beth looked disappointed. "Okay, okay. We can skip it."

"Absolutely not!" Casey said, walking toward the ride.

Beth looked over at me, and I shrugged. What was she doing? There was no way I was getting on that thing. I had managed to avoid it for the past fifteen years and had lived quite a fine life.

"Go on then, Beth. We'll wait for you."

Beth looked at the line and shook her head. "Nah. I'll do it later. The line's really long, and—"

"Go," Casey said, her eyes narrowed, one long arm pointing. Without another word, Beth headed toward the line of people.

I stared at the blonde in amazement. I had never seen anyone get Beth to do anything once she'd set her mind against it. Even I had a tough time. "How'd you do that?"

"What?" Casey asked, leading us toward a nearby bench.

"Beth is one of the most stubborn people I have ever known in my entire life," I said, glancing at my friend, then back to the grinning blonde.

"She is, isn't she?" We both laughed. "Yes, well, t'isn't very easy, but I am quite persistent and much more stubborn than she is." She turned to me and winked.

"So, what made you decide to choose medicine instead of law?"

With that question, Casey and I began the most intense, interesting discussion about law and the good and bad of it in the United States. She was incredibly insightful and even explained some of the practices of Europe. I watched her as she talked, watched how she moved, and suddenly something dawned on me: She and I were a lot alike. We saw things much the same way, especially where law and politics were concerned. I could easily imagine her in a courtroom, standing before the jury as she made her summation. I realized she'd probably be just as good at her chosen profession of medicine. She had charisma, intelligence, and the innocent face of an angel. Also, she was immensely likeable and had obvious compassion and kindness. Casey told me about her mother, who had died from MS, and how she had stayed by her bedside, working with the doctors and nurses, learning their trade. The thought of being able to help someone live, of being the force behind a person's survival or being able to help his death be as painless as possible had been the determining factor in her choice.

As I talked with Casey I saw what Beth saw, and I understood. My anger and jealousy dissipated with each word Casey spoke and each touch of my arm or knee as she explained something or emphasized a point. She was an incredible human being, and I felt honored to have been able to meet and talk to her. I felt at peace with Beth's choice. Until I caught them by the bathrooms.

After a long afternoon of going hoarse from screaming on rides like the Arctic Express, the Sea Dragon, and the bumper cars, we decided to get some lunch. With our baskets of cheeseburgers and fries in hand, we found a spot of grass under the shade of some tall trees. We laughed and joked, occasionally throwing a fry or two, mostly Casey and me ganging up on Beth. She never got mad; she just got even.

"You wouldn't. No, Beth, please, no!" I cried just before the cold water from Beth's cup spilled over my head and ran down my face and neck. The chunks of ice settled nicely in my bra and in my lap. Beth tossed the cup into a nearby trash can with a triumphant smile as she dropped to the grass again. I glared at her from under sopping bangs. "I can't believe you did that. You are evil, Beth. Do you know that?"

"Yup." She grinned, leaning back on her hands.

"I can't believe you just did that to your best friend, luv," Casey said, taking in my wet T-shirt and shorts.

"I warned her not to throw that fry."

"Well yes, but ..." One look at Beth told Casey all she needed to know. "Well, perhaps I should watch myself then." Beth winked at her.

We managed to find a bathroom near the Bud tent, and I hurried in to dry as much of myself as I could. The day was hot, and the water had actually felt good, but wearing a wet, white shirt was not high on my list of top priorities in life. I smiled and shook my head as I stared at myself in the mirror. I had no comb with me, and did I ever need one. I ran my fingers through the tangled strands as best I could before pulling it all back into a ponytail. With one final glance, I left the bathroom and re-entered the late afternoon heat. Beth and Casey were nowhere to be found. I heard a low giggle coming from behind the building, which backed up to a dark alley made of trailers from big rigs and tents. I followed the noise, but stopped cold when I saw Beth pushed up against the side of a green trailer, Casey pressed against her, their hands roaming as they kissed passionately. I could only stare. My eyes followed Beth's hand as she reached down and cupped one side of Casey's butt, pulling their bodies closer together. Casey moaned softly.

I wanted to leave, to just walk away and pretend I had seen nothing, but I couldn't move. Beth had told me about the nature of her relationship with Casey, but deep down, I hadn't accepted it; I'd tried to see Casey as just a friend of Beth's and no more. But there it was before my eyes in living color. Beth and Casey were lovers, and that meant that Beth was...that Beth was...

I turned and walked out of that darkened alley, heading back toward the crowds, wanting to be with them, to be where I understood and felt comfortable. I stood just at the edge of the main pathway, my arms crossed over my chest as I tried to catch my breath. I felt a hand gently touch my shoulder, but did not turn toward the owner.

"Em. Em, please look at me." I couldn't. I shook my head

and stared at my sandals. "Em, please." Beth's voice was soft and somewhat shaky. "I'm sorry. You weren't meant to see that."

I swallowed back my shock. "It's okay, Beth," I whispered. "No big deal."

I could feel her eyes as she studied me, weighing my words against what she knew of me. Finally she spoke, lightly squeezing my shoulder. "I guess we kinda need to talk when we get home, huh?"

"If you want to, Beth. We don't need to. I understand."

"Do you?"

I finally glanced up at her, seeing the tortured look in those blue eyes. *Did I? No, not really.* "I don't know. I think I'm a little confused right now."

"Fair enough."

~ ~ ~ ~ ~

Beep. Beep. Beep. Beep. Smack!

I sat up with a groan. I hated that damn alarm clock. With red, heavy eyes I looked around our dark room. Isn't the sun supposed to be up by...I glanced at the clock...four in the morning? Oh, God. I flopped back into the pillows.

"What time is it?" Rebecca mumbled as she cuddled against me, her warm breath tickling my neck.

"Early. Entirely too early," I answered, running my fingers through her hair.

"I thought so," she muttered. She hugged my side tighter as I continued to stroke her hair, which could nearly hypnotize her. She sighed contentedly. "You know you're going to give me a 'fro if you keep doing that." I chuckled and kissed the top of her head.

"We're supposed to get up about now, aren't we?"

"Yup."

She groaned again, but pushed herself up so that she lay over me, her weight supported by her arms. "How are you this morning, baby?" she asked, brushing a few stray strands away from my face.

I rubbed small circles on her back. "I'm okay. Didn't sleep much last night."

"Sweetie," she whispered, leaning down to gently kiss me.

I hugged her to me, needing to feel her warmth and strength. Hers was a stabilizing force I relied on, and I knew I would be needing it in the days to come. I certainly could have used it that afternoon at the state fair with Beth and Casey.

~ ~ ~ ~ ~ ~

I had tried to lighten up the mood as best I could, but by the time we reached Beth's house, the day was lost. Both Beth and Casey were uncharacteristically quiet. They didn't touch each other or really even look at each other. I may have been totally confused about how I felt, but I didn't want them to feel as though they had to walk on eggshells around me. It was my problem to figure out, and I could be adult enough to do it on my own. Casey cut the engine, and we all sat in the truck for a few moments, no one saying a word. I held my breath, not sure what would happen next. Finally, Beth broke the silence.

"Em, come with me." She opened her door and helped me out of the massive cab, then led me down the street. I knew where we were going and walked alongside her, both of us basking in the early evening breeze that began to ease the heat of the day.

"I had fun today, Beth," I said as we turned onto the path to the Bowl.

She turned to me with a partial smile and nodded. "Me, too."

We went to our regular spot and sat on the rock lip of the creek. I remained quiet, but I could almost hear the thoughts whirling around Beth's mind. She clearly needed a moment to collect them and find a good place to start. "You know, lately I've been thinking a lot about things. How different we are from when we were kids." She turned to me with that crooked grin I loved so much. "Remember when we were like eleven or twelve and we went camping with Billy?"

"Yeah." I smiled. "We had fun."

"Yes, we did." Beth picked a handful of rocks and, one by one, began to toss them into the still water, causing ripples to spread out and eventually disappear. "Remember when I asked you if we'd still be friends when we got older?"

I nodded, watching the light bounce over the tiny waves. "I said we'd be friends forever," I mumbled absently.

"Do you still believe that?"

I looked over at her for a short minute, just taking in how she looked at that moment; the dying rays of the sun had somehow managed to descend from the heavens and capture all that was Beth. The brilliant light brought out the red high-lights in her dark hair, the breeze picking up strands and holding them out to create a halo of gold around her face. She was beautiful. I stared into her eyes and nodded with a smile. She smiled back.

"I hope so." She turned back to the water and continued

to throw her rocks. "You know, you really weren't supposed to see that today. I'm sorry. Things just kind of got out of hand."

I chuckled quietly. "It happens, I guess." I couldn't help but think back to that night during New Year's. Apparently, she had not forgotten about it either.

"I think we already found that out, though, didn't we?" I turned and met her gaze. We both smiled, a secret smile that only we knew the reason.

"So, you're really into girls, huh?"

She nodded without hesitation. "Completely." She turned and stared over the treetops as the sun disappeared altogether. "I think I always knew, just didn't have the words to say, you know?"

"I think I always knew, too."

~ ~ ~ ~ ~

Chapter Ten

We rushed around the house to make sure we had remembered everything and that Simon had enough food and water to get him through for a couple days, then hurried to the garage to load up the Pathfinder. The early morning air was bone-chillingly cold as Rebecca pulled out of our neighborhood and drove in the direction of La Guardia Airport. I sipped coffee from my travel mug and stared out the window, watching the dark shops we passed on our way to the highway. In another hour or so, these streets would be packed with people commuting to work. Even on a Saturday. I listened as my lover talked about a student in her Biology II class whom she suspected was a lesbian and was struggling with it.

"It's hard being young," I said. Isn't that the truth.

~ ~ ~ ~ ~

Three days before Beth and I were to start high school, Casey flew home to England. Early in the afternoon before she left Pueblo, she came to my house and asked me to take a walk with her. We strolled down the street and turned toward the neighborhood park as she asked me different questions about certain houses that caught her eye or who a person walking on the sidewalk on the opposite side of the street was. Finally, we hit the park and headed toward the swings.

"I'm so glad I came here," she said quietly, watching some birds play in a nearby tree.

"Me, too," I said with a smile, which she returned.

"Beth spoke so highly of you; I couldn't wait to meet you. You don't know how deeply she loves and values you, Emily. It's quite extraordinary — the friendship the two of you share at such a young age." She was quiet for a moment and then spoke again, her voice low and serious. "Emily, I fear Beth will go through a great struggle in the next few years. I knew a girl like her in high school. Wanda was her name. She was sure on the outside, but not so sure on the inside." She looked at me to make sure I was paying attention; I hung on her every word. "Wanda killed herself during our junior year. I suppose why I'm telling you this is because Beth is young. She found out who she really is at a young age and will be very alone for a while. She is strong, but, Emily, please don't give up on her. Stay by her side and support her."

"I always have."

She smiled and gently tapped my chin with a finger. "I know. You and your family have helped her through so much. Lord knows that mother of hers is a complete hag." She hopped off the swing and reached for my hand. We walked around the park for a bit, hand in hand. "Can I write to you sometimes?"

I looked at her and smiled. "Yeah. I'd like that."

"Great. Me, too." She stopped us and leaned down to plant a small kiss on my cheek. "It was a pleasure to meet you, Emily. Do take care of yourself."

"I will. You, too, okay?"

~ ~ ~ ~ ~

"Did you ever hear from her again?" Rebecca asked, as she pulled into a space in the airport's long-term parking lot.

"Yeah. She wrote off and on for about two years, then not a word. I don't know what happened to her or where she ended up."

We arrived at our gate a bit early and took seats, placing our carry-on bags at our feet. Rebecca graded some papers that she didn't want to have to worry about over the weekend, and I stared out the huge windows into the pre-dawn morning. Or, to be more specific, I stared at my reflection in the window, my image hazy and double-edged.

With a sigh, I glanced down at the book in my lap, but I couldn't concentrate on the words or the story. Having read the current paragraph three times, I stared out the window again, but this time I saw neither the dawning New York morning nor my own face staring back at me in the glass. My eyes, like my mind, reflected back once again to the past.

~ ~ ~ ~ ~

My eyes opened, and I blinked several times as the bright, early morning light streamed in through my curtains. "Ugh."

I glanced at the clock across the room. It was almost seven. Time to get up. The first day of high school. As the thought entered my mind, I felt a wave of excitement and a touch of nervous energy fill me. With strong resolve, I slid my legs over the side of the bed and planted my feet on the floor. My alarm hadn't yet gone off; I'd been awakened by the sound of a car in the driveway. With drawn brows, I walked to the window and looked down to find my aunt's car. *What on earth is she doing here so early? Shouldn't she be at work?* I shrugged, let the curtains fall back into place, and headed for the closet.

As a freshman, I had to make a statement on the first day, let those upper classmen know who they were dealing with. I frowned as I pondered this. Just who were they dealing with? *Emily Thomas, Freshman Extraordinaire.* But then, why should they care about that? Darla's words bounced around in my head a bit, before I realized that Darla was full of shit. Beth was right; I just wanted to be myself.

I picked out a pair of comfortable blue jeans and a plain white sleeveless top. Not too flashy, not too boring. In all honesty, I didn't want to stick out. Well, not yet, anyway. Let a girl get used to her surroundings first.

Feeling pretty good about my appearance, with my long hair pulled back into a tight ponytail and my backpack hanging from one shoulder, I made my way down the stairs and toward the kitchen, where my mom and Kitty sat at the table talking quietly over coffee. From their positions, with their faces nearly pushed together nose to nose, I could tell the conversation must be pretty serious.

I stood in the doorway and watched them for a second, waiting for one of them to spot me and indicate whether or not I should enter the room. I didn't want to interrupt one of their infamous, top-secret talks. Unfortunately, I went unnoticed, so I had to resort to my own methods to get their attention. I cleared my throat softly, but to no avail. It really must be something serious. I cleared my throat again, a bit louder. Still no go. "Ahem!" My mother looked up first, Aunt Kitty looking away as she wiped one of her eyes with a napkin and then turned to look at me. I smiled as sweetly as I could. "Uh, sorry to bother you. You looked so intent on your conversation and all."

"Oh, honey. I'm sorry," my mother said, reaching for me.

Her gesture confused me, but I went to her and found myself engulfed in a monster, one-armed hug. "Is everything okay?" I asked, pulling away and looking down at them both.

Kitty smiled, but I could tell she'd been crying. Her normally bright green eyes were dull and bloodshot. "Yeah. Everything's fine," my mother said brightly. "Want some breakfast, baby?"

"Nah." I headed to the fridge for the lunch I had packed the night before.

"Are you sure, honey? You have to eat something, Emmy. Some toast?" I shook my head. "An egg?" Another shake of my head. "A bagel?"

"I'm fine. I'll take something with me." In truth my stomach was in knots, and I was in no way, shape, or form hungry. I just wanted to get the day over with and make it home in one piece. I poured a small glass of orange juice and sipped it as I leaned against the counter and stared at them. They stared back.

"I can't believe my baby's all grown up and in high school now." My mother's eyes began to fill. She grabbed a napkin and dabbed at them.

"I know. I remember when Billy started," Aunt Kitty said, sipping her coffee. She took a deep breath, then stood. "I better get going, Frankie," she said to my mother. She was the only person on the planet who could get away with calling Frances Thomas by the name Frankie and live to tell the tale. She leaned down and gave my mom a hug, then turned to me. "Want a ride, kiddo?"

A wide grin spread across my face. "Yeah!" Arriving on my first day of school in a car as opposed to a bus? *Hell, yeah.* "Can Beth come, too?"

"'Course." She turned back to my mom. "I'll call you later and let you know what I find out, okay?"

"Okay. Talk to you later, honey."

Aunt Kitty gave me one of her winning smiles and led the way to the front door.

Kitty's car pulled up in front of the high school, and I peered out at it. It was a large red brick building, four stories high. It was an old school, one of the oldest in the city. There were big, dark windows lining the front, and, for just a moment, I imagined I saw faces in those windows, staring out at me, sizing me up. It was a silly thought, I realized, but I was scared. With a deep breath, I opened the car door. Aunt Kitty stopped me with a hand on my arm, and I turned to look at her.

"Hey, you'll do fine, kiddo. You need anything, you don't be afraid to call, okay?" I nodded, and with an air of confidence that I absolutely did not feel, I climbed out of the car followed by my best friend.

Beth and I walked toward the building, my aunt's car disappearing from sight as we passed through the throng of other kids. Groups, couples, singles, any possible combination. I was so glad to have Beth at my side, part of me wanted to grab her hand. I glanced over at her to see her looking around, gauging people as she went. I was impressed by her demeanor. She actually *looked* the way I wanted to feel. She *always* looked the way I wanted to feel.

"Are you nervous, Em?" she asked out of the side of her mouth.

"Yup," I muttered back. "You?"

"Hell yeah," she said, smiling at some girl who walked by.

I narrowed my eyes and looked up at her. She was looking around, her body calm and relaxed. From all appearances, she didn't have a care in the world. "You're kidding me, right?" I asked, stopping us just outside the front doors.

She shook her head. "No. I'm not. I want to get the hell out of here."

I grinned and lightly punched her in the shoulder, then moved us on.

High school takes on almost mystical proportions to anyone who has not been there. To an elementary school student, the world is split into two distinct groups: children and adults. There was nothing in between these sacred positions. Because of this, the average high school student appears to be some sort of anomaly. To a middle school student, the high school student is a god or goddess. They have done the ultimate — they have left childhood behind but are not yet perceived as the enemy: an adult.

Now that I was the high school student, I realized just how screwed up my way of thinking had been. Being a teenager wasn't all it was cracked up to be. It was downright hard!

~ ~ ~ ~ ~

I was happy to find that Rebecca and I had three adjacent seats to ourselves on the plane. I hated being squished between Rebecca and some stranger. My lover always wanted the window seat and that was fine with me, since I usually slept on the plane anyway.

We got as comfortable as one could get in a big, metal, flying tube, and I settled in for a good nap. I listened with closed eyes as the pilots prepped the plane for takeoff, the folks around us got settled into their seats, and the overhead compartments were closed with quiet clicks. I took a deep breath as the realization of where we were headed stole over me once again. I thought about Nora Sayers. Was she even still alive? I had not talked to her or heard anything about her in at least a dozen years. If she was still there, I wondered if we'd see her at the funeral. Was Jim Sayers going to travel across the country to be there? He hadn't done so when Beth was a child, so I couldn't imagine what would make him change. My last thought before drifting off to sleep was that this whole situation was not going to be easy.

Chapter Eleven

~ ~ ~ ~ ~

My freshman year was a month old when I got some bad news.

Saturdays in my house were pretty much all the same. I would awaken to loud music blaring from the stereo in the living room, generally George Strait trying to persuade some naïve young woman that he loved her. No matter what the selection was, my mother would help the singer along by adding her own high-pitched, off-key vocals.

In theory, this practice was simply because my mother liked her music and liked it loud. But at 7:30 in the morning? In reality, this early morning concert was to get Billy and my butts out of bed to keep her company or to help with the housework. Now that my brother was gone, I was the only individual privy to the serenade. After a while, I got really good at tuning it out. Then, one Saturday in October, I awoke from the *silence*.

I raised my head and looked around my room, focusing on the pile of clothes on the floor, then rubbed the sleep out of my eyes. I pulled on a pair of sweats and my slippers to ward off the cold morning and left my room. At the top of the stairs, I stood and listened. I held my breath so I could hear better. Nothing. If I didn't know differently, I would have thought no one was home. Running a hand through my wild blonde locks, I slowly descended the stairs to the main floor. The living room was just as it had been the night before; the only indication anyone had been up this morning was the newspaper that sat, still rolled, in the recliner by the door. To my right, in the kitchen, I could just barely see my mother's socked feet.

"Mom?" I asked as I approached the kitchen doorway.

She sat at the table, one hand on her forehead, the other fingering the tea bag on the saucer next to her coffee cup. At the sound of my voice, she glanced up at me with sad eyes and beckoned me over. "Come here, honey." Her voice was nasal and thick. She'd been crying.

"What's wrong?" I asked, taking a tentative step toward her before heading straight into her outstretched arms. She pulled me to her, her head against my stomach, and wrapped her arms around my waist. I placed my hands on her shoulders and stared down at her, my heart beating wildly in my chest. "Is Dad okay?" She nodded, but said nothing. "Billy? Is he hurt, did he—"

"No, honey. It's not your brother. He's fine. Dad's fine." She sighed and gently pushed me away, nodding toward the chair next to hers. I sat and waited expectantly. She took a deep breath before she began to speak. "Your aunt started noticing problems some months ago, but she let it go. She didn't go to a doctor until a few weeks ago. Have you noticed how much weight Kitty has lost?"

"Yeah. I thought she was on another of her crazy diets."

My mother chuckled softly. "She has been on some wild ones, hasn't she? Remember the only corn diet?" We both laughed and I thought about how, to this day, my aunt still would not touch corn after having eaten nothing but for five weeks.

"But, no, that's not the problem. She started to get some aches that nothing would kick, and she is constantly tired. When she finally went to the doctor, they diagnosed her with chronic kidney failure." I drew back in surprise and confusion. My mother could read the question in my eyes and continued. "Aunt Kitty's kidneys are working at about twenty-five percent of what they should be. This apparently has been getting progressively worse for years, but she had no symptoms before and didn't know it."

"Is this bad?" My voice sounded weak, even to my own ears.

My mother nodded. "Yes. Right now they have things basically under control, but it keeps getting worse every time she goes in. The drugs they have her on just don't seem to stop it or slow it down. They are going to start her on dialysis next week."

My heart sank. Although I had no first-hand knowledge of it, I had heard that term before and knew it wasn't good. "What does that mean for her, Mom? How did she get this?"

"Well..." She took another deep breath and sipped from her tea. "They want to see how this goes for a bit, then they may have to look into transplants. They say she was born with it. It was just never caught until now."

I sat back in my chair and stared out the window over the sink. Kidney failure. Aunt Kitty was only in her late twenties, far too young for this sort of thing. I turned back to my mother. "So is this why Aunt Kitty was here so early the day we started school?" She nodded. "What does Ron say about this?"

"Well, he's upset and worried because he can't always be here. Aunt Kitty may have to stay with us off and on, honey. The Air Force sends Ron all over the place, so she'll be alone a lot. I don't want her to be while she's going through this. We'll just make up Billy's old room for her. I'll need your help, Emmy."

"Of course. I would never leave Aunt Kitty alone."

My mother smiled at me and patted my hand. "Want some breakfast, honey?"

After a moment's thought, I nodded. "I guess." My mother started to get up, but I stopped her. "No. Breakfast is on me this morning."

I spent a great deal of time thinking about my aunt and her condition. Aunt Kitty had always seemed so young and strong, so utterly untouchable by anything bad. The news of her illness definitely put a dent in how I felt about life and mortality. With just a snap of the fingers, anything could happen. As I walked through the halls of my school, I looked at all the life around me, realizing there were no certainties, no promise that could not be broken. No one was untouchable. I think I grew up a lot that day, shedding some of my innocence and naïve outlook. I also realized I wasn't going to like this transition from childhood to adult.

As the year progressed, I began to concentrate fully on my studies, determined as always to do my very best. With this change in focus came a change in friends. I no longer hung out with Darla, preferring instead a new group of academic-oriented students whose goal in school was not popularity but achieving the highest grades. By the end of my freshman year, I had been on the honor roll both semesters, had received an award for perfect attendance, and had distinguished myself as a member of the Honor Society, the English club, Future Business Leaders of America, and every advanced class I was allowed to take. Life was good.

Beth had immediately immersed herself in the school's drama program, led by Ms. Andy White, a beautiful recent college grad who was determined to whip the nearly nonexistent department into shape. Ms. White's predecessor had been on the verge of retiring for almost ten years, and the program he left behind when he finally made good on his threat to leave was marred by neglect.

"Okay, Em. You gotta tell me if this is believable or not."

I sat on the dry, winter-browned grass in the park near our neighborhood. Beth was rehearsing for a play that would start in three weeks in which she was cast as the villain,

Nadine Kidd, who was shot at the end of the show. I watched her as she faced an imaginary character, delivering her lines flawlessly while I read the part of her co-performer. Beth put so much into her rather psychotic role, I actually felt a chill run down my spine in fear.

"You won't get away with it, Nadine," I said, glancing up at her.

She glared at the air in front of her. "No? Just watch me," she hissed, then tried to walk past the hero.

"Bam!" I yelled into the cold, quiet afternoon.

Beth grabbed at her chest, a look of utter pain and surprise in her blue eyes. She fell to her knees, the hand that did not grip the imaginary wound reaching out for the other character. "Why?" she floated on a whispered breath that still managed to project her voice as she fell flat on her face and remained still. I watched her in awe. How had she gotten so good? With a wide smile, I stood and clapped. Beth rolled over and smiled up at me. "You like?"

I nodded vigorously. "Excellent. Had me fooled."

Beth reached her hand up, and I grabbed it to help her stand. "Cool." She took the script from me and read it over to make sure she had recited everything correctly.

I laughed as we headed toward the swings. "Your character is such a lunatic."

She glanced over at me and smiled. "I know. Isn't it great? She is such a hoot to play, too. I love being crazy."

"Hey, what was that you once said about being typecast?" Beth turned her head in my direction and stuck out her tongue.

In addition to her starring role, Beth also co-wrote and was acting as assistant director. She had certainly found her niche, and Ms. White had found her helper for the next four years.

Opening night arrived before we knew it, and I could tell Beth was nervous as she paced back and forth in my bedroom while she waited for me to get ready. Her mother had disappeared with her newest boyfriend two days prior, leaving Beth without a ride to the school. My mother stepped in, as always, and she was waiting downstairs to accompany us.

"Okay," Beth whispered seemingly to herself. She stared off into space as she paced, one hand running through her hair, the other buried in her pants pocket. Occasionally, she would wave both hands dramatically through the air as she rambled like a crazy person.

I sat at my mirror and gave my hair some finishing touches, glancing at her reflection off and on as she passed.

Beth had always been that way when it came to her art. It's a wonder she never managed to wear a trail in the carpet with her ritual. That night was a big one for her; she had invested a lot of herself in the play and would live or die with its reception. Of course, I knew in my gut she would blow them all away and leave them begging for more. I just wish she shared my confidence in her abilities.

It was a cold November night and I was dressed in a long skirt and shirt with a sweater over it. I stood and watched Beth for a long moment before I called her name to get her attention. I smiled at her startled reaction. She had forgotten I was even there. "It's time," I said with a genuine smile.

She let out a long breath and nodded. "You know what I like most about the stage? I can go up there and lose myself in my character, in my character's problems, and forget about my own. I like knowing that, whatever is happening to my character, by the end of the play, everything will be okay. There's nothing like it."

An hour later, I sat with my mother in that dark theater and watched with unimaginable pride as my best friend pranced across that stage, looking bold, unbelievably intimidating as her ruthless character, and utterly beautiful. Over the past year, Beth had filled out, her body catching up to her long legs and lanky features. Now she carried herself with a sense of dignity and a nonchalance that made you stop and watch. Her features were chiseled, and her eyes still shone that incredible incandescent blue that could burn with just one look. Her hair was long, black, and shiny. She no longer wore baseball caps all the time. Occasionally, she threatened to cut her hair, although I would've been surprised had she ever followed through. I glanced around me to see other's reactions to the show and especially to Beth.

When she first took the stage, I could tell from my vantage point in the first row that she was terrified. Her eyes sought out mine for reassurance several times. But, as the show went on, she gained momentum, and soon she owned that stage. During the last scene, Beth's Nadine was fighting with the male lead. He drew his gun and, with a deafening bang that echoed throughout the auditorium, shot Beth, who sank to her knees, reaching for him as he took a step back. She fell forward, taking one last breath before all became quiet. As the red curtain closed, I felt the stinging of unshed tears. Beth was utterly amazing. Pride surged through me again as I stood with the rest of the audience and clapped for all I was worth. The curtain opened, and the more minor characters ran onto the stage to take a bow, followed by the male lead and last, but certainly not least to this audience, Beth. The applause crescendoed, interlaced with shouts and whistles. Beth smiled from ear to ear, her face flushed with excitement. Her eyes scanned the crowd, then settled on me, and I tried to convey everything I could in that look as our eyes locked for just a moment. Then she stepped back to give Ms. White her due. The teacher reached back and grabbed Beth's hand, pulling her into the limelight with her and raising their joined hands as they bowed together.

My mother could not have looked any more proud if Beth had been her own daughter. She leaned over to me. "Nora Sayers should have been here to see this. That was incredible!"

~ ~ ~ ~ ~

I opened my eyes as my awareness returned to the present. We were in the air headed for Colorado. I had no clue as to how far into the flight we were; I only knew I was already sick of it and really wanted to feel the ground beneath my feet. I glanced at Rebecca and saw that she had nodded off, her unread magazine still open on the tray in front of her. I took a deep breath, unbuckled my seatbelt, and headed to the tiny bathroom.

The door clicked behind me and I stared into the small mirror above the even smaller sink, marveling at how the strange, bluish light warped my features. Running a hand through my hair, I thought back to the unofficial cast party after the play. I hadn't wanted to go, the "drama people" not being my group, but Beth had invited me and it seemed important to her. Even though she was only a freshman, Beth had made quite a lasting mark for herself already with the seasoned drama group and some of them were looking to her for ideas.

The party had been held at the family farm of one of the cast members. There had been an open field with a huge bonfire lighting up the darkness and warming the chilled air. There had also been loads of beer and other types of alcohol. I felt out of place there and did not like it.

~ ~ ~ ~ ~

I sat off by myself on someone's open tailgate, watching the action, an unsipped cup of beer in my hand. Beth talked and laughed with the others; she even danced off and on with a few. It was obvious to me that she was in her element.

"Hi."

I turned to see a guy standing beside the truck, half his face in shadow and half reflecting dancing orange from the light of the fire. I smiled shyly, but said nothing.

"Mind if I sit?" he asked. I thought for a moment. I really didn't feel like company, but wasn't completely averse to the idea either. I nodded toward the tailgate. "Do you talk?" He grinned as he sat, the truck bouncing slightly with his added weight.

"Depends," I said, looking back to the party.

"On?" He sipped from his cup.

"Who I'm talking to."

At that, he smiled and nodded. "Fair enough." He was silent for a moment as he watched the partygoers. "Why aren't you out there?" I shrugged, now feeling a bit uncomfortable and wishing he would just go away. "You here with someone?"

"Beth." I turned and got a better look at him. He was really a good-looking guy, with short brown hair and clean-cut, mature angled features. I couldn't tell what color his eyes were.

"Beth?" he asked, his brows drawn.

"Yeah. Beth Sayers. She's my best friend. She asked me to come with her."

"Oh." He nodded understanding. "Hey, you want to take a walk or something? I don't know about you, but I really don't like parties."

I stared at him for a moment and, without a word, hopped off the tailgate, leaving my cup behind. "So why are you here?" I asked, as we made our way toward a thicket of trees off to the right.

"Kind of the same reason you are, I suppose." He flashed me what he likely felt was a charming smile and reached down for my hand, which I quickly pulled away from his. "Sorry," he said, tucking his hands into his back pockets. "Wow, look at that." He pointed toward the full moon directly ahead of us. It was huge and gold and looked as though we'd be able to touch it if we walked just a bit further. "Let's stop for a sec and look." He placed his hand on my arm. I stopped and did as he said, my heart pounding slightly as my earlier discomfort returned. I glanced back over my shoulder and realized I could no longer see the party, only the light from the bonfire reflecting above the trees. When I faced the moon once more, I found it blocked by this guy's chest. I looked up into his face with questioning eyes. He smiled his "charming" smile again and said, "You know, I don't even know your name."

"I think we should be getting back now," I said and made a move to do so, but he tightened his grip on my arm, keeping me where I was.

"Why? Come on, what's your name?"

"No. Look, let's go back to the party, and I'll tell you anything you want to know, okay?"

"Nah. I think we should stay here."

He bent down and tried to kiss me, one large hand on the back of my head, holding me to him. I pounded my fists on his chest, trying to get away, but he was a lot bigger than I was. He pushed me back against a tree, using his weight to hold me there. I tried to scream, but with his tongue in my mouth it came out only as a muted groan. I was stuck and realized just how much trouble I was in when I felt his growing hardness press against my lower stomach. His free hand was all over the place, groping what he could, trying to get under my shirt. And then suddenly there was nothing but the cold night air. I looked around in confusion just in time to see him being slammed into the tree across from me. Beth was in his face, his shirt entwined in her fist.

"I should have your balls for doing this," she hissed, one hand reaching down to grab his crotch. His eyes squeezed shut in pain, and his arms waved uselessly through the air.

"What are you doing?! We were just—"

"*We* weren't just doing anything. *You* were just trying to do something very stupid to my best friend." His eyes opened, and he glared first at Beth then over at me. I ran a shaking hand down my sweater to try to calm myself. "Look at me, you fucker, not her." Wide, frightened eyes shifted back to Beth. "You do anything this stupid again, and I will have your balls. You got it?" He nodded, his eyes never leaving hers. She let go of his shirt and punched him in the stomach. He doubled over with a groan, then halfway righted himself and limped away.

I watched him go, my breathing becoming even more labored as the fear of what almost happened turned into the shock of what could have. The next thing I knew, I was enveloped in a strong, warm embrace. As I clung to Beth, my tears finally came. She caressed my hair, whispering soothing words into the late, quiet night.

Once I finally got myself back under control, I pulled away from her, wiping my eyes with the back of my hand. She held me by my shoulders, staring down into my face. "You okay, Em?" She ran her finger under my eye to catch a last tear. I nodded numbly. "I saw you talking to him, then when I saw you were gone...your cup on the tailgate...I had a bad feeling." Her own fear washed over her features. "If anything had happened to you, I never would have forgiven myself." Her voice broke on the last word.

I reached up and cupped the side of her face. "Nothing happened, thanks to you. I'm fine, Beth." She nodded, but I could still see the guilt written all over her face. "It's okay."

"That guy is known to be an asshole. I should have looked for you sooner. I'm sorry."

"Hey, it's okay." I drew her to me, this time comforting her. "I'm okay," I whispered into her shoulder.

~ ~ ~ ~ ~

I stared at myself once again in the small mirror while the toilet whooshed behind me. I always wondered what Beth had done to that guy later. Whenever I saw him in the halls at school, he went out of his way to avoid me. I shrugged off the memory and left the bathroom, returning to our seats.

"Everything okay?" Rebecca asked as I sat down and buckled my seatbelt.

"Yeah. Fine." I smiled and she returned it, placing her hand over mine and squeezing gently before she entwined our fingers in her lap and shut her eyes again.

I glanced out the window and watched the sky turn white as we flew through a thick group of clouds. With a sigh, I closed my eyes again, too.

~ ~ ~ ~ ~

"No way! That one does *not* look like a clown." Beth squinted and tilted her head.

"Yes it does. Look." I pointed with my finger. "See, there's his nose...that great big round cloud. ... Then see how it kind of goes up into a point? That's his hat."

"It does not go up into a point," she insisted.

"Well, it did before the clouds started to move." Beth looked over at me like I was nuts. I grinned. "Well, it did."

She shook her head and turned to look back up at the sky. "You know, you really suck at this game, Em. You try to make the shapes too elaborate. Whatever happened to just plain old-fashioned bunny rabbits and bananas?"

I shrugged. "I don't know. I just see what I see." I raised my arms over my head, feeling the cool, thick grass under my hands as I stretched my body. I closed my eyes in pleasure and groaned. "It is so nice out here." I relaxed again, laying my hands on my stomach.

"Un huh," Beth agreed, placing one hand behind her head and reaching down with the other to scratch her leg where a blade of grass was making her itch. "Your birthday ended up being a pretty nice day. Not too hot, like it usually is." She turned on her side, her head resting on her hand, and looked down at me. "Tonight, we're all going down to the lake on the east side. Wanna come?"

I wrinkled my nose. "No way. You remember what happened last time I went to one of your friend's parties."

"Different people. It'll just be me, Collin, Mary, and Sheila."

"Nah." I looked back into the sky. "Why tonight, though, Beth? Aren't you going to stay for my party here? Aunt Kitty and Ron are coming, and maybe one or two of my friends from Honor Society."

"Nah. We've had this planned for a while. Besides..." She rolled over and sat up, wrapping long arms around her bent knees. "Your friends from Honor Society look at me like I'm a leper."

"Oh, okay." I was hurt, but I knew she was right. None of my friends understood why I remained so devoted to Beth, and I suspected that her friends wondered the same thing. That was just the way things were now. "You guys going to drink again?"

"Probably some, yeah." Beth had started to do that a lot and I was worried for her. Her mother had made such a mess out of her own life and, in some ways, out of Beth's, and I didn't want to see Beth make the same mistake. I had heard that alcoholism ran in families. "Well," she said, standing and reaching down to help me up, "you said I could have the first ride in your Jeep."

We walked around the back gate to the front yard, and I couldn't help but smile as I spotted my birthday present. Never in a million years did I think I'd get a car for my sixteenth birthday. I guess it was good to have a father who managed a car dealership. The Jeep was a 1979 model and was painted bright yellow with a black rubber roll bar. It wasn't exactly the color I would have chosen, but I had to admit it had character. I sure would be able to spot it easily in a parking lot. Beth jumped into the passenger side, and I climbed behind the wheel and brought it rumbling to life. I grinned at my best friend and backed out of the drive. We drove around town in companionable silence, neither feeling the need to talk. I had left the hard top at home, so the warm, summer air blew through our hair. It felt so good just to be with Beth, no pressure from any of our friends or our new lives. Just us. Like it used to be. We rarely saw each other at school, and I was busy with after-school activities that kept me from home until nightfall most evenings. Times like these were increasingly few, and I grew to look forward to and treasure them.

Whatever happened, wherever we ended up, Beth would always be my best friend.

~ ~ ~ ~ ~

Chapter Twelve

"We are approaching Denver International Airport. Please make sure your chairs and trays are securely locked into their upright positions and that your seatbelts are fastened around you. We are preparing for landing."

I gripped the arms of my chair as I felt the plane lose altitude, glancing outside at the lowered wing as we banked around to face the airport. The town of Denver spread out below us, and the sight triggered an automatic smile. It had been far too long since I'd been back. As I looked down on the city, I felt home. It didn't matter that we still had a three-hour drive to Pueblo.

The landing was relatively smooth, and we collected our luggage quickly. Although I loved Denver, it wasn't our destination and I was anxious to move on. We rented a silver Toyota Camry and made our way south on Interstate 25.

~ ~ ~ ~ ~

I pulled into the driveway of my house feeling tired from the long day. It was dark, well after 8:00 on a warm late September night. I grabbed my backpack from the rear of my Jeep, slung it over my shoulder, and headed toward the front door, only to be met by my mother, who hurried onto the front porch when she saw me coming.

"Hey," I said.

"Honey, have you seen Beth?"

"What? Why?"

"Did you see Beth today at school?"

"No, I—" I paused, realizing I hadn't seen Beth for a couple days.

"Nora has been calling all day. Beth hasn't been home since Monday."

"It's Thursday!" I winced as I stated the obvious, but the thought seemed incredulous to me.

"Honey, you've got to go look for her." Even before my mother finished her sentence, I had turned back toward the Jeep, tossing in my bag as I hopped into the driver seat. The tires squealed in protest as I peeled out of the drive.

I began my search by visiting the places I knew Beth

hung out. Starting at the lake, I headed down Northern, checking all the bars. Beth was underage, but she was rarely carded since she looked as if she were in her mid-twenties. I drove by the school and stopped by the park. It was as though she had vanished.

"Damn." I slammed my hand into the wheel. *Where could she be?* I really didn't know any of her friends. Lately, she had been spending more and more time with a crowd that was notorious for partying, regardless of the time of day or day of the week. *What was the name of that girl I saw her with so often? Carrie? Corey?* Cora. I could picture her short, dyed black hair, pale skin, and dark makeup. She always wore black, usually leather. I remembered overhearing some kids talking about Cora and her group, about how they all hung out at some old run-down warehouse. *Where was it?* I tapped my fingers on the steering wheel as I thought, and then I remembered. *The Looms. That's what they called it.* I put the Jeep in gear and made a U-turn in the middle of the street.

It was nearly 11:00 by the time I finally found the place. The neighborhood was industrial and didn't exactly look safe. I was extremely nervous as I slowed the Jeep, pulling in next to an old gray cinderblock building with large blacked-out windows from which could be heard deep, pounding music. The only light was spewing from a door on the side, and with a deep breath and a small prayer to whomever, I headed inside.

The place was large and not very well lit, a scattering of naked bulbs hanging down from the high ceiling. The air was heavy and acrid, smelling of old cigarettes and the sweet odor of pot. I looked around to see various groups of people huddled in corners, some talking and some making out. My eyes bulged when I realized there was a couple actually having sex under a far table. I quickly glanced away, continuing to scan the room, the bone-shattering music vibrating up from the floor and causing a pulsing ache in my jaw. Two women were grinding together, dancing to the music. There was a lone figure slumped against an old loading dock door. She was dressed completely in black, as were most of the people, her upper shoulders against the metal door, her legs straight out in front of her, and her arms lying limply at her side. My eyes began to move on, but there was something familiar about this person. I studied her again and then froze.

"Beth," I whispered. "My God."

I ran to her, disregarding the strange looks thrown my way as I shouldered past different people and groups. Just before I reached her, Cora stepped into view, careening

toward Beth. "Get away from her!" I yelled, as I reached my
friend, throwing myself to my knees next to her. Beth's eyes
were open, but they were glazed and unfocused. Cora stood
over us, looking down at me, but said nothing.

"What is wrong with her?" I asked, reaching out to try to
straighten Beth's lolling head. Her pupils were so dilated; I
could barely make out the blue irises.

"I don't know. I think she had some bad shit." Cora's
voice was casual.

I looked up at her in disbelief. "Some bad shit?" I shivered, trying to maintain some semblance of control. "Does she
need a doctor?"

"Nah. Just get 'er home and let 'er sleep. Give her a
bunch to drink. Water's usually good."

"Beth, honey...come on. I'm getting you out of here." I
could feel my throat tightening and wanted to get the hell out
of that place before I broke down. "Help me!" I yelled at the
girl as I tried to lift Beth's dead body weight. With Cora's
help, I eventually managed to get Beth buckled into the passenger seat of the Jeep. As I strapped myself behind the
wheel, I growled, "You stay away from her."

Cora simply shrugged and took a step back toward the
door. "She needs to learn to hold her shit better. She's a good
lay, though." And with that, she disappeared into the warehouse.

I stared after her, my mouth hanging open, then turned
back to Beth. She lay with her arms hanging over the sides of
the seat, her head back against the headrest, mouth open
and eyes closed. "Beth? Beth!" When she didn't answer, I
shook her.

Her head lolled again, but then she righted herself and
glanced over at me. "Huh?" she slurred.

"I'm getting you the hell out of here!" I nearly killed the
Jeep as I ground the gears in my haste. My neighborhood was
quiet as I pulled into the driveway. I sat in the Jeep for a full
minute trying to decide what to do. A glance at the Sayers'
house confirmed that no lights were on. *Gee, Mrs. Sayers*
must have been really worried about her missing daughter.
"Bitch," I muttered as I climbed out of the car.

At Beth's side, I contemplated the effort it would take to
retrieve her from the car. "You've got to help me, Beth," I told
her as I unbuckled her seatbelt. She slid limply from the
Jeep, nearly taking me with her before I was able to maneuver
her legs until her feet touched the ground. I pushed her up
against the side of the car to hold her while I regained my balance. "Okay. We can do this." I shifted and slung her arm

around my shoulder. "Ready?"

"Huh?" I wrapped my other arm around her waist as we started very slowly toward the porch. I felt gratitude for my mom, who had thought to leave the light on to guide us. "One step at a time, honey. ... That's it. ... Good girl." Finally, we made it to the door, which immediately flew open, scaring the crap out of me and nearly making Beth fall to the grass.

"Thank God you found her!" my mother said, her eyes narrowing in worry at Beth's condition. She wrinkled her nose. "My God, where has she been? A landfill?"

"Long story, Mom. Just help me get her to my room, would you?"

"Honey, shouldn't she go home, or to a hospital? My God, she looks like she's half dead."

"Mom, please, I can't take her home. You know Mrs. Sayers will leave her to rot on the floor. And she doesn't need a doctor right now; she needs me. Please, Mom, please just let me take care of her."

My mother stared into my eyes and saw how serious I was. She sighed and nodded, then helped me get Beth to my bedroom. I pushed my mother out and shut the door. Beth lay spread across my bed. I wasn't sure what to do first, but decided to tackle the problem in a logical manner. First, I'd need to get a few things.

I headed for the kitchen, where I filled a huge plastic cup with cold water and grabbed some fruit and bread, figuring that would be easy stuff for her to eat. Returning to my bedroom, I set my offerings on my dresser and turned back to my friend. "Mom's right, Beth. You do stink." I walked to her and sat on the edge of the bed. With my foot, I scooted my metal trash can up against the side of the bed frame. Beth's breathing was more normal now, and she seemed to be coming around. Her eyes were still glazed, but they were open and they looked a bit better than they had. "Hey."

Her eyes tracked to my face. "Hey."

Her voice was scratchy and I retrieved the glass of water, bringing it to her lips and holding her head up as she sipped. She choked a bit, so I sat her all the way up, leaning her body weight against me. "Okay?" I asked. She nodded and buried her face in my neck. I could feel her body shake when she began to sob. "Hey, hey," I said, pulling her into me. She wrapped her arms around me, and I could feel her tears against the skin of my neck. "Shh, baby. It's okay."

"I'm sorry, Em." Her voice came out as a whimper. "I never meant for you to see me this way."

"Shh. I know. I was so worried about you." I was whispering now, my own tears close to the surface. "When my mother told me no one could find you, you don't know what went through my head." I lay back, taking her with me. She curled her body up to me, holding me so tight it almost hurt.

She cried for almost ten minutes before she began to calm, her tears turning into hiccups. "I didn't mean to scare you, Em." She moved down and laid her head upon my stomach. Just like old times. I reached down, my fingers trying to run through the tangles in her dark hair. "I feel so weird," she said.

I began to stroke her back with my other hand. "That girl, Cora, said you had taken some bad shit. What exactly does that mean?"

"I don't know. I took so much stuff, I don't remember. I don't remember much of anything, except seeing you barge in there like that." She chuckled quietly. "This little pint-sized thing rushing in there so tough. You're lucky Cora was pretty far gone, or she might have tried to kick you out." She took a deep breath. "I don't feel so good."

No sooner were the words out of her mouth when Beth leaned up and hung her head over the side of the bed. I held back her hair as she threw up into my trash can. She continued for some time, making the most awful noises, the veins in her neck standing out as her body continued to pump more and more of the stuff out of her system.

"Oh, God," she groaned, her strength gone. She remained on her stomach in that position and, within seconds, started all over again.

"Get it all out, Beth," I encouraged, rubbing her back as her whole body wracked with a spasm. Finally she stopped, completely spent. After a brief break, I helped Beth stand on weak legs and we made our way to the bathroom. She smelled of dirty clothes, smoke, sex, and now vomit.

"I need a bath or I'm going to make myself sick again just from the stench."

I flicked on the light and guided her to the toilet, where she sat and watched with half-hooded eyes as I began to run her a bath. "Will you be okay to do this by yourself?"

She looked down, then back over at me, shaking her head. "I think I'm gonna need your help."

While the tub filled, I knelt beside her to remove her shoes and socks. Tossing them aside, I moved up to her jeans, popped the button, and then unzipped the fly. "Lift," I instructed. When she did, I slid her jeans and underwear out from under her, all in one shot. I caught sight of a patch of dark hair, and a bolt of heat ran through me to land squarely in the pit of my stomach. I swallowed hard and continued with my mission.

Her grimy T-shirt came next, after which I reached around her to unhook her bra. With my arms around her, I could feel her breasts pressing against my own. I flashed back to the warehouse and to Cora. I realized that I despised the girl, not only because of where she'd taken Beth, but also because she and Beth were sleeping together. I didn't like that, not one little bit. I cleared my head of these thoughts and forced my concentration back to the task at hand. Beth was weak and needed my help. That's all that mattered at that moment.

"I have to pee." Her voice was quiet and betrayed her embarrassment.

I nodded and helped her to her feet so I could lift the lid. "Will you be okay for a sec while I get something for you to put on after your bath?" She nodded, looking relieved that she'd be left alone while she went to the bathroom. I hurried into my bedroom and dug through my drawers to find something that would fit her. Beth was so much bigger and taller than I was. In the bottom of one drawer, I found a pair of shorts my grandmother had sent me that were at least four sizes too big for me. I tossed them on the bed, adding a large shirt that I often slept in. Next, I took the opportunity to remove the smelly trash can from my room, leaving it just outside the back door to the house with the intention of cleaning it in the morning. Then I headed back to the bathroom, with a brief stop in my bedroom to pick up the clothes.

Beth was settled back onto the closed toilet lid again. She smiled up at me and I smiled back, locking the bathroom door behind me. I helped Beth into the bath, and she sighed deeply as she sank into the hot water, the steam swirling around us. I knelt beside the tub and tilted her head back so I could wash her hair. When I was done, I washed her body. I tried to use clinical detachment as I smoothed the soap over Beth's skin, but even in this state, she was just so beautiful. Her legs had always been long, but the rest of her had filled out, her thighs strong and shapely. Her stomach was flat and her breasts full and firm, the hardened nipples dark, but not too large. She held on to the sides of the tub to keep her balance, her fingers long and slender, with short nails that appeared well taken care of despite her recent activities. Her neck was also long, and I traced the washcloth over her well-defined collarbone and her wide shoulders. When I looked up at her face, I found her eyes closed. Her nose was straight and well proportioned. Her full lips were slightly parted, her breathing shallow. She was breathtaking, and I had a strong desire to run my hands over her, feeling her muscles flex under my fingers and learning all the planes of her body. I pushed that thought from my mind when the blue eyes opened and stared at me.

Beth scooted up and wrapped her arms around her drawn knees. She looked deeply into my eyes, which I prayed did not show what I was feeling inside. "Thank you, Em," she whispered. "I'm so glad you found me. You're the only person on earth that I would want to take care of me like this."

I smiled and gently pushed back some hair from the side of her face. "I'm always here for you, Beth. Just like you are for me."

With some effort, we got Beth dressed and back to my bedroom. She collapsed onto the bed and reached for me. I stared at her for a moment, but she just grinned shyly up at me. "I know it seems odd, and this isn't something I'd ask just anybody, but would you just...well...just hold me for a little bit?" Her eyes ducked to the quilt covering the bed, her cheeks coloring slightly. "I just seem to be embarrassing myself over and over again tonight."

My face broke into a soft smile and I lowered myself onto the bed next to her, opening my arms. Beth fell into the embrace, pushing her legs under the covers, and bringing the blankets up around us. I held her to me, her head against my chest, and we talked. We talked about everything that night — from favorite shows on television to politics to where we wanted to be in twenty years.

In all the years I had known Beth to that point, I had never seen her so candid and truthful about herself. The vulnerability she had experienced gave way to an unprecedented honesty that I don't recall ever again sharing with another human being. I cherished that night for what it was: a special intimacy that no sex act could ever equal.

"You know, I've been thinking about your aunt a lot lately," Beth said, her voice hushed. "So sad for someone so young." She was quiet for a moment then said, "Em, do you have any regrets?"

I ran my fingers through her dark hair as I thought about how to answer. "Yes."

She was quiet, letting me explain if I wished. The admission had flown out of my mouth before I even had a full answer. I had a lot of regrets where Beth was concerned, *that* I knew. I wasn't about to tell her that though. I regretted how our friendship had begun to deteriorate. Deep down, I knew we both loved each other as much, if not more, than we ever had. I would have done anything for Beth, and I knew the same was true of her. I regretted my weakness, my inability to admit that I felt equally as attracted to my best friend as I knew she was to me. My thoughts had betrayed me just a few hours before when I was bathing her. It was as though they were not my own, or perhaps they were more my own than ever. I didn't know, and I wasn't ready to face it that night.

I glanced at the window and saw the first rays of the sun peeking over the house behind ours. Beth and I had been talking all night. I turned my attention back to her. "Do you?"

"Yes I do. Many." She readjusted her head on my chest, wrapping her arm around me a bit tighter. "Someone told me once that to live with regret is to not live at all."

I sighed. "How true." I felt my body begin to respond to her closeness, tiny nerve endings reaching out to worship every part of her body that touched mine. There was just something about the silence of late night/early morning that made the body that much more aware of its surroundings and of its true desires. I closed my eyes and swallowed.

"Think maybe we should get some sleep," Beth said, her voice soft.

I opened my eyes and sighed with relief. *Sleep. What a good idea.* I wondered if Beth felt as affected as I did by our closeness. With that thought, I closed my eyes and let the darkness enfold me. I awoke with heat against my back and knocking in my head. As reality washed over me, I realized that Beth was spooned behind me, her arm holding me tightly to her, and someone was knocking on my door.

"Emmy? Honey, are you awake?"

I raised my head and looked around. My room was a disaster, clothes were thrown everywhere and the sun was blazing in through the open-curtained window. I groaned. "Yeah." I carefully climbed out of bed, trying not to wake Beth, and walked over to the door to unlock it. My mother stood in the hall in her robe.

"Honey, are you going to go to school today?"

"What time is it?"

"Almost 8:30."

I groaned again. Classes had started almost forty-five minutes ago. "No. We went to sleep only about three hours ago, and," I turned and looked at Beth's sleeping form over my shoulder, "Beth needs me today."

"Okay, Emmy." My mother's face turned serious. "You tell Beth if she pulls a stunt like that again, she won't have to worry about Nora Sayers. She'll have to deal with me."

"Point taken, Mrs. Thomas," said a groggy voice from

behind me.

I chuckled, and my mother glanced over my shoulder. "Better be," she said, waggling her finger at Beth, who smiled apologetically and laid her raised head back down with a moan. "You girls get some sleep." She gave me a quick hug before leaving us.

I returned to the bed, my body feeling like it had been hit by a Mack truck the night before. Beth grabbed me to her again, and I settled into her embrace and fell asleep.

~ ~ ~ ~ ~

Chapter Thirteen

Rebecca and I stopped for lunch at an IHOP in Colorado Springs. We sat at our table, and I stared down at my nearly untouched cheeseburger, a fry in my hand that I dipped over and over in my ketchup/mayo mixture.

"You know, I think that fry is about as covered as it's going to get." I glanced up and met Rebecca's twinkling eyes. With a grin, I popped the fry into my mouth. "So...that time she came to see you, where was Beth living? Was she with anyone?" my lover asked, using her napkin to wipe some ranch dressing from her lip.

I shrugged. "I honestly don't know. She never told me." Rebecca gave me an understanding yet confused look. "I was thinking about that last night. I have no clue if she still lived in Oregon, or whether she was living with someone. I don't know what she was doing either, though, knowing Beth, she was on stage to the end." I smiled in remembrance. "It was the only place on earth she ever truly felt at home, on that stage."

"She was very talented. I'm glad I was able to see her that one time."

"Yeah. Me, too."

"Did Beth like school?" Rebecca asked, sipping from her iced tea.

I shook my head. "Beth hated it. I think the only reason she went as long as she did was because of drama. That was her life. Well...that and partying."

Rebecca and I looked around as I drove the Camry down a familiar tree-lined street. In the past ten years, the neighborhood hadn't changed much, though my mother had told me many of the houses had been sold and turned into rentals. *What a shame.* The renters clearly weren't taking care of the properties the way an owner would.

I saw the old Donner house to the left. Townsend Donner had died the year before, and his house was still being fought over by his eleven children. It always amazed me that he and his wife had raised so many kids in just that small, three-bedroom home. My parents' house was just up ahead and to the right. Rebecca had never been here before. My parents had always traveled to New York to see us.

"You know, honey, you really need to get out here more," she said, her voice hushed in the quiet car.

"I know." I took a deep breath and pulled the Camry to the curb. My brother's truck was in the driveway, and I could not wait to see him and his family. My door was barely open when I heard a whoop, and I looked up to see Billy running across the front lawn. He grabbed me in strong arms, and I clung tightly to him, so happy to see him.

"Where've you been!" he exclaimed, his embrace nearly crushing me. "Don't ever stay away so long again, Emmy. I mean it." He pulled away and set me on the ground.

I looked up at him with appraising eyes, surprised by his full beard, which was dark like his eyebrows in contrast to his blonde hair. "God, you are such a good-looking guy." I grinned, and he smiled back.

"I know." He winked and turned to Rebecca, giving her nearly as breathtaking a hug as he'd given me. My parents and Billy's wife, Nina, were waiting on the porch for their turn. A seven-year-old girl stood behind Nina watching us with curious green eyes, much the same color as mine. A smaller boy ran around the front lawn with an airplane, making flying noises. In Nina's arms was yet another child, a baby girl who was asleep, her tiny head resting against her mother's breast.

I turned to Billy. "When did you get so many kids?"

"Well, if you'd come home now and then, maybe you'd know." He walked over to flyer boy and put a proud hand on his narrow shoulder. "This is Kyle. Little Heather is playing shy behind Nina, and our newest bundle of joy is Rachel."

Rebecca turned to me with a huge smile. She adored kids, and I could tell the new baby-sitter had arrived. I climbed the porch steps and was swept into a powerful hug by my father, followed by a warm, safe embrace by my mother.

"I'm so glad you're here, honey," she whispered into my ear.

"I am, too, Mom. I wouldn't miss this for the world."

~ ~ ~ ~ ~

I directed my father and Ron around the corner, opening the bedroom door as far as it would go so they wouldn't bang the headboard against the wall. With matching grunts, they set down the heavy piece of furniture and headed back upstairs to get the other parts. My mother and Aunt Kitty were in the kitchen making a schedule for my aunt's doctor appointments.

"Coming through!"

I backed up against the wall to let the guys by with the mattress they were carrying. After they'd passed, I climbed the stairs and went outside. It was early spring and the end of my junior year in high school. I would be eighteen in the summer and couldn't wait to get through my last year before I was off to CU Boulder to study pre-law. Aunt Kitty had gotten worse over the past year. The dialysis went fine at first, but then the tubes extending from her arm to the machine started plugging up with blood clots, and one by one her veins collapsed. Now, it was down to one last graft and a place on a donor list. I knew my mother was beyond worried.

I walked into the kitchen and leaned back against the fridge, watching the two sisters talk. Aunt Kitty looked nothing like her former self. About nine months ago, she had her hair cut short to make it easier to deal with. She'd also lost a lot of weight and it made my heart hurt to see the shadow she'd become. I fled the house and sat on the front porch, my gaze drawn to Beth's house. She and I had not spoken in nearly two months. I focused on the Nivens' house across the street in an effort to divert my attention away from Beth and the stupid thing that had come between us this time.

It was early February, and southern Colorado had been hit with a massive, out-of-nowhere storm that had dumped eighteen inches of snow on us. The town had been shut down for two days, and things were finally opening back up as the sun came out and began to melt the snow. I had bundled up in my winter jacket and was just beginning to shovel the sidewalk when something very wet and very cold hit the side of my face. I gasped in surprise and glanced to my right. Beth stood at the line between our two yards with a mile-wide smirk on her face, and a raised brow.

"Why did you do that?" I asked. My voice was calm, belying my incredible need to pick up a nice handful and chuck it back at her.

"Because I can," she answered just as coolly.

We stared at each other, neither moving, each waiting to see what the other would do. Then, as if an imaginary gun had gone off, I tossed the shovel and she hit the deck, as we both started making snowballs as fast as we could.

"Ready?" she called.

"Yeah. Go!"

We stood and began to throw as hard and far as possible while still remaining accurate in our aim. Within minutes, we were both screaming, our hair hanging limply in our eyes as the snowballs exploded on contact.

"Truce!" I cried when I ran out of ammo, but Beth's kept coming. "No!" I yelled, raising my arms against the onslaught while she moved forward, pelting me as she did. I fell to the wet ground, covering my head with my arms as I took her attack, our giggles echoing through the air. When she ran out of snow, Beth collapsed next to me and began to tickle me. I screamed out again as I twisted in the most bizarre ways to try to avoid her torturous fingers.

"Say it! Say it, Em!" She laughed.

"No," I cried, almost out of breath from laughing so hard.

"Come on, uncle. Say uncle!"

"Uncle!" I finally exclaimed, about to pee my pants.

"Good girl." She got off me and helped me up. "Snowman?"

Beth and I worked diligently, trying to gather as much snow as we could to build a mammoth snow creation. The bottom ball was at least four feet around, and the entire thing was close to six feet tall. We giggled and acted like children.

"I'm gonna go get us some stuff for him." I ran to the house, pausing only briefly to take off my boots at the front door.

"Whoa!" my mother called from the kitchen. "Where's the fire?"

I was halfway up the stairs when I yelled the answer. "Snowman!"

"I've got to see this," she said.

In my room, I grabbed a long scarf, some extra buttons from an old pair of pants, and my old cowboy hat. Just before I ducked back out, I glanced down from the window and gasped. "Shit." Beth was making our snowman into a rather voluptuous snowwoman. "God," I muttered as I ran down the stairs, nearly knocking my mother over at the front door, her Polaroid camera in hand. "Hang on a sec, Mom. Um...let us get her...it...set up."

I ran outside, nearly falling on my butt into the street. I turned on Beth, who was still quite into her creation. "What are you doing!" I became dumbstruck as her large hands sculpted the snow into realistic-looking breasts complete with very erect nipples.

She turned and grinned at me. "I'm making old Frosty here a Frosty-ette."

"So I see." I glanced back at the house to see my mother opening the front door. Turning back to the snowwoman, I threw the scarf around her thick neck and strategically hung the ends over her breasts.

"What are you doing?" Beth asked as I pushed her back to finish.

I motioned toward my mother with my head. "She can't see that!" I hissed.

"Why? Your mom has seen boobs before, you know." She grinned.

"This looks great, girls." My mother laughed as she looked over our creation. I glanced down to make absolutely sure the nipples could not be seen. "Okay. Emmy, Beth, both of you get on either side. I have to take a picture of this!"

My blood still boiling, I plastered a smile on my face as my mother took her picture. She smiled at us one more time and shook her head as she headed back into the house. As soon as the front door closed, I turned on Beth, my fury burning in my cheeks. "How dare you!" She smiled at me, pissing me off that much more.

"What? Come on, Em. Have a sense of humor."

"I have a sense of humor, Beth, but not when you have some Mae West made of snow on my front lawn!" My voice echoed through the neighborhood, much like our laughter had earlier. I looked around to make sure no one had heard me.

"Hey, if God can put balls on man, I sure as hell can put tits on a snowwoman."

"That's not funny, Beth." I turned to the creation, pulled the scarf off, and began to pat down the icy mounds.

"My, Em!" I could hear the anger in her voice. "You are so fucking worried what other people might think. Try and just be you for once!"

She turned and stormed toward her house. I stared after her, my fury rushing through my veins with every beat of my heart. *Was she right?* I turned back to the snowwoman. *No. I was.* This was all in fun, sure, but what if somebody walked by and saw this thing? They would think I had done this! Why the hell couldn't she do this kind of crap in her own yard?

I lay back against my pillows, legs crossed at the ankles, arms folded over Ruffles. I stared out through the curtains as night began to fall, the sky tinted a slight orange from the light reflecting off the snow. I was still hurt and angry with Beth. In fact, the more I thought about it, the angrier I became. True, she had just been having fun with the snowman, but all the same, she knew how I would feel about that; she knew how uncomfortable it made me. It was a total lack of consideration for me. She had been doing that a lot lately. And, in spite of everything, I couldn't help but be worried about her.

After the incident in the Looms, I had seen her coming home drunk so many times. She rarely went to school unless it was for drama practice. Considering her grades, I was surprised Ms. White even allowed her to do drama. However, I felt it wasn't my place to say anything, so I didn't.

~ ~ ~ ~ ~

I turned in a slow circle as I took in my room, smiling slightly at all the old posters that still hung on the walls. How outdated the stars were. I walked to my dresser and ran my fingers over its smooth surface, ending at my unicorn collection. I picked up one of the porcelain figures and turned it over in my hands, its mane forever blowing in an unseen wind. With a deep sigh, I turned to the window, small figurine still in my hands. As I looked out at the street, a red Mazda drove past. Everything looked so much the same, yet so very different. I tried to see the street through younger eyes, to bring back another time when I was another person. It was not so hard to imagine.

In the corner of the room, Rebecca's and my bags lay on the floor. We were going to sleep in my old room while we were here. I sat down at the end of the bed and fingered the blue-and-white bedspread. The only person I'd ever slept with in this bed had been Beth.

I flopped back onto the soft mattress and stared at the ceiling. How would I get through this? I could feel a lump begin to form in my throat and the familiar stinging in my eyes. I squeezed them shut, but still a tear slid out from under my lids. I held my breath and tried to get myself back under control as another followed the path of the first.

~ ~ ~ ~ ~

Aunt Kitty had finally fallen asleep after hours of my mother trying to soothe her raging headache. The pains had gotten worse, just as the doctor had said they would. Across the dinner table, my mother looked so haggard and tired. She had been taking care of her baby sister for two weeks, and it was beginning to weigh on her. I knew she didn't mind helping my aunt, but the emotional toll on her was awful.

My father glanced at her and shook his head. He had never been good at saying how and what he really felt, but it was clear to me he was worried about both his wife and his sister-in-law. I felt so sad, and I was tired of feeling sad.

"Can I be excused?" I asked quietly. The house was always so quiet lately. My mother had said Aunt Kitty was staying with us just while Ron was away and until she got better, but we were all privately coming to terms with the fact that we were taking care of Aunt Kitty until she died.

"Go ahead, sweetie," my mother said absently, picking at her chicken.

I headed outside to sit on the front porch and stare into the star-filled sky. Aunt Kitty's dementia was getting worse. She sometimes had no idea where she was or who she was with. She seemed to be hearing voices that nobody else could hear. I loved my aunt very much, and it was hard for me to see her suffer this way. I sighed and looked down at my tennis shoes. The sound of someone yelling brought me out of my funk and my head snapped to the right to Beth's house. Something crashed, followed by more yelling.

"You fuckin' stupid woman!" Beth's voice could be heard, followed by another crash. "Where is it? You took it from me didn't you? Didn't you?"

"Get off me, you God damn kid! I don't know where the fuck your pot is! Let go; let go!" The front door flew open, and Mrs. Sayers stumbled down the driveway to her car. She slammed the door shut, and a moment later, the old Pinto sputtered to life and carried her away.

I watched the scene with bulging eyes. Finally snapping out of it, I stood and walked over to the well-lit house. The door was open, and I could see through the screen that the house was in shambles. Somewhere deep within, the crashing sounds continued. With quiet deliberation, I opened the door and stepped into the hot, muggy place. It looked as though the house had been ransacked. Lamps were on the floor, and cushions from the couch and chairs were strewn about, as were books and bits of paper. "Beth?" I called, carefully making my way through the mess, not wanting to step on anything. "Beth?"

"Get the fuck out!"

I headed toward Beth's voice, which was coming from her room. When I reached the doorway, my jaw dropped in shock. Beth was in a rage, tearing posters off the walls and punching at the space behind them, her fist penetrating the drywall.

"Fucking bitch!" she yelled as she tripped her way over to the dresser, grabbing an eight-by-ten framed picture and throwing it across the small room, where it crashed into a hundred pieces. I recognized the ruined picture: it was of herself and her father taken the summer she had gone to camp.

Frightened by her temper, I swallowed, but I managed to take a step inside the room. "Beth?"

"I said get the fuck out!" she screamed at me.

My heart stopped. Beth's face was beet red with her hysteria, her eyes bright from all the tears; one eye was quickly darkening into a deep shiner. There was blood smeared on her face, trailing from her nose. Her hair was wild. She looked like some crazy Amazon woman, and her fury was quickly being shifted toward me.

"Get out!"

She walked over and pushed me. I nearly lost my footing but grabbed hold of the doorframe to keep my balance. "No. What's going on, Beth?" I stepped back into the room. She stared at me for a moment, then turned back into the mess, throwing and tearing at things. My God, I had never seen her like this! Then my heart stopped altogether as she grabbed one of her acting trophies from her dresser. Without a word, she chucked it at the far wall, the silver cup bouncing as it broke off the base. She grabbed another and did the same. "Beth!" I cried. Those trophies meant everything to her. "Please don't." My voice was thick, my vision blurry as I began to cry.

"What the fuck does it matter?" she roared, then she swept her hands across the dresser surface, sending all her prized awards, trophies, and ribbons clattering to the floor.

"Oh, Beth," I whispered through tears that made it difficult to speak. Beth seemed to sober for just a moment, realizing what she had done, and her legs buckled. She leaned against the wall, her head back and her eyes shut tight as she continued to cry. Not sure what to do, only knowing I needed to get to her, I swiped a hand at my eyes and hurried over. We both sank to the floor. She kept crying, not acknowledging that I was even there. "Beth?" No answer. "Beth? Talk to me. What happened?"

"What do you care?" she asked bitterly, her eyes still closed. I reached for her arm, but she pulled it away. "Don't touch me."

I was stunned. "I do care, Beth. Please talk to me." Finally she opened her eyes and looked at me. What I saw scared me. There was nothing there, only empty space.

"Careful, Em. People might think you have a weird friend or something. Can't have that." I flinched, feeling like I'd been slapped. All I could do was stare. She smirked. "Wow. Emily Thomas speechless. Should write this one down."

"Why are you saying these things?" I asked, my throat tight.

"It doesn't matter anymore, Em. It just doesn't matter." She was quiet for a moment, the anger seeming to drain from her like water out of a hose. She took a deep breath and leaned her head back against the wall again, staring up at the ceiling. "They're dropping the Drama Department." Her voice was dull and lifeless.

I glanced over at her, shocked. "What?"

"You heard me." She looked over at me. "That's it. Andy was laid off this week."

"Why?" Drama was everything to Beth. It was her life.

"Don't need it. Football is so important, you know. Gotta have that football." She chuckled ruefully. "Bastards."

"Are you okay, Beth?" I reached a tentative hand out to touch her arm. She did not move it away.

"Do I look okay, Em?"

She met my gaze, and my heart broke all over again. She was struggling. I could see it in her eyes. She was dying inside.

"That's all I ever wanted to do, the only thing that kept me in that fucking place."

Her eyes began to well up again. I wanted so badly to pull her to me, but didn't dare. There was still that dangerous look in her eyes. It was a look I had never seen there before and one I definitely never wanted aimed at me. She spoke again, pulling me from my reverie.

"What am I going to do now? I don't give a shit about school and homework and all that." She looked at me again. "I'm not smart like you, Em. Brains are your thing; this is mine. This is my craft, the one thing I have that only I can touch, only I can feel." Her eyes began to fill in earnest then. "The only time people look at me as if I'm something. Somebody." Her whole demeanor crumbled before my eyes, and she was in my arms in a heartbeat. I held her and she clung to me, her sobs wracking her body. "That's all I have, Em. How can they take it away from me?"

"I don't know, honey. I just don't know." I rocked her gently back and forth. I knew Beth needed the theater like most people needed food. She would be lost without it. I closed my eyes and listened to the labored sounds of her breathing against the backdrop of her tears. I remained quiet, knowing there was not one thing I could say that would ease her pain. Finally, I felt her pull away from me. She ran her fingers over her eyes and then wiped her nose.

"Please go, Em," she whispered, turning away from me.

"What? Beth—"

"Please."

I stared long and deep into those two pools of ocean. Finally, I nodded. I stood and headed to the door, but turned back to her, my hand on the frame. She hadn't moved from the floor. "Beth?" She didn't answer, but I knew she was listening. "You're wrong. You don't need that stage to be somebody. You've always been somebody to me."

I retraced my steps through the living room, staring at the mess. I righted an overturned chair and replaced its cushions. As I did so, a clear plastic sandwich bag slipped out from underneath. I picked it up and examined it. There were brownish flakes along with two tightly rolled joints. I had no doubt this is what Beth had been looking for when she started fighting with her mother. I held the bag for a moment, torn between what I felt I should do and what I knew Beth would want me to do. I put it in the pocket of my jeans, determined to get rid of it. I hated the idea that Beth was doing drugs of any kind. As I reached the front door, I paused and then turned back toward Beth's room, taking the bag out of my pocket and stopping in the dark hall just outside her now closed door. I raised my fist, ready to knock, when I heard the melancholy sounds of "La Traviata." I stared at the closed door for a moment, trying to decide what to do. With a small sigh, I lowered my hand to a hamper next to the wall by her door. I laid the plastic bag on top of it and headed out of the Sayers' house.

~ ~ ~ ~ ~

Chapter Fourteen

I stared up at the dark ceiling, my hands behind my head. Beside me, Rebecca was breathing softly. It had been a long day, filled with rediscovery, but all the same, I could not sleep. The clock on the dresser across the room showed it was almost midnight. A quiet knock sounded on the bedroom door.

"Emmy?" my mother whispered.

"Yeah?" I whispered back. The door slowly opened, the hall light spilling dimly into the room. Her head peeked around the frame.

"Midnight tea?" she asked, and I could barely make out a slight grin on her face. I quietly climbed out of bed, careful not to wake my lover. We descended the stairs to the kitchen, and I grabbed the tea bags as my mother filled the kettle.

"I'd forgotten about this," I said, smiling over my shoulder at her. She nodded, but she was still facing the stove.

"It's been a while." She turned to me, a package in each hand. "Oreos or chocolate chunk?" I pointed to the blue package of Oreos and met her at the table with two paper towels. We sat across from each other and dug in.

I closed my eyes as my tongue swept up the creamy filling. It had been so long. "Mmm." I bit into the dark cookie.

She smiled as she bit into her own. "When you were a kid, I told you not to grow up too fast, Emmy. This is what happens. You forget about Oreos."

"Yeah." I twisted the top off another cookie. "Seems I've forgotten all kinds of things." The teapot began to whistle, and I grabbed a couple mugs as my mom took the kettle off the burner.

"Do you know what today is?" she asked as she poured hot water into both cups.

"Saturday?" She raised a brow at me, and I grinned sheepishly.

"Very good, honey. I knew I had a smart daughter. Besides, smart-ass, technically it's Sunday." She poured sugar into her cup, then added the tea bag. I had always wondered why she did it in that order. Her reasoning that the sugar seemed to mix better made no sense to me; I say it makes the sugar sink to the bottom faster. "No, today...well, yesterday now...was the anniversary of Aunt Kitty's death."

I glanced at her with wide eyes and did a mental tally to come up with eighteen years. *My God, almost twenty years ago. Where does the time go?* "You keep track?" I asked, sipping to make sure it was strong enough; the minty steam wafted up to tickle my nose and cause instant perspiration on my forehead.

She nodded. "I put flowers on her grave every year. I went yesterday afternoon. I sat there for a while, telling her all about Beth. She always really liked her." She sipped her tea, scrunching her features at the hot liquid.

My mother was still a very pretty lady; her blonde hair was shorter than when we were kids, but it was very cute and looked easy to care for. She had just the slightest bit of gray showing. Her green eyes were bright, but the lines around them were more defined, and the smile lines never completely disappeared when she stopped smiling. If I hadn't known better, I would never have believed her to be in her late fifties. I turned my eyes back to the cookie I was about to eat. "Have you seen Ron lately?"

"Oh, I see him and his wife around town now and then. After he retired from the Air Force, he settled down back here. He's always very nice. Once in a while, when I go to put flowers on Kitty's grave, I see some there that are relatively new. I always wonder if they're from him."

"Could be." I drained my cup and stood to get a refill. I offered the kettle to my mother, but she declined. "He really loved her. You know, I haven't had tea in quite some time."

My mother stared at me, faking a pained expression. "Say it isn't so! You, my little girl, have switched to coffee?" I nodded, and she placed her hand on her chest. "No. I never thought you would become a traitor. Didn't I teach you better than that?"

I chuckled. "Yes, but I'm afraid coffee keeps me more awake than tea does."

We were both quiet as we got lost in our own thoughts. Then my mother broke the silence. "It's been wonderful. I've been baby-sitting for your brother and Nina now that she's gone back to work."

I smiled at her, and then realized she had no idea about my own attempts to give her grandchildren. It took a time like this to realize just how absorbed I had become in my own life, forgetting that perhaps my family might want to know what Rebecca and I were up to.

"Rebecca and I are trying," I said quietly, not sure what her reaction would be. I knew that over time my mother had grown to love Rebecca and to regard her as her own, but this was an entirely different matter. Not everyone thought gays and lesbians should have children. Once again, I had underestimated my mother.

"What? Children?" she asked, her face lighting up like a Christmas tree. I nodded, still trying not to get my hopes up just yet. Her eyes immediately filled, and the warmest smile spread across her face. "Oh, honey," she whispered, standing and pulling me to my feet. I found myself engulfed in a massive hug. "Oh, baby, why didn't you tell me?" She gently pushed me away to look into my face.

I smiled and wiped a tear away with my thumb. "Well, for one thing, I didn't know how you would react to it, what you would think... Oomph!" I laughed as I was squeezed again. "Okay, so I take it you're excited."

"Excited? Honey, I want as many grandchildren as I can possibly get!" She pulled away from me again, finally letting me go. We both sat back down, but she grabbed my hand, holding it within her own. She leaned over the table to give me her full attention. "How long have you been trying?"

"Just under a year. It's been slow going."

She let out a long sigh. "How wonderful to try for new life on top of all this death." She gave me a smile that melted my heart and dashed any remaining doubts or fears. "You two will make such wonderful mothers."

"I hope so," I muttered. I had wanted children since I was a little girl, but with the hours I worked and the life I created for myself, I often worried that I'd become too selfish for a child. I had never shared those doubts with anyone, not even with Rebecca, but they were valid and remained constant over the past year.

"Oh!" My eyes snapped up to look at my mother, who had hopped up from her seat. "I came across the most beautiful picture of you the other day while I was cleaning." She disappeared into the living room, only to return a moment later. She placed the photograph on the table next to my mug. I picked it up. The caption read, "Emmy in deep thought — 1980." I was bundled in a green winter jacket, standing outside during a cold day. The picture was taken on a mountaintop, the snow-covered Rockies behind me. My hair was blowing back from my face; my eyes were a dark green and squinted ever so slightly against the cold breeze. My eyebrows were drawn, and my posture was pensive.

I remembered well the day my brother took the picture. I had turned quickly toward him, flashed a wide, fake smile, and then turned back to look at the mountains. He snapped the camera as I turned away. It was our final trip together before he left home and I'd had nothing to smile about that day.

~ ~ ~ ~ ~

I glanced away, not wanting to see Mr. Buckley's sympathetic smile as I shoved my notebook into my backpack. I thought if I looked at the teacher, I would burst into tears, and I didn't want to do that in the middle of AP English. I made my way through the maze of desks and out into the hall. When she called, Mom had given me the choice of coming home or staying in school. Whatever would make it easier for me, she had told them.

It was the middle of fourth period and the halls were empty. I slung my backpack over one shoulder and walked down the long corridor, staring at the highly polished tile floor made blindingly bright by the reflection of the open doors at the end of the hall. It was a surprisingly nice clear day, considering we were in October.

I glanced inside the office as I passed and saw the secretaries typing away or talking on phones. Two students sat in the waiting area, and I figured they were there to see Mr. Edwards about Saturday school. One of them stared at me as I walked by, his look of curiosity quickly turning to boredom when he saw it was me.

The situation felt surreal. The corridors longer than ever before, and I walked them with the note from the office bunched up in my hand. The moment the office aide had entered my classroom, my stomach lurched. I had a bad feeling as the girl walked over to Mr. Buckley, handed him the message, then left. My eyes didn't leave the teacher while he read the note. His features fell and he looked up. I knew, even before his gaze settled, that his eyes would land on me. He beckoned me to his desk, and I stood on shaky legs and somehow managed to walk to him. He handed me the note with a gentle pat to the arm.

My locker was just up ahead and I reached for the lock. It felt like I was moving in slow motion as I dialed my combination, pulled the lock down with a metallic clang, and grabbed the books I'd need for homework. I felt detached, numb inside, like someone had reached in and taken all the important parts out of me. I knew it was just a matter of time before it hit me, but for now I concentrated on what I had to do to get home in one piece.

I re-zipped my backpack with the added books and, to my surprise, the whole bag fell to that highly polished floor. I stared down at it dumbly, not sure how it had gotten there. Then, before I could stop myself, I leaned back against the cold, metal lockers and slid down until I landed on my butt beside it. I sat there, my legs bent at the knee, hands at my sides on the cool floor and eyes fixated on my shoes. I didn't know what to do. *Was it real? Had she finally gone? Nothing the doctors could do? Donor didn't arrive in time?* My chin fell to rest against my chest, and my thoughts delved into the darkest part of my mind. I didn't want to think about this, but I couldn't stop thinking. I don't know how long I sat there before somewhere in the real world I heard the sound of soft-soled shoes approaching. They stopped just in front of me.

"Gee. Looks serious."

I could imagine the now ever-present smirk on Beth's face, so I didn't even bother to look up.

"What, did the captain of the football team dump you or something?"

I did not need this. "Go away. Leave me alone."

"No. Guess not. Maybe the captain of the chess club?"

"I said leave me the fuck alone." I heard the slight pop of bad knee joints as she knelt down to her haunches. I glanced up to see surprised blue eyes looking at me.

"Whoa. What's up?" Beth asked, her voice softening.

I didn't want to talk to her. Ever since the incident at her house, she had been a walking zombie, just a shell of who she was. There was no life left behind her eyes, only a bitter attitude that she doled out to anyone unlucky enough to provoke it. I felt like she was lost to me, and I didn't need to feel the weight of that loss right now along with everything else. "Please, just leave me alone," I told her, my voice losing its commanding force. Though I felt angry and hurt with Beth, I couldn't deny that she still represented a source of strength to me. I did not want to fall into that now.

To my dismay, she moved beside me and settled back against the lockers. I could feel her intense gaze, and I looked over and met her eyes for a moment. She stared deeply into what felt like my soul. She must have seen something there, because understanding washed over her features, and she opened her arms to me. With only slight reluctance, I fell against her, my fingers burying themselves in the front of her flannel shirt. Her arms around me were strong and capable.

"Ahh, Em. I'm so sorry, honey. So sorry," she murmured into my hair.

My resolve crumbled and my soul shattered into a million pieces. She held me, letting me cry. We had all known it was coming, but you can never be prepared for it, for someone you love to die and leave you alone on earth without their special brand of importance to you. I heard more footsteps and then voices that were like distant echoes down a long tunnel.

"What's wrong with her?" someone asked.

"Go away," Beth growled low in her throat.

"How rude!"

"You deaf?"

The footsteps moved away quickly, but I didn't care. Beth held on tighter, one hand in my hair and the other holding the back of my neck. My chest ached as the emotion poured out of me, leaving a wet trail on Beth's shirt. My throat felt raw, my face tight and my eyes burning. Finally, I was able to get myself under a modicum of control, and I pulled away from her. Beth ran cool fingers over my heated cheeks, brushing hair back from my face. She looked at me with such tenderness.

"You okay?" she whispered. My throat hurt too much to talk, so I nodded. She smiled. "Give me your keys. Let's get out of here."

"What about your class?" I managed to croak out.

"You think I'm out in these halls for my health? Let's blow this joint."

Beth helped me to stand and grabbed my backpack, slinging it over her shoulder. After signing out in the office, I left the building, numbly handing Beth the keys to my Jeep.

~ ~ ~ ~ ~

My mother had gone up to bed about an hour ago, but I sat there in the kitchen, the light above the sink my only illumination as I stared out the dark window into the backyard. Our trampoline had long since been sold, and the big yard looked empty without it. I sipped from my mug. Thank God Dad drank coffee or I would have been out of luck. The strong, dark taste pushed all need for sleep to the back of my mind. I felt alert, and I needed to walk.

I bundled up against the cold October night air and slipped out of the house. The street was quiet, and I heard nothing but the occasional sound of a dog barking some distance away. I stuffed my gloved hands deep into the pocket of my London Fog coat and stared into the sky. It had a pinkish hue, and I could smell snow in the air. I loved that smell, and I loved the snow. Living in New York, I miss the smell of fresh air. Crisp, clean, clear out the lungs. I inhaled deeply through my nose, letting the breath out through my mouth, watching as the crystallized air disappeared into the night.

As I passed the Sayers' house, I took in the chipped paint, overgrown grass, and neglected bushes. A truck was in the driveway, and I wondered if it belonged to Mrs. Sayers. Did she even live there still? Almost in answer to my unspoken question, I saw a puff of smoke rise above a massive bush that blocked my view of the front door. I stopped, unsure what to do, then I retraced my steps and walked up the driveway just enough to see who sat smoking. To my surprise, it was Nora Sayers. She followed my progress with her eyes, never missing a beat as smoke poured out her nose and mouth.

"Mrs. Sayers," I said quietly, standing just at the start of the path that would lead to the front stoop.

"How ya doing, Emily?" she asked, her voice deep and rough from too many years of hard drinking and smoking.

"Quite well, thank you." I took a small step forward.

She smiled, the lines around her mouth deepening more. "I ain't gonna bite, you know."

I completed my approach and stood in front of the porch. Mrs. Sayers had always made me incredibly nervous. Even now, as a woman in my mid-thirties, I didn't feel comfortable with her.

"So I hear you're some kind of lawyer?" She snuffed the half-smoked butt into an ashtray next to her.

I nodded. "Yes. I live in New York now."

"Good for you, hon. I always knew you'd be something special. Even when you was a kid."

The compliment meant nothing to me coming from her. Why couldn't she have had as much confidence in her own daughter? I thanked her anyway.

"So, what you doing up so late?"

I dug my hands deeper into my pockets and glanced at the sky. "Couldn't sleep."

She nodded and stood. "I hear you. Haven't been able to sleep a wink in about a week." She put a hand on my shoulder, and I got a good look at her. She was younger than my mother, but looked at least ten years older. Gone was the beautiful woman I remembered from my youth. "Freezing my ass off. Gonna go try and get some sleep. Good to see you again, Emily." With that, she moved back into the house.

I watched her and then proceeded toward the sidewalk. She hadn't mentioned Beth once. *Did she even give a damn?*

At the end of the Sayers' driveway, I turned right, not really thinking of a destination, just needing to walk. I studied the quiet houses around me, wondering who lived in them and what they did. My mother had told me that much of the old neighborhood was gone. New families moved in every year.

I wasn't surprised to find myself at the start of the trail to the Bowl. With a small smile, I headed into the semi-dark. I could have been walking back in time. It looked exactly the same: trees lined either side of the path, slightly overhanging it, blocking out the moonlight. As I got closer, I could see the sparse light reflecting off the rippling water of the small pond. It had seemed so much bigger to me as a kid. I walked in a circle, taking in everything around me, my eyes stopping when I saw a small tent in the trees with pictures of the Mighty Morphin Power Rangers imprinted on the canvass. The circular light from a flashlight lens could be seen through the thin walls.

~ ~ ~ ~ ~

"What was that, Beth?" I asked, my eyes the size of saucers. She looked around, her eyes just as big. We could see nothing through the blue walls of our tent, but that didn't stop us from imagining we could.

She slowly shook her head. "Don't know."

Being the brave soul she was, Beth grabbed our flashlight and unzipped the tent flap, crawling out of the small opening. I sat holding my breath as I waited for her to come back. It was our first night camping at the Bowl, and I was scared to death. I had been so glad to have Beth there. I knew she could protect me.

I jumped when someone tapped on the tent, my breath held in my throat. "Beth?" I whispered. She didn't answer. "Beth?" I asked again, my voice becoming desperate.

Another thump, followed by another gasp from me. Oh no! I just knew Beth had been captured, and now they were coming for me. I scrambled onto all fours to search for our other flashlight, when the flap suddenly opened and Beth's smiling face looked in at me. I glared back at her, rolling my eyes at her mischievous look.

~ ~ ~ ~ ~

I opened my eyes to find myself back in the present. I decided to leave before I scared the occupants of the tent. While heading for the trail, my long coat brushed some bushes. I couldn't help but grin at the whispered, "What was that?"

Our time at the Bowl was over; it belonged to the new generation. Now, I felt like an intruder, like a giant who had no place among the little people. It was a daunting feeling.

I headed back toward my parents' house. I had learned to ride a bike for the first time on this street and had taken part in an endless number of adventures and games of football. I had run over the mailbox twice. It all felt so strange to me as an adult. Did everyone feel that way about going home? I climbed the stairs to my room and stood in the darkness, removing my clothes.

"Babe?"

Rebecca lay on the bed with her head raised, but I couldn't see her face. "Yeah?" I tossed my shirt into the pile on the floor.

"You okay?"

"Fine." I walked over and crawled under the blankets. Rebecca grabbed me and pulled me to her. She was warm from being beneath the covers, and I snuggled up to her. With a soft sigh, I closed my eyes.

~ ~ ~ ~ ~

The drive to the church seemed to take forever. I sat in the backseat of my parents' car, my sweaty hands clasped together in my lap. At a soft touch on my knee, I turned to meet tender blue eyes. I tried to return Beth's smile but faltered. She gave me an understanding nod. I returned my attention to the street and the cars passing us, wishing I were in any of them, heading anywhere but where I was going.

The church was cold. I wondered why as I ran my hands down my legs to smooth the skirt of my black dress. My parents emerged from the side room, my mother wiping at her eyes with a Kleenex as my father led her by the elbow toward the sanctuary. I glanced back to that small room, unsure if I would be able to enter it. I felt the warmth of Beth along my right side; she was never more than a few inches from me. I could see just the barest hint of the shiny, brown casket from the doorway. I took a deep breath and stepped forward, then stopped. My heart was in my mouth, and I couldn't breathe.

"It's okay, Em," Beth whispered in my ear.

I leaned back into her a bit, then turned away from the door. "I can't."

"It's okay. You don't have to." She rubbed my back with her hand. "Kitty won't know the difference anyway." I turned to look into Beth's eyes. She wore a well-fitted black pantsuit and looked gorgeous in it. Her long hair was down, the colors streaming in from the stained-glass window turning its darkness into brilliant red and blue. "Let's just go sit down, okay?" I nodded and let her lead me to the sanctuary by my hand.

I sat in the wingback next to the fireplace and looked around the room. Beth was beside me on the hearth, her hand on my knee in support. People talked in that hushed tone that always seemed to befit a wake. They balanced plates of food as they looked for a place to sit. There was a nearly full cup of punch by my feet. Beth had been trying all afternoon to get me to eat something, but I couldn't do it. She never left my side, and I wondered if she knew just what her presence meant to me.

"There're a lot of people here," Beth commented quietly.

I nodded, but didn't answer. It had been a huge funeral, as is often the case when one dies so young. It made me proud to know my aunt had touched so many people in her short life. Ron walked out of the kitchen, his black tie loosened and the top button of his shirt open. He had held it together admirably in the church, but once we got to the cemetery, he just lost it. He stood there gripping his brother tightly, as if his life depended on it. There wasn't a dry eye as we all watched his anguish. My father, who had been sitting behind him, kept one hand on my mother's shoulder and the other on Ron's through the whole ceremony.

I glanced around our living room again, acutely aware that this was the last place Aunt Kitty had ever seen. She had lived with us for just under six months. My final conversation with her was a week before, just two days before she had died, and I replayed it in my head.

"Honey, your aunt wants some water. Will you take this down to her?" my mother had asked as I walked into the kitchen, a long day at school behind me.

"Sure." I took the small pitcher and glass and headed downstairs. I tried to go see my aunt at least once a day, but with the hectic schedule I had, she was usually already asleep by the time I got home. Both hands full, I quietly pushed open the door of my brother's old room with my shoulder. My aunt's head turned slowly, and she smiled when she saw me. I returned her smile. "Hey you."

"Hi," she whispered. It had been rare to hear her talk above a whisper for a month or so. I set the glass on the side table, poured water into it, and helped her to drink. She closed her eyes as the water hit her parched throat and she smiled her thanks. It was truly heartbreaking to see her. She was almost skeletal, with shrunken cheeks that made already big eyes bulge. Her hair, which used to be so rich and thick, was dull and looked like straw. "Have a good day?" she asked, her eyes full of interest.

"Wasn't bad. I had to fill out some more forms for my scholarship today. That's such a pain." I sat on the side of her bed, careful not to jostle her too much.

"I'm so proud of you, Emmy." She reached out her hand, and I grabbed it and held it in my lap, gently caressing the frail skin. "You make me happy seeing you so involved with your life." I smiled, but said nothing. "How's Beth?" she asked after a moment.

"I don't know. She won't talk to me." I stared off out the window. So much pain was attached to that name.

She looked at me with pleading eyes. "Don't let her go, honey."

"I don't have a choice, Aunt Kitty."

"Sure you do."

"How are you doing?" My brother's voice snapped me out of my reverie.

"Fine," I said with a nervous smile.

He patted my shoulder and bent down so he was mere inches away. "Listen, Emmy, you need anything, you tell me, okay?" I smiled at him and nodded. He gave me a light peck on the cheek and walked away.

The crowd seemed to be thinning a bit. On the wall above the couch, I saw the family portrait we had taken the previous fall. My gaze fell on my aunt and I felt my throat clench shut, the tears just below the surface.

"Are you okay, Em?" Beth whispered, squeezing my knee. I bowed my head, taking deep breaths so I wouldn't lose it again. I was so tired of crying. "Em?" I couldn't answer. "Come on."

I felt myself being pulled to my feet and blindly followed as Beth drew me by my hand. We walked through the crowd of people toward the stairs. My father was descending as we started to climb. He stopped, and I nearly ran into Beth's back when she did the same. My father recovered his surprise and glanced down at our joined hands, then his eyes traveled up to meet mine. I couldn't read his expression.

"Is everything okay?" he asked.

"Em's getting upset again. I'm taking her upstairs so she can calm down." Beth's head was raised defiantly, her protective mode emerging in response to my father's speculative gaze. He nodded and walked on. Once in my room, Beth let go of my hand and went into the bathroom. She returned a moment later with a warm washcloth. I was still standing in the middle of the floor, my shoulders slumped and my eyes feeling so heavy. I just wanted to lie down and sleep. Forever.

"Here." I looked up to find Beth in front of me, the washcloth in her hand. I ignored the cloth and collapsed into her. "Whoa."

She nearly toppled over backward, then recovered and wrapped her arms around me, holding me tight as my emotions rose and spilled over my reserve. I cried like I had never cried before. I was crying for my aunt. I was crying for Beth. I was crying for me. I was crying for all that could be but I knew never would. Soon, to my surprise, I felt Beth's body shaking against mine as she cried her own tears for her own reasons. Out of concern for her, my tears almost immediately dried up. I rested my face against the warm skin of her neck and rubbed my hands up and down her back, lifting to play in her hair, then back down to soothe across the wide expanse of her shoulders. The sensations under my fingertips were amazing. I felt her pull even closer and her tears slowed, finally drying altogether.

We stood where we were, just holding each other, our bodies swaying slightly. I closed my eyes and felt utterly content. Being in Beth's arms like that was like coming home. I needed to feel her, to know she was still with me. I opened my eyes only to close them again as I felt warm lips against my neck.

I buried my face deeply into her hair, intoxicated by her smell. The lips moved up to my ear, warm breath tickling the flesh there. I heard my name barely whispered, and I raised my head ever so slightly, almost on instinct, as if my body had gained a mind all its own. My fingers found their way into thick, dark hair. I felt hands on my back, reaching further with each caress. My lower body was on fire, begging to be next.

The lips moved from my ear to my throat, my head arching even more. One roaming hand found its way to my side, moving up my ribs to the curve of my breast, gentle fingers exploring increasingly sensitive areas. Another hand found its way down, cupping one side of my butt, pulling me ever closer to the warmth. My eyes remained closed, but my lips opened for what I sensed was coming. I felt those warm lips move up my throat, over my chin, and, finally, onto mine. I leaned into her as a sigh escaped me, and I gave in to the pressure against my mouth, willing it to crush me, to eat me alive. The softest touch of a tongue ran over my lip, and my own tongue reached out, desperate to touch and invite. Beth groaned deep in her throat as she filled me, her hand on the back of my head to bring me as close as possible. I was being barraged by sensations; then suddenly, I was transported back to the world by a soft knocking on my bedroom door.

"Emmy?"

I pulled away from Beth, my chest heaving. Her cheeks were stained red and I had no doubt mine were as well. I stared at her, backing up a step to put some distance between us.

"Yes?" I managed to call out.

"You okay?" Billy asked. "Sorry to bother you, but Dad

asked me to come up and check on you."

I closed my eyes and swallowed hard. "I'm fine."

I could hear my brother's steps as he walked away. My gaze was locked with Beth's and, as I stood there, realization of what had just happened, of what could have happened, set in. Beth's eyes began to wander, looking at anything but me. She reached into her jacket pocket, bringing out a hairband. With shaking hands, she began to pull her long hair away from her face.

"Why did you do that?" I finally asked.

Blue eyes darted to meet mine. She stared at me for a moment. "Why did you let me?" she asked, her voice deadly calm.

"I didn't." I ran my hands through my hair, my heart still pounding.

Her voice dropped an octave. "Well, I sure as hell didn't force you."

"Damn it, Beth! I'm not into that!" I yelled. My panic was quickly turning to guilt, which was quickly turning to anger.

"Then maybe you shouldn't have started something you didn't want," she growled, her eyes on fire.

I met her gaze, dagger for dagger. "I was vulnerable. You...you took advantage of that. I—"

"I don't have to listen to this shit." She took a step toward the door, then turned to look over her shoulder. "Especially not from you."

"Get out, Beth. Get out and don't come back." My voice was shaking. I couldn't believe I had just said that. I couldn't breathe.

She turned slowly to face me fully, searching my face to gauge my sincerity. She must have seen something she didn't like, because she took a deep breath, adjusting her shoulders as though she'd been slapped. "Later," she said, her voice barely audible, and she pivoted to open the door, closing it with a soft click behind her.

I stood where I was, staring at the door in shock. What had just happened? A wave of nausea raced through me, and I hurried over to the bed, plopping down face first as the tears overtook me yet again.

~ ~ ~ ~ ~

Chapter Fifteen

~ ~ ~ ~ ~

I squirmed in my chair. The hard seat was making my butt and back ache. I blew out a long breath, readjusting my hat as the speaker droned on and on. *Who cares! Just give us our damn diplomas already.* I played with the gold cord around my neck and looked around. My fellow graduates appeared to be just as bored as I was. I was sitting in the front row and that limited my ability to see everything that was happening around me. Mr. Edwards had already given the guy beside me the evil eye for not paying attention.

I snapped out of my dazed reverie when the speaker finally said, "And now we will call our graduates of the class of 1984, beginning with those honored with a gold cord, earning a grade point average of three point seven to four point oh."

Yippie! About time. I straightened in my seat and smoothed out my gown. Our row would be the first called. At the signal, we all stood, waiting in line as one by one our names were announced.

"Emily Jane Thomas! Three point nine five."

I smiled and walked onto the stage, feeling like a million bucks. I shook Mr. Edwards' hand as he handed me my diploma and then I moved toward the ramp that would take me back to my seat. I searched the audience, seeing my parents and Billy, who sat with his new girlfriend, Nina. My eyes quickly trailed over the other people around them, recognizing some of my friends' parents, but not seeing the one face I most wanted to. I knew she wouldn't come, but I had hoped in the deepest part of me anyway. I think I saw it like some movie where the heroine was surprised as the valiant knight rode up on his white horse, forgiving the naïve maiden. The fact was that I hadn't seen Beth since the day she'd moved out of her mother's house. That was back in early November. I had no idea where she had gone or whether she would ever forgive me.

I took my seat and tried to look interested as everyone else received his or her prize for four years of study. My heart cracked just a bit when I heard them say, "Toby Elliot Samson. Erika Lynn Serky." No Elizabeth Sayers. She had officially dropped out of high school and wouldn't be receiving a diploma that day.

The summer after graduation was a boring time for me. The longer I sat at home with nothing to do, the more admiration I felt for my mother, who had spent all those years as a housewife. My parents had told me I should enjoy this last summer before heading off to college, but I'd had enough joy and was ready to start feeling productive again. I sat at the kitchen table with the Pueblo Chieftain spread out in front of me, scanning the classifieds and the help wanted sections. There were tons of baby-sitting jobs. I didn't really know what I was looking for, per se, but I decided that since I was one of those lucky kids who didn't really have to work that summer, I could hold out for something a bit more interesting than that. My eyes suddenly stopped in their search. I squinted at the page, re-reading the ad to make sure I got it right. *Hot damn!*

> Help wanted in private law firm of
> Monica Nivens. Secretarial. Must be
> able to type, file, etc. Some training
> preferred.

I couldn't believe it. I knew absolutely nothing about secretarial work, but to work for a law firm! I had no idea my former neighbor had started her own firm. I was even more impressed by her than I had been.

I parked in front of the building and unbuckled my seat belt. I took a deep, nervous breath, then gathered my wits and my resumé and climbed out of the Jeep. The law firm shared space with another lawyer whose name I couldn't remember. There was a single receptionist desk in the middle of the small, well air-conditioned lobby. A woman sat at the desk, her brows drawn as she concentrated on a form in front of her.

I looked around as I approached and waited for the woman to notice me. She didn't seem to feel the need, so I cleared my throat. Her head snapped up, as if I had surprised her, and she looked at me questioningly.

"Hello." I smiled, but the question did not leave her eyes. "I'm here to see Monica Nivens." I still got no reaction from her at all. "Um, she is a lawyer here?" Maybe if I explained it to her a bit better, she'd pretend to be helpful.

"Yeah, that way." She pointed a long-nailed finger before returning her attention back to her form. I followed her finger to a darkly tinted glass door on which was stenciled in white letters *Monica J. Nivens, Attorney at Law.* A feeling of awe washed through me when I read the words.

I walked nervously to the door, pushed it open, and stepped inside a nice office decorated in maroons and dark greens. Two chairs sat against the wall by the door. Across the room was a single desk with a computer and tons of paperwork scattered on top. There was no one sitting behind it, however. I looked around, confused. A door in the short hall to the left opened and a man looking to be in his early twenties stepped out with a cup of coffee. He looked up, startled, and nearly threw the cup into the air. He closed his eyes and put his hand on his chest.

"My God, you scared me." He walked to the desk, set the cup down, and turned back to me. "Do you have an appointment?" he asked, dabbing at his tie with a Kleenex. "I guess it's a good thing brown is in this year."

"Sorry about that." I smiled, hoping I didn't look quite as stupid as I felt. "Um, I saw the ad in the paper for—"

"Oh, yeah. Right." He sat behind the desk and sipped from the coffee, wrinkling his nose as he did. "She keeps making it this strong, she'll have more hair on her chest than I do."

I grinned as he looked around for a pen. "How about the one there?" I asked, pointing to his head. He reached up and retrieved the Bic from behind his ear, rolled his eyes dramatically, and then began to write.

"Okay, sweetie, what's your name?"

"Emily Thomas."

"Emily Thomas," he murmured as he wrote it down. "Okay. Wait here. Oh, give me your resumé." He reached out his hand, and I handed him the paper that would tell Monica I had absolutely no useable experience whatsoever. The man walked toward another door in the hall, disappearing behind its dark paneling. I sat in one of the chairs against the wall and crossed my legs. I felt very self-conscious in my summer dress. I rarely wore dresses, but figured this was definitely an occasion for one. I smoothed out the skirt as I waited.

"Hon?" The man from the desk was standing in the doorway to what I assumed was Monica's office. He smiled and waved me over.

"Thanks," I said as I passed him. He pulled the door shut behind me, and I turned to look around. The office itself wasn't that big, but the space was used well. The colors were like those in the reception area, and the total décor boasted a surprisingly masculine motif. Monica was sitting behind a large cherry wood desk. I remained by the door, my arms crossed in front of me, and stared at her. She wore her dark hair very short, certainly shorter than I had ever seen it, but it complimented her thin face and dark eyes well. She was dressed in a red suit that made for a striking contrast between her dark features and pale skin. She was beautiful.

"Hello there, Emily." I jumped, startled from my appraisal, as she looked at me with amused dark eyes. "Come on in. I really don't intend to yell at you across my office."

I smiled nervously and sat in one of the two chairs that were placed before her desk. She looked so professional, almost regal, sitting there with her elbows on the desk pad, her fingers steepled under her chin. There was a pair of black-rimmed reading glasses sitting on a manila file below her arm.

"Hi," I said, again, feeling rather stupid.

"It's been quite a while."

"Yes." I cringed at my inability to articulate beyond single syllables.

"Well," she said, picking up my resumé and gesturing with it. "I have to be honest here, Emily. You really have no experience." She smiled at me. "And the paper was supposed to take that ad out on Friday. The job's been filled."

"Oh." My heart sank. "Well, thank you for seeing me." I began to stand.

"Hold on a sec." She sat back in her chair, studying me. "You still intend to go to law school?"

I nodded enthusiastically. "Yes. I got a scholarship to CU. Four year."

She raised her brows. "Good for you, Emily. It's a fine school." I knew she had graduated from Boulder herself. "Listen, I love to see young people follow their dreams, so I'll tell you what. I have a really big case I'm working on right now and could use an assistant. Would you be interested? I could show you a bit of the ropes."

My eyes lit up and my chest puffed out with pride. *Was she serious? God, please let her be serious.* "Absolutely!" I leaned forward in my chair.

"Great." She smiled, pleased. "I can't pay you much."

"Oh, that's no problem! To me the experience is priceless." My smile must have filled my whole face. *Okay, was I trying to win a beauty pageant or to get this job?* I had always felt such admiration for Monica, and the thought of actually working with her and learning from her was almost too much.

I strolled through the door of my house as if I were walking on a cloud. I was flipping through the stack of mail in my hand on my way to the kitchen to get some iced tea, when one of the envelopes caught my attention. I tossed the other stuff onto the table. The return address was the medical center from which Aunt Kitty used to receive treatment. Even though it was addressed to Kitty, I slid my finger under the flap, ripping it open. The neatly folded letter came out easily, and I covered my mouth with my hand as I read. My throat tightened and tears sprang immediately to my eyes. I dropped my hands, along with the letter, into my lap and stared out the window over the sink.

"Hey, honey," my mom said as she brushed by with a large bag full from gathering trash around the house. When I didn't answer, she turned to me. "Emmy? You okay, baby?"

I handed her the letter and spoke very quietly. "Apparently someone does not keep their records updated very well."

My mother read the notification, then her face paled and fell. She gently laid the paper on the table and walked to the sink, her shoulders slumped as she rested her weight on her arms. "Now they want to give Kitty a kidney?"

I went to her as she began to cry quietly, placing my hands on her arms and resting my chin on her shoulder. "You okay, Mom?" I swallowed back my emotions so I wouldn't upset her further, all thoughts of beginning my fledgling career in law momentarily abandoned.

It was my first day of work with Monica and she told me dressy casual was appropriate attire. I didn't know quite what that meant, but hoped my slacks and simple button-up shirt would do the trick.

"Okay." Jack, who I now knew to be the office manager, gave me the grand tour. "This is where she keeps all the files. They are in order by last name. Each case is given a number." He pulled one of the manila folders from a filing cabinet and showed me the number and the name printed on the front. He opened the folder and displayed the file. "This woman here, she is a total loser." He looked very serious as he eyed the details. "Now, don't do what I'm doing right now, because (A) Monica gets really, really mad, and (B) it's really, really illegal."

I grinned and followed as we exited the file room where the copier and coffee machine were, and we continued to his desk in the reception area.

"This is my desk, if you hadn't figured that out by now. I answer all the phones, make appointments, yadda yadda. Any questions about anything other than law stuff, ask me not Monica. Don't get me wrong, she's a great boss, with fabulous taste in clothes, but she has absolutely no clue what goes on here or how to run this office." He stopped to take a break and sipped his coffee, his finger reaching up to put a perfect piece of blonde hair back in place. "She'd be lost without me."

"Oh, really?"

I jumped, turning to see Monica walking into the office with her briefcase. She had a brow quirked and a grin on her face. "Don't listen to a word he says, Emily. He's usually full of it anyway."

"Am not," he said, his hand on his hip and an indignant look on his handsome face.

"Jack, I need you to pull the Reed case, please?" Monica didn't wait for an answer. She breezed by his desk and headed into her office. I stayed where I was, awaiting further instruction. Jack jerked toward Monica, then back to me, so I followed her.

Monica waited for me at her door, holding it open until I passed through and then closing it behind me. I stood in the center of the room, waiting for her to tell me what I was supposed to do. She walked to her desk, high heels sinking into the thick carpet.

"Jack is a pain in the ass, but I'd be lost without him." She plopped into her chair. I sat where I had the day before during my interview. She ran her fingers through her hair and sighed. "Okay, well, did he give you a basic tour of the place?"

"Yes. He showed me the file room—"

"Ah, yes. Where he goes through and reads the cases and pretends I don't know."

I stared at her, not sure whether she was joking. She cracked the slightest bit of a smile, giving me permission to share in the joke.

"Exactly. He showed me how he runs the front office."

"Good. Okay." She opened her briefcase and removed her reading glasses, a pen, and a stack of folders, after which she placed the case on the floor under her desk. "Here's the deal..."

Monica explained that she was working on a case for a Mrs. Rhoda Mills, who was suing her husband for domestic violence. Among other things, she wanted sole custody of their eleven-year-old daughter, whom, she had charged, he was sexually abusing. Monica had filed paperwork at the Family Courthouse and a restraining order had been served on Mr. Mills. I listened, transfixed, as my new boss outlined what she had already done in the case and what still needed to be done before the court date.

"How good are you at research?" she asked.

I looked up from the case I had been reading. "Really good."

She nodded and smiled. "Excellent. You'll be doing a lot of it here. By the time you go off to college, you'll either love it or hate it."

~ ~ ~ ~ ~

Still parked outside my parents' house, I sat in the driver's seat of the Camry and checked the scribbled address one last time. Monica's house was in Greenwood, which was a nice area. Impressed, I turned the key in the ignition and pulled away from the curb. As I drove through Pueblo, I recalled my mother's comments about how much the city had grown over the past five years. Looking around now, I could see she was absolutely right. There were so many businesses and neighborhoods that hadn't been there when I'd last visited. After the big quake in California, people had left that state in droves, and many of them found new homes in Colorado. Why not? The economy was booming, and Pueblo seemed as good a place to them as any other. They were opening new businesses or expanding ones already established on the West Coast. New York was now my home, but all the same, it felt good to be in a place where I knew I would always be welcome.

I drove by my old high school and saw cars in the parking lot. A line of yellow buses unloaded kids returning from a sporting event. It all seemed so long ago, and in many ways, it was another lifetime.

I decided to take the long way, driving through the park and watching families as they laughed and played together. The smell of grilled hamburgers and hot dogs wafted through the open window of the rental car. I smiled as I watched children chase each other, and braked abruptly when a big red ball rolled out into the narrow traffic lane of the park road. A man waved as he hurried in front of the car to grab the toy, then ran back onto the grass to lecture a careless child. It seemed as though all was well with the world.

~ ~ ~ ~ ~

"Where the hell is my wife!" a man's voice screamed out. I glanced up from my work to look at Monica with questioning eyes. She had already reached to pull her reading glasses off her nose and was glancing at the closed door.

"Sir, you need to calm down," we heard Jack say.

"Get your God damn hands off me! Rhoda! Rhoda, where the fuck are you?"

The voice was getting closer to us in the office, and the sound of the file room door banging open startled me. Monica sighed deeply and stood at her desk, her face like stone. Seconds later, her office door swung open. In the doorway stood a large man with a greasy baseball cap over what looked to be graying hair and a belly that overhung his pant waist. His face was red from the upset, his eyes like a shrew's. He looked around the room, his gaze stopping on me for a moment before roaming over to Monica. "Which one of you is that Nivens bitch?" When he spoke, the stench of his breath reached me, whiskey strong enough to make me feel sick.

"Sir, you have no business being in here," Monica said, her voice even and calm. I had no clue how she was keeping herself together. My knees were beginning to knock.

He glared at her and growled, "Where's my wife?"

"I'm your wife's attorney, sir, not her baby-sitter." He bared crooked, stained teeth, taking a step forward. Monica did not move an inch; she merely crossed her arms over her chest. "You must know this behavior will not help your case any." He stopped, briefly looking confused, but then the anger returned to his face. "Jack, call the police for Mr. Mills," she said, raising her voice enough for Jack to hear but never losing eye contact with the man.

Mills seemed to gain an awareness of the implications of his being there. He took a step back and out of the office. "You tell that bitch that she'll never take Carrie away from me." He took another step back.

"You can tell her yourself in court. Good day, sir."

Mills stared at her for a moment before, with a breath of disgust, he stormed away. I glanced at my boss, my eyes as big as saucers. Monica turned from the door, her fingers at her temples. I could tell she was shaken and was trying to get herself under control.

"You were brilliant," I finally said.

Monica chuckled. "That is one thing they don't teach you in law school — how to deal with irate husbands. I really thought he was going to pull a gun or something." She turned toward me, perching on the edge of her desk, her hands slightly shaking.

"Well, you were great. I can't believe you were able to talk him down like that." My admiration had grown by leaps and bounds.

Monica glanced at her watch, then clapped her hands together. "I don't know about you, but I could use a break." She smiled at me, and I returned it eagerly. "What do you say to some lunch?"

Jack had other lunch plans, so we found ourselves alone together in the historic district of Pueblo on B Street, sitting at an outside café. It was a hot day, and I ran my hands through my hair, pulling it back away from my face. On days like this, I understood the inclination to chop hair short. I looked across the small, round table at my boss as she picked at her salad, taking a bite now and then. My own cheeseburger and fries were long gone. "Are you okay?"

Monica glanced up at me and nodded. "Yeah. That just shook me up." She set down her fork and sat back in the wrought iron chair. "You know, I try to do so much for this community. When I finished my four years of college, then headed to law school, I had the typical idealism of youth and I was so naïve." She took a drink of her ice water. "I really thought I could make a difference, you know?"

"But you do."

She chuckled. "Oh, Emily, I look at you, and I see myself all over again."

"Do you regret it? Going into law?" I stirred my straw around in my Coke before taking a sip.

Monica was quiet for a moment as she thought about her answer. Then, with a sigh, she shook her head. "No. I don't."

We talked for another hour, and she told me all about law school and what I had to look forward to after my pre-law degree. Excitement soaring through me, I ate up every word. I wanted to move on with my life, to get far away from my childhood. What I didn't understand at that age and level of experience was that those would be some of my best years, years that I would return to in my mind.

~ ~ ~ ~ ~

I pulled the Camry to a stop at a red light and tapped the wheel with my fingers as I waited for it to turn. A large part of me was glad to be back home, although I would have preferred it to be under better circumstances. It amazed me to think that my twenty-year class reunion would be coming up in a few years. I hadn't attended the ten-year. At the time, it seemed pointless. Now, I wasn't so sure.

As I began to drive again, I came to the realization that I had, in my arrogance, thought that nothing pre-New York mattered, when in retrospect, everything pre-New York had shaped me into the woman I had become. I think everyone needs a good lesson like this every now and then, as painful as it may be at the time.

Chapter Sixteen

~ ~ ~ ~ ~

As the weeks went by, I realized just how much research Monica had been talking about that first day. Was she ever wrong. There wasn't just a lot of research; there was a ton of it. I didn't mind, once I got past the overwhelmed feeling. I also found out that during law school I had to serve some time in an internship and this could qualify as some of that time. It certainly didn't hurt that Monica was the most amazing person to work for. She was tough, but extremely fair and very generous. And, to my surprise, she was a lot of fun.

I stared at the dark ceiling of my bedroom, tired from another long night of depositions. After we'd left the office, Monica and I had headed to her small house over on Park. We sat on the carpet eating take-out from Burger King and went to work to determine every angle of the case we'd need. She went over every point, line by line, so I would understand the ins and outs. I was impressed with Monica's extensive knowledge, and with the way her mind worked. I was looking forward to going with her to court the following Thursday to watch the proceedings. It was a simple custody case, but, nonetheless, I was buzzing with excitement and anticipation. I'd never observed an actual case, and as her assistant, I would get to sit at the table with Monica and her client. As if that weren't enough, Monica told me that after the trial, she had a surprise for me.

A car passed outside, and through my window the headlights shone across the ceiling like an apparition. I hugged Ruffles to my chest and studied the light overhead. I thought about my new boss. I wondered if she was married, which I doubted, or had a boyfriend. I'd sort of brought it up one day, and she had made it pretty plain that the subject was off limits. I wondered why. Was it too painful to discuss? Had she been through a really terrible break-up? My God, I sounded to myself like one of Beth's stories.

Beth. It had been so long since I'd seen her. I'd heard through the neighborhood grapevine that she'd gotten some job doing Community Theater. I hoped she was happy. Beth deserved a bit of happiness after such an unhappy childhood.

That night, I realized just how much I had taken Beth for

granted, thinking she'd always be there. But, wasn't she the one who told me that she always would? I would be nineteen in a few days and Beth would soon follow in October. We were growing up.

I sat at the table in the courtroom, digging out anything Monica asked for. She was brilliant, pleading her case to show why Laura Martinez should have sole custody of her daughter. I scrutinized the judge and the jurors, studying their responses to Monica. They seemed to watch her with interest, and perhaps I was just projecting, but I thought I detected the occasional glimpse of out-and-out awe. This was definitely what I wanted to spend the rest of my life doing; if I hadn't been convinced before, I sure was now.

Monica was a sight to behold. My eyes trailed over her well-cut suit, the way the gray pinstriped skirt clung to her hips, and the jacket that dipped in at her waist, then flared out at the shoulders and bust. She wore a silk blouse and a simple silver necklace that matched the small hoops in her ears. Her legs, long and shapely, ended in sleek, black heels.

I was jolted from my thoughts by her low voice asking for her notes. I shook myself out of the daze and handed her a yellow legal pad, which she took with a grin and turned back to her witness. I tried my best to concentrate on the content of the trial, but couldn't help watching her every move. I mean, I admired and wanted to be like her some day. It was only natural that I should look. Right?

Monica was elated as we exited the courtroom. She laughed and talked with her client, who thanked her over and over for helping to get her daughter back under her roof. Monica was gracious and kind. "Please take care of her, Laura," she said softly, grasping the younger woman's hand as we waited for the elevator doors to open.

Laura Martinez nodded enthusiastically. "Of course, of course!" she said in heavily accented English, then her happiness seemed to fade. She looked at the floor. "Miss Nivens, I talked with my father this morning and he is not going to be able to get the money." She looked up at Monica as tears began to roll down her cheeks. "Will you let me make payments to you?"

Monica patted her hand and smiled. "Tell you what, Laura; you just concentrate on your daughter right now, okay?"

The young woman's eyes widened, as did her mouth. "What are you saying?" Her dark eyes filled with hope and disbelief.

"I'm saying that you should focus on yourself and little Maria."

The small woman gasped and grabbed Monica in a tight, crushing hug. Monica smiled, surprised, and returned the sobbing woman's embrace. "Oh, thank you, thank you! I pray for you."

Monica slowly pulled away and smiled down at her. "That works for me."

I stood to the side, not wanting to intrude on such a touching moment. I couldn't believe Monica had just waived her fees. *All that work, for what?* That question was answered when I saw the happiness on the young mother's face when the bailiff brought her two-year-old daughter to her. I knew from the case file, and from what we'd heard in court that day, that the woman had been through hell with her ex-husband and his family, and she just needed some peace with her daughter.

"Come on." Monica motioned me to the elevator, and I hurried after her.

As the doors closed, I turned to her. "I can't believe you did that. I thought that sort of thing only happened on *Matlock* or *Perry Mason*."

She chuckled, switching her briefcase from her left hand to her right. "Well, sometimes you have to do what's right instead of what's practical. Martinez was real scum, and she needed to get that baby away from him." She pushed the button for the lobby. "Tell you what, Emily, why don't you go on home, get ready, then I'll pick you up at your house in an hour, okay?"

Outside Monica's office, I climbed into my Jeep and blew out a breath. I was surprisingly tired; the day had been more emotionally draining than I'd expected. As the engine fired up, so did the radio, and Wham began to sing, "Wake Me Up Before You Go-Go." A smile on my face, I sang along as I pulled out of the parking lot and headed home.

My mother sat on my bed, watching me finish with my hair, and I gave her a brief description of the trial while I got ready to meet Monica. My mother had been so thrilled when I told her where I'd be working and what I'd be doing.

"There's a client that we're sort of worried about, though," I said as I tucked in my shirt and stuck my comb in my back pocket. My mother looked at me strangely.

"Honey, why are you taking a comb with you when you have enough hairspray in there to keep a small community together?"

I shrugged and looked into the mirror, patting my feathered bangs. "I don't know. Guess it just looks cool." I watched her reflection in the mirror as she shook her head in confusion. *Parents.* They never understood anything about fashion.

"So, tell me about the client you're worried about."

"Oh! Well, we have this client whose name is...well, actually I can't tell you that. Confidentiality." I felt rather important that I knew something my mother didn't, and I was slightly irritated when I saw her try to hide a small grin. "Well, anyway, so this client is trying to get her little girl away from her husband, who is a complete monster. Just two weeks ago, he barged into the office and threatened Monica. The man's crazy!" I turned back to the mirror as I put on my lip gloss and smacked my lips together. "The wife is afraid of what he might do. I know Monica is really worried about him, too."

"Sounds exciting."

"It is."

She smiled, leaned back on her hands, and cocked her head to the side. "Where are you going tonight, honey?"

"Monica has some sort of surprise planned for me. Don't know what's up."

"Oh." She looked down at her hands as she sat up and then twined her fingers together.

"Why?" I asked, grabbing my purple Velcro wallet and sticking it into my pocket.

"Well, it's just that it's your birthday, and you're never home lately. I know Dad and I aren't as exciting as Monica, but I thought you might want to spend some time with us." She looked up at me shyly, then returned her gaze to her hands.

I stared at her dumbly. Not spend time with Monica? It had never even occurred to me. I sighed. *Try and be diplomatic, Em.* "I'm sorry, Mom." I walked over and sat next to her. "If she hadn't already made plans for us, I would stay home. Tell you what," I put my arm around her shoulders, "tomorrow is Saturday, and I don't have to work, so why don't we go down to the mall and just window shop all day like we used to? We can even go into that music store and laugh at all those crazy groups coming out." She nodded and I could tell she was pleased with my idea.

"Okay."

"Thanks, Mom." I gave her a quick hug, but when I heard the doorbell, I shot up from the mattress, nearly knocking my mother off the bed. "She's here." I was running out the door when my mother stopped me.

"Emmy?"

I turned back to her, my hand on the doorframe. "Yeah?"

"I'm so proud of you, honey. Have a good time."

I smiled my goodbye and raced down the stairs. When I jumped into the passenger seat of Monica's white Jeep Cherokee and glanced over at her, my eyes were nailed to the spot. "Wow. You look really good," I muttered, then blushed deeply. I hadn't meant to say that out loud, but she wore a red tank top that showed off trim, well-tanned shoulders and arms. That simple silver chain was still around her neck, a nice contrast against her skin tone. She wore jean shorts and sandals, and her hair was clean and shiny and combed back.

She smiled. "Thanks. So do you."

I smiled back and looked down at my own T-shirt and shorts. I felt like just a kid compared to her grace. She backed out of the driveway and we were off.

"So where are we going?" I stuck my arm out the open passenger window to try and catch the breeze.

She smiled and shook her head, her eyes fixed firmly on the road. "Not going to tell you. However, we do have a quick stop to make. Is that okay?"

"Fine by me." Inside, I was jumping for joy. Monica made me feel so important, as though what I said really mattered. She treated me as an equal. My happiness was plastered across my face as I stared into the early evening sky, everything turning gold as the sun set.

"... And now, a big hit for Rick Springfield, 'Jesse's Girl'." Monica reached for the radio, intending to change the channel.

"No, wait. I love that song."

She pulled her hand back as the car filled with the song about a guy who had fallen in love with his best friend's girlfriend. We jammed to the music as we drove through downtown and headed toward Santa Fe Avenue. Then Monica turned onto a back road that I was unfamiliar with and eventually parked in front of a small building that was low to the ground, almost as though it were hiding from something. There was a dirt parking lot off to the side with a few cars scattered about.

She turned to me and smiled. "This will only take a sec."

"Wait, I want to go in with you." There was a Budweiser sign in a front-facing window of the building and I figured it must be a bar.

Monica's face darkened slightly. "Uh, well, are you sure?" Her voice took on a nervous tremor, which only served to pique my curiosity. I nodded enthusiastically. "Okay. Come on."

We walked toward the door, which was a piece of wood painted black, and were nearly bowled over when it swung open and somebody came barreling out.

"Monica! Where you been, girl?"

He was the tallest man I had ever seen, with dark skin that looked like polished onyx. He was extremely thin with very feminine features, chiseled cheekbones, and straight, white teeth. I squinted as I stared up at him. *Was he wearing eye makeup?*

"Hi, Magenta!" Monica succumbed to a powerful bear hug. When they parted, the large man looked at me. "Who's this precious young thing?" he asked, extending a long, narrow, yet surprisingly elegant hand for me to shake. As I did so, I noticed his fingernails were painted a deep pink. *What the hell?*

"This is Emily. She's working for me this summer."

"Well, it's sure nice to meet you, sweets." He let go of my hand and turned back to my boss. "Sweetheart, I'd love to chat with you, but I must be going. You need to come in some time. We miss you, girl." He motioned dramatically and gave an affectionate pat to Monica's shoulder.

"I will. I've been so busy lately."

"Well, catch you two cuties later."

He winked and walked past us into the parking lot. I glanced over my shoulder and watched him sashay to his car, then turned back to Monica to meet amused dark eyes.

"Come on, Emily." She chuckled, holding the door open for me.

I walked ahead of her, looking around. The place was dim, and obviously not open for business. There were small bulbs strung around the ceiling and support poles, and they looked to be the only source of light. Small round tables were scattered liberally, with chairs stacked neatly on top; there was a hardwood dance floor in the center of the largish room. The long bar was to the left toward the back. Two women were sitting on bar stools talking to a male bartender. Other than the three of them and us, the place was empty. I had no clue why we were there, so I moved to the side to allow Monica to walk by. The trio at the bar looked in our direction, and one of the women stood but made no move toward me. Her eyes darted briefly to me before resting on Monica. She was a short woman, not much taller than me, with clipped blonde hair tucked under a cowboy hat. She wore tight-fitting Wranglers and black boots. Her western-style shirt was half unbuttoned, revealing some of her cleavage, and I quickly found the juke-box in the back incredibly interesting.

"Hey, Mon," she said in a low, smoky voice.

"Hi, Lee. Thanks for meeting me."

They embraced and then stepped back from each other. I moved away a couple steps, not wanting to eavesdrop. I walked onto the dance floor and slowly pirouetted in a small circle. I had never been in a bar before. It didn't seem so bad. I could see the bathrooms near the pool table in back. A large picture of James Dean appeared on the door to the men's room, and a picture of Marilyn Monroe was on the door to the women's room. The back walls held liquor signs, mostly of different beers, and there was a giant upside down pink triangle on one of the mirrors. I thought that a bit strange, having no clue what it was supposed to mean. When I turned toward the bar, Monica was sitting with the other three, talking to the bartender and laughing. I decided to see what the joke was.

"You guys have got to behave!" Monica was chuckling, rubbing at her eyes with her fingertips. "See, you're making me cry."

"You big baby," the blonde woman called Lee said, lightly punching her on the arm. "Always was a problem." Monica sobered slightly and glared at her.

The bartender, who had been leaning on the bar, straightened and smiled. "Hey, kid," he said.

I hated it when people called me kid. I clenched my teeth, but smiled back. "Hi."

"This her?" the blonde asked, looking over at me and taking in my shorts and tee. Then her eyes traveled to my bare legs and shoes before making their way back up.

"Lee," Monica warned in a low voice.

I was utterly confused, and I'm sure it showed on my face. I looked from one to the other, then back to the bartender, who was trying to stifle his amusement. The blonde, because of her arrogant stance and condescending gaze, irritated me. "I'm Emily," I said, my chin raised high in defiance of her stare.

She continued to look at me with hooded brown eyes. Finally, after further inspection of my legs, she swiveled her barstool around to face me fully, her boot heels hooked on the metal of the stool. "Lee," she said, tipping her hat.

I felt a strange flush course up my neck and over my cheeks. She was a very pretty lady, and something in that stare made me uncomfortable. She looked as though she was taking in all of me with that gaze, my outer as well as inner persona. It was disconcerting, but it spurred me on. Suddenly, I felt a boldness flow through me that I'd never felt before. "Well, now that we've got that straight, why don't you ask *me* if I'm her or not?"

Except for the slightest lift of a dark blonde eyebrow, her expression didn't change, then she grinned a bit and nodded. The bartender and other woman both whistled quietly under their breath and glanced at Monica, then back at me.

"Fair enough." Lee tipped her hat again and swiveled back around to grab her beer. I took a deep, shaky breath, amazed I had done that. I was not the type to confront people like Lee. I glanced at Monica to meet impressed, albeit surprised, eyes.

She smiled and shook her head, turning to the others. "We better go. It's this one's birthday today." Her voice was proud and she stood, putting a hand on my back. Part of me was annoyed that she'd let Lee know that. I didn't want her to know anything about me. I didn't even like her!

"Hey, congrats, kid. Happy birthday," the bartender said with a genuine smile.

Monica grabbed a book off the bar. "Thanks for bringing it by, Lee. It's only been nine months." She smiled, but just as quickly it was gone.

"Well, get everything next time," Lee said, crossing her arms over her chest, which caused her shirt to open a bit more. I blushed and tried to look away, but caught myself sneaking a peek.

"Come on, Emily. Later, all."

With a round of goodbyes, we finally left the bar. It was much darker on the street than it had been when we'd gone in. I took a deep breath of fresh, summer air and let it out with a smile.

"You look happy," Monica said as she unlocked the driver's side door.

"I am." Somehow that place had revived me, cleansed me. It had only been a bar, I assumed like any other, but despite the blonde, I had felt a kinship to those people, even to that strange guy, Magenta. I couldn't explain it to myself let alone to Monica, so I didn't tell her. "It's a great night," I said, in answer to her silent question, but only revealing half the truth. "It's my birthday, it's my last year as a teenager, and I have something wonderful to look forward to."

She reached over and unlocked my door, and I climbed in and reached for my seatbelt. I stared out the window, looking back at the place just in time to see the sign outside suddenly light up. *Campy's Bar.* "I like that place."

Monica raised her eyebrows. "Really?"

"Yeah. I want to come back some time. When they're

open."

Monica took me to eat at a crazy place called Papa's Bag
that had clowns running around, squirting unsuspecting
guests with flower squirt guns or honking their noses. It was
great fun. After dinner, we went to see the newest Molly Ring-
wald movie. We laughed, talked, and laughed some more. It
turned out to be one of the best birthdays I'd had in a long
time.

~ ~ ~ ~ ~

I slowly scanned the large, old houses that had lined the streets
of Pueblo for a century or more. I pulled the Camry to the curb and
double-checked the piece of paper in my hand to confirm the
address. The house was on the left-hand side of the street and stood
tall, a three-story Victorian. The dark green paint was accented with
white shutters, and there were columns on the porch. Monica and
Connie's house was truly breathtaking. Two cars were parked in the
narrow drive, one behind the other. I assumed they were both home.
I hadn't called to say I was coming, preferring instead the element of
surprise. I pulled back into the street and performed a U-turn so I
could park at the curb in front of their house without facing the
dead-end of the cul-de-sac. I knew it was silly, but my nerves were
getting the better of me, and I wanted to be able to leave quickly if I
had to. I cut the engine and sat for a moment, staring at the well
cared for winter-yellow lawn. I inhaled deeply and got out of the car.
It was time to confront the past again.

Chapter Seventeen

~ ~ ~ ~ ~

I had called Jack earlier at the office to tell him I was going to be late, because I had some things to take care of before I would be ready to leave for Boulder in a month. The summer was passing too quickly, and part of me didn't want to go. I almost wished I could just stay in Pueblo and continue to work for Monica at her practice. As I drove to work, I recalled what she said to me when I mentioned the thought to her.

"Emily, I'm flattered, believe me. And you have been of immense help to me. But this is not your dream — to be stuck here, working for an attorney. Your dream is to be the attorney. Don't give up on that. Ever."

As I pulled into the parking lot at the office, I saw a policeman getting into his cruiser. I followed the black-and-white with my eyes until it disappeared around the corner, then hurried to the side door of the building that would take me into the hall by Monica's office. Her door was closed, so I by-passed it and went into the reception area to ask Jack what was going on. As usual, he was sitting at his desk, chewing on the end of a pencil. "Jack."

He looked up at me, surprised. "Hey." He tossed the yellow Number 2 to the desktop. "Glad you're in. You should really go talk to Mon."

"What happened? I saw a police car outside. Did someone break in?" I looked around, but didn't see anything awry.

He shook his head, his perfectly styled hair not moving an inch. "No. Mon can explain it to you." He patted my hand where it rested on the edge of the desk, and pointed to the closed office door. "Besides, I think you're the only one who can help her right now."

Confused and worried, I hurried over to Monica's door and knocked softly. "Monica?" There was no answer. "Monica?"

"Come in" was the very faint response.

I opened the door; Monica sat behind her desk, her head in her hands. "Monica?" I asked again, my voice low, careful. "Hey."

Her voice was thick and wet from crying. I pulled over one

of the chairs and sat, never taking my eyes off her. Finally, after a moment of silence that seemed to stretch on forever, she looked up at me. Her eyes were heavy, and her face was pale.

"What is it?" I whispered. "What happened?"

"Rhoda Mills is dead." I stared at her in shock, my stomach immediately seizing up in knots. "I knew it, Emily. When her husband came slamming in here that day, I knew I should have called the police." Fresh tears began to form in her dark eyes.

My heart went out to her. I could see she was assuming the complete blame for what had happened. "Oh, Monica, there was nothing you could have done. Nothing." I felt totally helpless and knew there wasn't anything I could say to make her feel better. Guilt was a hard thing to alleviate.

"I knew he was dangerous, though! He just walked into the house this morning, pointed his .38 at his wife and their daughter, and pumped three bullets into each of them. They never had a chance." She swiped at her falling tears. I took her hand, hoping to offer some semblance of comfort. "Why am I doing this, Emily? I don't make a difference. These people in this town are screwed. Just plain and simple. They're screwed, and no one and nothing can help them, least of all Monica Nivens, Attorney at Law. What a joke."

"No, Monica. Please don't say that." I fought back tears of my own. "Just think about all the cases we've worked on these past six weeks." Suddenly, the face of one of our former clients flashed before my eyes. "Just think of what you did for Laura Martinez!" I exclaimed, grasping at anything that might help break through to her. "Her face that day in court when you waived your fee." I stopped to take a breath. "Monica, do you know how profoundly you changed the lives of that woman and her daughter?"

She looked at me through tear-puffed eyes. "Do you really think so?"

Her voice was childlike with hope. I nodded enthusiastically. "Absolutely!" I moved around her desk until I was kneeling next to her chair. "Monica, I wanted to be a lawyer before, but watching you makes me want it that much more. I want to be just like you." She continued to stare at me, her eyes unwavering as my words sunk in. I could see the moment of acceptance; she smiled suddenly and it was like sunlight bursting through clouds.

"Thank you, Emily. I think that's one of the nicest things anyone has ever said to me." She brought her hand up and gently cupped my jaw. We held that pose for a moment, until she took a deep breath and turned back to her desk, the spell broken. "Come on, woman, we have some cases to work on."

On rare occasions, Monica asked me to work on a Saturday. Some unpleasant surprises had come up on our latest case, and they had to be dealt with pronto. After an evening of going over new depositions, trying to find holes in the defense's case, I had spent the previous night crashing in Monica's spare bedroom. The new day didn't made the task any easier, and I sat on the floor with my head resting against my hand as I pored over the file open before me on the coffee table. I was going cross-eyed and wanted to fall asleep again.

"Monica?" I called out while continuing to study the file, "Did you fall in or what?" I heard the toilet flush and had just turned the page when I felt something wet dribble on my head. "What the..." I looked at the ceiling. No leaks; it hadn't even rained lately. I shrugged it off and refocused my attention on the file, only to feel it again a moment later. This time, when I turned around, I was hit smack in the face with a thin stream of water at the hands of a laughing lawyer. "You!" I stood, shielding my face with my hands so I could protect myself from the onslaught of the squirt gun. Monica chortled with joy as she completely soaked me. Once it was emptied, she put down the gun and stood grinning at me. My T-shirt stuck to me like a second skin, and my bangs hung wetly in front of my eyes. I stared back at her, my hands on my hips. "You think this is pretty funny, don't you?"

She nodded. "Unh huh."

I made my move and she screamed and took off running through the small house, me on her heels. She made the mistake of detouring to the backyard, and I immediately went for the hose, turning the faucet as fast as I could, and then chasing her while trying to spray around potted plants, trees, and even the house. She disappeared around a corner, and the hose would not reach that far, so I decided to lie in wait. Patience is a virtue, after all. I grinned to myself as I thought of just how wet she actually was as a result of my efforts. Her white polo was virtually see-through, her cotton shorts hung on her frame, and her hair was pasted to her skull. That would teach her to try to sneak up on me!

"Huh!" I gasped as I felt ice-cold water cascade over my head and down my shirt. I closed my eyes as my body adjusted to the temperature of the water after the heat of the day. When I was finally able to lower my hunched shoulders, I turned to see Monica holding a water cooler at her side. "You are evil!"

"Yup."

"Went around the fence?"

"Yup."

I nodded, then got my bearings and brought up the hose. She giggled as she screamed and tried to protect herself from the stream of water. She advanced on me blindly, spitting water out of her mouth and occasionally peeking through one of her tightly closed eyes, until she reached me and we began to struggle with the hose for control. We were laughing and screaming like schoolgirls.

"Noo!" I yelped as she began to get the upper hand. She laughed evilly and managed to wrestle the hose from my grasp. I took a step back to flee, but my foot got caught in the hose and I went down, pulling her with me. We hit hard, me on the grass and her on me, which knocked me breathless.

"Ow." I giggled and opened my eyes to look up at her. She was giggling, too. She put her hands on the grass on either side of me and pushed herself up a bit, but then stopped as she stared down at me.

I got my breath back, only to lose it again as I stared into her eyes. The smile slowly faded from her face. I didn't know what to do, but I wasn't so sure I wanted her to get up, so I just laid there, my arms out to my sides. Monica seemed to get closer to me and I could feel her warm breath on my face, which in turn spread that warmth to other areas. Her eyes lowered, staring at my open mouth. Then, as suddenly as it had happened, she blinked, pushed herself off me, and got to her feet, reaching a hand down to help me up.

"You okay?" she asked, focusing her attention on gathering up the hose and returning it to the sidewalk by the house, where she turned the faucet handle until the flow of water stopped.

"Uh, yeah," I said, still in a daze.

Once she had the hose wrapped around the stand, she turned back to me, her hands wringing the water out of her shirttail. "Sorry, Emily. We've both been working so hard, I figured we could use a break."

I smiled at her and began to wring out my own clothes. "That was fun." It was a hot day. Not just regular want-some-ice-cold-lemonade hot, but let's-run-and-hide-in-the-air-conditioner hot.

Monica and I walked down the street, doing some window shopping on Main on our way to our favorite little outside café to eat lunch. She was dragging me from window to window as she gawked at the different types of candles. Monica wanted to redecorate her house, and I was to help her. "Oh!" I stopped, my gaze riveted on one of the most beautiful candles I'd ever seen. It was a large wolf, standing at the edge of a cliff, howling at a full moon. It was carved from ivory wax, and the detail was exquisite, right down to the wolf's fur and the tail tucked between its legs. "Look at that." When I got no answer, I turned to see my friend's attention had completely shifted elsewhere. Annoyed, I tugged at her sleeve. Then I followed her gaze to the street and my own eyes bulged in surprise.

A woman was walking down the sidewalk in our direction, still a good fifteen to twenty feet away. She was tall, with long legs in loose-fitting worn blue jeans that had matching holes in each knee. She wore a tight, ribbed black tank that showed off tanned skin and an incredible physique. She had dark, nearly black hair, cut short, but with long bangs that flanked each side of her forehead. As she came closer, I stared into blue eyes that seemed to glow against the reflection of the sun, and when those blue eyes crinkled in recognition, my stomach fell.

"Beth." Monica turned to me, startled from her strange daze. "And she cut her hair," I added dumbly.

"You know her?" she asked.

I nodded, sticking my hands in my pockets to stop them from fidgeting with the sudden attack of nerves I felt. As she approached, I noticed Beth's eyes darting back and forth between Monica and me, and there was a question in her lopsided grin. My God, she was more beautiful than ever.

"Fancy seeing you here, Em."

I was speechless and merely watched as she turned to Monica. "Hi," she said to my boss.

"Hello," Monica said with a sweet smile. "Friend of Emily's?"

I was curious about how Beth would answer that. She glanced at me for a moment, then looked at Monica. "We know each other," she said finally. "You're Monica from across the street." Beth cocked her head to the side to take in all of Monica in her cream-colored, lightweight suit. "Right?"

I watched, torn between the two, not sure I believed what I was seeing. If I didn't know better, I would have said from Beth's tone and the play of her eyes that she was flirting with Monica. Was...was Monica flirting back? I was baffled by another strange feeling that washed over me: jealousy. My awareness of the present resurfaced.

"... Yeah, I'm Beth Sayers. Lived next door to Em, here." Recognition seemed to dawn on Monica's face, and she nodded. "Of course."

Beth looked back at me with a smile of wonder on her face. "My God. You have definitely grown up."

"Well, it does tend to happen. And so have you, by the way."

The two of them continued to talk, but I blocked them out, my own feelings raging like a tempest inside my head. How could I be so glad to see Beth, yet wish she'd go away? I never in my wildest dreams pictured Beth as a threat of any kind, but at that moment, I saw her as just that. *Why?* How could I feel jealousy aimed at Beth *and* at Monica? It was obvious to the densest person that something was crackling through the air between those two. However, I was not yet ready to put a name to it or even to try to identify it.

Every once in a while, I sneaked a peek at Beth only to find my gaze meeting blue. As always, no matter what she did, she still seemed to keep me in her sights. That was both comforting and unsettling at the same time. Old habits die hard.

~ ~ ~ ~ ~

I took the keys from the ignition and opened the Camry door, mindful of oncoming traffic. The walkway to the large green house was done in flagstone, with bits of colored pebbles thrown into the mix of mortar. The porch swing swayed slightly in the light breeze. I glanced at the increasingly darkening sky. It was beginning to get cold again and I hoped a storm wasn't coming in. On the porch, I took a deep breath and reached to press the doorbell. I could hear chimes from the interior of the house and then the barking of a dog followed by footsteps on a hardwood floor.

"Emily?" I looked up to meet the dark gaze of my old friend and boss. "Oh my God." Monica stepped forward onto the porch to wrap me in a tight hug. "Why didn't you tell me you were coming?"

"I guess I wanted to surprise you," I explained as we parted.

I looked into Monica's face, now that of a woman in her mid-forties. She was still beautiful, with just the tiniest bit of gray mixed into her shiny black hair. It was longer than it had been the last time I'd seen her. She wore a baggy sweatshirt and matching pants, her feet in thick wool socks. She held me at arm's length and looked me over.

"You look wonderful." She beamed. "My God, you've grown up." She shook her head. "Come in; come in."

Monica stepped aside to allow me into the large entryway, a long, narrow hall leading from it. A small beagle rubbed my leg and looked up at me with big brown eyes, its tail about to wag off.

"This is Molly."

"Hey, Molly." I bent to give the excited dog some attention, and then Monica led me through the house, showing me the antiques she'd accumulated over the years and her prized collection of candles. This was the house she had always wanted.

"You have got to meet Connie," she said, tugging me by the arm up the stairs. As we got closer to the third floor, I could hear hammering. "Honey?" she called out, leading me through a maze of rooms and doors until we finally ended up in a well-lit room filled with windows. A woman was at the far end, up on a ladder, working a nail into the rafters. "Connie?" Monica said, but the woman obviously didn't hear. "Connie!"

"What?" The woman jerked in surprise, nearly tumbling from the ladder. She put her hand to her chest and glared at Monica. "Are you trying to kill me?"

"Sorry, babe. I want you to meet someone. Connie, this is Emily Thomas. Emily, my partner Connie."

I smiled, glad to meet the woman who had finally given my old friend what she'd always wanted: love and a stable home.

"Emily. Hi." Connie stepped down from the ladder, wiping her hands on her paint-stained pants. "Sorry about the mess. We're remodeling." She smiled, extending her hand.

"Not a problem."

"I certainly wish we were meeting under better circumstances, but I'm glad to meet you all the same," she said, covering our joined hands with her other one.

"Same here." She had deep blue eyes. Kind eyes. Her hair, which was swept back into a messy ponytail and had specks of white paint in it, was a deep blonde color, almost butterscotch. She was a simple-looking woman, but beautiful in that simplicity, and I immediately pegged her as a person with a good heart.

"So where's Rebecca?" Monica asked.

"She stayed at the house to baby-sit. She just adores kids, and Billy and Nina jumped at the opportunity."

"Well, let's go downstairs and you can tell us all about life in the Big Apple."

~ ~ ~ ~ ~

I stood from the stack of files on the floor and walked over to the window, looking out at the dark street and the single streetlight that illuminated part of the front yard. I crossed my arms over my chest and leaned my shoulder against the wall. "Emily?" I heard quietly from the room behind me.

"Hmm?" I asked absently, my mind far away.

"You okay, hon?"

I could hear the concern in Monica's voice. "Yeah. Just thinking."

"About?"

About what, indeed. I watched as two boys raced down the street, lit for just a second beneath the orange glow of the streetlight, then they disappeared, leaving only the echo of their laughter in the still night air. I tried to focus my thoughts, to get them in order so they'd make some sort of sense to my friend. They made absolutely no sense to me. I turned away from the window. "I'm so confused, Monica," I said quietly, my gaze locked on the coffee table.

"About?"

Her voice was soft and encouraging. "Remember last week, when we ran into Beth?" She nodded. I turned back to the window, staring at my reflection in the glass, not wanting to see her face as I told my story. My eyes tracked to the west as a large bolt of lightning lit the night sky, briefly transforming night into day and making my reflection disappear for just a moment. "How can..." I stopped, trying to find the words. "How can you miss something you never had?" I stared into the reflection of my own eyes, eyes that were transparent to me now. I wondered if I had always been that transparent. Had I known what I wanted all along, but was just never strong enough to grab it?

"What do you mean?"

What did I mean? "Beth." I spoke her name almost like a prayer. "When you two were talking that day on the street, I was jealous. And that's not the first time those two have been in the same sentence — Beth and jealousy. As I watched her talk to you, I realized the word 'Monica' had to be added to that sentence, too." I didn't dare look at her, terrified of the implications of that admission. "I was scared. I am scared."

"Of what, Emily?"

I still did not turn around, but I was able to make out the hazy reflection of Monica's face behind me. I had gotten myself in this deep, might as well finish it. I would be leaving for school soon anyway. "Of losing either one of you. To each other." I smiled ruefully. "Silly, huh?" I finally garnered the courage to turn and face my friend. She had a look of understanding on her face. I shrugged in defeat. "I don't understand this, Monica."

She smiled sympathetically. "You're so young, Emily. You have no idea how much you remind me of myself ten years ago: so ambitious, intelligent, yet utterly confused and blind.

I once asked myself how I could be so smart and yet so dumb at the same time." She took a step toward me. "Emily, go to Beth. She is where your heart really lies. You look up to me, see what you want to be; don't confuse that with something it isn't."

I could feel the sting of emotions behind my eyes. "What if it's too late?"

She reached out her hand and placed it upon my cheek. "You'll never know until you try. You've managed to get yourself this far, to figure out this much. Don't stop now."

Later that night, I lay in bed, staring at the dark ceiling and listening to the distant thunder that continued to rumble deep in the night sky. I held Ruffles to me, needing to cling to something that was a reminder of who I really was, of who I thought I was, and of who I pretended to be. Ruffles had been through it all, had seen all the changes. He'd seen all my wishes, dreams, and disappointments. If he had the capability, he would probably know me better than I knew myself. I released my grip and turned the bear until he was sitting on my stomach, his familiar worn face opposite mine.

"What do I do, Ruffles?" I ran a finger over the tiny line of stitching where he had ripped once and been sewn back together for a teary-eyed five year old. "I wish you could talk, fella." With a sigh, I pulled him back to me and looked at my closet doors where Bonnie Tyler and Olivia Newton-John smiled at me. Their features, frozen in the pictured poses, were as familiar to me as my own, but they somehow seemed more beautiful that night. Olivia's big hazel eyes and innocent smile called out to me. I could hear her voice inside my head singing "Hopelessly Devoted To You," and I chuckled low in my throat at the irony of that. "What do I do, girls? Should I go after her?"

My thoughts, never far from her lately, returned once again to Beth. Why was I only seeing it now, rather than when we were kids? I knew deep in my gut Beth had always known what I had been purposely blind to. Her heart had always been in it, and I realized at that moment just how badly I must have hurt her so many times. Why had she always come back? Why hadn't she run away from me? Then I realized, she had run. I kept trying to draw her back. She had been happy with Casey, spreading her wings and learning about who and what she was from someone who would accept her for who and what she was. Just Beth. No pressures, no expectations. And I loved her for that. I could finally admit to myself that I had always loved her.

Monica gave me the day off, and I stood in front of my full-length mirror dressed only in a towel, staring at my reflection. I studied my face, my eyes, and my hair. My skin was clear; the summer tan still visible. My body, though short, was well-proportioned and compact, with narrow hips and full breasts. Slowly I opened the towel, staring at what lay beneath. Pleased with what I saw there, I dropped the towel and began to get dressed. I took special care in what I wore that day, wanting colors that would bring out my eyes and the golden tones of my hair. I pulled tight cut-offs up freshly shaved legs and struggled into a snug-fitting baby-doll tank, leaving just the barest hint of my stomach showing. I kept a careful eye out for any imperfection as I put myself together. I was ready. Ready to finally tell Beth how I felt, what I wanted.

The Rogers Theater was in the center of town, an old two-story building that had once been a library. The sculpted molding around the edges and the Roman columns gave it a historic feel. My stomach in my throat, I walked up the long staircase. The theater was kept dark, the whir of fans filling the near silent space. I looked around, trying to find anyone helpful. Or just anyone at all, for that matter. In the auditorium, the house lights were off completely to keep down the heat level, the lights on the stage making the actors feel like fast food as it was. I stood in the back and watched the rehearsal for a moment, but it didn't involve Beth and she was why I was there. I descended the long slanted aisle toward the stage, looking for someone who wasn't busy. A woman sat in the front row, her legs stretched out before her, her eyes glued to the stage. I stopped a few feet away and cleared my throat. She glanced at me and raised impatient brows. "Hi," I said. "Um, have you seen Beth Sayers?"

"Yeah," she said, turning her eyes back to the stage.

"You have seen her?"

"Yeah, several times."

I rolled my eyes. "Where is she?" I tried to keep the impatience out of my voice. Without giving me a second glance, she waved her arm behind her, pointing in the general direction of the back of the auditorium. I hurried in that direction, not sure where to look, but figuring it to be a starting place.

Along the back wall, past the window of the raised lighting booth, there was an exit sign. I pushed the door open and found myself in a long cinderblock hallway with harsh, fluorescent lighting. It was quite an abrupt change from the darkness of the theater. I squinted for a moment until my eyes could adjust. When they did, I stopped dead in my tracks.

Toward the end of the hall were two women. One was pushed against the lime-painted wall, the other pressed up against her. The one against the wall had short, fiery red hair, and the other was Beth. I watched as they smiled at each other, engrossed in a conversation too low for me to hear, and then they kissed, long and deep. The redhead had wandering hands, and she slipped one beneath Beth's shirt and one into her hair. Beth pulled the woman to her, her hands fastening to the woman's rear end.

I was speechless, frozen to the spot and wanting nothing more than to find a hole, crawl in, and never come out again. I felt like such a fool. I quietly turned, wanting to slink away without Beth ever having known I was there.

"Em?"

I cringed, stopping just short of the door. I closed my eyes, took a deep breath, and pivoted to face them. Beth had disentangled herself from the redhead and had taken a couple steps in my direction. I looked at her, unable to say anything. She smiled in confusion and took another step.

"What are you doing here?"

Still leaning against the wall, the redhead watched me with curious eyes. Beth's question hung heavy in the air.

"I, well, I...um...I saw you were in the play, and so I wanted to come by and, well, I wanted to tell you...to..." My mind was a mess, and the evidence of that was starting to flow out my mouth. I stopped myself, took another deep breath, and then looked into her eyes again. She was confused, and I couldn't tell if she was also amused or annoyed. "I wanted to tell you that I, well, that..." I took yet another deep breath. "I wanted to come by and say goodbye."

She blinked, taken aback. "Goodbye?" She repeated the word, tasting it on her tongue.

"Yes," I said, my heart breaking. "I'm leaving for Boulder on Saturday, and I wanted to wish you luck on your play," I glanced at the redhead, "...and everything."

Beth smiled slightly, but I couldn't read her at all. She had totally blocked herself off to me. I had never hit a brick wall with Beth and found it to be extremely disconcerting.

"Oh," she said quietly. "I'm glad you did. Good luck to you, too." I smiled weakly and nodded, turning again toward the door. "Em?" I glanced at her over my shoulder. "Don't I even rate a hug?"

I felt my chest expand suddenly, my emotions threatening to explode both in relief and in regret. I walked toward her and she met me halfway, reaching for me and pulling me to her in a bone-crushing embrace. I wrapped my arms around her neck, as hers slid around my waist. I could feel her breath against my skin, her body against mine, and my eyes closed against the tremendous sense of loss I felt already, even with her in my arms. Her hand moved up to cup the back of my head, and she placed the softest kiss against the side of my neck before she slowly released me. She smiled at me, the old Beth, the Beth I knew inside and out; then, without a word, she let me go and walked back to the redhead.

I wanted to watch her as long as I could, but my feet had other ideas. Before I realized it, I was out on the sidewalk heading for my Jeep. I sat behind the steering wheel, my hand on my chest, which continued to expand until I thought it would burst. Then I grabbed the wheel in a death-grip as my emotions exploded, and the overflow slipped from my eyes to soak through the thin material of my shirt, a tiny spot that got bigger and bigger as the flood kept coming.

"I never thought I knew what love could be, but now I find out." Blue eyes stared in wonder, eyes that were full of life and passion. "I was such a fool, and I pray that you can forgive me. Someday." I shot to my feet, my hands stinging as I clapped, my heart in my throat, and tears in my eyes. The curtains closed, and I felt the impact of Beth's last words hit my heart yet again. She had touched me, and as I looked around, I could see that I wasn't the only one. The curtains opened again for the cast curtain calls. Beth finally came out, her smile wide and satisfied. It had always amazed me that no matter how many plays she performed in, Beth never lost that look of wonderment and awe. Each time, it was as though she realized for the first time that she could evoke a strong reaction from a group of total strangers.

Wanting to beat the crowd, I left my aisle seat and exited the theater. The warm summer night air hit my face with a soft, comforting touch, drying the trails on my cheeks. I had wanted to see Beth on stage just once more. She was as stunning as ever, and I was gratified to see that she just kept getting better. I felt very sad then, my heart heavy, as I sat behind the wheel of my Jeep. Just two days prior I had sat in that very place, crying for all the what-ifs and the missed chances. They were lost forever, and I just had to learn to accept it. Beth had waited as long as she could for me, but I couldn't expect her to put her life on hold forever. I had nobody but myself to blame.

~ ~ ~ ~ ~

Chapter Eighteen

I visited with Monica and Connie for a couple of hours, catching up on their lives and sharing with them details about Rebecca's and mine. During a lull in the conversation, I couldn't help thinking about Beth's funeral the next day. I knew it was going to be extremely difficult, and part of me dreaded it deeply.

"Emily, walk with me," Monica said finally, dragging me from my thoughts. I looked up at her, and without a word I set my coffee cup aside and stood. "Hang on. Be right back." She disappeared up the stairs as I pulled on my coat. Moments later, Monica returned, and I followed my friend as she led the way to the front door after gently kissing Connie. We stepped into the late afternoon, the air crisp and much colder than when I'd arrived earlier in the day.

"I sure hope it doesn't snow," Monica said as we walked along the sidewalk.

"Me, too."

"I'm so glad you came, Emily." She smiled at me and shoved her hands into the pockets of her jacket.

"I am, too. This has been a tough trip, though." I knew I could tell her what was on my mind, how I really felt about things. She would not judge me; she never had. "I should have come back a long time ago, Monica. It was selfish and pretentious of me not to. I see that now."

"Don't be too hard on yourself."

"No, Monica. I've never even met my brother's kids!" I stopped her with a hand on her arm. She looked at me with sympathetic eyes. "What kind of a sister does that make me? What kind of an aunt?"

"A very busy one."

"That's a good excuse; however, I'm afraid it's grown old and thin."

"Sometimes we can get our priorities all messed up and backward. It happens to the best of us." We were both quiet as we continued to walk for a while. "Beth came to see me last year, Emily. She came home."

"I know. She told me," I almost whispered.

"She gave me something for you."

"What?" I asked, my voice revealing my surprise. Monica stopped, unzipped her jacket a bit, and reached inside to pull out an envelope. She handed it to me, and numbly I took it. I turned it over in my hands, seeing my name scrawled on the front in Beth's typical large, bold writing. It simply read *To Em*. I could only stare, not sure what to do. I knew I didn't want to open it then. I was not ready.

"Are you okay?" I heard whispered near my ear. I nodded, unable to speak for fear I might choke on whatever I'd say.

~ ~ ~ ~ ~

We closed the office early in honor of my leaving the next day. Monica wanted to do something special for me, but I had to choose what it was.

"I told you, Emily, it's your choice," she said for the tenth time.

I shut the blinds around the office, while she locked her desk and threw some papers into her briefcase. I drew my brows, frustrated. I didn't know what I wanted to do. There really weren't any good movies playing that I hadn't already seen with her, and I wasn't hungry. Suddenly an idea hit me, and I turned to her, my hand on my hip and my head cocked to the side in curiosity. "Would you take me to that place?"

Monica looked up, one brow raised. "Care to be a little more specific?"

"That one place, that bar."

She hesitated. "You mean Campy's?" I nodded. "Oh, Emily, I don't know." I walked over to her, leaned on the desk, and gave her my most beseeching look. She grinned and rolled her eyes. "What's with the puppy-dog eyes?"

"I want to go," I said simply.

"You're too young. That *is* a bar, Emily."

"Oh, come on, Monica. Don't try to tell me that you can't get me in."

She crossed her arms over her chest and chewed on one side of her lip. Finally, she nodded her decision. "Okay. We'll go to Campy's."

As I dressed, I thought of our destination. It hadn't occurred to me while I was there the first time what kind of bar Campy's was, but I figured it out later. I had heard of places like that before, of course, but I had never paid any attention to things like that. I felt a surge of energy; my curiosity about it would soon be satisfied. What the hell, I was out of Pueblo soon anyway.

I decided on conservative attire: loose-fitting blue jeans and a T-shirt. At first, I tried pulling my hair into a ponytail, but when I saw myself in the mirror, I looked like I was twelve. Instead, I combed it down around my shoulders. That helped a bit; I looked at least fifteen. I sighed and sat on my bed to put on my shoes. I wondered if Beth had ever been to Campy's. Part of me, a large part actually, wished she were going with us. Or with me. I missed her so much. I'd seen her twice in the past couple weeks, after not having seen her at all for seven months, and I was craving something only she could give me. I knew it was crazy of me to wish for something that was never going to happen. I was usually far too logical for that. But my feelings for Beth seemed to defy logic. I wondered if the pretty redhead from the theater was her girl-friend. Had she been another actress? I didn't recall seeing her in the play. Maybe she was just a fan. Like me.

"Okay. You're sure about this?" Monica asked as we sat in her Cherokee outside of the bustling Campy's. I stared at the building at the end of the parking lot, listening as the heavy beat of music pounded out the open door. I nodded. "Okay. Let's go."

Monica had to do some pretty fast talking to the bouncer so I could get in. My eyes absorbed everything as we walked through the door. It certainly looked different than it had when I'd been there the first time. The air was filled with a foggy glow as the thousands of twinkling lights caught ciga-rette smoke. It also seemed to vibrate with the beat from the music, which was Motley Crüe, the heavy guitar and vocals almost deafening. Faces were hard to distinguish in the red hue of the place, but I could see tables jam-packed with crowds of people who were talking, drinking, and laughing. The patrons were mostly women, but there were a few men wandering around, too.

"Do you want something to drink?" Monica asked, leaning in close so I could hear above the noise. "*Non*-alcoholic," she said pointedly.

I shrugged innocently. "What? A Coke?"

She smiled and headed toward the bar. I tried to follow, but ran smack into someone or vice versa. Startled, I looked up to see short, curly blonde hair and half-lidded brown eyes.

"In a hurry?" Lee asked.

"Sorry."

She shrugged bare shoulders and looked at Monica who stood at the bar. "What're you two doing here?" she asked.

"I'm leaving for school tomorrow, so I wanted to check the place out. When it was open." I don't know why I was bother-ing to explain things to her. She nodded and walked away, and I stared after her, shaking my head. What a strange woman.

"What?" I turned to discover Monica standing next to me, searching to see what had caught my attention and caused my frown. I nodded with my head toward the table where Lee now sat with a large group of women. "Oh. I'm not surprised. She's here all the time. That was part of the problem."

I turned to her, curious. "Part of the problem?" Then it dawned on me, making me want to whack myself in the forehead. "You two were together?" I looked back to the blonde with new understanding. "So you are, well, into...this?" I asked, my hand out to include the whole room.

"Have been for almost ten years now." She smiled. "Come on." She walked toward an empty table in a corner. We sat, me with my Coke and Monica with her beer, which I eyed. "You like beer?" she asked, taking a sip.

I scrunched up my face and shook my head. "Tastes like carbonated horse piss."

She set the bottle down and threw her head back in a howl of laughter. "Something you've tried recently?" I stuck my tongue out at her.

"Good evening, ladies." A woman with a tray approached our table. "For you." She set another beer on a small, round cardboard coaster in front of Monica.

"Who?" my friend asked, glancing around the bar. The waitress pointed three tables down and walked away. Monica strained her neck to look behind her at the table, seeing a woman raise her glass in salute. Monica smiled and raised her beer. I watched in fascination. The woman was attractive, with long brown hair. "I'll be right back, Emily. You be okay for a sec?"

"Yeah, go ahead."

She chugged the rest of her first beer, then got to her feet, taking the new one with her. I settled back in my chair, watching as couples rose from their tables and headed toward the dance floor, which was already filled with a steady throng of dancers. It was such a new experience for me to see women together like this. They were dancing with each other, talking close, some even kissing. It was almost an overload of images, and my body was thrumming with new revelations. How had it happened so suddenly to me? It was like a brick fell out of the sky, thumping me on the back of the head. I suppose I just wasn't ready before. It is a fundamental truth that everything happens in its own time.

"You look lost." Lee was standing at the table, an amused grin on her face.

God knows I certainly felt lost at that moment, but I

didn't want the blonde to know that. I shook my head. "Just thinking."

She pulled out a chair and dropped into it, sipping from her water. "Penny for your thoughts," she said, leaning back in the chair and bringing her booted foot up to rest on the chair beside her.

I studied her for a moment, wondering what she wanted. Seeing nothing but genuine curiosity, I decided to indulge her question. "I've never been to a place like this before." I felt really young at that moment.

"Kind of interesting, isn't it? Whole new world, kid." She wiggled her brows. "Monica teaching you the ropes?"

I glared at her. "She's my boss."

"All the better."

I rolled my eyes and looked toward the dance floor.

She chuckled. "I'm just kidding, Emily. Hey, just a joke." I glanced back at her, annoyed. "Come on. Let's dance." Fear gripped me immediately, and I shook my head. "Come on, I won't bite. Let's go."

She stood, scooting her chair back under the table. I glanced over to see Monica talking to the woman who had bought her drink. When I looked back up at Lee, I saw she was patiently waiting for me. On shaky legs, I stood and slowly followed her to the dance floor. The song was fast-paced, and bodies were thrashing about. I tried to be careful not to get smacked in the face by a weaving hand or arm. Lee found us a place near the edge of the floor and began to move. I watched her for a moment before I joined her. I loved to dance and decided to just let go. The blonde smiled and I returned it. Maybe this wasn't so bad.

The song ended, and Cyndi Lauper's "Girls Just Wanna Have Fun" began. I giggled as Lee sang along, her voice often getting lost in the loud volume of the music, her movement wild and silly to match the song. I was having a ball until I turned around and noticed Monica sitting at our table. She was watching us, an unreadable look on her face. Lee noticed where my attention had gone and turned back to me.

"She tell you we used to date?" she asked, moving a bit closer to be heard above the beat. I nodded. "What did she tell you?"

"Not much." Part of me wanted to ask questions, but then I thought better of it. Any questions I asked should be directed at Monica, not at her ex.

"We lived together," she continued. I remained silent, hoping she'd tell me more. "For just over a year." She turned, grinding with a friend of hers who danced next to us. I watched them as they laughed and hugged each other. Lee turned back and inched her way to me, until she was behind me, where she placed her hands on the sides of my thighs and hunched down, taking me with her, her front grinding into my rear end. I wasn't sure what to do, but I did realize that, despite my discomfort, I was getting turned on. Dismayed, I scooted away from her, and when I turned to face her, I found her grinning at me.

"Why'd you break up?" I asked, just this side of sarcasm.

"I like to have too much fun," she said with a shrug. I couldn't believe she was so nonchalant about it. Looking at Monica, I saw she was still staring at us, the slightest pained expression on her face. "But..." I turned my attention back to Lee. She had dropped the careless smile and was watching Monica. "I do have my regrets." I was surprised at the wistful tone in her voice. The blonde seemed to shake herself out of her reverie. "Come outside and have a smoke with me."

"I don't smoke."

"Well, I do. Come on."

I followed Lee off the dance floor and out the front door of the club. She walked us over to a large Ford, yanked down the tailgate, and hopped onto it. I did the same, our legs dangling back and forth. Lee removed a pack of Marlboros from her shirt pocket and stuck a slim, white cigarette into her mouth. She offered me the pack.

"You sure?" she asked when I shook my head. With a shrug, she stuck the pack back into her shirt, taking out a lighter and flicking the wheel to ignite the small, yellow flame. I stared into the night as she took a deep drag, expelling the smoke from her nose and mouth with a sigh. "Gets so crowded in there." She placed her hands on the cool metal of the gate on either side of her legs.

"You come here a lot?" I asked, glancing at her.

She nodded, taking another drag. "Few times a week."

"Don't you work?" I asked, incredulous.

She chuckled. "Sure do. This is how I relax." To me this seemed far more stressful than relaxing, but to each her own. "So, you like working for Monica?" That seemed safe enough territory, so I nodded. "She a good boss?" Again, I nodded. "Good." She took another long drag, staring at the cars that drove by on the highway. "She seeing anyone?"

I fidgeted, not at all comfortable with the question. "I really don't think that's any of our business, Lee."

"Fair enough. I'm sorry. Don't mean to get you involved."

"S'okay." I gave her a small smile, because I understood. If I had run into that little redhead who had been with Beth at the theater, I would have picked her brain, too. *Does she talk about me? Does she think about me? Does she miss me?* All questions that I would probably never know the answers to. My head drooped slightly as I thought about the ramifications of those thoughts.

"You okay, kid?"

I glanced over at Lee, who was studying me. "Yeah."

"You really are new to this world, aren't you?"

Was it stamped on my forehead? I couldn't help but wonder if there was some sort of rite of passage I was supposed to take. Was "this world" like its own community? Could I just continue to be myself? It was all very confusing. I sighed. "Yes."

"Thought so. Tell your folks, yet? I mean, I assume you still live with them."

I stared at her. *Tell my folks?* It hadn't even occurred to me. Suddenly I was mortified. *What would they say? How would they react? Did I have to tell them?* Maybe they didn't need to know. After all, I was no different than I had been all my life. I shook my head.

"Yeah, it's tough to do." She blew a puff of smoke into the dark sky, watching as it got lost above the reach of the parking lot lights. "You know, my mother kicked me out when I told her." She glanced at me from the corner of her eye and grinned at my look of shock, a small dimple playing near her mouth. "Sorry. Guess that's not the kind of thing you need to hear." She dropped the cigarette to the ground, reaching down with her booted foot to crush the butt into the gravel. She stared up at the sky, so I did the same. A star fell across to our right. Lee pointed at it. "See that? Make a wish, kid. Hope it sticks."

~ ~ ~ ~ ~

I couldn't remember the wish I had made that night sitting on Lee's tailgate, but I thought of the moment now as I drove away from Monica and Connie's house. The envelope lay on the passenger seat of the Camry. What did Beth have to say? I stopped at a red light and stared straight ahead, my hands on the wheel, thumbs caressing the leather. I looked at the letter again and then snatched it up. I saw only my name, and I traced my fingertip over the bold writing, a small smile playing across my lips. *Just like Beth — bold but solid.* The light turned green, so I laid down the envelope and drove on. To distract myself from the thing I was so obviously not ready to face, I continued my reminiscence about my final night as a full-time residence of Pueblo.

~ ~ ~ ~ ~

"So, what did Lee have to say?"

I was sitting in the passenger seat of Monica's Cherokee dwelling — almost to the point of obsession — about the idea of breaking the news of my sexual leanings to my parents. I blinked twice as it registered just what she asked me. "Oh, ah, not much. Just talked about when she was younger. Her mother. That sort of thing."

"Yeah. You know the way Beth and her mom used to fight?" She didn't wait for a response. "That was Lee and Ann all over again. God, night and day." She shook her head sadly.

"You remember Beth, then?" I asked, trying to hide my surprise with nonchalance.

She nodded and grinned at me. "Yeah. I do. I didn't pay much attention to you guys growing up, but when I saw her the other day, I remembered her. Poor kid."

"Beth's not a kid," I pouted. "And neither am I." I glanced out the side window. At the bar, I had hoped Monica would ask me to dance with her, and I had felt left out when she spent most of her time with that other woman. After Lee had finished her cigarette, she had wished me good night and good luck and headed home. Monica was nowhere in sight when I went back to our table, and I had felt young and vulnerable sitting there alone.

Monica didn't immediately respond to my childish retort, but I could feel her eyes on me. "Okay, Emily. What's wrong? Are you mad because I talked to Arlene?"

"Who?" I asked, knowing full well whom she meant. I was feeling the need to be difficult.

"The woman who bought me the beer?" Monica's voice dripped with sarcasm.

I tried to hide a slight smile, but failed miserably. She saw right through my brooding and refused to play along. I could never stay mad at her long anyway. "Actually, I just felt really alone," I muttered.

Monica pulled into her driveway, set the brake, and turned off the engine. I was surprised to see she had taken us to her house. It was late, and I had wanted to get an early start the next morning. I turned to her, and she read the obvious question in my eyes.

"I want to give you a going away gift. Come on." She opened her door. "I'm sorry about the bar, Emily. Really I am. I saw you talking to Lee, so I figured you didn't want me around. I mean, I got you in, the rest was up to you." She spoke quietly as she searched for the right key on her ring.

I put my hand on her arm. "Monica, why did you think that? I wanted to go there, yes, but I wanted to go with you." Her face brightened, but she said nothing, so I continued. "You're such a good friend and so much fun to be with." She smiled shyly and turned back to the door, holding it open for me. "You know, Lee brought up a really good point tonight; one I hadn't thought of."

"What's that?" Monica asked absently as she knelt in front of her stereo, adjusting the dial until she stopped at a station playing Laura Branigan's "Gloria". "Oh, love this song." She moved to the couch and took a seat, kicking off her shoes with a contented sigh.

"My parents." I sat in the chair across from her. Monica glanced at me under her bangs, clearly confused. "Telling them? About me?" I said.

"Oh." She took an audible breath and sat back against the soft, green material. "Well, you could *not* tell them, I suppose." She chuckled. "I'm sure that would go over well."

I sighed. "Don't you think maybe I should wait to tell them until I'm *really* sure?"

"Aren't you?"

"I don't know!" I buried my face in my hands.

"Hey," I heard spoken quietly. I peeked an eye open to see Monica kneeling beside the chair. She looked at me with the softest smile. "Believe me, Emily. You'll know. When the time is right, you'll know." She smiled encouragement, and I tried to smile back but only managed for a millisecond. Monica stood, offering her hand to me. "Come on. Let's dance."

I was taken off guard by the sudden change of subject. "What, now? Here?"

She nodded. "Yeah. I didn't get to dance with you at Campy's."

I no longer felt like dancing, but I took her hand and followed her to the middle of her living room, where she turned to face me, letting go of my hand. A fast song by Def Leppard played, and we began to dance, laughing as we got into it and each tried to outdo the other. She began to twist, her arms tucked into her sides and her knees together as she got lower and lower.

I stopped, my hands on my hips. "How the hell can you twist to this?"

She grinned. "All's fair in love and rock and roll." Her voice was breathy from the exertion.

"Um, isn't that love and war? Oomph!"

My head flew back as she suddenly pulled me to her, sliding one of her hands around my lower back and taking my hand with her other. She began to hum along to the fast beat of the music as she led me around the limited space. When she reached the wall of the room, she twirled me under her arm, then led me back in the other direction. I could not stop giggling when she tried to dip me, managing only to drop me on the floor. She helped me up, and we both paused to get our breath back as we laughed. God, it felt so good to laugh. Monica could always make me do so.

"Oh. Oh, yeah. Now here is a song to dance to," she said with a wistful smile as the beginning chords to Foreigner's "I Want To Know What Love Is" began. "Come here." I felt a bit strange, but walked to her anyway. She grabbed me, and we settled into the same position as before, her hand on my back, mine on her shoulder, and our other hands joined. She set a slow pace, staying with the song, and began to talk softly. "This used to be our song, Lee and mine."

"We can stop if—"

"No." She smiled sadly. "No. That's over now. I really thought we had something special, though. Lee just liked to have a bit too much fun."

"That's what she said."

Monica looked into my eyes for a moment, trying to read me. "Did you two talk about me? About her and me?"

"A little. Nothing major. She just told me that — the too-much-fun thing." Monica nodded acknowledgment and pulled me closer, surprising me when she laid her head on my shoulder. I glanced around the room, not sure what I was supposed to do now that I was leading. I just kept us moving.

"I really wanted to dance with you tonight," I heard muttered near my ear. "I'm sorry."

"That's okay." I expelled a small nervous laugh. "I knew you were busy."

I was lying, of course. The truth was that the main reason I had wanted to go in the first place was to dance with Monica. She had been such a good friend, invaluable in helping me prepare for college and what I would face later on in law school. I would truly miss her, and I told her so.

She lifted her head from my shoulder, a smile across her lips. "Really? I'll miss you, too. After all, who will I get to file for me?" I gave her a dirty look, which earned me a chuckle. "Just kidding. Though I will miss you, Emily."

Her voice softened and she looked into my eyes. I returned her gaze, studying her dark irises. I felt butterflies attack my insides, as if they might try to fly right out of my chest to be free. When her head inclined just the barest inch, it hit me. She was going to kiss me. My heart began to pound, my stomach doing a series of somersaults. I tried to steady my breathing, to ready myself for it. Beth was the only woman I had ever kissed like *that*. My God. What should I do? Say? Then I was ripped out of my fantasy as Monica backed away, her eyes wide with surprise.

"Uh," she stumbled. "It's getting late, and ah..." She took several steps back from me. "I need to give you your gifts." That said, she quickly disappeared into the back of the house.

I stood where I was for a moment, stunned into silence, nailed to the spot. I could still feel her breath against my face; the urgency had washed off her in waves, flowing straight into me. I swallowed and tried to get my still-thrumming body under control.

"Okay." My head shot up when I heard Monica's voice coming from down the hall. She held two wrapped packages in her hands. "Here ya go."

I shook myself out of my daze and put a smile upon my face. I took the smaller package first — wanting to save the larger one — and walked to the couch, where I ripped the colorful paper that read *Good Luck* in silver letters all over it. It was a hand-held tape recorder.

"Trust me. You'll need that."

I smiled my thanks and set it next to me on the couch. I could tell as I hefted the second gift that it was a book of some sort and I tore into the paper with gusto. It was a brown leather book with pages edged in gold. The gilded lettering on the front revealed it to be the first volume of a set of law books.

"Um, thanks. Should I get the others in the set from the library?"

"No. I'm giving you the whole set. I just didn't feel like wrapping a million books, thank you."

I smiled, truly astonished. "Monica." I knew a set of these books were ridiculously expensive. "Why...you shouldn't...wow."

She chuckled. "They're used. My mother gave these to me when I went to college. Some of it might be a little dated, but you can always look up the new stuff in the law library."

"My God. Thank you." I smiled from ear to ear. I was speechless. I jumped off the couch, book still in hand, and ran to her, wrapping my unburdened arm around her neck.

"Whoa!" she exclaimed as I nearly knocked her to the ground.

"Thank you, thank you, thank you."

She rubbed my back, hugging me tight. "You're welcome.

Just do me proud, okay?" She pulled back from me, holding me at arm's length and looking deep into my eyes. "I really am going to miss you, Emily."

"Me, too," I said, feeling the tears stinging at the back of my eyes. Why was it that the women I most cared about seemed to disappear from my life before I was ready?

~ ~ ~ ~ ~

Chapter Nineteen

I stopped the rental car just in front of my parents' house, since Billy's truck was in the drive. I tapped my fingers on the wheel, unsure what to do. I really didn't want to go in yet. There was so much more I needed to clarify in my mind, so much more history I needed to dig through before I could confront the next day. I needed to face Beth with understanding and commemoration.

Making my decision, I headed for the park. I zipped my heavy winter coat against the bitter cold, which still blew my hair around my face. I tucked my hands into my pockets and veered toward the swings. I had to chuckle to myself at how small everything felt to me. The swings had never seemed to sit that low to the ground, and surely these black rubber seats used to be wider than this?

I pushed off with my booted feet, the wind picking up slightly as I gained altitude. The gray sky moved closer, then farther away in turn. Maybe if I just reached out, I could touch it. I smiled as I did just that, my gloved hand reaching for something so deceptively close and yet unattainable. How many such things had I reached for in my past? Anyone examining my life at face value might find me admirable and accomplished; sitting here in the city of my youth, I felt like a fraud. The people and the things from which I'd fled so many years before surrounded me, but back then I never acknowledged them. I couldn't wait to get out of this city; I had planned to never look back.

~ ~ ~ ~ ~

The morning sun rushed in at me, making me squeeze my tortured eyes shut. I had stayed at Monica's far too late the night before. I opened one eye and looked at the clock, only to groan at the time. Damn. I had wanted to be on my way out of the city first thing. Finally, with a sigh, I rolled over and sat up, rubbing my eyes. When I opened them again and looked around, it suddenly occurred to me that the previous night had been the last I would spend in this room for quite a while. The realization hit me in the stomach. I glanced over to the corner and saw my bags, packed and ready to go. *Ready for me to go.* My posters were still hanging where they'd been for a few years, displaying the same faces that had greeted me every single morning, the last faces I had seen every single night. And then there was my unicorn collection, all but forgotten over the past few years.

I stood and stretched my arms over my head with a half-yawn, half-groan. I needed to get myself together, and the shower seemed a good place to start.

Monica had asked me to stop by her home to pick up the books on my way out of town. I hoped I would have space for them in my dorm room. Hell, I hoped they'd fit in my Jeep, which was loaded, with all my worldly possessions crammed into every available space. I had only to extricate myself from my parents and I could get underway. To this end, I stood in the living room, my mother and father flanking me on either side.

"You sure you don't want us to go with you, honey?" my mom asked, her shaky voice just on this side of all-out bawling.

I shook my head. "I'm sure. You guys have more important things to do than waste three hours driving to Boulder with me."

"Well, you know it's really no trouble," my father chimed in.

I smiled and hugged him. "Thanks, Dad. I'll be fine." Even as I said that, I had to wonder if *they* would be. I pulled away from him and kissed his cheek. He smiled at me, saying with his expressive eyes all that he couldn't put into words. I nodded, our silent communication complete. I turned to my mother, knowing I had to stay strong for her. She was already battling her emotions, and I knew if mine slipped even just a little, that would be it, and she'd be a puddle.

"I love you, Mom." I embraced her tightly, and I felt her body jerk as she swallowed a sob. My own tears began to burn, but I pulled away with a solid, if forced, smile on my lips. "I'll be home for Christmas before you know it," I said with exaggerated enthusiasm. My parents nodded silently. After one more round of hugs, I climbed into my Jeep.

Monica met me at the door with a cup of coffee in her hand. "Morning."

"God, how can you drink that stuff?"

She chuckled. "Give it time, you'll be downing it like it's water." She stepped away from the door, allowing me to enter. "Come on in, grumpy." I hissed at her and she laughed. "Your books are in the spare bedroom."

Together we managed to load the three boxes into my Jeep, and it was time for me to go. We stood by Monica's front door, neither of us wanting to say goodbye. Finally, she smiled and grabbed me for a hug.

"Good luck, Emily. I know you'll do well," she said into my hair. I nodded, holding her just as tight, my eyes closed. She gently pulled away and looked at me. "I have one more gift for you," she said quietly. I stared at her, the butterflies from the night before returning to my stomach. She smiled softly, seeming to sense my nervousness. She placed a hand on either side of my face and took a step closer. "I don't think you give yourself enough credit, Emily." I could only stare. "I think you are ready. Whenever you doubt yourself, think of this." She moved in, and my eyes closed instinctively as she touched my lips softly with her own. Her kiss was simple but incredibly pleasant. When she drew back from me, my eyes opened to find her smiling. "Good luck, Emily. I'll miss you."

I pressed my fingers to my lips as I drove the long, straight highway that would take me to college. I could still feel Monica's kiss, soft and tender. Maybe she was right, and I was ready. My thoughts inevitably turned to Beth. I had replayed the scene at the theater in my mind so many times. Each time it turned out differently. My favorite scenario was one where she turned to me, her back to the redhead, and smiled that cocky little smile of hers as she told me she was glad I had finally come to my senses. Then she took me into her arms, just as she had the redhead, and it had been her lips against mine, not Monica's. She kissed me the way she had the day of my aunt's funeral — a deep kiss, filled with passion and love.

Did Beth love me? The way I loved her? Or thought I did, anyway. I had been so confused at that time; I didn't know much of anything. And, in all honesty, I had been glad to head off to Boulder, to head anywhere that was away from Pueblo. It was too much drama, and it was too much to try to figure out at nineteen.

~ ~ ~ ~ ~

As I reflected on the past, I sat with my head resting against the cold chain, the swing just barely moving, my feet dragging in the hard dirt. Boulder and the CU campus. What an amazing time that was for me, and I hadn't even realized it until now. It was that whole hindsight thing again. I sighed, recognizing just how simple life had been then. Go to class, do homework, attempt to get enough sleep, and live off of Ramen noodles and PBJ. How hard could that be? Of course, that wasn't all there was to it. I went through a few of the normal, and even some of the "not so normal", growing pains.

~ ~ ~ ~ ~

I gripped the pen tighter between my teeth and growled when the shade fell into my hands again. "Odamit!" I exclaimed around my Bic, nearly falling backward off my chair. I recovered my balance and attempted to reach up again, my brows drawn in concentration. I wondered if any of the people walking around down below could see me standing on my desk chair in the window of my third floor dorm room, pressed so tightly against the glass I must have appeared to be kissing it. I managed to get one of the side pegs into the hole, then began a similar struggle with the other side. Sometimes it sucked to be short. With a victorious whoop, I leaned back, wiping the saliva off my chin that had squeezed out around the pen.

"Nice going."

"Ah!" I screamed, falling back against the window and jarring loose the shade, which then fell on my head, causing me to cry out in pain. I spit out the Bic and peeked from under the shade. Dana, my roommate, was lying on her bed with her hands behind her head and her legs bent and spread. She grinned at me. "Damn it, Dana!" I threw the shade to the floor. "Don't do that!"

"Oh, you are just too cute when you're mad, Embo."

"Yeah, well you should know. Lord knows you piss me off enough." I hopped down from the chair. "And don't call me Embo. How many times do I have to tell you that?" I plopped onto my own bed, scooting so my back was against the wall and my legs were hanging off the side. I was thoroughly exhausted from my efforts to hang and re-hang the shade. I got mad all over again when I realized that I would have to hang it yet *again.* "I should make you hang that thing back up, Dana."

"You can try to make me," she said, wiggling her eyebrows.

I shook my head. "Give it up. I'm not gonna sleep with you."

"Why not?" She sat up, her hands resting on her knees, and blew her long blonde bangs out of her eyes. "You just might enjoy it." Her voice was low and teasing.

I simply glared at her. "Right. That'll happen."

She lay back down with a quick raise of her eyebrows. "I know."

Dana stared up at the ceiling on which she had plastered posters of naked women. I could almost see those wheels turning. I took her in: her long legs clad in torn blue jeans; scuffed, worn sneakers; a sweater that was actually hole-free for a change. Dana had been my roomy for the past three months, and she never ceased to amaze me. I often wondered just exactly what she was doing at CU. She never went to class, never opened a book. In fact, I wasn't sure she had ever even bought a book for a class. I knew she wasn't stupid. In fact, she was far from it. She just had a little too much partying to do.

I shook my head sadly and stood. "I have a study group to go to. See you later." I grabbed my backpack from the floor by the closet and slung it over a shoulder. When I got to the door, I glanced back at her, but she had not moved. With a shrug, I left and headed across campus to the library. *Face it, Em. Your roommate is strange. Strange and obstinate.* But even so, she was cute as anything, sexy in her own unusual way.

The first day I met Dana had certainly been an adventure. I had just arrived on campus, and after many tries, had found the dorm where my room was. She was already there, her things strewn all around the room. When I opened the door, I found her sitting on her bed wearing just a pair of extremely brief underwear and a tiny bra, her legs folded Indian-style, her hands on her knees, and her eyes closed. I stopped in the doorway, my arms loaded with my stuff, and stared. I couldn't tell if I was interrupting something.

"Enter, you sexy thing," she had said, her eyes still closed.

"Excuse me?" I had taken a step into the room.

"Why certainly." She gave me a winning smile.

I wasn't sure whether to laugh or run screaming. Though Dana would prove to be a laugh a minute at times, at that moment I wondered if perhaps running would have been wiser.

"Emily? Hello, Earth to Emily?"

"Huh?" I snapped my head up, staring wide-eyed at my study partner, Katherine. She was grinning at me, a question in her eyes.

"Where'd you go?" she asked, turning the page of her bio-chemistry book.

"Sorry." I shook my head to clear it. "What were you saying?" I also turned the page in my own text, trying to figure out where we were.

"I said that you took really great notes. The ones I copied." I nodded, finally with it. "You ready for this test? I've heard it's a real bitch."

I listened as Katherine prattled on about the class, the professor, and the test. Well, I sort of listened. My mind actually wandered back to Dana. Should I just give in to her? She was certainly persistent. One night, when I had found her in a semi-serious mood, I began to ask her questions. Questions which, to my discomfort, led to her asking me on a daily basis to sleep with her. I had wanted to know what the life of a lesbian was like, what I would be in for if I turned out to be one. I thought I might be, but I just couldn't get myself to definitively admit it, not even to myself.

Dana saw different people constantly, never remaining with the same girl. I never understood that. She told me she was simply trying all the different flavors. That was way more information than I had needed, but I guess I understood. I couldn't quite decide what I wanted to do, though. I had never had sex, per se, and was very curious. I hadn't looked for anyone to date, wasn't sure I wanted to, or *who* I wanted to. Maybe it would be a good idea with Dana. Hell, I didn't know. Ideas for and against flew through my mind like smoke.

As I walked down the hall of the dorm, I stopped to get a Dr Pepper from the machine. When I opened the door to my room, I froze. Dana was lying on her bed in much the same position as when I'd left, but unlike before, she wasn't wearing a stitch of clothing. I watched, part in horror and part in wonder, as her hand moved between her legs. I could not stop my eyes from trailing up her body to her breasts, which moved up and down with her slow, easy breathing. Her breasts were small but firm, the light brown nipples erect. I was utterly transfixed and had no idea what to do. Part of me wanted to leave, yet I couldn't move.

"Hey. Was just thinking about you." I stared at her smile, suddenly seeing that mouth in an entirely different way. "You look like a deer caught in the headlights there, Embo," she said in a husky voice.

"Don't call me that." I barely recognized my voice, which was soft and deep, like from a dream. I was suddenly flooded with embarrassment. "I'm sorry. I'll go—"

"No." Dana pulled her hand away from herself and sat up. "Don't. Come here," she whispered.

Utterly bereft of thought, I dropped my backpack and walked over to her bed, sitting down next to her, my hands in my lap. I dared not look at her. The heat radiating from her body was almost scorching me.

"Don't be nervous, Emily," she said into my ear, her fingers pushing my hair back off my shoulder. She tipped my face toward her, and I finally met her eyes. They were dark with arousal, and I had to gasp at that look. She grinned. "I have, you know, been thinking about you."

"Why?" I asked, my voice stronger, but still a bit breathy.

"Because you, dear Emily, are scrumptious. I want you. I want this." She ran her fingers down my neck and dipped them just below the collar of my sweatshirt. "May I?" she asked, a small smile playing across her lips. I nodded dumbly. Her smile got wider, and she leaned in and kissed me.

I laid there, the room dark and cool in the early November night. Thanksgiving break would start in just over two weeks. I could feel Dana sleeping next to me; I was on my back and she on her side. One of her arms was draped over my stomach as she slept. I thought about what we had just done. I didn't regret it. I was glad it had happened and it certainly helped me to figure out more about myself. So much made sense to me at that moment. I was filled with a sense of clarity I had never before experienced.

Naturally, my thoughts turned to Beth. Why couldn't it have been her who kissed me like that? Touched me like that? Made me feel like that? I sighed. It had been her at one time, but I hadn't been ready. Why had we come to terms with who and what we were at such drastically different times? I sighed again and turned to my side, Dana scooting up behind me and pressing her body close. I closed my eyes and imagined it was Beth whose body was spooned against mine. I was too young for regrets, but I sure had them. Perhaps it was just time to finally let Beth go. There was nothing I could do about the past, and she had her own life back in Pueblo, filled with new people. She didn't need a bleeding heart around. I loved Beth, and I believed she loved me and always would. But all the same, things had changed, and sometimes you just couldn't change them back, no matter how badly you wanted to. It was time for me to begin anew in Boulder, to discover more of this woman Dana had helped reveal me to be.

After that night with Dana, I came into my own, wanting to see just exactly what kind of stuff I was made of. In short, I went nuts.

Dana had made it very clear to me that she was not even remotely interested in a relationship. If we happened to enjoy the occasional tumble, that was fine, but there would be nothing else. I was hurt at first, until I realized the possibilities. If neither of us had a date on a Friday night, we'd make a date with each other. We actually became very good friends, sharing intimate conversations. I guess having sex on a semi-regular basis with someone will do that. Don't get me wrong, I was not a player by any means. I stayed completely faithful to whomever I was dating. It's just that on a college campus as liberal as CU Boulder, it was tough finding women who lived by the same principle.

My first year in college flew by, and I dedicated myself to two things: the pursuit of academic excellence and the pursuit of women. I was trying to understand this attraction I had to its fullest, and I made some wonderful friends and was having a ball by the time the middle of my second year rolled around.

I had promised my friend Patty that I would help her at the spring career fair. I hated doing those, but I had been suckered into it both springs so far. I hadn't enjoyed the first one, and I hated even more that I was such a sap that I couldn't say no to this one.

"This sucks," I muttered as we sat at our designated booth. How many people in this world really feel the need to pick up brochures on accounting? I knew there were some, but they obviously decided to skip this career day. I glared at her. "We have not had one bite."

"Oh, come on. You're doing your duty to the school." She re-straightened the already straightened pile of brochures.

"I pay them a lot of money every semester. Now, *that* is doing my duty to the school." I pouted and hoped she wouldn't call me on the fact that I was attending on a scholarship. "God, wasting an entire Saturday for this. I could be studying right now." I sat back in my chair, my arms crossed over my chest.

"That doesn't sound like too much fun."

My head slowly rose and my mouth fell open. Wearing an old pair of black jeans, a tank with a flannel overshirt, and a backpack slung over one shoulder, there stood Beth.

~ ~ ~ ~ ~

Chapter Twenty

~ ~ ~ ~ ~

Beth.

I could only stare. Who would have thought?

She grinned at me, that familiar twinkle in her blue eyes. "Careful. You'll catch flies that way."

My mouth closed with an audible snap. "What are you doing here?" I finally managed. Patty looked from me to Beth and back.

"What does it look like?" she said, running her hand up the strap of her backpack. "I happened to glance through the door and see you in here." I had not yet regained my wits enough to do more than nod. She chuckled. "Listen, I can see you're busy. When do you get done? Maybe we can get some coffee?" she asked, the tiniest bit of hope sounding in her voice.

Again I nodded. "Well, I'm stuck here until five, but—"

"Hey, I can wait," she said, shrugging the pack down her arm and setting it on the table with a loud thud.

"Just go, Emily. It's not as if I'm going to get bombarded or anything."

I turned to Patty and stared. I didn't know how to react to this. I felt silly, like a child. I looked back at Beth, almost as if to reassure myself she had not disappeared. Then, out of the blue, I felt a tiny spurt of anger surge through me, taking me by surprise. The last time I had seen Beth had been at the theater when she was with that redhead. Well, at least, it was the last time she'd seen me. It all washed over me again, the hope and fear that had mixed in my chest, spurring me on to tell her that I loved her and wanted to be with her. It had seemed like the right thing to do at the time, until I saw her kissing that other woman. I had been too late. *Too late.*

And now, here she was again, and I realized how much I had missed just her presence in my life. I had vowed two years earlier to forget about her, to tie up all the loose ends and move on. She had been a big part of my past, but that was the past, the past that now stood before me, staring me in the face. And I realized it would never be possible to forget about Beth, and I had been a fool to think otherwise.

The C Ground was nearly empty. I knew from many

months of experience that this was the best time of day to go. I often retreated to the café just to get away from school, to study, or whatever. Beth followed behind me as I led the way to my usual table in the back corner. I took my regular seat, tipping my chair back against the corner where the two walls met. She sat across from me, grinning at my childish antics.

"What?" I asked, my whole body jolted as the front two legs of the chair landed solidly onto the tile. "Ow."

"Nothing. I've missed you, Em," she said, her voice low. I stared at her, my mouth open. "There you go again. You majoring in fly catching?"

"No. I guess I'm just shocked to see you here, is all. Who would have guessed?" I waved to Barney, my usual waiter, and he walked over.

"Hey, ladies." He smiled and set his sights on Beth. Barney flirted with anything in a skirt, but he was definitely barking up the wrong tree. Beth glanced at him with vacant eyes. I put my hand in front of my mouth, chewing on my lower lip as I watched.

"Yes?" Beth drawled at Barney's continued stare.

He seemed to get the drift and cleared his throat, looking over at me. "The usual, Squirt?" he asked. I glared, and then turned the glare on Beth when I heard her laugh. She sobered immediately, giving me that innocent look I had missed so much. I realized just how much I had missed everything about her.

"Call me that again, Barney, and you'll be missing a very integral part of your identity." I smiled sweetly at him.

He rolled his eyes and walked off, before turning back to our table. "I, um, forgot to get your orders."

I felt Beth's eyes on me and I looked at her, that familiar gleam in those baby blues telling me I had done well. I smiled. I had missed that silent communication, too.

People were beginning to flow into the café in earnest. The sun was going down, and Beth and I still sat across from each other. I sipped from my coffee cup, the hot fluid sliding down my throat, engulfing my stomach in heat.

Beth narrowed her eyes. "You hate that stuff."

I glanced down, confused, then it came to me what she was saying. "Never." I smiled. "Are you kidding me? I owe my sanity and my grades to this stuff." I sipped to prove my point all the more, smacking my lips together. She shook her head, one of her trademark smiles firmly in place. "So," I said, taking a bite of my cheeseburger, "after you spent that summer in Wyoming, what did you do? Where did you go? And why did you leave in the first place?"

"Well, after I left Cheyenne, I drove that old rickety pick-up back into Colorado. I went to Denver. And I left because I was sick of the place. I was tired of roaming from one place to another. When I got back to Denver it occurred to me to..." She sighed and stared toward the door, her thoughts a million miles away. "I wanted to get my life going, settle in somewhere." Her eyes turned to me. "You know I didn't graduate?" she asked, her voice quiet, almost ashamed.

I nodded. "Yeah. I know."

Her eyes drifted down, staring at the remains of her pancakes. "I'm tired of running from things, Em. I'm tired of running from me." She paused, looking as though something had just occurred to her. "Can I ask you a question?"

"Sure." I held my breath. I didn't know why I was nervous, but I was.

"You came out, didn't you?"

I stared at her, seeing those half-hooded eyes; she knew the answer to her own question, but wanted to hear what I would say. I decided not to be coy. "How did you know?"

She shrugged. "There's a confidence about you, a sense of self you didn't have before. It's like you are who you are, and you don't give a shit what anyone else says or thinks. It looks good on you."

The drive back to campus was a quiet one. I took Beth to her dorm building, which was next to mine, and we sat in the Jeep, neither of us speaking. We had spent nearly four hours at the café and had covered a lot of ground. I felt at peace with her, as though I no longer had any regrets or pain. Beth had told me the redhead at the theater had meant nothing, just a fling. She had not had any real steady relationships in the past two years; her only goal had been to keep moving. She was trying to figure out who she was and where she was headed.

"I decided school was it. I want to make something of myself," she said. I felt so much pride at that moment. She stared out the windshield. "You know why I chose CU?" She turned to me then. I shook my head. "I saw you that night in the theater. You got up before everyone else, and I saw you. You walked out through the rear exit door and out of my life."

"You saw me?" I was shocked. "But it was so dark. How could you?"

"I don't know. I think mainly I recognized the way you move, the way you walk. It was just a gut feeling, I guess."

"Yeah, I was there. I had to see the show. I've never missed a production of yours, Beth. I wasn't going to start then. Or now. You *are* in the drama department, right?" She gave me a small smile and a nod. "Of course. If that wasn't a stupid question." I smiled back, and then both of us stared out the window again. We had said all there was to say for one night, but I think neither of us wanted to be separated again. Finally, Beth sighed.

"I'm going to go. Have to be at work early in the morning."

"Okay," I said quietly, not sure where this would go. Was that it? We made our peace and now that would be all? I wanted her friendship back. I wanted her back in my life, but I didn't quite know how to say it. So I said nothing.

"Well, good talking to you. Maybe we can talk again later." Beth grabbed her pack and hopped from the Jeep, her hand still on the roll bar as she stood still for a moment. She smiled at me, then walked away.

~ ~ ~ ~ ~

I sat on the closed lid of the toilet, a towel wrapped around my body, the ends held together in my fist. I stared out the frosted-glass window above the shower, not able to see anything clearly, just the light from the morning. I knew the sky was gray. A storm was due later in the evening. That was fine by me. Perhaps a little snow would do me good. It would reflect the feelings in my heart, which felt like a lump of ice in my chest. I took a deep breath and crossed my legs at the ankles, feeling the cool porcelain of the toilet against my shower-heated skin. A small shiver passed down my spine. Tearing my eyes away from the window, I squeezed them shut, trying to stop the stinging behind my lids, the tightness in my throat. Never in my life had I thought I'd have to face such a day; never had I any clue how difficult it would be. At that moment, I wanted to find some deep, dark cave, curl up and cry. I felt my lips part, and I whispered one word.

"Beth."

Finally, I stood, unwrapped the towel, and dried my skin. I swiped a hand across the smooth surface of the mirror and was captured by my reflection. I stared at myself and willed myself to be strong; I had to be. I just wished I knew how.

I dressed slowly, fastening the last button on my silk blouse, running my hands down the front to feel the smoothness under my fingertips. I flipped my hair back over my shoulder, wanting to wear it down. Beth had always liked it down. I wore black slacks and black heels. The final touch would be the jacket that went with the suit. I could see in the mirror above the dresser that my face was pale, so I applied just the barest touch of makeup and a light lipstick. I was ready to go. Well, that is to say, I was dressed. I would never be ready to do this.

I slipped my arms through the sleeves of the jacket, picked up my purse, and moved toward the closed bedroom door. Rebecca met me in the hall just before the stairs. She looked beautiful in a black skirt suit and green silk blouse, her long red hair bound on top of her head and small ringlets falling around her face and neck. I smiled when I saw her.

"You ready?" she asked.

"As I'll ever be."

I stepped from my parents' car in the parking lot and right away saw Monica and Connie walking toward the church. The air was heavy and wet with the impending storm. Monica saw us and veered over to me.

"Hey, honey," she said, gathering me into a tight embrace. We pulled apart, and she smiled at me, everything she thought and all she wanted to say reflected in her dark eyes. I nodded, her words not necessary. "You must be Rebecca," she said, stepping over to my lover.

Rebecca smiled and grabbed Monica's outstretched hand. "Hello, Monica. Nice to meet you; though I certainly wish it were under different circumstances."

Monica patted the hand within hers. "Yes. If this one here is up to it, Connie and I would like to have you both over for dinner tonight."

Three pairs of eyes focused on me, and I looked from one to the other. I recognized sympathy and love in turn. *How could I feel so loved, yet so alone?* I truly didn't believe any of the three understood just what was going through my head. Hell, I wasn't quite sure I was completely aware of the extent of my feelings. Rather than try to explain, I just nodded, figuring it was a safe gesture.

"You ladies ready to go in?"

I turned to see my father standing just outside our little circle of women and my mother standing beside him. She reached out and grabbed my hand, pulling me with her. Rebecca followed us into the church.

The pew was cold and hard, but my body slid easily against its polished wooden surface. I sat between Rebecca and my mother, with Rebecca on my left. My mother held my hand, and Rebecca placed her hand on my knee. It appeared they both were trying to comfort me through contact. I thumbed through the little pamphlet that had been handed to me at the door. The pamphlet cover exhibited a smiling picture of Beth, probably taken a few years prior. She looked healthy, happy, and beautiful. I read the information provided about her, her theater credits and even a commercial I had not been aware of. Then I had to smile at the part about her childhood. I saw my name and what her mother had dubbed us many years before, "Trouble Twins". Lord, hadn't that been the truth.

It occurred to me that I had yet to see Nora Sayers. Scanning the crowd, I spotted her standing near the door to the sanctuary. She was talking to a good-looking man. To my surprise, I realized it was Jim Sayers. I had not seen him in years, and neither had Beth, as far as I knew. It was a fine time for him to decide to show. Standing with him was his wife, Lynn, whom I remembered from a photograph. He nodded a few times at something Mrs. Sayers said and then, with a dismissive smile, led Lynn toward a pew near the back. Mrs. Sayers watched them walk away, and then turned to make her way toward the front. *Shouldn't Beth's father be sitting up front?* I watched Beth's mother, her graying hair teased to a ridiculous height. Her red-and-black dress, mostly red, was a bit tight for her body, which had become pudgy through the middle with age. She looked tired and had on too much makeup to cover her heavily lined face. She turned and her eyes landed on me, causing her to smile, the red lipstick a bloody slash through a pale face. I smiled back wanly, nodding slightly. She sat next to a blonde woman.

I gestured over my shoulder at Monica, who sat behind me. "Who is that?" I asked, nodding toward the blonde. Monica leaned up and looked at the back of the woman's head. "I think that's Lana. She and Beth were living together when...well, they were living together." She sat back, squeezing my shoulder, leaving me to stare and wonder. A very large man approached the dais and began to sing "Ave Maria", his powerful voice filling the large space.

My throat tightened as the sound of wheels rolling along carpet, the slightest squeak foretelling their approach, drifted to my ears. I could not look, could not make myself see it. If I were to see the coffin, then it would mean I was seeing the finality of the situation. There was no end to Beth. There just couldn't be.

I stared straight ahead at the crucifix placed above the front of the church and at the large, brightly colored stained glass windows on either side. I thought back to those days in college. Those days of new discovery with Beth. My best friend. I felt a hand tighten around my own as the squeaking passed our row and moved toward the front of the church, the obvious weight keeping those wheels turning at a slow, steady pace. I could not look. Could not look. Could not.

~ ~ ~ ~ ~

I unlocked the door to the room I shared with a freshman named Candice Parker. I was surprised she wasn't home, since I couldn't recall her ever going anywhere on a Saturday night. But, perhaps she'd gone to get something to eat. Part of me was glad, because then I could relax and think without any interruptions. Another part of me was disappointed. I felt the need to talk at that moment, about life, school, Beth, or whatever. I took a deep breath, expelling it as I plopped down on my bed, extending my arms over my head and staring at the ceiling. I jumped when I heard a knock at the door. "Who is it?" I yelled.

"Me," came a muffled reply.

I rolled my eyes. "Me, who?" I was irritated and in no mood for games. I sat up, swung my legs off the bed, hurried to the door, and yanked it open. A stunned Beth stood in the hall, her mouth open as if to speak. She closed her mouth and grinned at me.

"Uh, hi," she said with a little wave. I waved back, still looking at her as though she'd lost her mind. "Um, well, it's later. Wanna talk?" I grinned and nodded as I closed the door behind me.

The campus was dark, the sporadically placed lamps not bright enough in places to break through the night. I felt perfectly safe, however, as Beth walked at my side. We had been strolling for about half an hour, each lost in our own thoughts and neither saying much. As usual, I felt no need to make frivolous conversation. With Beth, it was just a matter of *feeling*. Words were not necessary.

"It's very peaceful out here," she said finally, her voice hushed, as if she didn't want to disturb the quiet of the clear night.

I nodded. "Yeah. I used to go out walking all the time, but then last semester a girl was raped over there." I pointed off toward the library.

Beth followed my finger, her brows knit together, shaking her head. "Well, if you want to walk at night, come get me." She smiled at me.

It dawned on me that I had never told her where I lived. "Hey, how did you find me, anyway?"

She shoved her hands into the pocket of her jeans and shrugged. "I followed you in."

I shook my head again, grinning. What a goof. "I do believe you've turned into a stalker, Beth Sayers."

"Guess so." We continued to walk for a moment. "You don't mind, right?" She looked down at me, the moonlight catching in her eyes, making them seem transparent.

I smiled. "Nope."

"All right then." She stopped walking, fell to the ground.

I looked down in shock, wondering what the hell she was

doing. She sprawled on the grass, her hands behind her head and her legs crossed at the ankles, and stared into the sky with a big, goofy grin on her face. "Um, hello," I said, my hands on my hips. "What are you doing?"

"Stargazing," she said, as if it were the most natural thing in the world to just plop down in the middle of a college campus at nearly midnight and look up at the stars.

I stared at her for a moment, trying to decide if I should join her or if she'd only pop back up and tell me she was kidding. Biting my bottom lip, I decided on the former. I lowered myself to the ground next to her, resting my hands on my stomach, and stared into the sky.

"Look," she said, her voice quiet, as she pointed. "A shooting star."

"Make a wish," I said, reveling in the feeling of peace that stole over me. I glanced at her in time to see her close her eyes for a moment, her lips moving as she silently mouthed her wish. Eyes made gray by the night opened and looked over at me with a smile. She raised her brows and looked back into the sky. I heard her chuckle softly.

"You know, it's funny. When I decided to come here, I thought I'd be starting out new. Fresh. Then I run into you."

The slight smile that had been on my lips fell. I stared back at the sky. "Well, I'm sorry I ruined that new start for you, Beth." My voice was soft, but it was obvious I was trying not to let the hurt or surprise surface. I had been so happy to see her, to maybe have a chance to rebuild our lost friendship.

"No, Em. No. I mean," Beth sat up, pulling her knees to her chest and wrapping her arms around her shins.

"What I mean is that I thought I'd get here and have to start over. Meet new people, make new friends. Something I was not really looking forward to, you know?" She glanced back at me over her shoulder, her long bangs partially covering her eyes. I met her gaze but said nothing. A soft smile spread across her lips. "Here, I was, thinking I'd know no one, be alone, and I find you. My best friend."

My chest swelled. She always knew just what to say to allay any fears or worries I had.

"Heads!"

I ducked just in time to see a football whiz by my nose, the resulting wind blowing my bangs off my forehead. As the ball plowed into my books and scattered papers all over the blanket that covered the grass, I looked up, aiming to pin the person who dared interrupt my study time with a critical gaze. My green daggers met two sparkling blue eyes. "You," I growled. The blue eyes got closer until they were right across from me. Beth dropped beside me on my blanket, her shorts-clad legs crossing Indian-style, her hands on her knees. She grinned at me as she reached for her ball. "You are evil, Beth. Leave me alone." I pouted.

"Uh huh. I believe you wanted me to do that." She tossed the ball in the air from hand to hand, daring me to take it from her.

"I'm warning you, Beth," I said through clenched teeth, the ball in my peripheral vision. "I'm gonna shove that ball right up your—"

"I'd love to see you try," she challenged. Beginning to get more than a little annoyed, I raised an eyebrow at her, which caused her to cock one of her own. "Yes?" she drawled, as I bit my bottom lip, then the inside of my cheek, my brain calculating. I eyed the ball for a moment, then with lightning fast movement, I grabbed it and stood, nearly stumbling onto my face in my effort to get away before she could take it back. "You're asking for it, Em."

I stood away, tossing the ball up into the tree, only to catch it as it fell. "Really?"

"Yeah, really."

"I'm shakin' in my boots here."

"Should be." Beth stood, her legs set wide apart, her hands rubbing together.

For just a moment, I did feel a bit of fear, knowing Beth was a bunch taller than me and that much faster. "You know, I can just about smell the smoke from the wheels turning in there," I said, my voice casual, though I did not feel even remotely casual in my idle threats. I saw that brow of hers quirk again, but nothing else. I took a step back, still casually tossing the ball into the air, a little higher each time, my body ready to take off at a moment's notice. She lunged, and I screamed as I took off at breakneck speed, hearing her growl behind me as she chased, still a bit behind, but gaining with every heartbeat.

"Run, little girl. Run!" I heard chanted behind me. I couldn't help but grin as I continued to pump my short legs as fast as I possibly could, determined to give myself at least half a chance by sheer willpower alone. To no avail. I screamed again as I felt hands wrap around my waist, and I was suddenly pulled back against her, breath in my ear as she demanded, "Say it!"

"No!" I said as I attempted to bring my heart rate under control. I struggled against the arms that held me captive, the ball tight against my body.

"Say it."

I managed to twist out of Beth's grasp and ran, only to stumble and fall to one knee. I winced as I felt a rock embed itself into my skin. I rolled onto my back in time to see her coming at me, and she fell onto me, straddling my hips and pinning my arms to the grass with her own.

"Say it," she demanded again, her eyes wild, a half-smirk on her lips. I closed my eyes and tried to squirm out of her grip, which I knew was absolutely useless. Her grip was unbelievably strong. "This isn't hard, Em." She chuckled. "You're so stubborn. Just say it. Uncle."

"Never!" I opened my eyes to see her grinning.

She relaxed her grasp a bit, but maintained her determination. Suddenly, those blue eyes flashed, and I knew I was in trouble. She brought both my wrists up to one hand and with the other began to tickle me.

"No!" I cried, wriggling for all I was worth as her fingers attacked my ribs, my sides, my stomach, under my arms. "Oh, God, no! No! Won't, ugh, won't say, uhhh!" I could hear her laughing as she assaulted my poor body. Feeling like I could pee my pants, I shouted, "Okay! Uncle! Uncle! Aunt! Brother! Whatever you want! Just let me up."

"Ha," she said with satisfaction, and the weight that was holding me down was gone, my wrists released. Trying to catch my breath, I opened my eyes to see Beth kneeling next to me, a grin on her face. "How ya feeling?" she asked, her words dripping with sarcasm. I stuck my tongue out at her, which got me another quirked brow. "Careful what you do with that," she warned, tapping her thumb and index finger together.

"You are evil," I said, finally able to speak as I held myself up on my elbows.

She grinned. "Yes, that I am."

~ ~ ~ ~ ~

Chapter Twenty-One

I stood at the pulpit, the bible laying flat against the inclined board. My fingers caressed the thin, tissue-paper-like pages, the book open to the scripture I had been given the previous night. I didn't see the lines that were before me, the words I was to read. These were words Beth never said; they meant nothing to her.

Clearing my throat, I looked up, meeting the gaze of the audience before me. A small smile spread across my lips, and with a soft thump, I closed the heavy Bible. "I am supposed to read this scripture," I said, raising the Bible for all to see. I looked around the congregation, filled with faces I didn't know, save for a handful. Who were these people to Beth? Would she be able to stand here and identify all of them? My gaze went to Mrs. Sayers, and I saw the confusion in her eyes, so much like Beth's. I smiled at her. I was not sure exactly what I was doing, and I think she understood that.

"I'm standing here looking out at all of you staring up at me, wondering what I'm doing. And I'm wondering myself what I'm doing. I think...I think this is the sight Beth loved the most." I smiled warmly at the rows of people. "She did love an audience," I nearly whispered, the microphone catching my words, filling the large quiet space with them. Someone coughed near the back. "I don't really want to read these words, as beautiful and meaningful as they may be." I placed the Bible back on the pulpit. "I just have something very simple to say." I could feel my eyes beginning to sting. *God, not now.* If I could only hold it together for a minute. This would all be over in a minute. "Beth was my best friend for many, many years. We were children together, teenaged demons together." A few chuckles filled the room. I smiled and memories from the past flew by my eyes.

~ ~ ~ ~ ~

"Oh, my God! Strickland is, like, the absolute best director I have *ever* worked with!" Beth gushed, her eyes wide with excitement. I sat across from her at our regular table in the café, a smile on my lips. I had not seen her so happy about anything in a long time. The bells above the door dinged as someone rushed in to escape the falling snow. "He has this incredible vision for this production, Em. I mean, his ideas are incredible!"

Beth's voice began to echo in my head, filling it as I stared at her. I noticed for the first time a small scar above her right eye. I had to wonder if that had been from the time she'd banged her head against the swing set in the schoolyard in fifth grade. Her head had bled like a stuck pig. But then, head wounds always seemed so much worse than they actually were, as she had reminded me at the time. Then I noticed the tiny specks of darker blue that glittered in her eyes, the color of the bluest June sky. *So beautiful.* Her dark eyebrows rose and fell with her excitement level, a couple tiny dark hairs straying away from the others, marring what would otherwise be a perfectly arched brow. But it didn't matter. Nothing could mar Beth's beauty. Her beauty shone from the inside, blinding in its purity. She left me in awe.

My eyes roamed down her face, down that straight nose, the tiniest beginning of a line on the right side. In another ten years that line would stick more, stay a little longer after a smile. I focused on her lips, moving quickly as she spoke, the words now mute against my unhearing ears. Her straight, white teeth flashed repeatedly as she formed words, made sounds, breathed. A tiny bit of saliva escaped the corner of her mouth, only for an errant tongue to snake out and catch it before it could go anywhere. Her lips were moist from her words and looked soft, just the slightest bit chapped from the cold Boulder air. That dry Colorado cold played havoc with skin. My eyes began to retrace their path until they fell upon twin orbs, half-hooded, one brow raised.

"Are you listening to a word I'm saying?"

I was snapped back into the café. "Um, incredible." I blinked hard to knock myself back into the conversation. "His ideas are incredible." I smiled, proud I could remember what she'd been talking about.

She bit the side of her lip, wiping her hands on her napkin. "Uh huh. His ideas were incredible about five minutes ago." She threw the napkin onto her empty plate and sat back in her chair, one arm hanging over the back.

"Oh," I said, thoroughly embarrassed. Where had my mind gone anyway? To cover the feeling of stupidity, I grabbed my cup of coffee and sipped. I felt Beth's eyes on me, but I could not meet her gaze. *I was staring again, wasn't I?* I'd been doing a lot of that lately and had no idea why. Beth was Beth. The same every day, the same she'd been for the past ten or so years, but I just couldn't help myself! My eyes refused to behave.

"You going to Laney's party tonight?" I heard her ask. I met her amused look, but shook my head. "Why? Should be fun." She tried to entice me, but it wouldn't work.

"Have to study."

"God, Em!" She whipped her head back, her hands waving with exasperation. "Live a little, for crying out loud."

"Beth, we've had this conversation before. I am here to study, not party." Beth and I would just never see eye to eye on this subject.

"What, and I'm not?" she said, suddenly sobering.

"I didn't say that. I was not talking about you, Beth. I was talking about me." My voice reflected my irritation. Why did she always have to infer I was talking about her? I tried to catch her eyes, but she would not look at me. Then, like a ton of bricks, it hit me. Beth still thought of herself as beneath me. I felt my heart sink, and I reached across the table to take her hand in mine. Her gaze rose to meet mine; she looked so shy. *Jackpot.*

"Beth, don't feel you have to compete with me," I said in a soft voice. "We are different people." She opened her mouth to speak, but I stopped her, holding up a hand. "I could never do what you do on stage. Ever."

We must have sat there for five minutes, just staring at each other, holding hands. I didn't want to let go and was surprised when I felt her thumb rubbing over the back of my hand. A small, soft smile spread across those lips, and she nodded, as if coming to some sort of decision in her head. "Thanks," she said, her voice just above a whisper. I smiled back, squeezing her hand a bit tighter. She looked away, out the glass door; the wind had slowed, but the snow continued to fall. She turned back to me. "Wanna go walk in it?"

Without hesitation, I nodded. It was one of my favorite pastimes. We stood and tugged on our heavy coats, tossed some bills onto the table and headed into the early winter evening.

~ ~ ~ ~ ~

I swallowed hard, trying to make those snow-filled images leave my mind. I closed my eyes for a moment, only to open them to see the church still before me. "Beth..." I stopped to clear my throat. "Sorry," I whispered, smiling slightly. "Beth was the kind of person who...who you could count on for anything. For everything."

I glanced out the window, seeing the snow begin to fall lightly. "How many of you from the neighborhood remember Beth's snow creations?" Again, chuckling around the sanctuary, as I saw heads bobbing with the memory. "What about the year she made the anatomically correct reindeer?" I looked to Billy, who had helped her. He tried to hide his smile behind his hand. "Or how about that horrible victory cry she'd yell when we played street football?" I found myself chuckling along with that one, seeing and hearing it as plain as day in my mind's eye. "And could she ever make a good snowball..."

~ ~ ~ ~ ~

The campus was nearly empty; the later at night it got, the colder it became. Beth and I strolled along the path, my hands tucked inside my coat pockets and hers tossing a ball of snow from hand to hand. We talked for a while, and then she said something that made me pause. "I've decided to take out that cute little blonde." Her tone was casual.

"Oh" was all I said.

"You know the one I'm talking about, right?" She threw the snowball in the air, catching it mid-fall.

I nodded. "Yeah. Madeleine Briggs from your *Aspects of Theater* class." I kept my voice low and even.

"Gee, don't sound so excited about it, Em."

"Sorry." I plastered a smile on my face. *Why the hell was I ticked?* Just because we had been spending every single free minute together for the past semester didn't mean I had any claim on her. She smiled back, though it was obviously forced. For just a second, I got the strange feeling she wasn't all that excited over the prospects of Madeleine Briggs either. "What are you planning to do?" I asked, trying to pry information out of her that I could later take home and dissect.

She shrugged. "I don't know. I was thinking about taking her to Laney's party."

"Oh." Now I really didn't want to go.

"But, I don't know."

I sucked in my breath as I felt incredibly cold fingers slide incredibly colder snow down the back of my shirt. I stopped, bringing my shoulder blades together in an attempt to stop the progress of the snow down my back. "You are evil," I managed through clenched teeth. She laughed then backed away to gather more snow as I tried to get myself composed enough to attack or, at the very least, to defend myself. "You're gonna get it!"

~ ~ ~ ~ ~

I heard those words echoing in my mind as I lowered my head. My eyes closed, and a lone tear managed to escape past the walls of my heart, which were quickly weakening with every memory of every moment I ever spent with Beth. Every time I saw her look at me in that special way that only Beth could look, making me feel special, separate from the rest of the crowd. The tear slid down my cheek, falling to the Bible on the pulpit, making a dark spot on the already dark leather.

"Beth was a presence," I continued shakily, "not a person. She had a gift. A gift to be able to reach down inside you, touch a part of your soul, and take it with her." I did not raise my head when another tear slipped out to follow the path of the first. I could not face the eyes that watched me struggle, watched the internal battle I was quickly losing. As my voice began to quiver, I heard the sound of someone blowing a nose and of someone else crying quietly. I could not look into the tortured eyes of someone else, when I could barely face my own torment. "She was my best friend," I whispered and stepped away from the microphone, from the eyes of the others, from myself, and from my self-control. I needed air. I needed to be alone.

~ ~ ~ ~ ~

"Hello?" I said into the receiver, more than a bit annoyed. I hated being bothered when I was writing a paper. I should have remembered to unplug the phone.

"Ha ha! Got you at home. Goody."

"Beth. What do you want?" I asked, flipping through my dictionary to look for the perfect word.

"Come out with me."

"Can't. Give me a synonym for alike?" I said as I continued my search.

"Um, let me think. Oh, got a good one." I could hear the smile in her voice, and I looked up from my dictionary, waiting to hear the term. "I'll give you this wonderful, great, terrific word if you come out with me."

"Beth, I have a dictionary in my hands as we speak."

"So? It wouldn't come from me."

I took off my reading glasses, tossing them to the desk. "Okay. Where?"

"To Laney's party."

I groaned. "Beth..."

"No whining. Yay or nay?"

With a loud sigh, I agreed. "Fine. Spill it." My fingers were poised above my keyboard. "And this better be good," I warned.

"Symbiotic."

I re-read my sentence fitting in Beth's word, and had to admit that it worked perfectly.

She was obviously proud of herself. "I did good, right?"

"Yes. You did good. Fine. I'll go." I was about to hang up, but stopped. "What about Madeleine? I thought she was going to go with you?"

"Nah. Decided I'd rather go with you. See you in fifteen minutes."

The phone still in my hand, I sat there and tried to process what she'd said. What did she mean by that? Or had she meant anything at all? I buried my face in my hands. I seemed to be reading into everything she said, and that was not good. "Why?" I moaned into the empty room.

Beth drove us to Laney's house in the piece-of-crap car she'd bought over the summer. "Hey, it was cheap and gets me where I need to go," had been her defense. "Okay. Well it sort of gets me where I'm going," she had grudgingly amended.

Laney Wilson was one of my best friends at CU, and she had taken to Beth right away. In fact, Beth was so charming and so much fun, everyone had fallen in love with her when I'd introduced her. Sitting in the passenger seat, which had been taped together with duct tape, I thought about that. I was glad Beth got along with my friends; it made it much easier for us. However, part of me — the childish, selfish part — wanted Beth all to myself.

She looked great that night, wearing a pair of loose cords and a flannel shirt. Her hair, which she had begun to grow longer the year before, was shiny and clean, and her long bangs were tucked behind her ears. But then, Beth would have looked great in a potato sack.

I watched the scenery through the windows, the darkness tinged with a pinkish-orange hue from the snow reflecting off the streetlights. It was truly a wondrous night. Laney's house was well lit, and cars were everywhere they could possibly find a place to park, even one or two on the front lawn. I wondered if Laney knew that. A pounding bass beat bounced around the night, vibrating through the air. "Head Over Heels" by the Go Go's pulsed out the front door, bringing a smile to my face. I had fond memories of that song. Beth and I walked up the path and into the house.

~ ~ ~ ~ ~

Blindly, I made my way down the side aisle of the church, the tears in my eyes making it impossible to see the sympathetic faces I passed. I didn't want to see them anyway. I had to get myself together. Once out in the cold October air, I leaned against the brick building, my eyes closed as I took in deep breaths.

"Emily."

I turned my head to see Rebecca standing just outside the door.

"Are you okay, babe?" Her voice was quiet as she walked over to me.

I pushed away from the wall, crossing my arms over my chest to ward off the chill. I know I was also trying to push her out, to make myself inaccessible to her. "Yes. I'm fine," I said with a sigh. I really just wanted to be alone. She stepped closer, placing her hand on my arm. I could feel her eyes on me, the worry radiating off her in waves.

"What is it, Emily? Please don't shut me out. Talk to me."

"What would you like me to say?" I asked, turning on her, taking a step back. She sucked in a surprised breath, her eyes wide. "I just..." I stopped, looking out into the parking lot, trying to think just what I wanted to say. "I think I just need to be alone right now, Rebecca. I need to think." I looked back at her with pleading eyes.

She nodded, but her eyes wandered, not able to meet mine. "Okay."

I could see the slump in her shoulders as she walked away. She was hurt and confused. I felt terrible. Why was I not able to let her in, to explain to her what was going through my head?

~ ~ ~ ~ ~

"Hey, you two." Laney grinned when she saw us. She came over and hugged me, patting Beth on the shoulder. "Good for you, Beth. Don't know how you got her to come, but good for you."

Beth grinned down at me. "I gave her a word."

Laney's face showed her confusion, but she just shrugged when Beth did not offer any further explanation. "Um, okay. Well, anyway, have fun, ladies." She winked at me and disappeared between dancing bodies.

"Alrighty then," Beth said, rubbing her hands together. "I want a drink." She looked around. "Aha!" she exclaimed, tugging me by the hand toward a distant place in the corner of the room.

"You know, it really must be nice to be tall," I grumbled as I tried to avoid a nasty collision with a writhing person on the dance floor.

"What are you having, Em?" I heard asked. I stopped looking at the other partygoers and turned to Beth, who was holding two bottles in each hand. I scrunched up my nose. "Come on, Em. Just have one drink. For me?" she begged, her bottom lip sticking out.

I had such an urge to nip that protruding lip between my

teeth. Taken by surprise by my thoughts, I actually took a step back. "Okay. One. I don't care. Whatever you're drinking."

Beth handed me a bottle of beer with the comment, "Eh, figured you'd be able to handle a Coors and still study later."

I grinned and followed her through the throng of people until we ran into a few of our other friends. We were all standing around talking when I noticed a woman enter the house with another girl, neither of whom I knew. The woman had long brown hair pulled back into a ponytail. She spotted our little circle of friends, looking first at me before her brown eyes moved to Beth, where they stayed. I watched her as she stared at my best friend. I wanted to find some way to warn her off, to get her to leave Beth alone even if she was just looking. I hated the feeling of jealousy, but it commandeered my body, making me angry.

"Hello? Earth to Emily?"

I snapped my attention back to the conversation and noticed Richard was gazing at me with expectant eyes. "Sorry. What?" I took a casual sip of my beer, trying not to wince. Beer was nasty, nasty stuff. I managed to become reengaged with our friends and lose track of the brown-haired woman. The party dragged on, as parties tend to do. I was not a fan of them and never anticipated a change of opinion on that matter. I turned away from Richard and his girlfriend, Ann, to ask Beth a question, but she was gone.

"She went dancing, Emily," Richard said.

I looked back at him, shocked. I hadn't noticed her leave, and, suddenly, I felt very alone. Many beers, a few dances, and many discussions later, I began to wander through Laney's house, looking for Beth. I was ready to go home. It was late, I was beyond tired, and I had a test the next day. I peeked into the bedrooms, the kitchen, even the bathroom, but she was nowhere to be found. I tossed my half-empty beer into the trash under the kitchen sink and glanced out the window, where I saw some people scattered around the backyard. Curious, I opened the back door, stepped onto the porch, and then froze. Out in the yard, just visible in the porch light, stood a huge cottonwood tree. Sitting on the ground, her back against the massive trunk, sat Beth, the cute brunette on her lap, straddling her. They were kissing, hands everywhere. The brunette, with closed eyes, broke the kiss, arching her neck for Beth's mouth to probe. Past images crashed into my mind: stepping out of the bathroom at the State Fair to see Beth and Casey ducked behind the trailer of a rig making out; opening the big, metal door at the theater only to find Beth and the redhead at the far end of the hall-way. I felt hurt, betrayed, and downright nauseous. *Why couldn't she see me like that? Why couldn't it be me on Beth's lap, tasting her mouth?*

Suddenly feeling suffocated, I needed to get out of there. I wiped an impatient hand over my eyes before the tears could fall and searched my pockets for my car keys before remembering Beth had driven us. "Damn it!" I found Laney and called to her, and when she turned to look at me, concern immediately filled her face.

"Emily? What is it?" She approached me and placed a hand on my shoulder.

"Please take me home, Laney."

"What? Why? Are you okay?" She pushed me further away from the group she'd been talking to, taking us to a place a little less populated.

I was grateful. I felt ridiculous enough as it was. "Please, Laney?"

"Where's Beth? I thought—"

"Laney!" I exclaimed, not wanting to go into it and getting extremely irritated. Damn it, why couldn't I just go home? She could read it in my eyes and nodded, her face softening. "Okay. Let me get my keys."

I sat in the passenger seat of Laney's little Honda, my coat folded in my lap, staring out the window. Laney drove in silence, and I was glad. Finally, we reached my building. The car idled quietly as we sat there. Despite my hurry to get there, I wasn't quite ready to go in yet, and Laney wasn't ready for me to go, either. I knew she wanted answers, but I wasn't so sure I had them.

"What do you want me to tell her?" she finally asked.

I took a deep breath followed by a shrug. "You know, I really don't know. I guess just tell her I had to go home."

My friend smiled sadly at me, but nodded. "Okay."

I gathered my belongings and myself together and stepped from the car.

Laney leaned across the passenger seat and looked at me. "You know, I don't know why you two don't just do it and get it over with." She smiled and drove away.

I could only stare. *Why, indeed.*

~ ~ ~ ~ ~

Chapter Twenty-Two

~ ~ ~ ~ ~

I was aware of rough bark against my hands, my fingers digging into it as I felt soft lips beneath mine, parting for me. My eyes were closed, but I knew whose lips they were. "Beth," I whispered, feeling her beneath me as I sat straddling her lap. Her hands were in my hair, running down my back, trailing lower until they slipped beneath my sweater. I sighed, the wetness of her tongue suddenly against my neck. I shifted my head to grant her greater access...

Bam! Bam! Bam!

My eyes popped open, and my body lurched upright, although I remained disoriented. I spent a moment trying to figure out what the hell was happening. I was in bed in my dorm room. There was the banging again, and I realized it was my door.

"What?" I called out, irritated. The bedside clock indicated it was barely 8:00 in the morning. More banging. "Jesus." I threw back the covers, stalked to the door, and swung it open. "It is too God damn early—" I stopped when I saw it was Beth. I just looked at her, not sure what to say, and she stared back at me. Then I remembered my dream, and I was flooded with the vision of her mouth on mine, her hands on me, and I knew my face must have turned every color known to man. I took a step back. "Hi."

"Hi." She did not sound like a happy camper. Then, after just a moment's hesitation, she strolled past me into the room.

"Come on in." I remained standing near the door, turning to look at her. She removed her leather jacket and tossed it on Candice's made bed. I was glad my roommate had a morning class.

"So what's the deal?" she asked, her arms crossed over her chest and her stance very imposing.

"With what?" I asked, crossing my own arms.

"Why did you leave the party?"

"I had to get home."

"Yeah, that's what Laney said, but I want to hear it from you. Why did you leave?" She took a step toward me.

I held my ground. "Like I said, I had to get home." My

voice wavered slightly and I knew I sounded weak.

She took another step. "I don't believe you, Em." Beth's voice was low and deep, almost menacing.

I raised my chin in challenge. "I don't care what you do or do not believe, Beth. You knew I had things to do. I needed to get home. I was tired. I went to find you, but—" I cut myself off, not wanting her to know I saw her with that girl.

"But?"

"But I couldn't find you," I lied.

"You saw me, didn't you?"

"Beth, please just go. I need some sleep. I don't have class for another three hours."

"Don't lie to me, Em." Beth grabbed her jacket and headed toward the door.

I stared at the ground until she stopped in front of me. I could feel her breath against my bangs, tickling my forehead. Somehow, I gathered the courage to look up at her. She stood not half a foot away, staring into my eyes, looking at my face, down to my mouth, then back up to my eyes. Her expression was guarded, and I could not read her at all. I hated when she did that. I looked deep into those baby blues, trying to see past the wall. Was she angry with me? I didn't think so. There was a palpable tension between us, but I didn't dare give voice to what I thought caused it.

"Get some sleep," she finally said, her voice low and husky. She turned away and stepped into the hall, closing the door softly behind her.

I stared at the door, trying to gather my thoughts. Beth had come to get answers from me, but instead left so many questions. I covered my face with my hands and leaned back against the wall, sliding down until I sat on the carpet. *Oh, Beth.*

As the holidays quickly approached, I tried to concentrate on school and my upcoming finals. I had stayed clear of many of my friends, as was my custom around that time of year. They knew me well enough to expect this and left me alone. But, truth be told, there was really only one person I was actively avoiding. I didn't want to be feeling things I should not be feeling. Although I had a nasty suspicion it was too late, I was determined to discover whether the old adage "out of sight; out of mind" really worked.

It didn't. Thoughts of Beth obsessively consumed me, and I didn't know what to do about it. She had called my dorm a few times, and Laney had told me she constantly asked for and about me. I just could not do this again. I only had a year and a half of school left before advancing to law school. I needed no interruptions and I couldn't handle another disappointment. I did, however, hear that Beth had turned into quite the heartbreaker. She would date a woman once or twice and then move on to the next. Just what exactly she was trying to prove, I had no idea. I figured it was not my problem to worry about anymore, not that it ever had been.

I was studying at the library one day when I went to retrieve a book from the shelf. I nearly jumped out of my skin when I heard Laney's voice. She stood on the other side of the stack and grinned at me through the gap between books. "That was hardly funny, Laney."

"I thought it was." She chuckled and then disappeared, only to stroll around to my aisle. "Okay, woman, here's the deal. Richard is having a small, intimate get-together at his place before Christmas. I figure we can all exchange gifts, that sort of thing." I just stared at her, already not interested. I began to shake my head when she held up a hand. "Ah. Wait, before you say no. It's on Friday, the week before finals start, so don't even try that one."

I rolled my eyes, not wanting to get boxed into anything. I just wanted to study in relative peace. "Laney, I have to study," I whined.

"So study Saturday."

I sighed. I knew I should go to the party. I hadn't spent any time with the gang in over a month. Finally, with a resigned nod, I agreed.

Laney clapped her hands together with glee. "Yay!"

I donned my coat and grabbed my keys, ready to head to Richard's. I didn't want to go, but I had promised. The prior week, we had all drawn names for the gift exchange. I had Ann. Since I knew she was into Def Leppard, I bought her their newest release, which I pitched onto the passenger seat of my Jeep. The weather was cold, and we'd had a bad storm the previous weekend. Evidence of holiday spirit was everywhere, with decorations all over campus and the town. I had to smile when I saw a Santa Claus talking to a little girl on the street corner, his big bulk kneeling to be at her eye level. An old holiday tune sung by Elvis blared from my speakers, and I could not help singing along, beating my palm against the cold steering wheel. I truly loved the holiday season and looked forward to getting home. My mom and I always did our annual Christmas shopping together in Denver. I just wanted the semester to be over.

I pulled up to Richard's apartment building, locked the

Jeep, and jogged up the two flights of stairs. I only had to knock once before Richard threw the door open.

"Merry Christmas," he said with a big smile as he pulled me to him for a hug.

"Um, merry Christmas to you, too." His near giddiness surprised me. I placed my gift with the others under a four-foot tree that stood on a table in the corner of the room.

"Give me your coat, Emily," Ann said as she approached me with another coat tossed over her arm.

I struggled out of mine and handed it to her. She disappeared down the hall, and I turned to see who else was there. Richard, of course; Laney and her boyfriend; our friends Tanya and Lauren. And then I saw her, sitting in the recliner by the window. It never ceased to amaze me how Beth could just pop in and out of my life at the strangest and often most inopportune times. She looked up from her chair and smiled at me.

"Merry Christmas, Em."

"Merry Christmas." I stood there for a minute just looking at her and then walked over to the kitchen where Richard and Ann were piling snacks on trays. "Can I help?" I asked, leaning against the breakfast bar.

Richard looked over his shoulder at me. "Yeah. Get drinks ready." He nodded toward the fridge with his head. I opened it and grabbed as many cans of soda as I could, balancing them against my chest with my hands and arms.

"Want some help?" Beth stood beside me, her hand on her hip. She wore a festive red and green sweater and black cords. On her head she had placed a Broncos baseball cap.

I chuckled. "Do you have any idea how much you clash?"

She looked down at herself and smiled. "Hey, a true die-hard fan does not care. They're in the play-offs, and I've got to support my boys. Elway's first Super Bowl, you know."

"They're not there yet, Beth," I pointed out, indicating she should take a stack of cups to fill with ice.

"They will be. Mark my words."

"Uh huh." This had been a point of contention between us for so many years, and I purposely tried to tick her off with my lack of interest.

Later, after many Christmas cookies and glasses of spiked eggnog, we all sat on the floor in the living room ready to play a game.

"Okay. This is the way to play 'Conscience'," explained Richard, holding up an empty tequila bottle. "Couple 'Spin the Bottle' with 'Truth or Dare'. You spin the bottle, making you the conscience of the person who it points to. You ask that person any question you want. They have a choice of either answering it *honestly*," he looked around the circle, eyeing us all with that word, "or taking a drink."

I felt the smooth glass of the bottle in my fingers. It was once again my turn to spin, having already suffered the embarrassment of answering Laney's question about the time I'd lost my virginity. I placed the bottle on the piece of cardboard that served as our spinning surface and let it go. It spun round and round, and then, with one final shaky spin, it stopped. I looked up, following the path of the mouth of the bottle, and met blue eyes. *Oh boy.* I stared at Beth for a moment, trying to decide what I wanted to ask her. The entire night she had stuck by me, hanging on my every word, which only served to confuse me all the more. She had been very physical, something quite unusual for her. Even Laney had noticed and asked me about it. "Okay," I said finally. Everyone waited in breathless anticipation. "Beth?"

"Yes, Em?" She quirked a brow.

"If you could kiss anyone in this room, who would it be?" My voice was quiet but definitely daring.

There were audible chuckles. Everyone in the room knew the situation, and I believed they had been secretly making bets. So far, almost everyone had answered whatever question was posed to him or her, and a nearly full bottle of tequila sat waiting for someone to choose the drink option. Beth stared at me, her eyes never leaving mine as she thought about my question. Part of me wanted so badly to look away, almost ashamed for asking. It had been a bit manipulative, and I hoped I knew the answer.

Beth sighed deeply and then cleared her throat, never breaking eye contact with me. "I think I'm going to have to choose to take a shot." Her voice was just as low and daring as mine had been. Without a word, she reached her hand out to grab the tequila Richard poured for her. She raised the small shooter to me in salute, then downed it in one gulp, her face contorting as the liquid fire slid down her throat. My face fell, but I tried to hold it together. I didn't want to give anyone there the satisfaction of knowing I was crushed. Beth had hurt me. And she had hurt me bad.

~ ~ ~ ~ ~

A light drizzling snow had begun to fall, the type where you could easily catch tiny flakes of near liquid on your tongue. I walked carefully around the graves, trying not to step on them. That had been something Beth had drilled into me the one time we'd been at a cemetery together: *"You can't step on 'em, Em! That's just rude."* Just up ahead I could see the green tarp that covered the gravesite. A few chairs had been set up under it for the immediate family. Rebecca walked beside me, but she said nothing and didn't try to touch me. I knew I had some apologizing as well as some explaining to do later. My parents and Billy brought up the tail end of our little parade. We stood under the tarp but did not take seats.

Mrs. Sayers sat front and center, flanked by Mr. Sayers and his wife to her left, and the blonde Monica had identified as Beth's lover to her right. Monica and Connie walked up to me, and Monica squeezed my fingers. With a deep sigh, I faced forward. The casket was beautiful; it was white with silver handles and decorations. Flowers of different colors and types adorned the top of it. I wondered where they had found such beautiful flowers this time of year. They must have paid a premium for them. The minister approached the other side of the casket, facing us, and opened his large book. He reached up, straightened his glasses, and then began to speak. I heard nothing the minister said as I stared at the stone near the casket. ELIZABETH SAYERS OCTOBER 23, 1967 OCTOBER 12, 2001 SHE LIVED AS SHE LOVED.

My mind focused only on those few lines. My brain refused to believe it was true, that Beth was permanently gone. Mrs. Sayers sat quietly, a blanket provided by the funeral home spread across her legs. She raised her hand to her face every few minutes, the white Kleenex she clutched becoming more and more saturated with her tears and with small black marks as her mascara was cried off. Mr. Sayers remained dry-eyed. He looked almost as though he felt nothing, or perhaps he was just numb. *Like me.*

I felt as if I were just a doll, waiting for my owner to pick me up and take me home. It was surreal. My eyes were heavy and my lungs felt even heavier from the cold air. Then, to my surprise, I realized the cold was coming from inside me. There was something I couldn't quite define, but I felt it die inside me, and I wondered if I would ever get it back. Would I ever even figure out what it was? People began to leave around me, but I just stood still and stared at the spot where Beth's casket had passed below ground level, disappearing into the earth. It was so final. I had found my emotions; apparently, I wasn't as numb as I thought. My face felt tight from the seemingly endless supply of tears that had streamed down my cheeks. The numbness, like the snow, melted into tracks down my face. My sorrow as they had begun to lower Beth to her final resting place was unbelievable. I couldn't stop the tears, hadn't wanted to. I knew I needed to cry, to feel this release. I needed to grieve.

I became frozen to the spot on which I stood, unaware of those who were around me; the numbness began to reappear even though tears still slid from my eyes, freezing my face as the cold air hit them and making me shiver.

"Honey," I heard my mother say to my left, her hands wrapped around my arm. "Come on, honey." She spoke in a reverent whisper, her voice thick from emotion.

"No." I paused. "I'm going to stay for a bit."

"Are you sure, baby?" Rebecca asked. I nodded in a robotic manner, not really feeling the motion of my own head. "Okay. See you at home." Rebecca hugged and kissed me, then left with my parents. For a moment, I thought I was alone, but then I felt a presence beside me, and I turned to find Beth's blonde.

She looked at me and smiled sadly. "You must be Em," she said, and I was surprised by her use of Beth's name for me. She was very beautiful, with long hair swept back over her shoulders and clear, honest blue eyes. "I'm Lana." She extended her hand, which I took on autopilot. "I...well...Beth and I lived together for five years." She turned and looked at the stone marker that had kept my rapt attention. "I was with her when she..." Her voice broke just a bit. She cleared her throat and turned back to me with a smile. "I heard a lot about you over the years. I always wanted to meet you. And here we are."

I smiled weakly. "I guess so."

"She used to talk about you all the time. At first, I was almost jealous." She smiled again, and I could understand how Beth had fallen in love with this woman. Her pure heart was on her sleeve as was her undeniable grief. "Um, Em...I want you to know that Beth was happy. She was loved. Very much." Her voice dropped to a whisper and she ducked her head for a moment. She seemed to get herself under control and smiled again. "Anyway, just wanted to say hello."

"Thank you, Lana," I said, trying to smile through the newest assault of tears. *God, how could anything be so painful?* Lana took a step closer, and before I knew it, I was enveloped in a strong hug. I returned the embrace, and then she pulled away from me, not even looking at me again as she made her way out of the cemetery. I watched her depart, her black pantsuit clearly visible against the white ground as she retreated, until she faded from view.

~ ~ ~ ~ ~

"Emily? Emily, wake up."

I opened my eyes to see Candice standing over me. "What?"

"Come on. The study group?" She patted the backpack

that hung from her arm.

"What about it?" I asked groggily, turning to my other side and giving her a nice view of my back.

"Remember? We're all getting together for the lit class final?"

"Not goin'," I muttered, and then closed my eyes. I had no desire whatsoever to get out of bed, let alone to go to some stupid study group. I'd felt such a heavy weight on me since the party at Richard's the previous night. Nothing mattered, not even finals. Why the hell should I care if Beth didn't give a shit? I was tired of being the only one to care. *Why did she have to come back into my life? I was doing just fine without her!* I felt liquid warmth seep out my closed lids, wetting my pillow, until mercifully, sleep claimed me once again.

The darkness dissipated as I heard pounding. Pounding that wouldn't stop. *God, what now? Can't they just let me sleep?* "What!" I bellowed, my head ringing with the yell.

"Em?" came the muffled reply.

I quirked open an eye. "Go away!"

"Let me in!"

The doorknob rattled, and I just got more irritated. "Go the fuck away!" I yelled again, throwing one of my pillows to emphasize my point. Then I jumped as she kicked the door. My God. With a growl, I tore myself from the bed, unlocked the door, and then returned to my perch. The door opened just as I sank back down on the mattress, grabbing Ruffles and holding him close to my chest. Beth stormed into the middle of the room. She looked worried, angry, and all sorts of other things, none of them happy, as she stared at me with her hands on her hips. "Go away, Beth," I said into the fur on top of my teddy bear's head.

"What the hell are you doing, Em?" Her voice was hard and angry.

"What do you mean, what am I doing? I'm attempting to sleep, that's what I'm doing. My God, you'd think the world had never heard of sleeping in, for Christ's sake."

"Sleeping in?"

"Yeah. I know you sure as hell know all about that."

"You've been sleeping in, all right. Do you have any clue what day it is?" She took a step forward.

I glared back up at her. "Saturday. At ..." I glanced over at the clock, "one-thirty in the afternoon."

"Try Monday at one-thirty in the afternoon, Em," she barked. I looked at her, incredulous. "Your roommate was worried about you. She hunted me down after class today. Said you didn't do any studying this weekend. That you didn't get out of *bed* this weekend. Em!" She took yet another step closer. "What the hell are you doing?"

"What do you care, Beth? You get pissed that I study so much as it is." She stared at me, stung by my tone. It felt good. It felt good to hurt her. My heart was still reeling from her rejection at Richard's party.

She was quiet for a moment, her hands running through her hair while she studied the floor. "What is this about, Em?" she finally said, her voice unsure.

"Nothing, Beth. It's about nothing." I tossed Ruffles aside. "Why are you here? Why don't you just go find one of your flavor-of-the-week girlfriends and leave me the hell alone, okay?"

Her face fell, as did her shoulders, but she quickly regained her composure. She took in a deep breath and glared at me with fire in her eyes. "Is this about that stupid game? Is that it, Em?"

"You took the shot, Beth. That was your prerogative." My voice matched hers in hardness.

She smiled, though no humor reached her eyes, and nodded to herself. "That's it. Because I wouldn't fucking admit to—" She cut herself off.

"What?" I challenged. "Admit to what, Beth?" I unfolded myself from the bed and stood. "Admit to what, Beth?"

"Stop it. This is ridiculous."

"Is it?"

She glared at me. "Stop it, Em. I'm warning you."

I took a step closer. I could feel the heat radiating from her. "Or what? Huh?" I reached her, staring up into her face.

Her fists were clenched at her sides. "You want to hear it? Hmm? You want me to answer your fucking question? Is that it?"

"Would be nice."

"Don't do this, Em." To my surprise, I saw fear flash through her eyes. Just as quickly, it was gone. "Fine. I'll answer your fucking question."

I sucked in my breath as she lunged, grabbing two handfuls of my shirt and whipping me around until my back was slammed against the wall. A picture crashed to the floor next to me. I wrapped my fingers around her hands, which still held my shirt. Beth's body pressed against mine, and her jean-clad leg pushed into me.

"You want to hear who I'd kiss?" Beth rumbled, her face mere inches away. She had me pinned firmly to the wall, but I wouldn't have moved had I been able to. I stared into her eyes, twin pools of icy fire. "You, Em. I would have kissed you." Her eyes traveled my face, starting at my own wide eyes, then moving to my nose, and finally settling on my lips, where they stayed. "I've always wanted to kiss you, Em. Still do." She whispered the last words.

"Then do it," I whispered back.

Her eyes left my lips and locked onto mine. So many things passed between us: uncertainty, fear, hope, and mostly desire. The room was filled with the sound of our heavy breathing as we stared at each other. My fingers squeezed her hands, begging her. She clutched my shirt tighter and roughly pulled me to her, crushing her lips against mine as she pinned me tighter to the wall and slid her leg between mine. Her tongue pushed through my closed lips, forcing me to let her in, and a whimper escaped her throat. Her hands loosened their hold on my shirt, grasping my shoulders instead. My hands slid up her forearms until they snaked around her neck, pulling her that much closer. Her mouth began to slow and she softened her actions, the kiss becoming tender.

"Beth." I breathed into her mouth, amazed that she was here, that she was kissing me, that I was wrapped in her arms.

"I'm here," she whispered.

Her hands slid down my shoulders, her fingers sneaking up the short sleeves of my T-shirt, rubbing the bare skin of my upper arms. My hands stroked her neck and then buried them into her thick hair, until finally I grasped the collar of her jacket and tugged it down her arms. Beth tossed the coat to the floor and pressed herself fully against me again. I could feel her breasts through the thin material of her shirt. I moaned, feeling as if I had never been touched before, as if Beth's kiss was a lifeline and I a drowning woman.

Beth's hands begin to roam, stroking my sides on their way to the hem of my shirt. At last, she slipped those hands underneath and tugged my shirt over my head. I lifted my arms to aid the removal and she tossed it behind her to the floor. Beth returned to my mouth, but her hands cupped my breasts, the nipples already hard against her palms. I needed to feel her skin against mine, and I pulled at her shirt, freeing it from the waistband of her jeans and yanking it over her head. Beth had never been one for bras and she wasn't wearing one now. Her breasts were magnificent. She shook her hair free and pressed our naked torsos together, both of us moaning at the touch.

Fire swept through me at breakneck speed. I gasped when she pushed her thigh further into me, pressing against me as

228 ❖ Kim Pritekel

her mouth devoured mine. My fingers dug into her shoulders and her lips left mine, kissing and licking down my jaw. I lifted my head to give her more access; my skin was in flames, and I needed to feel her everywhere. She sucked and bit my neck as her hands slid down my back, dipping into the waistband of my boxers to caress the smooth skin of my rear end. I lowered my hands to the front of Beth's jeans and fiddled with the fly, popping the button and then unzipping her. When I pushed her pants down her legs, Beth paused briefly to step out of them, kicking them behind her. At last, we stood before each other in just our underwear. It struck me while Beth returned to my mouth, kissing me long and deep, just exactly what the term "making love" meant. Before that moment, I had never had any clue as to the real significance of the words.

I powered away from the wall, pushing Beth toward my bed. She let me guide her, our lips never losing contact. The back of Beth's legs hit the mattress, and she fell backward, taking me with her. It felt unbelievable to lie on top of Beth, and I prayed this wasn't another dream. Beth rolled us over and positioned me against the pillows at the head of the bed. She held herself up on her arms above me. I ran my fingers up and down her back, looking into those eyes that had haunted me.

"I've waited so long," she whispered.

"Me, too."

"I love you, Em." She leaned her head down, bestowing upon me the softest kiss.

"I love you, too, Beth."

She stared at me for a moment and then kissed me for all she was worth, pouring everything she felt into it and leaving me breathless. She pulled away to remove her underwear, flinging them off the side of the bed, then she reached for my boxers, once again locking her gaze to mine as she slid them down my legs. I laid back and let her stare at my body. She used her right hand to trace a line up my leg, fingertips briefly teasing the wiry hair at the junction before continuing to trail up over my stomach. When she reached my breasts, her other hand joined in and she grabbed two handfuls, causing me to suck in a breath. I arched into her touch, craving it. She pulled me onto her lap so I was straddling her, my arms around her neck and my fingers in her hair, as once again she found my mouth. Her hands stayed on my breasts, and her thumbs played with my nipples, the sensation shooting through my body directly to my groin. When her hands moved to my shoulders, I sighed at the loss, but she immediately moved to replace them with her mouth. I closed my eyes and moaned as Beth's lips wrapped around my right nipple and began to suckle me, her tongue swiping across it, sending fresh jolts of desire squarely south.

One hand left my shoulder and blazed a path back down my body, disappearing between my legs. I leaned up a bit on my knees and Beth pushed into copious slickness. She moaned as she slid those fingers through the wetness, caressing me, stroking me, and finally entering me. I breathed into the side of her neck as her fingers filled me and began to slowly slide in and out of my body. I moved against her, matching her rhythm until I was gasping as I rode her hand, my hips pumping faster and harder. I closed my eyes, no longer able to keep them open; all I could do was feel.

"Beth."

With her free hand, Beth guided my mouth back to hers, and our breathing mingled in a soul kiss. She swallowed my escalating moans as I teetered on the edge. Then she reached up with her thumb, pressed down on my clit, and pushed me over the precipice. Light burst behind my closed eyelids as I exploded. Beth continued to pump, her thumb stroking until my body stilled, jerking slightly with a small aftershock. She pushed me back and lay on top of me, her body between my legs. We kissed, long and hard, my heart still pounding out of control. Finally, I got my breath back only to lose it once again as I thought of all the things I wanted to do to Beth.

I had to have my mouth on her, so I flipped her over and straddled her hips. We were breast to breast, and as I stared down at her, I could see the hunger in her eyes. It was like being struck by a bolt of lightning. I kissed her, softly at first, waiting for her to open her lips and invite me in. It didn't take long. I explored her mouth thoroughly, until with a sigh, Beth wrapped her arms around me, running her hands down my back and cupping my rear to pull me against her. The kiss began to heat up, setting us both on fire again. Her tongue chased mine, first fighting for space in my mouth then in hers, and she began an animalistic response, her hips grinding against me, searching for some sort of relief.

I broke from her lips and began to kiss down Beth's body, sucking on her nipples, worshipping her breasts with my hands, fingers, and mouth. Beth moaned my name and pushed down on my shoulders, trying to position me at the apex of her need. I allowed her to guide me, able to smell and feel her heat as I got closer. When I reached my goal, I placed my hands on the insides of her thighs and spread her legs wider. I paused in my task and looked up at her, meeting her gaze.

"Please," she groaned, and I smiled, gladly obliging. I lowered my mouth between Beth's legs and took in her smell before snaking my tongue out and laving her entire length. Her wetness gathered on my tongue, and I smiled in satisfaction when she shivered. I lowered my head again, and Beth's hands tangled into my hair, fingers stroking my scalp. I brought her to the edge of her release, and her hips bucked wildly as her hands pressed my face into her, grinding me against her need until her entire body convulsed in orgasm.

I had never wanted to please a woman as badly as I did that day. Beth meant so much to me, and I wanted her to know it. I kissed the insides of her thighs one last time and worked my way up as Beth fought to regain control of her breathing. When I lay on top of her again, I kissed her gently. She wrapped her arms around me, holding me close and whispering soft words into my mouth.

As we kissed, we started to move together, neither of us completely sated in our desire for each other. Beth's hips began a slow grind, and our tongues mimicked the action. I pushed myself up onto my elbows, digging my fingers into the pillow on either side of Beth's head as our kiss deepened and the pace of our hips quickened from slow and leisurely to fast and hard. Beth began to pant into my mouth, her hands squeezing my butt and pulling me further into her, deepening the contact until both our bodies began to tremble. Our skin was slick from sweat and the remains of our earlier lovemaking. I broke the kiss, burying my face against Beth's neck, biting her skin as I came again, thrusting hard against her, my cries muffled.

"My God," Beth whispered, holding me close.

"My God," I repeated.

Sometime later, I opened my eyes to see that it had gotten dark outside. A smile played across my face as I soaked in the heat that ran along the back of my body. Beth was spooned behind me and her arms held me fast, her breath warm against the back of my neck. With a contented sigh, I closed my eyes and joined her in sleep.

I rolled onto my back, my smile firmly in place before I even opened my eyes. I knew it was morning and reached my arms up over my head to stretch. I felt glorious, and I looked to my right. No Beth. I sat up to check the rest of the room. Candice's bed was already made, her bag tossed onto it. I squinted at the alarm clock and saw it was nearly 8:00. I had a final at 9:30. I rose from the bed, pulling yesterday's discarded T-shirt over my head, and looked around. There was no note. I had a bad feeling in my stomach and dressed hastily before leaving the room. I didn't even bother to brush my hair, pulling a baseball cap on instead, as I ran to the next building. I stood outside Beth's door, impatiently waiting for my knock to be answered. In the hall of the dorm, everything was quiet, but I heard movement behind her door. Finally, it opened. I blinked in surprise when I saw Kelly, Beth's roommate.

"Hey, Emily," she said, her voice groggy. She rubbed her eyes.

"Sorry to wake you, Kelly. Where's Beth? Did she already go to her class?" I didn't think she had a final that morning, but I could only hope.

Kelly looked puzzled. "Emily, you mean you don't know? I mean, I figured of anyone, you would have known."

"Known what?" I tried to keep the worry from my voice.

"Beth left."

"What?"

Kelly nodded her dark head. "Yeah. She left early this morning. Got all her stuff, shoved it into her bags, and off she went. Didn't even wake me up. Heard her as she was leaving. I asked her what was up, and all she said was goodbye."

I stared at Kelly, her dark eyes looking sad. "She just went home for the holidays, right?" I said, my voice weak, already knowing the answer.

Kelly shook her head. "I don't think so, Emily. I think she's just gone."

I swallowed and took a deep breath, trying to put on a smile. "Thanks, Kelly."

I turned away, hearing the soft click as the door was closed behind me. I bit my bottom lip and walked toward the stairs.

~ ~ ~ ~ ~

Chapter Twenty-Three

I looked at Beth's stone and was surprised to see they had already finished positioning it. Glancing around, I saw the workers driving the utility vehicle further into the cemetery. It truly was just Beth and me now. Taking a step forward, I stood at the edge of the new dirt and wiped a wet snowflake from my eye. Or was that a tear? I wasn't sure anymore.

"Well, Beth. Looks like we finally made it to Pioneer, huh?" The wind provided the only answer. "You're right. It is beautiful."

My thoughts traveled back to college and Beth's departure. She disappeared from my life for ten full years. I could still feel the pain of waking up to find her gone.

"Why did you go, Beth?" I asked the gray winter sky. "Why? Was it a way of running again? You know, after that I didn't date for a very long time." I smiled ruefully. "I thought it was bad luck. I decided to just study, worry about classes, and try to be the best. It worked, too. I *was* the best." I buried my gloved hands into the pocket of my overcoat. "Until I met Rebecca seven years ago, I really thought that was it for me. I thought you had ruined it for me, Beth."

The snow was beginning to fall in earnest, though the air temperature didn't penetrate the fog in my brain. I lifted my head, closed my eyes, and stuck out my tongue, catching half a dozen flakes into my mouth. It brought a bleak grin to my face and I looked back at Beth's stone.

"Remember our snow days? God, we had fun, didn't we?" The winter-dead grass was brittle and the blades crunched under my shoes as I shifted. "You know, for ten years I tried to get you out of my mind. Yet, I couldn't stay away from your plays. Go figure." I chuckled quietly. "I took Rebecca to see a performance of yours on our first date. You were playing Pippa in a production of 'Storage'. Very strange play, might I add. But you were great. As always." I kicked at a small gathering of snow. "Ten years, Beth. Ten years too long."

~ ~ ~ ~ ~

I walked in the door after a late day at the office. Rebecca had gone out with a friend and the house was empty. I dropped my briefcase and jacket onto the couch and noticed the light on the answering machine was beeping. I pressed play as I began to sort through the mail.

"Bill, bill, junk, bill, junk, hmm...coupons."

"Hi, Em. This is Beth."

I froze, the stack of mail in my hand immediately forgotten. Beth's voice sounded far away and metallic over the speaker. "I'm in town this week and would really like to see you. You know, kind of touch base with my old roots. So, if you'd like to get together, um, give me a call at my hotel." I listened dumbly as she recited her number, my heart beating erratically. I pushed play again and listened to the message repeatedly, trying to get the nerve to return her call.

I could hear my blood pounding in my ears as I listened to the phone ring; part of me was so tempted just to slam the phone down and not deal with it. I had cleared my head and heart of Beth Sayers long ago. I did not need a reminder. I—

"Hello?" came the low, husky voice I remembered too well. I was struck speechless for a moment. "Hello?"

"Uh, hi." I closed my eyes, feeling really stupid.

"Hi. Em?" came the quiet question, the hope unmistakable.

"Hello, Beth. How are you?" I opened my eyes and plopped down on the couch, my fingers playing nervously with the phone cord.

"I'm fine. You?"

"Fine."

"Well. It's been a while."

I could hear the faintest bit of a smile in Beth's voice, but she also sounded very tired. I glanced at my watch; it was only 7:15. "Did I wake you?" I asked.

"No. No, just taking a nap. So tired these days. I swear, I'm getting old." I smiled, but said nothing. "Listen, I really would like to see you, Em. Is that possible?"

I remained silent for a moment, trying to make an impromptu decision. My brain refused to work. "Okay."

"Great." I heard the sigh of relief and was surprised. "When? I leave Thursday."

"Well, how about lunch? Tomorrow? There's a park outside my building. Say around 12:30?"

"Yes. Absolutely. I'll be there. But, you must let me bring lunch. I know of this great little deli around the corner—"

"Lonny's? Yes, I know it. I go there a lot. Perhaps a bit too often." I heard the low chuckle on the other end of the line. I had missed her laugh, then was angry with myself for thinking that. I wanted to forget that part of my life. Beth and I had

234 ❖ *Kim Pritekel*

been over for ten years.

"Okay, well. I'll see you at 12:30 then."

I was jumpy the entire next morning. Rebecca must have thought I was on drugs. At 12:20, I gathered myself to go meet my best friend.

"Here you go. I hope you still like turkey," Beth said, handing me a six-inch sub and a Styrofoam cup filled with Dr Pepper.

I nodded and she smiled. I studied her. She was so thin, I hardly recognized her when I'd first descended to the lobby of the office building and found her waiting for me. Her hair was cut short again, but it looked good on her. Her blue eyes were not as bright as I remembered, and I noticed that her clothes hung from her tall frame. I wondered about that, but didn't ask.

We walked to the park, found an empty bench, and sat to eat. Neither of us said much. I had many questions for her, but I had packed those away so many years before, and I didn't want to dig them out again.

"How have you been, Em?" she asked, licking a bit of mayo off her lip.

"Good. I've been doing real well. The firm is wonderful, and I've been successful here. I'm due in court tomorrow actually."

Beth nodded, eyes wide with a look of pride. "I always knew you'd do just fine." She smiled, sipping from her Coke.

"And you?" I asked, taking a bite from the sub.

"Can't complain. I live in Oregon now. Who would have guessed, huh? I did, however, go home a few months back. You know, just to touch roots."

I smiled politely. Part of me wanted to run, to get away from my past. I did not need this. I had a new life, a good life, with Rebecca, and my career was booming. All this making up for lost time and catching up was for other people, not for me.

I rewrapped the remainder of my sandwich and put it into its plastic bag, standing from the bench and smoothing my skirt. I tossed the bag into the trash can next to the bench and turned back to Beth. "Listen, it was nice to see you, Beth. But I have to get going."

She looked up at me in shock, like I'd just hit her with a baseball bat. She quickly composed herself and stood beside me. "Well, I'm glad you were able to get away for a little while, anyway." She also tossed her lunch. We stood there for a few minutes, neither sure what to do. I don't know why I felt so indecisive. "Take care, Em," she said finally with a sad smile.

"You, too. ... Goodbye." I made a move to head back to my

office, when she called out to me. I stopped, but didn't face her.

"Em? Don't I even rate a hug?"

There was real pain behind her words. Slowly, I turned around and looked at her. She remained standing beside the bench, her hands in her pockets. I thought I recognized a look of regret in her eyes. I took a few steps toward her until we were little more than a yard apart. "You want a hug?" I asked, my voice low and even.

She nodded. "Very much so."

"After all this time, after all that has happened, you want a hug?"

"Yes. Especially after all this time, and especially after all that has happened."

"I don't think so."

Again, I turned in the direction of my office, but she caught my arm, gently shifting me back to face her. I looked into her eyes, a strange lump in my throat. Then I fell into her, wrapping my arms around her waist and burying my face against her neck. I felt her arms circle my shoulders, one hand at the back of my head. For just a moment, I felt at peace. It was like I had come home, the missing piece had been found. My Beth was here. *My rock.* I could feel her heart beating, and I'm sure she could feel mine. Even so, there was something very different in that hug. It seemed desperate and final. I couldn't understand it, nor did I want to. I was filled with the need to run, to escape this warmth before it beckoned me again. I just couldn't afford to embrace it one more time.

I pulled away, and without another look back, I hurried toward my office, toward the safety of my life.

~ ~ ~ ~ ~

God, was it only last year? I stared at the rows of graves leading up the hill; many of the markers were more than a hundred years old. The rich history of this cemetery had been one reason Beth loved Pioneer so much. I wiped away one last errant tear and took a deep breath. "I have to go now, Beth," I whispered. "I love you. My best friend. Always." I kissed two of my fingers and placed them on Beth's name then turned away.

As I headed up the hill toward the road, I was surprised to see the rental car parked there, Rebecca leaning against the side. Her hands were stuffed into the pockets of her wool overcoat. I walked to her and, without a word, leaned into her, wrapping my arms around her neck. I felt her arms slowly, almost hesitantly, wind their way around my waist.

"I'm sorry," I breathed into her neck, then began to cry.

Epilogue

I listened to the sound of the shower as I sat in our bed, looking over a client file so I would be prepared for my return to work in two days. Satisfied that I knew the case details well enough, I put the file aside and reached up to remove my reading glasses. Out of the corner of my eye, I caught a glimpse of the night table and, on it, the white envelope whose contents I had not yet read. Breathing deeply, I grabbed it, fingering the smoothness of the paper and tracing the bold letters on the front. Finally, I dug up my courage and carefully tore open the envelope.

Em,

How to start this? Should it be something so dramatic as: If you are reading this letter, then I am surely dead!? No? I agree. I played too many roles in my life. Now isn't the time.

I know you have a lot of questions. Probably about as many as I do. But, see the thing is, a long time ago, I came to the realization that chances were good I would never get the answers to those, so I stopped searching. But I never stopped believing. And I never stopped loving. You, Em. I never stopped loving you.

So many years ago in college, when you and I made love, I can't even begin to explain to you what that was like for me. Well, I probably don't have to now, do I? I think you know. You felt it, too. I'm sorry things happened the way they did, Em. I was a coward. I had made a promise to myself that nothing would ever happen between you and me again. When I started at CU, I had every intention of sticking to that decision. But there you were, big as day. The apple for my temptation. I fought it, Em. Really I did. Finally, I just couldn't anymore. I wanted you so badly, and I wanted to be able to show you. So I did. We did. But then my heart couldn't take it. Early that morning after, I lay awake and watched you. I must have watched you sleep for hours. Trying to decide what to do. I decided to do what I always did. Leave. Flee. Run. I ran from you, Em. Now as I look back, I can't help but wonder if it was the wrong thing to do. Part of me is resigned to the belief that it should, could, have happened no other way. Even all these years later, I still don't have the answer for that, though I wish I did.

During my decade away from you, I tried to get into the real world, the world of acting and living, and I had to struggle, doing meaningless jobs like waiting tables or whatever happened along. I always thought of you then. Imagining you in my mind's eye got me through it, Em. If I wanted to take a serving tray at a restaurant and bang the customer over the head with it out of frustration, I would think of you. Wonder what you were doing. Wonder if you could ever forgive me. I never seemed to be able to forgive myself.

If I had to describe what you are to me, other than my best friend, then I'd have to say you are my first. My first best friend. My first kiss. My first crush. My first sex. My first love. You are so many firsts for me, Em. Even now. My first thought when my doctor told me I would be gone in six months was of you. Ha! I showed him. I hit six months last week. All joking aside, I know it's coming. And I'm ready. I've had a full life in just thirty-four years, experienced many things. You were a part of so many of those things, Em. You are a part of me. You always have been, and you always will be.

I love you, Emily.

Be well,

Beth

I laid down the letter, staring across the room with unseeing eyes. I slowly removed my glasses, absently setting them on the table. Deep inside myself, I felt Beth. And for the first time, I understood. This letter was not a goodbye. It was a beginning...of peace, of understanding, of love. A slow smile spread across my face.

"What are you smiling about?"

I glanced toward Rebecca's voice. She was standing in the bathroom doorway, wearing only a towel, her red hair wet from her shower. She held something in her hands.

I smiled up at her and shook my head. "Nothing."

"Well," she said, seeming to understand that my smile was the key to a secret not for sharing. She looked me in the eye, making sure she had my full attention. She raised a white stick for me to see. "It's blue."

I blinked, not sure I had heard her right. Those two precious words sunk in, and I felt my newfound peace grow. I understood it, now. Rebecca approached the bed and fell into my waiting arms. As I held her, I realized something. Life was full of experiences. Some were good. Some were bad. But none were ever to be forgotten. Beth was a force from the past that propelled me into my future. She was a cornerstone of the building that was my life. Even the worst of times with her helped me to be who I was today, and although Beth was gone, her energy would remain forever. For that, I would always be grateful.

Kim Pritekel was born and raised in Colorado, where she still lives with her two pesky furry, four-legged children Sebastian and Emily, a.k.a. Bubba and Munchkin. Writing is her life, and she's been at it since she was nine years old. She can be reached at XenaNut@hotmail.com.

Breinigsville, PA USA
08 September 2010

245027BV00002B/226/A